APOCALYPSE
of the
DEAD

APOCALYPSE of the DEAD

JOE MCKINNEY

PINNACLE BOOKS
KENSINGTON PUBLISHING CORP.
www.kensingtonbooks.com

PINNACLE BOOKS are published by

Kensington Publishing Corp.
119 West 40th Street
New York, NY 10018

ISBN-13: 978-0-7860-2359-2
ISBN-10: 0-7860-2359-7

First printing:November 2010

10 9 8 7 6 5 4 3 2 1

Printed in the United States of America

For Clay McKinney and David Snell.
Thanks for making it happen.

ACKNOWLEDGMENTS

We're about to take a long walk together through the wasteland, but before we get started I want to take a moment to thank a few people who deserve a lot more than the mere mention I'm about to give them. No book is ever a solo journey, and this one was no exception. These kind folks helped me get from beginning to end:

Jacob Kier, David Snell, Arthur Casas, Jim Donovan, Gary Goldstein, Lisa Morton, David Wellington, Brian Keene, Kevin Luzius, Amy Grech, Bruce Boston, Marge Simon, Mitchel Whitington, Michelle McCrary, Tobey Crockett, Mark Onspaugh, Mark Kolodziejski, Michael McCarty, Lee Thomas, Charlie Delgado, Michael Starnes, Adam Zeldes, Donald Strader, Gabrielle Faust, Shawn and Grady Hartman, Joe and Jennifer McKinney, Alexander Devora, Tiffany and Clay McKinney, Thomas McAuley, Beckie Ugolini, Caren Creech, Joel Sutherland, Harry Shannon, Kim Paffenroth, Matt Staggs, Angie Hawkes, Chris Fulbright, Greg Lamberson, Corey Mitchell, Michelle McKee, Ray Castillo, A. Lee Martinez, John Picacio, Sanford Allen, Matt Louis, Norman Rubenstein, Richard Dean Starr, Michelle Mondo, David Pruitt, Steven Wedel, John Joseph Adams, Nate Kenyon, Bev Vincent, Brian Freeman, Louise Bohmer, Weston Ochse, Judy Comeau, Graeme Flory, Fran Fiel, and Gene O'Neill.

And, as always, to my lovely wife, Kristina, and my daughters, Elena and Brenna, who make this a world worth living in.

They asked him, then, whether to live or die was a matter of his own sovereign will and pleasure. He answered, certainly. In a word, it was Queequeg's conceit, that if a man made up his mind to live, mere sickness could not kill him: nothing but a whale, or a gale, or some violent, ungovernable, unintelligent destroyer of that sort.

—HERMAN MELVILLE

CHAPTER 1

Down there in the ruins it was low tide. Galveston Bay had receded, leaving the wreckage of South Houston's refineries and trailer parks up to their waists in black water. Moving over the destruction at eight hundred feet in a Schweizer 300, the thropping of the helicopter's rotors echoing in his ears, Michael Barnes scanned the flooded ruins for movement. The Schweizer was little more than a pair of lawn chairs strapped to an engine, but its wide-open bubble cockpit offered an unobstructed view of what had been, before Hurricane Mardell ripped the skin off the city, a vast cluster of tankers and docks and refineries and arterial bayous, the breadbasket of America's domestic oil and gas industry. Now the world below Michael Barnes's helicopter looked like a junkyard that had tumbled down a staircase.

Flying over the flooded city, Barnes remembered what it was like after the storm, all those bodies floating in the streets, how they had bloated and baked in the sun. He remembered the chemical fires from the South Houston refineries turning the sky an angry red. A green, iridescent chemical scum had coated the floodwaters, making it shimmer like it was alive. That mixture of rotting flesh and chemicals had produced a stench that even now had the power to raise the bile in his throat.

What he didn't know—what nobody knew, at the time—was the awful alchemy that was taking place beneath the floodwaters, where a new virus was forming, one capable of turning the living into something that was neither living nor dead, but somewhere in between.

Before the storm, Barnes had been a helicopter pilot for the Houston Police Department. Grounded by the weather, he'd been temporarily reassigned to East Houston, down around the Galena Park area, where the seasonal floods were traditionally the worst. The morning after the storm, he'd climbed into a bass boat with four other officers and started looking for survivors.

Everywhere he looked, people moved and acted like they'd suddenly been transported to the face of the moon. Their clothes were torn to rags, their faces glazed over with exhaustion and confusion. Barnes and his men didn't recognize the first zombies they encountered because they looked like everybody else. They moved like drunks. They waded through the trash-strewn water, stumbling toward the rescue boats, their hands outstretched like they were begging to be pulled aboard.

The city turned into a slaughterhouse. Cops, firefighters, National Guardsmen, and Red Cross volunteers went in thinking they'd be saving lives but emerged as zombies, spreading the infection throughout the city. Barnes considered himself lucky to have escaped. When the military sealed off the Gulf Coast, they'd trapped hundreds of thousands of uninfected people inside the wall with the zombies. Barnes emerged with his life, and his freedom; nearly two million people weren't so lucky.

And with the rest of America in an unstoppable economic nosedive after the death of its domestic oil, gas, and chemical industries, he considered himself lucky to get a job with the newly formed Quarantine Authority, a branch of the Office of Homeland Security that was assigned to protect the wall that stood between the infected and the rest of the world.

But all that was two years ago. It felt like another lifetime.

Today, his job was a routine sweep with the Coast Guard. Earlier that morning, a surveillance plane had spotted a small group of survivors—known as Unincorporated Civilian Casualties by the politicians in Washington, but simply as "uncles" by the flyboys in the Quarantine Authority—working to wrest a wrecked shrimp boat loose from a tangle of cables and nets and overgrown vegetation. Most of the boats left in the Houston Ship Channel were half-sunken wrecks. And what hadn't sunk was hopelessly, intractably mired in muck and garbage. There was no chance at all that a handful of uncles could get a boat loose from all that mess and make a run for it. And even if they could, they'd never be able to beat the blockade of Coast Guard cutters waiting just off shore. They'd be blasted out of the water before they lost sight of land. But the Quarantine Authority's mission was to make sure nobody escaped from the zone, and so the order had gone out, as it had numerous times before, to mobilize and neutralize as necessary.

Now, along with three other pilots from the Quarantine Authority, Barnes was slowly moving south toward the Houston Ship Channel. Once there, they'd rendezvous with the boys from the Coast Guard's Helicopter Interdiction Tactical Squadron, known as HITRON, and act as forward observers while the H-Boys took care of any survivors who might be trying to escape to the Gulf of Mexico.

"Good Gawd, would you look at them?" said Ernie Faulks, one of the Quarantine Authority pilots off to Barnes's right. In the old days, Faulks had made his living flying helicopters back and forth from the oil rigs just offshore. He was an irredeemable redneck, but cool under pressure, especially in bad weather.

Barnes glanced up from the ruins below and saw a string of seven orange-and-white Coast Guard helicopters closing on their position. Even from a distance, Barnes could pick out the silhouettes of the HH-60 Jayhawks and the HH-65 Dolphins.

"You know what those babies are?" said Paul Hartle, a former HPD pilot and Barnes's preferred flanker. "Those are chariots of the gods, my friend. Ain't a helicopter made that can hold a candle to those bad boys."

"I'd love to fly one of them things," answered Faulks. "I bet they're faster than your sister, Hartle. Sure are prettier."

"Fuck you, Faulks."

Faulks made kissy noises at him.

"All right, guys, kill the chatter," Barnes said.

Technically, he was supposed to write up the guys when they cussed on the radio, but he let it slide. A little friendly kidding was good for morale. And besides, as pilots, Barnes and the others were seen as hotshots within the Quarantine Authority. They were held to different standards, given special privileges, looked up to by the common guys on the wall. Being pilots, they had to do more, take bigger risks. It was why all these guys loved flying, why they kept coming back.

But in every profession there is a hierarchy, and while Barnes and his fellow Quarantine Authority pilots had a firm grip on the upper rungs of the status ladder, the very top rung was owned by the H-Boys from the Coast Guard's HITRON Squadron. Originally created to stop drug runners in high-speed cigarette boats off the Florida coast, the H-Boys now did double duty patrolling the quarantine zone's coastline. They flew the finest helicopters in the military, and their gun crews had enough ordnance at their disposal to turn anything on the water into splinters and chum.

The pilots in the Quarantine Authority worshiped them, wanted to be them when they grew up. It was the Quarantine Authority Air Corp, in fact, that had come up with the H-Boys' nickname.

"Papa Bear calling Quarter Four-One."

Quarter Four-One was Barnes's call sign. Papa Bear was Coast Guard Captain Frank Hays on board the P-3 Orion that was circling overhead.

"Quarter Four-One, go ahead, sir."

"I'd like to welcome you and your men to the show, Officer Barnes. Now, all elements, stand by to Susie, Susie, Susie."

"Mama Bear Six-One, roger Susie."

Barnes scanned the line of orange-and-white helicopters until he saw one to the far right dipping its rotors side to side. That was Mama Bear, Lt. Commander Wayne Evans, the senior officer in the squadron and the quarterback for this mission. Once the sweep got under way, he would be the link between the individual helicopters and Papa Bear up in the P-3 Orion. Barnes had worked with Evans before and knew the man had a talent for keeping a cool head and an even cooler tone of voice on the radio when things got sticky.

"This is Echo Four-Three, roger Susie."

"Delta One-Six, roger Susie."

"This is Bravo Two-Five, roger Susie."

The pattern continued down the line of Coast Guard helicopters, each one answering up with their call sign and the code word "Susie," which was the signal for the sweep to begin.

When they'd all answered up, Mama Bear said, "Quarter Four-One, you and your men drop to three hundred feet and recon the quadrants north of here. Sound off if you spot any uncles."

"Yes, sir," Barnes answered.

He gave the orders for his team to drop altitude and spread out over the area. They had done this many times before, and they all knew the drill. And they all knew that the order to sound off if they spotted any uncles was superfluous. The HITRON boys had the finest heat-sensing equipment in the world. Their cameras would spot any bodies down there long before Barnes and his men could. What Barnes and the others were expected to do was identify whether or not the bodies spotted were uncles or zombies. The HITRON boys would only get involved if they had uncles.

But telling the difference under the current conditions wasn't going to be easy. They had maybe thirty minutes of usable daylight left, and there was a spreading shadow over the ruins that gave everything, even at three hundred feet, a monochromatic grayness.

Barnes recognized the ghostly outlines of Sheldon Road beneath the water. Its length was dotted with tanker trucks and pickups that, even at low tide, were a good five or six feet beneath the surface. He looked east, across a long line of metal-roofed warehouses that shimmered with the reddish-bronze glare of sunset. From frequent flyovers, Barnes knew that at low tide the water was only about two or three feet deep on the opposite side of those warehouses. If they were going to find uncles, that's where they'd be.

Within moments his instincts proved true. Boats and cranes and even a few larger tankers had been spread by the tides across the flooded swamp that had once been a huge tract of mobile homes. In and among the debris and stands of marsh grass he spotted a large number of people threading their way toward three medium-sized shrimp boats waiting just offshore. One of them already had its engines going. Barnes could see puffs of black smoke roiling up from beneath the waterline.

Several faces turned up to track his movement over their location. He felt like he could see the desperation in their expressions, and he turned away. He didn't like doing this, but it was necessary.

"Quarter Four-One, I've got uncles east of the warehouses."

There was a pause before Mama Bear answered up. "Quarter Four-One, roger that. You sure they're uncles?"

Barnes could hear the indignation in the man's voice. Though they were all on the same team, the H-Boys knew they were the all-stars. Barnes was sure the man was cussing to himself that a Quarantine Authority pilot in a Schweizer POS had spotted their objective before his boys did.

Barnes enjoyed making his reply. "Oh, I'm sure, Mama Bear. I estimate between forty and sixty uncles. Looks like they've got themselves three shrimp boats, too."

There was a pause. *Must be on the private line to Papa Bear*, Barnes thought.

Finally, Mama Bear answered. "Roger that, Quarter Four-One. Go ahead and give 'em Mona."

Come again, thought Barnes.

"Uh, Quarter Four-One, I didn't copy. You said to give 'em Mona?"

"Roger."

"Mama Bear, did you copy they got three shrimp boats in the water?"

"Roger your three shrimp boats, Quarter Four-One. Echo Four-Three and Delta One-Six will fall in behind in case you need assistance. Now give 'em Mona."

Give 'em Mona was the strategy most commonly employed by Quarantine Authority personnel when they spotted uncles trying to breach the wall. The expression came from the amplified zombie moans the Quarantine Authority personnel played over their PA systems. The moans carried for tremendous distances, attracting any zombies that might be in the area. Usually, the moans were enough to send the uncles into hiding.

But this isn't a bunch of uncles throwing rocks at troops up on the wall, Barnes thought. *Those people are a viable threat. They have boats. They have boats in the water, for Christ's sake. You guys are underestimating the situation.*

Barnes reached forward to the control panel in front of the passenger seat and flipped the PA system power switch. Instantly, the air filled with a low, mournful moan that Barnes could feel in his chest and his gut.

He hated hearing that noise. He squeezed his eyes shut and tried to block out the images of bodies festooned in the branches of fallen pecan trees, of people screaming for help in flooded attics, of his brother Jack getting pulled under the water by a nest of zombies they'd wandered into when they were less than two miles from safety. But it was no use. Sometimes the images were too powerful, too vivid, and when he opened his eyes, he had tears running down his face.

Barnes didn't even hear the first shots. He heard a loud plunking sound, like a rock dropping into water next to his ear, and when he looked over his shoulder, he saw a bullet hole in the fuselage.

Missed my head by six inches, he realized.

He heard another sound below him. Glancing down, he saw what appeared to be a faint laser beam between his shins. The bullet had pierced the lower section of the fuselage and entered the supports right below his seat. He had daylight pouring through the bullet hole.

"Quarter Four-One, they got a shooter on the ground!" Barnes heard the panic in his voice but couldn't fight it.

"Take it easy," Mama Bear answered.

More shots from below. Barnes could see the man doing

the shooting, the bursts of white-orange light erupting from the muzzle of what appeared to be an AK-47.

"I'm hit," Barnes said.

Instinctively, he pulled back on the stick and started to climb. He couldn't see the Coast Guard Jayhawk that had moved into position above and behind him, but he heard the pilot's angry shouts as he turned his aircraft to one side, narrowly avoiding the collision.

"Goddamn it, watch yourself, Quarter Four-One!" the pilot said.

Barnes's Adam's apple pumped up and down in his throat as he fought to get himself back under control. He scanned the airspace around him, then made a quick instrument check. Everything appeared to be holding steady.

Out of the corner of his eye, Barnes saw the Coast Guard Jayhawk rotate into position over the uncles below. Barnes could see several uncles shooting now, while farther off, people were jumping into the water and trying to climb aboard the shrimp boats.

"Kill that Mona, Quarter Four-One," shouted one of the H-Boy pilots.

"Roger," Barnes answered.

He leaned forward and killed the PA switch. But as he did, he saw a flash of movement that grabbed his attention. A man was kneeling in the shadows between a wrecked fishing boat and what appeared to be the rusted-out pilothouse from a tugboat. He had a long, skinny metal tube over his shoulder and he appeared to be zeroing in on the Jayhawk to Barnes's right.

Barnes recognized it as an RPG and thought, *Where in the hell did the uncles get an RPG? That's impossible. Isn't it?*

Barnes glanced to his right and saw that the Jayhawk had rotated away from the shooters so that its gun crews could bring their 7.62-mm machine guns to bear on the targets.

"That guy's got an RPG," Barnes heard himself say. "Heads-up, Delta One-Six. That guy's got an RPG. Clear out. Repeat, clear out!"

"Where?" the other pilot asked. "Where? What's he standing next to?"

"Right there!" Barnes shouted futilely. He was pointing at the man, unable to find the words to describe his position amid all the rubble. It all looked the same.

"Where, damn it?"

But by then the man had fired. Barnes watched in horror as the rocket snaked up from the ground and slammed into the back of the Jayhawk, just forward of the rear rotor. The Jayhawk shuddered, like a man carrying a heavy pack that had shifted suddenly, and then the helicopter started spewing thick black smoke.

"Delta One-Six, I'm hit!"

"Fucker has an RPG!" shouted the other H-Boy pilot. He was moving his Jayhawk higher and orbiting counterclockwise to put his gun crews in position.

"Delta One-Six, she's not responding."

"Come on, Coleman," said the other Jayhawk pilot. "Pull your PCLs off-line."

"I'm losing it!"

Delta One-Six made two full rotations, wrapping itself in a black haze as it drifted toward a partially capsized superfreighter. As Barnes watched, the Jayhawk clipped the very top of the superstructure and hitched forward toward the ground in a dive. One of its gunners was holding onto his machine gun with one hand, the rest of him hanging out the door like a windsock in a stiff breeze. The pilot tried to level off the aircraft right before they hit, but only managed to snap the helicopter's spine on impact.

A moment later, a thin plume of black smoke rose up from the wreck.

Then the radio exploded with activity. "He's down, Echo Four-Three. Delta One-Six is down."

"Get him some help over there. You got one moving!"

It was true. Barnes saw the pilot stumble out of the cockpit, his white helmet smoking. The man threw his helmet off and he fell into the water. When he bobbed back up to the surface he was holding a pistol in his hand.

"Oh, shit, Echo Four-Three, we got problems. I got infected moving into the area."

"What direction?" asked Mama Bear.

"From the ten. I got a visual on thirteen of them."

"Uh, Mama Bear," said Faulks. "Ya'll got a whole lot more than that. I got a visual on about forty or fifty over here at your two o'clock."

"You want me to go down and extract your man?" Barnes asked.

"Negative, Quarter Four-One," Mama Bear said. "Echo Three-Four, give me your status."

"One second," said the pilot. "We're about to smoke out this RPG."

A moment later, a steady stream of tracer rounds erupted from the Jayhawk's gunners, slamming into the little pocket of debris beneath the tugboat's pilothouse.

The shooting went on until the pilothouse collapsed.

"Echo Three-Four, RPG neutralized."

"Your boy's in deep shit over here, guys," said Faulks.

Barnes rotated so he could see the downed pilot. The man was standing in the middle of a ring of zombies. The way he was standing, it was obvious he'd broken one of his legs, but the man fought bravely, placing his shots carefully, not rushing them.

"You guys gonna help him?" Faulks said.

"Roger that, Echo Three-four."

The Jayhawk and the three other Dolphins moved into

position, but Barnes could tell it was too late for the man on the ground even before the H-Boys started shooting. The man was pulled down below a sheet of corrugated tin by one of the zombies, and a moment later the water turned to blood where he had been standing.

"Echo Three-Four to Mama Bear, Delta One-Six has been compromised."

A pause.

"Roger that, Echo Three-Four. Status report."

Instinctively, Barnes swept the area, taking it all in. He saw the smoking helicopter, the zombies advancing through an endless plain of maritime debris, the uncles scrambling to escape the zombies, jumping into the channel and swimming for the boats. One of the boats had already made it a good fifty yards from the bank.

Echo Three-Four completed his status report. There was another pause while Mama Bear conferred with Papa Bear, and then Mama Bear gave the order that turned Barnes's stomach.

"Smoke 'em all," said Mama Bear. "Disable those boats and neutralize any targets in the water."

A moment later, the air was alive with tracer rounds.

Barnes watched as the machine guns chewed up people and zombies and boats, and something inside him went numb.

Three miles to the east, on a small shrimp boat chugging quietly away from the darkened coastline, Robert Connelly heard the guns and saw the smoke columns rising up into the darkening sky.

"You okay, Bobby?" he said to his son.

The boy nodded into his shoulder and Robert hugged him.

Robert turned and looked over the faces of the forty

refugees who had commandeered this boat with him. Several of them coughed. Half of them were sick with one kind of funk or another. Their faces were gray and gaunt, their eyes dull and languid in the darkness. They were all too tired, he realized, to understand just how lucky they were. The others had insisted on going to the main docks just above San Jacinto State Park, claiming there'd be more places to hide there. But Robert and his people had refused to go that route. They decided to take their chances, alone, down around Scott Bay. And now, as he listened to the explosions and the gunfire, it looked like that gamble was paying off.

He listened to the water lapping against the hull, to the steady droning thrum of the engines. He felt the wind buffeting his face.

He could feel the anxiety and the frustration and two years of living like an animal among the Houston ruins lifting from him. He took a deep breath, and though his chest hurt, it felt good to breathe air that didn't taste like death and stale sweat and chemicals.

He squeezed Bobby again.

"I think we're gonna make it," he said.

Chapter 2

"Bobby?"

A hard thud against the door.

"Bobby, let me see you. Bobby?"

Robert Connelly looked through a yellowed, grimy window, trying to catch a glimpse of his boy out there. He saw a few of the infected staggering around in the dark, trying to keep their balance as the boat pitched on the dark waves.

A hand crashed through the window and Robert stepped out of reach. The zombie groped for him, slicing its arm on the glass stuck in the frame. There was a time when seeing the zombie's arm cut to ribbons like that would have made him vomit, all that blood. Now the arm was just something to avoid.

Robert got as close as he dared to the broken window. "Bobby, are you out there? Bobby?" Sometimes the infected remembered their names, responded to them. He had seen it happen before.

He waited.

There was another thud against the door, and this time something cracked.

"Bobby?"

He heard the infected moaning, the engines straining at three-quarters speed. The waves slapped against the hull.

He stepped over to the controls and looked out across the water. Far ahead, shimmering lights snaked across the horizon, sometimes visible, sometimes not, depending on the pitch of the bow over the waves. He thought for sure it was Florida. They had almost made it.

The thought took him back almost two years, to those lawless days after Hurricane Mardell. He remembered the rioting in the streets, the terrified confusion as nearly four million people scrambled to safety. Bloated, decaying corpses floated through the flooded streets. Starvation was rampant. Sanitation and medical services were nonexistent. Helicopters circled overhead for a few days after Mardell, picking up whomever they could, but there were so few helicopters, and so many to be rescued.

And then the infected rose up from the ruins.

At first, Robert believed they were bands of looters fighting with the authorities. He didn't believe the reports of cannibalism. Paranoid hysteria, he called it. But then he saw the infected trying to get into the elementary school gym where he and Bobby and about a hundred others had been living. After that, he knew they were dealing with something more than looters.

He took Bobby on a desperate three-day trek north, and they made it as far as the quarantine walls, where they were turned back by soldiers and police standing behind barricades.

"We're going to survive this," he told his son. "I will keep you safe. I promise."

He had said those words while they were sitting on the roof of a house less than half a mile from the wall, sharing a can of green beans they'd salvaged from the kitchen pantry. There was no silverware, none that they trusted the look of anyway, and they had to scoop out the food with their fingers. In the distance, they could see helicopter gunships sprinting over the walls. It was late evening, near dark, and they could hear the sporadic crackle of gunfire erupting all around them.

"It doesn't matter, Dad."

Robert Connelly looked at his son. The boy's shoulders were drooped forward, the muscles in his face slack, like somebody had let the air out of him. "Bobby," he said, "why would you say something like that? Of course it matters."

There were two green beans floating in the bottom of the can. Robert offered them to Bobby.

The boy shook his head.

"There's no point."

"Bobby, please. It matters to me."

The boy pointed at the wall. "Look at that, Dad. Look at those walls. Look at all those helicopters, all those soldiers. Think how fast they put all this up. They're not ever going to let us go. They want us to die in here."

Robert hardly knew what to say. Bobby was only thirteen years old, too young to think his life was valueless.

But he'd already noticed there were no gates in the quarantine wall.

He hoped they'd simply missed them.

They hadn't.

For two years, Robert kept them alive, fighting the infected, rarely sleeping, scavenging for every meal. The struggle had carved a fierce resilience into his grain, a belief that his will alone was enough to sustain them against the cozy, narcotic warmth of nihilism.

With a small band of like-minded refugees, he found a serviceable boat in the flooded debris field of the Houston Ship Channel. There wasn't a sailor among them, and yet they'd dodged the helicopters and slipped through the Coast Guard blockade undetected. For a glorious moment that first night, holding his boy, he'd believed they were really going to make it.

Now, he knew better.

One of the forty refugees on board the *Sugar Jane* was infected, and that first night, while they were at sea, he turned.

Robert Connelly was the only one left. He'd made a promise to his son and he'd almost kept it. He'd sought to escape the criminal injustice his government wrought upon him by locking him up inside the quarantine zone, and he'd almost succeeded.

But almost only counts in horseshoes and hand grenades, he thought, smiling faintly at the memory of one of his father's favorite expressions. And now the *Sugar Jane* was a plague bomb bound for some unsuspecting shore.

But what was the sense in worrying about it? It didn't matter anymore.

Not without the boy it didn't.

Not to Robert Connelly.

There was another thud against the door and it splintered. A shard of plywood skidded across the deck, landing near his feet. Bloody fingers tore at the hole in the door. A face appeared at the widening crack, the cheeks and lips shredded to a pulp, the small, dark teeth broken and streaked with blood. The moaning became a fierce, stuttering growl.

That might be Bobby there; it was hard to tell. But it didn't matter.

Robert looked over the controls. The boat would run itself. And it looked like they had enough fuel to finish the voyage. There was nothing left to do here. He stood as straight as the rolling deck of the boat allowed and prepared to run for it.

There was a hammer on the chair beside him.

He picked it up. Tested its heft.

It would do.

The door exploded open.

Bobby and two others stood there. Bobby's right hand was nearly gone. So, too, were his ears and nose and most of his right cheek.

"Ah, Jesus, Bobby," Robert said, grimacing at the wreckage of his son.

They stumbled forward.

Robert moved past Bobby and swung at the lead zombie, dropping it with a well-placed strike to the temple.

The other closed the gap too quickly, and Robert had to kick it in the gut to create distance. He raised the hammer and was rushing forward to plant it into the thing's forehead when Bobby grabbed his shoulder and clamped down with a bite that made Robert howl in pain.

He knocked the boy to the deck and swung again at the second zombie. The claw end of the hammer caught the zombie in the top of the head and it dropped to the deck.

Bobby was on him again.

He grabbed the boy and turned him around and hugged him from behind, determined not to let go. A group of zombies was bottlenecking at the door. Robert knew he had only a few minutes of fight left in him. He charged the knot of zombies at the door and somehow managed to push them back. Hands and arms crowded his face, but he wasn't worried about escaping their bites. Not at this point. All that mattered was getting on top of the cabin and up into the rigging.

Bobby struggled against his hold, but Robert managed to get his left arm across Bobby's chest and over his right shoulder, pinning the boy's arms. With an adult, it wouldn't have been possible. But with a boy, and especially with a boy who had existed at a near-starvation level for two years, Robert managed fairly well.

The zombies clawed at him. They tore his cheeks and

arms and neck with their fingernails. One of them took a bite out of his calf. But they couldn't hold him.

He was breathing hard by the time he reached the top. He could feel his body growing weak. The infection felt like somebody was jamming a lit cigarette through his veins. But he reached the top of the rigging, and once he was there, he slipped a small length of rope from his back pocket and looped it around Bobby's left hand, then around his own.

"It's all right," he whispered into Bobby's ear. "Don't you worry. We're together now and nothing else matters."

In the distance, he could see the bobbing string of lights that marked the Florida coast. Fireworks exploded above the horizon.

It was the Fourth of July.

"It's beautiful, isn't it?"

The zombie, his child, struggled against him. It wouldn't be long now. He felt so weak, so sleepy. Soon, nothing else would matter.

They were together. And that was enough.

"That's what counts," he said. "I love you, Bobby."

CHAPTER 3

It was a cloudy, humid morning. Some of the prisoners were trying to sleep. Others were gazing vacantly out of the bus windows as it made its way southward through the heart of Sarasota, Florida's coastal district. Billy Kline had his head against the wire mesh covering the windows, watching the others as they swayed in their seats to the motion of the bus. Beside him, Tommy Patmore was absently pulling at the loose threads of his work pants. The mood was subdued, quiet, each man lost to his own thoughts.

A few of the guys had their windows down, but not even the occasional draft of sea air that managed to find its way into the bus could cover up the smell. Their work clothes were little more than heavy-duty orange hospital scrubs with SARASOTA COUNTY JAIL stenciled across the back, and though they were supposedly washed after every use, they nonetheless stank of mildew and sweat and something less definable that Billy Kline had only now identified.

It was the rank odor of despair.

He'd been thinking a lot about despair lately. There were times when he felt it as a physically immediate and distinct sensation, like the burning itch between your toes after a few days of taking communal showers; or the painful swelling in your bowels that came with your first few meals; or rolling over at night and seeing the man in the cot next to you enveloped in a living haze of scabies. But there were other times when it was more tenuous, like when you heard the resignation in your mother's voice when she said good-bye at the end of your ten-minute Tuesday-night phone call; or when you seethed with a cold, mute rage every time some bored guard emptied everything you owned onto his desk from a paper grocery sack and picked through it like he was looking for a pistachio kernel in a pile full of shells.

He felt so much rage.

Billy was twenty-five, halfway through an eight-month sentence for selling stolen property to undercover officers. Before that, he had done two months for car burglary, charges dismissed. And the year before that, he'd done three months, again for car burglary, and again with the charges ultimately dismissed. There had been other visits, too.

But this time was different.

This latest round of trouble had finally pissed his mom off to the point where she no longer asked for explanations or feigned credulity when he provided them unsolicited.

This time, he had finally hit bottom.

Beside him, Tommy Patmore sucked in a deep breath.

Billy leaned over and whispered, "You're gonna unravel those pants you keep picking at 'em."

A murmur.

"What'd you say?"

"Be quiet."

Tommy glanced furtively around the bus. No one was paying any attention to them.

Billy followed Tommy's gaze and frowned. "What's wrong with you?"

One more look around.

"Ray Bob Walker came to see me this morning before we left. They asked me if I wanted to join."

Billy sighed inwardly. He'd been dreading this.

"And? What'd you say?"

Tommy looked at him. It was enough.

"Ah, Tommy, you gotta be shitting me. What were you thinking?"

"Be quiet, Billy. They'll hear you."

"Fuck them. Tommy, I told you those Aryan Brotherhood assholes will get you killed. Is that what you want? You know what those guys do. What the fuck's wrong with you?"

"Be quiet," Tommy said. "They'll hear you."

He looked around the bus again. Billy looked, too. He saw a lot of bald heads: a mixture of blacks and Mexicans and white guys. The Mexicans and the white guys all had prison tats on their necks. The white guys came in two body types. You had the big guys, stout, meaty, biker types. They tended to be the older ones, doing time for robbery or check kiting. Then you had the lean ones, wiry, wild-eyed. They were the loud ones, the meth heads, the fighters, the ones with something to prove.

Tommy is going to fit in well with the younger ones, Billy thought. He had the body type. He had the same desperate air about him, an urgent need to fit in somewhere, anywhere. But then, all the young white guys who joined the Aryan Brotherhood started out that way. They were all angry, frustrated, a little frightened to find themselves alone in a world that demanded so much and yet seemed to promise so little in return. The Aryan Brotherhood offered safety. It offered direction. It offered a society that gave its members rank and made them something special within their own little world. It offered an "us" and a "them." For someone like Tommy Patmore, the appeal was irresistible.

But they hadn't looked twice at Billy. With a last name

like Kline, they all assumed Billy was Jewish. But if he was, his family had neglected to tell him about it. And yet his name was enough to brand him a Jew in the eyes of his fellow prisoners. It made him a sort of nonentity, a prisoner like the rest, yet distinct enough that he didn't fall inside any of the racial lines that sharply divide all U.S. jails and prisons. At six-one and a hundred and ninety pounds, he was big enough and tough enough to stand in the no-man's land between the gangs, but it was a precarious existence. He was always watching the man behind him, because that man could turn on him at a moment's notice, and maintaining that nearly constant state of vigilance wore Billy down, exhausted him.

That was the big reason why he hated to see Tommy Patmore get sucked into the gangs. He liked Tommy. Now, Tommy was one more individual he'd have to watch out for.

"Just do me a favor, would you?" Billy said. "Do your time smart. If they try to talk you into hurting somebody, get the hell out. The last thing you want to do is spend the rest of your life in a state pen someplace."

Tommy swallowed the lump in his throat. Then he looked down at his hands folded in his lap.

That was all Billy needed to see.

"Ah, Tommy, you are one dumb son of a bitch. What did you agree to do?"

"Please don't say anything."

"What are you going to do? Tell me."

Tommy looked around, then folded down the waistband of his pants, exposing a five-inch-long piece of tin that had been hammered into a crude shank, some duct tape wrapped around the blunt end as a handle.

"They haven't told me who yet."

"Ah, Tommy. For Christ's sake."

"Don't say anything, Billy. Please."

"I won't," Billy said.

He looked away in disgust.

In his mind, he tried to wash his hands of Tommy Patmore, though it wasn't as easy as it should have been.

They were pulling into Centennial Park. The Gulf of Mexico stretched out before them like a flat green sheet of cold pea soup. Gulls circled over the water, filling the morning air with noise. The smell of the ocean was thick and pungent and pleasant. Billy closed his eyes and breathed in deeply. For a moment, he imagined that all his problems were somewhere else.

But it was the last quiet moment he would ever know.

The driver parked the bus in the middle of a nearly empty parking lot, and things started to happen quickly after that.

Billy shuffled off the bus with the others.

A few of the men stretched.

A guard came by and collected their SID sheets, the 3 x 5 index cards that contained all their personal information and that they had to present to the guards every time they moved from one place to the next.

Billy and three of the others were pulled off the line and brought over to the equipment stand.

A guard handed Billy a canvas sack with a strap meant to go over one shoulder and a sawed-off broom handle with a dull, bent spike shoved into one end.

"Collection detail," the guard said. "You're with Carnot. Over there."

Deputy Carnot, who the prisoners called Deputy Carenot because he didn't seem to give a shit about anything except talking on his cell phone, waved his men over and pointed them toward a large plain of grass south of the parking lot. He didn't even have to stop talking on the phone.

Billy and the other members of the collection detail had all done this before. They knew the drill. Fan out. Fill your bag. Empty it into the garbage sacks brought up by the runners.

Billy worked steadily for the better part of an hour, going up and down the grassy expanse of Centennial Park, spearing trash, while the others went around emptying garbage cans into sacks and carting them off to a Dumpster that had been brought in for their use. It was easy work, mindless, and in his head he was drifting.

All that morning, the wind off the Gulf had been trying to clear the clouds from the sky, and it was finally starting to succeed. It was getting hot. Billy walked over to where Deputy Carnot was sitting in a lawn chair next to a yellow watercooler, talking on his cell phone.

"Hey, boss, you mind if I get a drink?"

Carnot gave him a frown and a dismissive wave of his hand. *I don't give a shit. Do what you need to do and lemme alone.*

It sounded like he was talking to his girlfriend. Billy shook his head and smiled. Then he filled a paper snow cone cup with water and leaned on his trash spike while he drank it down in one quick gulp. It felt good going down, cold and clean.

He leaned down again for another drink, and that's when he saw it.

He froze.

About a hundred feet away, DeShawn James, one of the younger black guys on the work crew, was wrestling with a heavy trash can, trying to pull it out of a wooden bin so he could empty it. Behind him, hugging a line of shrubs and coming up fast, was Tommy Patmore.

Billy could see the tin shank glinting in Tommy's right hand.

Damn it, Tommy. You are one dumb son of a bitch.

Billy glanced at Carnot. The man was oblivious, still talking on his phone. No one else seemed to have noticed Tommy making his move either, and that was good.

Billy filled his cup, stood, and looked away, anywhere but at what Tommy was doing.

And that's when he saw the man coming down the sidewalk toward him. His right arm was dark with dried blood, but he was walking normally, which is why Billy didn't clue in right away that he was looking at a zombie. Like everybody else, he had seen the news footage from Texas. He had seen the infected wading through the flooded streets of Houston, their movements jerky and uncoordinated. He had seen the fighting in San Antonio and Austin and Dallas. He had read about them in magazines and seen the public service announcements on TV, telling you what to do if you should ever encounter one of the infected. But none of that occurred to him just then. All he saw was a man who didn't look right but who sent a shiver down his spine just the same.

It wasn't until he saw the man's milky eyes that everything clicked.

And then he knew what he was looking at.

"Hey, boss," he said.

Carnot rolled his eyes up at Billy. *What the fuck do you want?*

Billy pointed at the approaching zombie with a nod of his chin.

Carnot looked over his shoulder, then did a double take. "Holy shit," he said. He stood up and backed away from his lawn chair, still holding the cell phone to his ear.

The zombie stepped off the sidewalk and onto the grass. It raised its arms, its hands outstretched and clutching for them in a gesture of supplication that Billy found strangely funny.

But he stopped laughing when the zombie started to moan. When you do nothing but sit around the common room of a jail pod all day, you watch a lot of TV. He had heard that moan before, on the news. Once, he'd seen a news spot where hundreds of the things had been moving down a San Antonio street. The things had been packed in tightly. And even with the volume turned down and the other guys talking and laughing and making asses of themselves all around him, he could still feel the gooseflesh popping up on his arms. But seeing it on TV was nothing like hearing it in person. The real thing took his breath away.

"Shoot it," he said to Carnot.

But Carnot just stood there, the phone still stuck to the side of his face.

"Hang up the fucking phone and shoot," Billy said.

Carnot groaned. Then he seemed to find himself. He looked at the phone like he was surprised it was still there. Then he said, "Babe, I gotta go."

He flipped the phone closed and slid it into his gun belt.

Then he pulled his gun.

"Sir, you need to stop."

"He's not gonna stop," Billy said.

"Shut up," Carnot snapped.

He raised his gun and pointed it at the zombie's chest.

"Stop, police!" Carnot shouted.

The man lumbered forward.

"Jesus, Carnot, he's not gonna stop. Fucking shoot him already."

"Stop," Carnot said. But his voice was barely a whisper. He lowered his gun, raised it again.

"Oh, for Christ's sake," Billy said. He stepped around Carnot with his trash spike raised like a javelin and jammed it into the zombie's temple.

The zombie didn't go down. It stayed on its feet and even turned a little toward Billy, its hands coming up to clutch at him. Grunting with the effort, Billy held on to the spike and worked it around inside the wound until the zombie's arms dropped down to its sides and it sagged to the ground. Billy guided it down onto its back and then yanked his spike free.

"Holy shit," Carnot said. "What the hell did you do?"

Your job, you idiot.

But he didn't say that. His gaze went right past Carnot to the parking lot. Three more zombies were limping toward them. They looked different than the one Billy had just put down. They were shabbier. Their clothes were gray, filthy rags. Their faces were gaunt, smeared with blood. They looked like the zombies he had seen on the news, the ones inside the quarantine zone.

He heard moaning to his right and looked that way.

"What the hell?" he said.

There were two zombies there, a man and a young boy, their wrists tied together.

"Hey, boss," he said. "We're gonna need that pistol."

"Yeah," Carnot said.

But the deputy was shaking so badly he could barely point his gun at the approaching zombies, all of whom had started to moan loudly. The sound carried with disturbing clarity across the park. It seemed to be coming from everywhere at once.

"We have to get to high ground," Billy said.

Carnot nodded, but didn't move.

"Come on," Billy said.

He grabbed the deputy by the shoulder and pulled him toward the bus. There was enough of a gap between the zombies that Billy thought they'd be able to make it at a brisk walk, but they hadn't gone more than a few steps when one of the prisoners tumbled out of the bus doors and landed on his back in the parking lot. It looked like his throat had been torn out. One of the guards climbed down after him, his face and the front of his uniform soaked through with a reddish-brown stain.

"Get on your radio," Billy said to Carnot. "Call for help."

Carnot reached down to his belt and felt for where the radio should have been, but wasn't. He looked back at the water-cooler. Billy followed his gaze and saw the radio in the grass next to the lawn chair.

"For Christ's sake," Billy said.

One of the other prisoners was coming across the grass toward them. Most of his face was gone. Billy stared at the man. He'd heard the infected could ignore pain that would put an uninfected person over into unconsciousness. There were recorded instances of the infected walking around with their intestines hanging out of their bellies. But Billy hadn't really believed those things until now. That man, his face had literally been chewed off. And he was still coming.

Billy looked around for a place to take cover. The news had said to seek the high ground, if possible. There was a gap between the approaching zombies and through it he saw a car parked off by itself.

"There," he said to Carnot. "That car over there. Come on."

They ran for it, Billy pulling Carnot along behind him. The car was a fairly new Buick in decent shape. It was empty, and Billy was glad for that. He jumped onto the roof, turned, and pulled Carnot up next to him. Then they got on the roof and stood side by side, watching the zombies getting closer.

"You're gonna have to shoot," Billy said.

Carnot raised his weapon. Billy watched him take aim at a man in running shorts and the remnants of a bloodstained white T-shirt.

"Shoot him," Billy said.

Carnot fired. The bullet smacked into the man's shoulder and spun him around, but it didn't drop him. He turned back toward them and came on again.

"Head shots, damn it," Billy said.

"I'm trying," Carnot said. His voice was trembling.

He fired three more times and managed only one hit.

Within moments they were surrounded. Mangled hands clutched at their feet. The moaning was deafening. Carnot was shaking badly now. He was firing wildly, completely missing zombies that were less than three feet from the tip of his gun. Billy, meanwhile, was kicking at hands and spearing at faces, making his movements count.

He got one of the zombies in the forehead, and the man slumped forward onto his knees, his face pressed against the back driver's-side window by the bodies pushing in from behind him. One of the zombies in the back managed to ramp up over the fallen zombie's back and came up onto the roof.

Billy sidestepped around the zombie's outstretched arms and pushed him down onto the trunk.

He heard a click.

Carnot was standing there, pointing his empty Glock at the zombies below him. The slide was locked back in the empty position.

"Goddamn it. Reload!"

Carnot pointed the empty pistol at another zombie and tried to pull the trigger.

"Reload your fucking—"

But Billy didn't get a chance to finish. Carnot vanished. It was like Wile E. Coyote in those old Road Runner cartoons. One second he was there; the next he was gone, his feet pulled out from underneath him. The back of Carnot's head smacked against the edge of the roof with a sickening crunch and then they pulled him down to the ground.

As Billy watched, they swarmed Carnot, tearing at him with their teeth and their fingers.

His screams lasted only a moment.

Billy didn't waste time watching Carnot twitching in his death throes. Instead, he jumped to the ground and ran for it. A few of the zombies tried to follow, but they were slow. Billy was able to weave through them easily. Once he created some distance, he stopped, caught his breath, and looked for an escape route.

There were, he guessed, maybe sixty or seventy of the zombies walking across the park. Most were close by, already in the parking lot. A few were crossing the street into the hotels and green belts opposite the park. In the distance, he could hear police sirens getting closer.

"Never thought I'd be happy to hear that," he muttered.

Out of the corner of his eye he saw movement, a splash of orange coming around a line of shrubs.

It was Tommy Patmore. His arms and his stomach and his thighs were soaked with blood, but he didn't look infected. He looked shell-shocked, confused. The shank was still in his hand.

From behind Tommy, one of the other prisoners was coming up fast. He was limping, a bad bite wound just below his knee, but he was still moving with frightening speed.

A fast mover, Billy thought. The articles he'd read had mentioned how some of the zombies, the ones who were in really good physical condition before they became infected, sometimes managed to maintain a measure of their former physical prowess when they turned. But the same article had also said that it took longer for those people to turn. They'd only been out about two hours. How had this happened so fast?

He shouted, "Tommy, look out!" and ran for his friend.

He got there just as the fast mover was closing on Tommy, and he jammed his trash spike into the zombie's ear. The zombie fought like a big fish on a hook, but it eventually went down.

Billy pulled his spike out of the zombie's head and turned to Tommy.

"Are you okay? Did you get bit?"

Tommy's mouth was working like he was chewing gum, but he wasn't making words.

"Tommy, answer me."

"I . . . I killed him. I did it."

He was crying, his body shaking all over.

"What? Who?"

"DeShawn James. They wanted me . . . They told me to . . . I stabbed him in the belly and then I stopped, you know, I . . . I had changed my mind. I didn't want to hurt him. I didn't. But then he started fighting me."

Tommy glanced down at the shank in his hand like he didn't know what it was.

He said, "I didn't want to. God, there was so much blood."

"Yeah, well, you did. Now it's time to cowboy the fuck up and deal with it. We're in a world of shit here, Tommy. Are you bit anyplace?"

"Bit?"

"Oh, for Christ's sake, Tommy. Are you hurt?"

"No."

"Good. We got to get to someplace safe." He scanned the buildings across the street. The hotel would be no good. Zombies were already walking up to the covered carport at the main entrance. But farther south, he saw a place that looked promising, a few low structures behind a large pink stucco wall. "Over there," he said. "Come on. Stay close."

And together, they ran for it.

CHAPTER 4

From the notebooks of Ben Richardson

Houston, Texas: July 5th, 3:15 A.M.

I saw my first zombie from the window of a registered charter bus on the Gibbs-Sprawl Road as we entered the quarantine zone around San Antonio.

That was eight months ago.

She was weirdly sexless, not anything like what I expected. I remember she was standing barefoot in the weeds that had grown up at the edge of the road since the city was abandoned, and her greasy, stringy hair hung down over her face like a wet curtain. Her body was thin and rickety looking. She was wearing a baglike, bloodstained hospital gown, and to me she looked like an emaciated crack whore. She never even looked up, not even as our bus rolled on by. She just stood there, hugging herself with her bone-skinny arms in the cloud of dust our bus had kicked up. I wasn't disgusted like I thought I would be. I just felt sad.

But, like I said, that was eight months ago. I've seen a lot of zombies since then, a lot of death. I've studied them. I've gotten closer than I would have liked at times. Eventually—

hopefully—all of these notebooks will get turned into some kind of cohesive whole, some narrative of the zombie outbreak that has brought our great nation from superpower status to the level of a ticking time bomb for the rest of the world, and in that narrative I'll try to find a reason for it all.

If there is one.

Somehow I doubt there is.

I'm growing more and more convinced that there aren't reasons to explain this world we live in. Not good ones anyway.

Maybe that's what makes catastrophes so horrible—the lack of a reason. I mean in a teleological sense. Our brains are wired to see the world in terms of cause and effect. Even the atheists among us find some small measure of comfort knowing that there's a reason things are so bad.

These days, I find myself more interested in the zombies themselves than I am with the traditional things with which a historian and commentator should be concerned. Xenophon, Plutarch, Sallust, Suetonius, Geoffrey of Monmouth, Raphael Holinshed, Francesco Guicciardini, Edward Gibbon—those great chroniclers in the history of historians—they all sought to cast a wide net, giving equal attention to personal agenda and facts. I would like to cast a wide net, too. And I have plenty of opinions. The economic impact of the outbreak at home and abroad, the political flare-ups, the big, empty speeches on the floor of the U.N. and on the White House lawn—all those things have their place in a history with any claim to completeness. But I find it hard to give a rat's ass about them. The politicians aren't out here on the street dying with the rest of us. They're all stashed away in some secure, undisclosed location, waiting it out. And their eloquent speeches don't tell the part of the story that needs telling.

I read Eddie Hudson's book and a dozen others just like it. I know what they described—all the shambling corpselike people flooding the streets, attacking every living thing they could find. Well, I've seen what happens after almost two years. The infected aren't dead. And like all living things, they've changed, adapted. The ones who have survived since the first days of the outbreak—and granted, there aren't many of them—have become something different. And yet, for all that, they are still dangerous; they are still unpredictable. They still attack. They're like alcoholics who can't help coming back to the bottle. Even if they don't want to.

That's the side of this thing I want to talk about.

July 5th, 5:40 A.M.

We've got about twenty minutes until takeoff and I wanted to jot down a few notes about the quarantine zone. Sometimes I find it hard to wrap my mind around how big it is. The logistical scope of the project is simply staggering.

Back in its heyday, the U.S. Customs and Border Protection Agency patrolled the 2,000 miles of borderland between the United States and Mexico. Of the agency's 11,000 agents, more than 9,500 of them worked along that 2,000-mile stretch of desert. They hunted drug dealers and illegal aliens with a huge array of tools, everything from satellite imagery and publicly accessible webcams to helicopters, horses, and plain old-fashioned shoe leather. Even still, the border had more holes in it than a fishing net.

In comparison, the Gulf Region Quarantine Authority only has a wall of some 1,100 miles to patrol. The wall stretches from Gulfport, Mississippi, to Brownsville, Texas, paralleling the freeway system wherever possible to aid in the supply and reinforcement of problem areas. The GRQA keeps this stretch of metal fencing and sentry towers and barbed wire secure with just over 10,000 agents, most of them former CBP and National Guardsmen and cops. They are aided at sea by the U.S. Coast Guard and in Mexico by federal troops.

Yet despite their numerical advantage over the old U.S. Customs and Border Protection Agency, their job is infinitely harder. Nobody in the old CBP thought too much of it that a steady stream of illegals got through the border every day. They just shrugged and went on with life. But the GRQA can't afford to let even a single zombie through its line. That would spell disaster. The pressure is high; the price of failure is apocalyptic.

Their job terrifies me. These guys are frequently posted outside of major metropolitan areas where the zombie populations are thickest. Day and night, they have to listen to that constant moaning. They have to stand by and listen to the plaintive cries for help from the Unincorporated Civilian Casualties, the Gulf Region Quarantine Authority's official designation for the people who were unable to make it out of the quarantine zone before the walls were put up and were sealed inside with the zombies. Hearing all that noise for just a few weeks is demoralizing. I can't imagine what it would be like to hear it every single day for months and years at a time.

Even worse, I can't imagine what it would be like to grow used to hearing it.

It is little wonder that so many of the GRQA go AWOL at least once or twice a year. Or that they are never punished for it when they do. Most don't even get their pay docked.

And it's no wonder that the leading cause of death among GRQA agents is suicide.

Actually, I'm surprised it doesn't happen more often than it does . . .

From the copilot's chair of a Schweizer 300 helicopter, Ben Richardson looked out across the flooded ruins of southeast Houston. They were at two hundred feet, skimming over what had once been wide-open cattle-grazing land. It was under twenty feet of water these days. Here and there, he could see the top of an oil derrick just below the surface. Dead trees poked skeletal fingers up through the water. Every once in a while, they'd pass over a perfectly round metal island, the remains of oil tanks. Dawn was spreading over the flooded landscape, dappling the water with reds and yellows and liquid pools of copper.

"Looks pretty, don't it?" Michael Barnes said.

"Amazing," Richardson said. They were talking through the intercom system built into their flight helmets, but even then they had to nearly yell at each other to hear over the noise the little helicopter made.

"All those colors you see . . ."

"Yeah?"

"That's oil in the water. Most of this area is so thick with it you'll be able to see a film over the water come midday."

Nice, Richardson thought.

This area had once been the hub of the oil and gas industry in the United States. Now, all of it was gone. It was no wonder that gas had gone to more than twelve dollars a gallon in the last two years.

"You see many people down in this area?" Richardson asked.

"You talking about uncles or zombies?"

"Either."

"You see dead bodies every once in a while. You know, floaters. Hardly ever seen anybody alive, though. The water's too deep."

Richardson stole a sideways glance at Michael Barnes, the Gulf Region Quarantine Authority pilot who had been assigned to fly him around for the next two weeks. Barnes was a former Houston Police officer, and he still looked the part. He wore a blue flight suit with a black tactical vest over that, his sidearm worn in a jackass rig under his left armpit. He was thirty-eight, tall, lean. He never seemed to smile.

Richardson had a knack for understanding people. It was why he was so good at writing about how people dealt with disasters. But Barnes was a tough nut to crack. He answered all of Richardson's questions, even the personal ones, with plainspoken ease. But even still, Richardson sensed a hard grain of meanness in the man that was like a warning not to get too close.

"Hang tight," Barnes said. "I'm gonna swing us around and head north toward downtown. I want to show it to you while it's still at high tide so you can see the Hand."

"What's the Hand?"

"That's what we call the shape made by the floodplain. Due to elevation and runoff and the tides and all that stuff, the outline of the flooded areas changes throughout the day. If you catch it during high tide, the waters look like an outstretched hand about to grab downtown."

"You're joking?" Richardson said.

"Nope. You'll see it right away."

"How come I've never heard that before?"

Barnes shrugged. "The powers that be don't like to make a big deal of it. We have a bad enough time with treasure hunters trying to sneak in. I guess they figure it would make our job even harder if we become some kind of tourist attraction."

Richardson nodded.

After a moment, Richardson said, "I was going to ask you about the treasure hunters. What do you think makes people want to risk sneaking in through the quarantine? Is there really that much worth stealing in here?"

"I guess so. You think about it, really, there's probably a fortune down there. I mean, all our banks and museums and jewelry stores and all that. Those places weren't cleaned out before the storms, and as far as I know they weren't cleaned out afterward. Not with the infected roaming the streets. And with the economy being what it is, can you really blame people for wanting to risk busting the quarantine for some potentially huge profits?"

"No, I guess not."

"Hell, even in good times, just the rumor of treasure is enough for some folks."

Richardson looked down again. They were passing over some kind of refinery now, pipes and trucks and mangled debris visible through the water.

"You're not thinking of going in with some of the treasure hunters, are you?"

Richardson smiled sheepishly. He was never very good at concealing what he was thinking.

"The thought had occurred to me."

"Well, don't think about it too hard," Barnes said. "I mean, you're a nice guy and all, but if I see you trying to come through the quarantine wall some night, I'll shoot you in the head, same as anybody else."

He said it breezily enough, but there was still something there that made it pretty plain he wasn't joking.

"Point taken," Richardson said.

The helicopter's engine hiccupped and they lost altitude momentarily as Barnes wrestled with the controls.

Richardson's stomach went halfway up his throat.

"What the hell was that?"

"Nothing to it," Barnes said. His voice was glassy smooth. "These old Schweizers, they're finicky."

"Are we okay?"

"Yeah, we're fine. Don't worry about it."

Richardson looked doubtful. The helicopter ride was scarier than he thought it would be, and it occurred to him that it wouldn't take more than a strong wind to hurl the thing to the ground.

"Where'd these bullet holes come from?"

Barnes glanced at the holes. "The uncles."

"They shoot at you?"

"Sometimes."

Richardson groaned. "That doesn't make me feel any better."

"It's no big deal," Barnes said. "Here, look down over there. I want you to see this. Whenever I come through here, I always try find some dolphins."

"Dolphins?"

Barnes pointed through the cockpit bubble to the water below. Richardson leaned over to see. They were flying over what had once been I-45, the street lamps and overhead road signs just poking up through the water. Barnes dropped the altitude even lower and cut their airspeed to a crawl. From a height of some sixty feet or so, Richardson could look through the fairly clear water and see the cars and debris down at road level.

"You see 'em?" Barnes said.

Richardson scanned the water for a long moment before he saw what Barnes was trying to show him. There were dolphins down there, three of them. They were headed northbound, toward downtown, paralleling the freeway below them. Richardson guessed the water was between fifteen and twenty feet deep, just deep enough for the animals to skim over the roofs of the sunken cars and still stay submerged. They almost looked like motorcycles zipping through traffic.

"That's amazing."

"Yeah," Barnes agreed. "There aren't many perks to this job, but that's one of 'em."

Richardson watched the dolphins until they finally turned off and swam into the deeper water east of town. They were getting closer to Houston proper now and seeing larger and larger buildings, the ground-level floors flooded to the ceilings.

Richardson crinkled his nose. "Hey, you smell that?"

Barnes looked aft and cursed under his breath.

Richardson turned around in his seat, as much as his seat

belt would allow, and saw a long, thick cloud of brown smoke trailing out behind them.

"Holy shit, are we on fire?"

"No, we're not on fire," Barnes said. He sounded annoyed. "The smoke is brown. We're burning oil. The smoke from a fire would be dark black."

Barnes turned back to his controls and started checking gauges.

"Are we going down?"

"We're fine," he said, a bit peevishly. "Just keep quiet and don't touch anything."

Barnes keyed his radio and said, "Quarter Four-One to Dispatch."

"Go ahead, Quarter Four-One," said a woman's voice.

"Quarter Four-One, we're losing oil pressure. I'm smoking pretty bad. I'm gonna try to get us back to Katy Field."

There was a pause on the dispatcher's end that Richardson didn't much like.

"Ten-four," the dispatcher said at last. "What's your location, Quarter Four-One?"

"Quarter Four-One, we're over Bay Area Boulevard and El Camino Real. You have any other units in the area?"

"Negative, Quarter Four-One."

There was a pause on Barnes's end that Richardson liked even less than the dispatcher's.

"Ten-four," Barnes said.

"Quarter Four-One, be advised. I have Katy Field standing by for your approach."

"Ten-four," Barnes said.

Richardson watched Barnes's hands flying over the controls. He had no idea what the pilot was doing, but he could tell plain enough that they were in some serious trouble.

"Officer Barnes?"

"Shut up."

Several tense moments went by. Barnes continued to work

the controls. A terrible acid fear spread through Richardson's gut as the engine continued to sputter and smoke. Despite Barnes's best efforts, they were losing altitude and their airspeed was slipping.

The engine sputtered once more, and smoke began to pour into the cockpit. Warning lights lit up all across the control panel.

"Quarter Four-One, we're going down. Repeat, we're going down. Coming up on El Dorado and Galveston Road."

Richardson didn't hear a reply. The helicopter shook beneath him, and the next moment they were going down way too fast, coming up on a large grouping of trees and some overhead power lines.

"Hang on," Barnes said.

They hit the water with a hard smack that knocked the air from Richardson's lungs and threw his whole world forward like he was caught on the crest of a wave. The blades of the helicopter's props struck the water with a series of loud slaps before they snapped completely free of the fuselage. The control panel sparked, and for a moment there was so much smoke that Richardson couldn't see.

Then water started to pour over his legs.

He screamed.

He felt hands groping at his chest. He tried batting them away, but couldn't. "Stop it," Barnes ordered him. "I'm trying to get you loose."

And a moment later, Richardson felt himself coming out of his seat, strong arms pulling him across the cockpit of the helicopter and into cold water that came up to his waist. He coughed and tried to rub the acrid smoke from his eyes. The water in his mouth tasted nasty, oily.

"Are you okay?" Barnes asked.

Gradually, Richardson's vision cleared. He looked at the officer and nodded.

Barnes turned on the helicopter and then punched it.

"Fucking piece of shit," he said. "Goddamn worthless fucking piece of shit."

Richardson was still too stunned to take in the fact that he had just lived through a helicopter crash. It was all he could do to stand on his own two feet.

Barnes, meanwhile, was digging through the cockpit for the emergency kit and his AR-15. He came up with an orange backpack and two rifles. He came over to Richardson and stuck one of the rifles into his hands.

"You know how to use that?"

Richardson took hold of the rifle, gripping it like they'd taught him in the army twenty years earlier.

He nodded.

"Good," Barnes said. "Because we're about to have company."

Only then did Richardson get a sense of their surroundings. They had landed in what looked like a grocery store parking lot. He could see the tops of cars and trucks just rising above the water. Off to their right was a subdivision, the houses sagging in on themselves, empty black holes where the windows and doors had been.

There was movement all around them.

The noise of the crash, he thought. *It'll be like a beacon for the infected.*

Ragged shapes that hardly looked like people anymore stumbled into the water from the subdivision, filling the air with the sounds of their splashing and their moaning.

He looked down at the gun in his hands, then at Barnes.

"Let's move out," Barnes said. "We're on the clock now."

CHAPTER 5

Art Waller was eighty-four years old and suffering from the classic one-two punch of gastrointestinal nuisances that nature so generously doles out to the elderly: a fixed hiatus hernia and a peptic ulcer.

Add to that two bad knees, a back that screamed at him every time he had to reach below his thighs, and a palsied shake that he was pretty sure was the advance calling card of Parkinson's, and his life was basically an object lesson in misery.

Still, for all that, right now, he had no intention of giving it up.

He turned slightly. Just enough to see that the thing behind him was still gaining.

Art needed a walker to get around. The tennis balls on its legs softened the noise, but the contraption still clanked each time he put his weight on it.

Clank clank. Clank clank.

He was creeping along, but it was as fast as he could go.

He chanced another look at his pursuer. There, on the sidewalk, less than ten feet behind him now, was one of the infected. It shouldn't be here. They were supposed to be quarantined. He had seen them on TV, and they had said they were all locked up behind the wall. It shouldn't be here.

But it was. And it was about to catch him.

The zombie used to be a nurse here at the Springfield Adult Living Village, but she was nothing but a mess now, no legs. They'd been torn off below her thigh. Now, she was pulling herself along on her belly with raw, bloody, mostly fingerless stubs that had once been her hands, leaving a thick blackish-red snail trail behind her.

And she was getting closer.

He gasped. The sound came up inside him like the rattle of dried beans in a coffee can. He was ashamed at the weakness he heard there, angry at himself. Damn it, he'd fought in Korea. Now, this miserable body of his was moving like the hour hand on a clock.

And that zombie behind him, she was the minute hand.

It was a slow-motion pursuit, but she was going to catch him. It was just a matter of time.

Clank clank. Clank clank.

He tried a few doors, but it was the Fourth of July weekend, and there was almost nobody left here at the Village. Just a skeleton crew of staff and a few residents.

He tried another door.

"Help me," he cried. "Please."

Behind him, the thing crawling on the sidewalk began to moan.

The sound of it unhinged something inside him. Union troops, he remembered, waiting on one knee in some cornfield someplace, their rifles ready at their cheeks, told stories of hearing the Confederates coming toward them, the rebel yell echoing off the surrounding hillsides. It did something to you deep in your bowels, they said, rattled you.

This was infinitely worse.

He tried to go faster.

Clank clank. Clank clank.

Just ahead, there was a hallway. He could hear voices. A man's deep voice. A woman's laughter.

The man's voice again.

Ed Moore, he thought. *The retired U.S. Deputy Marshal.*

"Help me," he said. "Ed?"

He put everything he had into it.

Clank clank. Clank clank.

Ed Moore had moved to Florida back in February because he liked the weather. For eleven years after his retirement from the U.S. Marshals Service, he'd lived in Amarillo, the Texas panhandle, where the winters were an endless parade of icy sleet and gray skies and wind that never stopped howling. Compared to that, Florida, with its comfy little villas nestled among the bougainvillea and palm trees and the live-in staff who wandered the place in their golf carts, was an absolute paradise.

The woman, Julie Carnes, was new to the Springfield community. She'd moved in at the end of June. She'd caught his attention right off, slender, a pretty face. Not handsome, but pretty. Still wore her hair long. He liked that. He leaned against the doorway to her private cottage and tipped his cowboy hat to her through the screen door. Ed said he thought it was time he introduced himself.

She was knitting something. She folded the needles together and rested them on the lap of her white dress.

He was wearing loose, faded blue jeans, black boots, a clean white shirt open at the neck. He doffed his cowboy hat to her as he entered, exposing a thick, uncombed tangle of white hair before sliding the hat back onto his head. There was a weatherworn look about him, like he should be trailing a cloud of dust.

She said, "You the resident cowboy?"

He smiled. He didn't mind smiling. He still had all his own teeth. "You're just like I figured," he said.

"Oh? And what did you figure?"

"Well, I figured I'd found somebody I could talk to."

"How do you know you can talk to me?"

"Well," he said, "I ain't never seen you in purple. I hate purple on a woman. All the women around here, they wear purple like it's some kind of uniform."

"You mean an old-lady uniform? I'm seventy-five years old, Mr. Moore. I don't need a uniform for people to know I'm an old crone."

"You ain't a crone," he said. "You wanna know the truth? I think you're about the best-looking woman in this place. I mean that. I'm talking about the staff, too. And by the way, you can call me Ed."

She nodded. There was a lull.

"So, you're here by yourself?" she said.

"For the last six years."

"You've been here six years?"

"I've been here since February. I've been on my own six years."

"Ah," she said. "Two years for me."

"You get lonely?"

She shrugged. "Sometimes. A girl can knit only so many scarves. Why, you asking me out?"

"Jerry Jeff Walker's gonna be in Tampa next Friday."

She laughed. "I knew it. A cowboy. The hat isn't just for show, is it?"

"Been wearing it all my life. Don't see any reason to give it up now."

"You mean now that you're not a marshal anymore?"

"How'd you know about that?"

She looked down at her knitting needles, fidgeted with them. "I asked around about you," she said. He thought he saw a blush, but that might have been the light.

Encouraged, he said, "They'd don't have cowboys where you come from?"

"I'm from Monroeville, Pennsylvania. They got George Romero, and that's about it."

"Ah."

"You like living here?" she asked.

"It's okay. Actually, to tell you the truth, not as much as I thought I would. I don't play golf, and I don't read like I planned on doing. Most of these other guys here, they sit around all day and watch the news and talk about how much better things were when Ronald Reagan was in office. It makes me wanna pull my hair out."

"So what do you do?" she asked. "Sit around with them and wait for something to happen?"

"Well, I had kinda thought that something just did happen."

She blushed that time. He was sure of it.

He was about to ask her if she wanted to come back to his place for a drink when they heard panting outside the door.

"Help me," came a man's voice. "Ed?"

Julie looked at Ed. He frowned. He went to the screen door and poked his head out, a silhouette standing there in the sunshine.

"Art? What's wrong there, buddy?"

"The nurse," he panted. "Out there. She's infected. Oh, Jesus, after me. Ed . . . please help me."

"Hold on there, Art. I'll help you." He turned to Julie. "You mind if I bring him in here?"

"Of course not," she said, and rose from her chair and started clearing skeins of yarn and magazines from a couch in the living room.

They sat Art down on the couch, the two of them lowering him onto his seat even as he went on frantically babbling about something going on outside in the hallway.

"What happened to him?" Julie asked.

Ed shook his head.

"Out there," Art said. He was gasping. "She's out there."

"Who's out there?"

"The nurse. She doesn't have any legs."

"What?"

"Ed," Julie said. She looked frightened.

"I'll go check it out. You stay here with him."

He slid out the door and stood there for a moment, looking around, then headed off in the direction from which Art Waller had come.

The hallway was empty, quiet, checkerboarded with patches of sunlight and shadow, but Ed could still feel the hairs standing up on the back of his neck. Something felt wrong.

Back in 1992, he'd gone into a house in Hugo, Oklahoma, with an arrest warrant for a militant white supremacy nut accused of a church bombing that killed two black women. The house had looked empty, but Ed wasn't so sure. All his internal alarms were blaring. He'd stepped into a back bedroom, and something told him to stop. Looking down, he saw a tripwire under his foot that led up the doorjamb to a shotgun mounted in the ceiling. Another inch, and they'd have been cleaning him up off the floor with a sponge and some hot, soapy water.

He had that same feeling now. Moving slowly, he stepped up to the corner of the hallway and looked around. He saw a long, dark smear of blood on the sidewalk. The trail turned in to a room a few doors up the walk. He glanced behind him and saw Julie standing in the doorway, watching him. He motioned her back inside. Then he set off toward the blood trail.

The door was propped open, and inside he saw two paramedics and Art Waller's legless nurse feeding on the body of a supine woman, her torso ripped open like a canoe. The body shook and twitched as the zombies tore into her.

Ed nearly vomited.

Three blood-smeared faces looked up at him.

Ed backed away.

One of the zombies, a tall, slender kid in his twenties whose only injury seemed to be a small but festering wound on his shoulder, got to his feet.

The next moment he was running at Ed.

Fast mover, Ed thought. But before he could react, the thing had closed the distance between them. The zombie raised its hands for Ed and Ed sidestepped him, coming up behind him and pushing him headlong as he swept his feet out from under him.

The zombie crashed headfirst into a bougainvillea bush and got wrapped up inside its dense inner branches.

When Ed turned back to the cottage, the second paramedic was already on his feet and limping more slowly than the first toward him. The legless nurse was dragging herself toward him on her belly.

He stepped out of the doorway and almost ran down the hallway to Julie's cottage, but he stopped when he realized the zombies would follow him.

He couldn't lead them straight to Julie and Art.

He looked around for a way out.

The first zombie, the fast mover, was pulling himself out of the tangled bougainvillea. The second one stepped out of the doorway. And now he could hear their moans. The sound carried through the courtyard and it made his blood run cold.

Without a plan, he took off running across the courtyard, away from Julie's cottage.

They were still behind him, but he had a pretty good lead. A few quick turns, and he lost them somewhere near the path that led down to Tamiami Road and Centennial Park.

And that's when he heard voices.

One voice, actually. A woman's. "It was such a lovely wedding," he heard her say. "Your Daddy was so proud. I remember watching the two of you come down that aisle, you holding on to his arm, just smiling ear to ear. I think it was the only time I ever saw him cry."

Ed followed the woman's voice. It belonged to Barbie Denkins, whose husband had died thirty years earlier and left her obscenely rich. The woman was in her late eighties now and thoroughly senile, Alzheimer's. Her cottage door was standing open. There was blood on the door frame. Inside, her quarters were packed with unopened boxes of sporting goods and picture frames and vegetable juicers and miracle cleaning products, all of it sold to her by unscrupulous telemarketers she was too starved for attention to hang up on.

Off in a far corner of the room, a zombie was bumping into boxes, trying to fight its way to where Barbie Denkins sat, chattering happily away.

"You didn't want those red flowers on your cake," Barbie said. "But I went ahead and did it just the same, and it was a better cake for it. You tell me it wasn't."

The zombie saw Ed and turned his way.

Beside Ed, next to the door, was an umbrella and a wooden Louisville Slugger baseball bat.

He picked up the bat.

The zombie stepped around a row of boxes, its head leaning to one side at an unnatural-looking angle. One of its cheeks had been torn open so that the mouth was elongated, the bloodstained rows of its teeth visible all the way back to the molars.

It moaned as it raised its hands at him.

Ed took a step forward and swung for the fence, planting the sweet spot of the bat on the side of the zombie's head.

The thing went tumbling backward against the wall, then landed in a heap on the floor.

It didn't move.

There was a pain in Ed's left shoulder, and he worked it around in the socket. The joints were protesting the sudden exertion.

"Stay here," he said to Barbie.

Outside her door, the first of the two paramedics was coming around the corner about fifty feet away.

The second one wouldn't be far behind.

He flexed his shoulder once again and raised the bat for another blow. He'd take care of these two, then go back inside and get Barbie.

Piece of cake.

CHAPTER 6

"What are we gonna do?" Richardson asked.

He was following Michael Barnes as best he could, wading through water that looked like melted caramel, holding his AR-15 up above his shoulders to keep it from getting wet.

"Be quiet," Barnes ordered him. "I'm gonna get us to a secure position. A roof, if possible. From there, we're gonna call for extraction."

"They'll extract us? You're sure?"

Barnes put a finger to his lips. Then, using hand gestures, he indicated that they were going to go around the back of the grocery store and into the buildings behind it.

They couldn't use the roof of the grocery store. Richardson knew that. Scared as he was, he'd been able to tell from the air that the building's roof had collapsed in on itself. It wouldn't be safe.

He turned and looked back at the wreckage of their helicopter. The thing looked like the jumbled exoskeleton of some enormous insect. A thick column of smoke rose into the air. Beyond the wreckage, he could see the infected already coming into the area. They were attracted to noise. All their senses worked, but their sense of hearing was the strongest. And the moaning of those already in the area would only make things worse.

He'd read Eddie Hudson's book about the first night of the outbreak in San Antonio, and like a lot of others had, he found it hard to believe that so many of the infected could pour into a street that was completely empty only moments before. But after seeing it for himself, he knew it was true.

Michael Barnes clearly knew it, too. Like all members of the Gulf Region Quarantine Authority, Barnes was a graduate of the Shreveport Survival School. Richardson had interviewed some of its instructors and had even been through an abbreviated version of the program before being allowed to go inside the quarantine zone with GRQA agents. He had a sense of what Barnes was trying to do by guiding them against the side wall of the grocery store. Richardson was ready for the slow but steady pace of their advance, stay quiet, stop, listen, scan, and move out again. While at the Shreveport School, he had felt like a kid playing cops and robbers. But this was the real deal.

Ahead of him, Barnes stopped and looked around. He motioned for Richardson to come forward.

"When we go around this corner, we're not gonna stop, okay? You'll see a strip center just ahead of you. We're gonna stay to the right of that. You got me?"

"Yeah," Richardson said.

"That weapon you've got there can fire through a magazine in a hurry, so don't lose your cool and empty the whole thing into the first zombie you see. Every shot counts, or you don't take it."

Richardson nodded.

"Okay, let's go."

Barnes stepped around the corner and Richardson tucked in right behind him. Ahead of them was a long stretch of water, the strip mall Barnes had told him about on the opposite side. In between, a few cars were sunken up to their windshields. Here and there they saw a tree.

Richardson counted sixteen zombies, all of them within fifty yards of their position and closing fast.

"Let's go," Barnes said.

He was already moving out, going quickly, but without splashing. It was harder for Richardson. He was terrified of moving through water, especially when he couldn't see his feet. He had a terrible feeling that the infected were just below the surface, waiting to grab him, even though he knew that to be impossible. The infected weren't truly dead, after all. They needed to breathe to go on hunting.

As they were moving forward, he tripped over the curb of a traffic island and went face-first into the water. When he came up, spluttering and blinking the water from his eyes, he saw that Barnes was already a good ten yards ahead of him.

He ran forward, making a terrific splash.

But Barnes didn't try to quiet him. One of the zombies had closed the distance between them, and Barnes leveled his AR-15 and dropped him with one shot.

Two others were close by and he dropped them as well. The pools of blood spreading out around the dead zombies turned green as they sank.

Barnes turned back to Richardson and said, "Heads up. Behind you."

Richardson twisted around.

A male zombie, the face a blotchy pattern of scabs and abscessed wounds, was less than ten feet from him. He hadn't heard it moving behind him, he realized. And then another thought occurred to him. This was one of the later-stage zombies. It didn't move with the same clumsy gait. The milky film had cleared from its eyes. The dead, vacant stare was gone. In its place was a feral intensity, the deliberateness of a hunter.

"Shoot it," Barnes ordered.

Richardson muttered an acknowledgment and raised his rifle and fired.

His first shot hit the zombie in the neck and sent it spiraling backward into the water.

Richardson got it in the head with his second shot.

He heard firing behind him. Barnes had zombies on three sides, but he was still calm. His firing was controlled, his pattern deliberate. One after another, the zombies went down until only a few remained, and those farther off, not yet a threat.

The battle had lasted perhaps twenty seconds, but Barnes had managed to drop a dozen or more of the infected. Richardson was in awe.

"Be careful," Barnes said. "Don't get too close to them. They may look dead, but it's always possible for one of them to pop up suddenly."

Richardson nodded.

"Come on. Let's go."

Barnes led him to a five-story building a couple hundred yards away. All the windows and doors had been blasted inward during the storms and the first floor was choked with debris, lath visible through the walls. Water came up to the bottom of the few pictures still on the walls and lapped at the top of the receptionist's counter toward the back.

"Come on," Barnes said. "We're headed for the roof."

They found the stairs and started up, water pouring out of their flight suits as they moved up to the second floor.

Richardson stayed behind Barnes, letting him make sure the way was clear before they proceeded upward again. Every floor was a repeat of the one below it, wrecked, the walls peeling, the carpet dark and moldy beneath their boots. The place smelled of seawater and sewage and rot.

When they reached the roof, Barnes moved immediately to the edge and looked down.

Richardson moved in beside him.

Below, a few zombies were moving toward the fallen corpses. Richardson knew that these later-stage zombies were cannibals, and wouldn't hesitate at an easy meal.

He was watching one pack of zombies eating a floating corpse when all of a sudden the corpse was yanked under the water. One of the zombies refused to let go of his meal and was pulled down with it. He resurfaced about twenty feet away, but with one arm bitten off at the elbow.

"What the hell was that?" Richardson said.

Barnes watched the zombie get to its feet and just stand there with a vacant expression on its face.

A moment later, it was pulled under again.

"What's down there?"

"Tiger shark, probably."

"A tiger shark? You're kidding."

"They've been known to come in this far during high tide," Barnes said. "And we did put a lot of blood in the water."

He stood up then and took the radio from his tactical vest.

"Quarter Four-One to Dispatch," he said.

"Go ahead, Quarter Four-One."

"Quarter Four-One, we've set up on the roof of the Clear Lake Title Office. Our situation is stable at present, no injuries. Request evac A-sap."

There was a long pause.

"Quarter Four-One?" Barnes said.

"We read you, Quarter Four-One. Negative on your request. Evac is not possible from your current location."

Barnes looked at Richardson and frowned. "What the fuck?" he said. He keyed up his radio again. "Quarter Four-One, you did copy my transmission, didn't you? Our situation is stable, but urgent. We are not injured. We need immediate evac."

The radio was silent.

Barnes tried again, but got nothing.

"Fuck," he said, and clipped his radio back onto his tactical vest.

"What does that mean?" Richardson said. "Why won't they answer you?"

"What the fuck do you think it means?"

Barnes sat down against an air duct and took a Snickers bar from his vest. "Might as well get comfortable," he said. "We're not going anywhere for a while."

CHAPTER 7

Her grandkids said they wanted to go down to the estuary, and Margaret O'Brien figured, sure, that'd be okay. She had them for the weekend while Grace, her daughter, was on a business trip in Atlanta, and frankly, she thought she was doing pretty well. The kids fought and bickered with each other every chance they got, that was true, and Randy, who was seven, tattled constantly on his sister, Britney, who was ten, but the trick to kids was just to keep them occupied. They had something to do, they behaved. Grace acted like Margaret had forgotten everything about children. Ha! She'd raised three daughters, hadn't she? And she'd done it as a young widow, too. She didn't have a wealthy ex-husband paying her alimony. She hadn't forgotten everything she'd learned about raising kids. She was sixty-eight, sure, but she wasn't senile. Not yet, anyway.

"Look, Ma, I'm not saying you forgot anything," Grace had said, once again holding out the book she'd been trying to unload on her for the last twenty minutes. "All I'm saying is—"

Margaret held up one of her small, chubby hands.

"Don't," she said. Margaret, short, thick about the middle

with a generous bust and a full head of brown hair that was only now starting to turn gray, was born Margaret Stephanides, and sometimes, when she argued with her daughters, the Greek blood in her fanned hot. She took one look at the book, *Siblings Without Rivalries* it was called, and said, "This is the book you think is going to teach me about taking care of children? Bah. Grace, you're going away for the three days. You don't think I can handle myself for three days? What do you think, I'm going to let them steal a car or something?"

"No, Ma, I just—"

The palm again. "You keep your book, Grace. You leave me the kids. Have a good time in Atlanta, okay?"

And so there'd been a few fights, sure, and Randy, he looked mystified when Margaret told him to stop tattling instead of yelling at his sister for calling him a turd brain, but it was okay. She was doing fine.

Now they were on the way down to the estuary, where the pamphlet up at the nurse's office said they had over sixty species of migrating birds during the summer months, the path lined by bougainvillea and palmetto swaying in the warm ocean breeze.

Britney, who was tall and skinny and beautiful like her mother, liked birds. Randy, he didn't. He looked bored.

"Nana," he said. "Where are all the birds? You said there'd be birds."

That was a good point, Margaret thought. She didn't see any.

"Nana, what's that man doing?"

"What man, Randy?"

"That one."

With her thumb, she pushed a pair of bifocals up the bridge of her nose and leaned forward, trying to see where Randy was pointing.

What followed was a moment of confusion. Her mind

gave her a merciful sort of reprieve from the shock of too sudden a revelation. Like bad news, the full impact of what she was seeing took a moment to filter through the buffer of her disbelief. But gradually, the obvious could not be denied. That man, she realized, was a zombie.

"Nana?"

She grabbed them both by the shoulder and squeezed. "Come on, kids. Let's go back."

"Nana," Britney said. She shook herself loose.

Together, they watched the man in orange as he stood up and slowly turned around. His face was covered with blood. Something long and limp, like wet, raw bacon, was hanging from his mouth. Even at this distance, Margaret could tell there was something wrong with the man's eyes.

The man in orange climbed onto the bank, pond water leaking out from between his cracked teeth. None of them saw the others coming out of the trees farther down the path, not until Randy heard sirens from the main road and turned that way.

"Nana," he said, pulling on Margaret's shirt.

Margaret pulled him close to her. A man in a bloodstained T-shirt and khaki shorts was coming toward them through the grass. A big piece of meat was missing from the side of his face and dried blood covered his hands. The hands kept opening and closing, like he was begging for food. His mouth opened, revealing teeth black with blood, and he began to moan.

The sound was answered all around by the other zombies.

"Nana," Britney shouted.

It was too much for Randy. He was pulling against Margaret's grip, trying to run away. Randy was small for his age, but God he was strong, and he nearly pulled her down with his struggles. And then Ed Moore, wearing a cowboy hat and jeans and holding a baseball bat, stepped into the grass in front of them, and Margaret couldn't believe how fast he moved. He planted the bat right up against the zombie's head.

Laid him out with one swing.

The zombie didn't get up. Ed stood over the body, looking down.

Blood dripped from the end of the bat.

Then he turned and smiled and tipped his cowboy hat to Margaret, winking at her. "How you doing, Margaret? You okay?"

Margaret whimpered.

Beside her, Randy, who was thoroughly awestruck, just nodded.

Ed Moore looked the three of them over. Margaret O'Brien was sixty-eight, frumpy, a little overweight, but still confident on her feet. The kids looked young, early elementary school aged. One look at Margaret and he knew she had already figured out what was going on. That was good. Having to explain it to her would take too long. The kids he wasn't so sure about. That age, did they know about the infected? Did they have any idea what it meant to see them outside the quarantine zone?

"We have to get somewhere safe," he said.

Margaret O'Brien nodded. The kids didn't say anything, just latched onto Margaret and stared at the infected coming at them from all sides.

"My cottage is over there," he said, pointing with the bat over their shoulders. "Can you guys make it?"

Margaret pulled the children close. Ed figured that was answer enough. He turned and gauged the distance to his cottage. There were three zombies between them and safety, two others that might be able to close the distance if he didn't get the other three with the first hit.

"Let's go," he said.

And with that, he went for the zombie nearest to them and got behind it. He stroked it in the back of the knees and dropped it. While it was down, he hit it in the back of the head.

He gave a quick look behind him, saw that Margaret and her two grandkids were still with him, and went on to the next one.

"Where did they come from?" Margaret asked him.

They were in his cottage now. Margaret was standing in the middle of his living room. The children had backed themselves into the corner behind his TV. Neither one of them had said a word since he first met them, and that was okay with Ed. He liked children, always had, but the quieter the better. He figured scared and quiet kids beat scared and crying kids any day.

"Ed?"

He was in his closet, getting his guns down from the storage box on the top shelf. After retirement, he had shelved his beloved .357 revolvers and figured he might never wear them again. And up until today, he had even convinced himself that it was nice not having to carry the things around.

"Ed? Where'd they come from? I thought . . . the quarantine. Aren't they . . . How could this happen?"

He stepped out of the closet with his gun belt in his hand. He slipped it around his waist and buckled it, then put his gun case on the coffee table and took out a pair of Smith & Wesson .357s. He dropped one into the holster and tucked the other into the small of his back.

The boy was looking at him, his eyes wide.

"I don't know, Margaret. I really don't. It's spreading, though. I saw three of them attacking Linda Beard."

Margaret looked sick.

"Do me a favor," he said. "Check the window. Tell me how many you see."

"Where did you get those guns?" the boy asked.

Margaret was peering through the blinds. She let them fall back into place and said, "Mr. Moore is a retired U.S. Marshal."

"No way! You're a marshal?"

"Used to be," Ed said. He smiled at the boy. "What's your name, son?"

"Randy Hargensen."

"Well, hello, Randy Hargensen. And how about you, little lady?"

"This is Britney," Randy said. "She's ten."

Ed tipped his hat to her. "Pleased to know you, Britney."

The girl didn't speak. She was trembling all over.

Randy said, "I like your hat. It's cool."

"Randy's into Westerns," Margaret said.

"Great. I like a good Western myself. You ever read Elmer Kelton, Randy?"

The boy cocked his head to one side. "I'm seven."

"Oh. Good point. Tell me, Randy, you ever seen a real marshal's badge?"

"No, sir."

Ed took out his wallet. Inside was a gold badge. He slid it out, removed it from its backer, and then handed it to Randy.

"You put that on, okay? You and your sister are gonna be my deputies."

The boy's smile was huge. The girl was still trembling, though. It was going to take more than trinkets to reach her.

"Margaret," he said. "What's the count?"

"Eight of them," she said.

"Okay, that's no problem."

He loaded each of his revolvers in turn from the speed

loaders in his gun case. Then he stepped up to the door, a revolver in each hand.

"Margaret, come over here and do the door for me. When I tell you to, you throw it open, you hear?"

"Where are we going, Ed?"

"I left Barbie Denkins in her apartment. We're gonna go get her. Then we're gonna make our way over to Julie Carnes's place. She should still be with Art Waller. From there, I don't know. You ready?"

She nodded.

He turned and winked at the kids. Then he said, "Okay, throw her open."

Margaret opened the door and Ed rushed outside. There was a zombie right in front of the door, and Ed put a bullet in its forehead.

He stepped over the body and went for the others. He didn't waste time letting them come to him. The sound of gunfire would bring more of the infected, and they had to be gone before that happened.

Careful to make every shot count, he dropped five of them in short order.

"Ed!"

He turned at the sound of Margaret's voice.

Two of the infected had gone for the open door instead of for him. They were on the sidewalk now, one on either side of the door.

Ed stepped between them, raised his revolvers, and dropped both zombies simultaneously.

When he turned his attention to Margaret and the kids, the boy was looking at him strangely. His eyes were wide, and he wasn't crying. He was smiling.

"Whoa," the boy said. "Mister, that was cool!"

CHAPTER 8

Ben Richardson was looking over the side of the roof at a small group of zombies clustered around the doorway of the building opposite them. There was another group doing the same thing around the door to their building. What exactly they were doing he couldn't tell, but something was going on. It almost looked like they were communicating, discussing something.

He and Barnes had spent most of the morning on the roof of the Clear Lake Title Company, waiting for the infected to get bored and wander off. But they hadn't. If anything, there were even more of them down there than before. The sound of their moaning chilled some deep interior part of him, something vital. It hadn't been like this in San Antonio.

"Hey, Officer Barnes."

No answer.

Richardson looked back. Barnes was sleeping with his back against the stairwell door, a white hand towel draped over his head. Richardson had heard stories of U-boat captains who sometimes took their boats deep to avoid a depth charging and fell asleep, even as the boat creaked and groaned and shuddered all around them. It was one way to show their men there was nothing to fear so as to keep up their morale. For a moment, he wondered if Barnes was trying to do something similar now, but just as quickly he chased the thought away. He didn't get that sense from Barnes. The man had a stoniness to him that didn't seem to allow room for compassion for another man's fear.

"Officer Barnes."

"What do you want?"

"Can you come here for a second, please?"

Barnes lifted the towel, annoyed at having his nap interrupted.

"Please?" Richardson said, and waved him over.

Barnes crawled over to him.

"What do you want?"

Richardson pointed at the zombies clustered around the doorway across the street. "Look at them over there," he said. "Why are they doing that?"

The tide was starting to ebb again, and most of the zombies were only up to their knees in water. They were all at a fairly advanced stage in the infection. Their skin was gray and leprous, open sores on their arms and neck and face, but they moved with a confidence that the more freshly turned Stage One and Stage Two zombies couldn't match.

Beside him, Barnes studied the crowd. He was frowning. He pulled himself up and peered over the side of the building at the group that was gathering around the door to their own building.

"How long have they been there?" he asked.

"I don't know," Richardson said. "I just saw them."

"Shit," Barnes muttered.

"What is it?"

"They're getting ready to make entry," Barnes said. "We're gonna have company pretty soon."

"What do you mean? How can you tell?"

Barnes pointed at the zombies out in the street. "I thought you went through the Shreveport School."

"Well, I—"

Barnes cut him off with a wave of his hand. "You see those zombies there? The ones walking there? If you watch them long enough, you'll notice that they're circling the building. The same ones have been doing it all morning, making that god-awful racket. These others have broken away from the main group, though. They've given up trying to flush us out. They're coming in to get us. Those ones over there, they've probably trapped something inside that building. A dog, maybe. There's still lots of dogs around here."

Richardson was shocked.

"You're serious? They're capable of that kind of cognition? They can set up a diversion?"

"Of course," Barnes said. "They'll fuck you up if you're not careful. Bubbas like these guys can do basic problem solving. They can open doors and crawl through windows and hunt in packs. I watched four of 'em trap a raccoon once. I don't know if you ever tried to catch a raccoon, but it ain't easy."

"You call them Bubbas?"

"Stage Three zombies, like those guys. They're not real bright, but they're bright enough to get the job done."

Richardson shook his head in amazement. He'd heard rumors that some of the Stage Three zombies had limited cognition. At Shreveport, they told him some of the more advanced zombies could respond to their names or cooperate on kills, that kind of thing. But he hadn't believed those rumors. It seemed more like wishful thinking from the growing sector of the American public that wanted the government to go in and try to administer a cure for the necrosis filovirus, even if that meant risking the quarantine.

Richardson had seen it before with Dr. Sylvia Carnes's

expedition into San Antonio. She'd taken twenty-eight college kids, all of them members of the University of Texas at Austin's Chapter of Ethical Treatment for the Infected, into the quarantine zone, and gotten most of them killed in the process. Richardson had been along as an embedded reporter on that disastrous trip, and was one of three to make it out of San Antonio alive. It was there he'd solidified his opinion that the infected were beyond help. But seeing the infected like this complicated things.

"So what are we going to do?" he said to Barnes.

"We're gonna need to get out of here. You ready to move?"

There was a loud crash from somewhere downstairs.

"What was that?"

"Shit," Barnes said. His rifle was leaning against the wall next to the stairwell door. He ran over and picked it up, ejected the magazine, checked it, slapped it back in. "How you doin' for ammo?"

"I only fired twice."

"Okay, good."

Barnes leaned against the door, listening. Even from where he stood, Richardson could hear moans inside the building below them. Something was crashing around inside the stairwell, making its way up.

Barnes looked back to Richardson. "We're about to get some company. Remember, make your shots count. Don't rock back and start firing or you'll burn through that magazine in a heartbeat."

Richardson nodded.

There was a booming crash against the metal door. It rocked against its hinges.

Another crash.

"Next one and they'll be through," Barnes said.

Richardson swallowed the lump in his throat and tried to focus. His vision was tunneled around the door.

There was a final crash and the door exploded outward. A

zombie stood there, three more behind him. The first one lumbered out onto the roof. He looked half-starved. His shirt was little more than a scrap of soiled cotton looped around his neck and his left shoulder. Richardson could count the man's ribs down his right side. They protruded like ripples in a pond through his yellowish-gray, abscessed skin. But his eyes were clear, intent on aggression, full of feral intelligence behind a curtain of wet, dark hair.

Richardson's finger twitched against the trigger, but he didn't fire. Barnes did that for him. Four quick, well-aimed shots. The man looked like he was practicing on the range. He kept himself in a crouch, making every move count.

The exchange lasted maybe three seconds.

Barnes advanced into the doorway without saying a word.

Richardson went after him.

There was one more zombie in the stairwell but Barnes put it down with another well-aimed shot.

In the stairwell, the sound of the AR-15 was like two boards being slapped together. It echoed inside Richardson's head.

A moment later, they stepped out onto the fifth floor. From there, they were going to have to take the exposed interior stairwell that led down through the center of the building and into the lobby. Debris had collected all over the floor, and Richardson had to scramble over it just to keep up with Barnes.

They were on the second-floor landing when they spotted their next zombie. It crashed out of an office to Richardson's right, and Richardson gasped in surprise as the thing clapped a mangled hand on his shoulder.

He ducked away from the woman and spun around, bringing the muzzle of his rifle to bear on the woman's head.

He fired, and the woman's head exploded all over the wall behind her. The headless corpse fell backward against the wall and sagged to the ground.

Richardson lowered his rifle and looked at the damage he had caused.

"My God," he whispered.

But when he turned around, Barnes was out of sight.

"Officer Barnes?"

He heard the sound of footsteps below him. He looked over the railing and saw Barnes moving in a crouch across the lobby.

Realizing that Barnes had no intention of waiting for him, Richardson ran down the stairs as fast as the debris in his way allowed. All sorts of trash had floated into the lobby with the ebb and flow of the tides, and scrambling across it was hard. Barnes made it look easy, never letting his weapon dip from the low ready position, but for Richardson, it was humiliatingly difficult to navigate the mess of chairs and tables and plastic boxes and piles upon piles of plywood that seemed to be everywhere.

He came up next to Barnes and looked out into the street. The noise of their firefight had attracted scores of the infected. They stumbled out of every doorway, from around every corner, advancing through the knee-deep water with varying degrees of skill. Some almost seemed to bound through the water. Others moved in fits and starts, like badly handled marionettes.

Richardson raised his rifle, but Barnes put a hand on the muzzle and forced it down.

"No," he said. "Save your ammo."

"What are we gonna do?"

"We're gonna move fast. Come on."

They ran up the narrow street, zigzagging through the wreckage, hugging the walls of buildings wherever possible. Richardson kept as close to Barnes as he could, but the man was fast. By the time they reached the corner of the building, Richardson was a good ten yards behind him, and losing ground.

But then Barnes stopped. He peered around the corner, then looked back at Richardson. His gaze didn't stay on Richardson, though. It drifted to the area behind him, and his face took on an odd, puzzled expression.

Richardson stopped and turned to see what Barnes was looking at. None of the infected had followed them. They had run right through the crowd, but now the infected were all turning away and forming a tightening ring around a knot of people who had just emerged from the building across the street from the Clear Lake Title Company.

Even from a distance of two hundred feet or so, Richardson could tell they weren't infected.

"Oh, my God," he said. "Officer Barnes, do you see—"

"Uncles," Barnes said. "Come on."

He made a move to duck around the corner.

"Hey, wait," Richardson said. "We have to help them."

"They're uncles," Barnes said. "They're dead already."

"You're kidding. You're just gonna leave them? You can't."

"Just fuckin' watch me."

Barnes turned away. Richardson stared at his back, amazed that the man could disengage from the scene so effortlessly. He only had a moment to make up his own mind: follow Barnes or do what his gut told him was the only humane thing to do.

He went with his gut.

While Barnes slipped around the corner, Richardson ran out into the middle of the flooded street and began to scream at the top of his lungs, "Hey, hey, hey. Over here."

He jumped up and down, splashing water everywhere. He waved the rifle over his head and shouted some more.

From the shadows, Barnes hissed, "What the fuck are you doing?"

Richardson glanced at him. "Help me," he said.

When he looked back to the street, some of the infected

had broken away and were stumbling toward them. Most were still advancing on the small crowd of people.

"Fuck it," Richardson said, and charged.

Running and shooting was not easy, and Richardson's shots were mostly misses. He burned through his entire magazine in seconds and scored only four hits.

Now he found himself in the thick of the fight.

He grabbed the rifle by the still-hot barrel and used it as a club. A zombie in the remains of a business suit staggered forward. Richardson could see its wide, intensely wild eyes. Dark ropes of saliva oozed from the corners of his mouth and down his neck. As it reached for him, Richardson brought the rifle over his head and slammed it back down again on top of the zombie's skull.

The gun sent a painful shudder up his forearms, like he had hit a baseball with the neck of the bat instead of with the sweet spot, but the zombie folded to the ground and went facedown into the water. Dark blood oozed from the wound and into the water like a curl of smoke coming up from a pipe.

When he looked up, four more zombies were right in front of him. The one to the far left looked emaciated to the point she could barely hold her arms up. Her face was dark, the cheeks sunken, and her eyes appeared to protrude oddly from the sockets, like the skin had puckered around them.

He flanked her, intending to use her as a barrier between himself the others. Then he brought up his rifle again and prepared to swing it at the woman's head.

He heard gunshots instead.

Two of the zombies behind the emaciated woman dropped. Then the third. Then the woman.

Richardson looked toward the sound and saw Barnes strolling almost casually down the center of the street, firing as he advanced, dropping zombies with every shot.

He stopped a little forward of Richardson's position and kept on firing. His skill with the rifle was almost beautiful to watch. He was so smooth, every gesture one of complete control, the shots coming like the ticks of a metronome. He shot through his magazine, ejected it, slapped in a fresh one, and with barely a pause went right back to firing.

More zombies were coming into the street from all directions.

"They've got us surrounded," he yelled to Barnes.

Barnes stopped firing just long enough to scan the scene.

"Get them," he said, pointing at the crowd of people.

"Where are we going to go?" Richardson asked.

"Through there," Barnes said. He was pointing at a narrow alleyway between two buildings off to his right. "Hurry," he said.

Richardson made his way over to the crowd and did a quick count of eleven people, four women and seven men. One of the women was Hispanic, about forty, dressed in clothes so worn and weathered they looked gray, though they had clearly once been some brighter color. Next to her, clinging tightly to her waist, was a scrawny white kid about fourteen years old. All of them were armed with makeshift clubs, pieces of rebar, baseball bats, metal pipes. Richardson got a sense right away that the woman with her arm around the fourteen-year-old boy was the leader of the group, the others seeming to gather behind her.

"I'm Ben Richardson," he said. "We're gonna help you. Come with me."

"Okay," she said.

Richardson pointed the others through the alleyway. They crossed the street behind Barnes, who fell in behind the group and covered their retreat. The woman moved into the alleyway with confidence, and Richardson realized that she almost certainly knew her way around here. She and her group had probably been living as scavengers in these ruins since the first days of the quarantine. He fell in behind her and let her take the lead.

They emerged into a jumble of wreckage. A seemingly endless field of wheels, paint cans, sheets of plywood, refrigerators, TVs, a huge metal frame like the skeleton of an overhead street sign, toppled trees, light poles, cars, the frame to somebody's boat trailer, and a whole profusion of bricks and pillows and mattresses and mud stretched out before them.

"Can we get through that?" Richardson asked.

"Yeah, through here," the woman said.

But before they could move out, there was the sound of a scuffle behind them. An infected woman in a blue dress had stepped out of the doorway of the building to their right and fell on one of the group.

The man wrestled with the woman for a moment and then managed to toss her to one side. Two other members of the group stepped up with their makeshift clubs at the ready and battered the infected woman into a motionless pulp with a few well-placed blows.

"Okay?" the woman leading the group said.

The man who had tossed the zombie to the ground nodded.

Behind them, Barnes was firing. He paused long enough to shout, "Get moving up there," and went back to firing.

"This way," the woman said.

She led them through the maze of debris with surprising ease, pointing out the tricky parts for Richardson to avoid.

"It isn't easy for the infected to get through here," she told Richardson. "They get confused easily."

He nodded. He noticed that even as they threaded through the densest parts of the debris field, she never let go of the boy's hand.

* * *

Ten minutes later they were standing in a parking lot, not a zombie in sight. Off to their right were the remains of a shopping mall. Richardson could still read the signs on a few of the buildings.

"Where are we?" Richardson said to the woman.

"South side of Baybrook Mall," Barnes said, coming up behind them. He had a GPS in his hand.

"Thank you for helping us back there," the woman said. "We would have died if you hadn't helped us."

Barnes just grunted, didn't even look at her.

She turned to Richardson. "We saw your helicopter go down. We were going to see if we could help you, but we got caught in that building across the street from you guys."

Barnes moved off from them and took out his radio.

Richardson watched him for a moment, then turned to the woman.

"I'm Ben Richardson," he said.

"I know," she said. "You said that already."

And then she smiled, and it was a surprisingly pretty smile. Even after two years inside the quarantine zone, her teeth looked white and healthy.

"I'm Sandra Tellez," she said. She put her arm around the boy and said, "This is Clint Siefer."

The boy didn't speak. His face was lean and dirty, yet his forehead had a thoughtful heaviness to it that left his eyes in shadow. Richardson had always prided himself on his story radar, that gift he had for spotting the people in a crowd whose story seemed to capture the essence of a disaster. That radar was going full tilt in his head right now, looking at these two. They had a story. He only hoped there'd be time to hear it.

A young man was standing next to Clint. He looked to be about twenty-five, though it was hard to tell for the layers of grime on his face. His eyes kept darting to the pouch clipped to Richardson's shoulder.

"What's your name?" Richardson asked him.

"Jerald Stevens," he said. "Hey, do you have any food on you?"

His eyes flicked to the pouch again.

"Uh, yeah," Richardson said. "I think I got a candy bar."

"Can I have it?"

Richardson laughed, though a bit uncomfortably. There was disturbing urgency in the man's attitude, something that didn't seem quite sane.

"Yeah, sure," he said.

He unzipped the pouch and removed a Snickers bar and a small bag of smoked almonds.

"You want the almonds, too?"

The man nodded, and in that moment, Richardson had him pegged. He reminded him of that hyperactive weasel from the old Foghorn Leghorn cartoons, and Richardson had a sudden image of the young man with his tongue hanging out the side of his mouth, his hands dangling limply in front of his thin, spoon-shaped chest, eagerly bouncing on his toes in nervous anticipation of a morsel.

"Here you go," he said.

The young man, his hair a matted, out-of-control mess, snatched the food away and walked off from the group to devour it.

Richardson watched him go, then looked back to Sandra Tellez.

She shrugged. "Things are hard inside here. We eat whenever we can."

"I'm sorry I don't have any more."

"That's okay," she said. "I'm sure you guys didn't plan on crashing."

"No, you're right about that."

"What happened?"

"I'm not really sure what happened. There was a lot of smoke. Officer Barnes over there said something about an oil leak. We lost oil pressure, and the next thing I know we're crashing into that parking lot."

"You're not part of the GQRA?"

"No," he said. "I'm a freelance journalist. I was doing a piece on the Quarantine Authority when this happened."

"And now you're screwed here with us?"

Richardson laughed. He liked the way she said it, like there was still a part of her capable of appreciating a sick joke. He hadn't expected to find that among the uncles.

"And you guys?" he said. "What's your story?"

She started to tell him when they heard Barnes cussing at his radio.

They both turned and watched him throw it down to the pavement, where it shattered.

"What's wrong?" Richardson asked.

"What the fuck do you think is wrong?"

Sandra said, "They're not coming for you, are they?"

Barnes kicked a piece of the radio, looked off into the distance, and huffed.

"No, they're not," he said.

She looked at Richardson. "Looks like you guys really are screwed."

Barnes walked over to the rest of the group and eyed them each in turn. One of the group was standing off from the others, and Barnes's gaze locked on him.

Richardson noticed it was the man who had been surprised by the zombie in the alleyway. He was sitting on his haunches, hugging himself, rocking back and forth. His breathing sounded ragged. His face was pale and sweaty.

"You," Barnes said, pointing at the man. "Stand up."

Barnes advanced through the crowd. Sandra followed him.

The man rose painfully to his feet. He kept his left side turned away from the others.

"You're infected," Barnes said.

"No, I'm not," the man said, but you could hear it in his voice.

"Bullshit," Barnes said.

He grabbed the man by the shoulder and spun him around. The man had his hand clamped over his bicep, but blood oozed between his fingers and rolled down the back of his hand.

"Show me," Barnes said.

Sandra came up behind him. "Rob? Are you okay?"

The man's gaze dropped to the ground. He took his hand away, exposing a nasty bite mark that was already showing the first sign of decay. It smelled bad.

"Oh, no," Sandra said.

Beside her, Barnes drew his pistol.

"Hey," Sandra said. "Hey, wait!"

But she couldn't stop what happened. Barnes leveled the pistol at the man's face. The man put up his hands and Richardson could see the man's lips starting to form the words *No, wait,* but it was wasted effort. Barnes fired a single shot that took the top of the man's head off and laid him out on his back on the pavement. Then Barnes holstered his weapon with a casualness that suggested he did stuff like this every day.

"What is wrong with you?" Sandra said. She was practically screaming at him. Her face was pulled tight in a grimace of rage and pain and shock. "Why did you do that?"

"He was infected."

"We have a way of dealing with this," she said.

"You have a cure?" Barnes asked sarcastically.

"No, we have a way of letting somebody take care of themselves when they get infected. We give them the choice of how they want to—"

"I'm not interested," Barnes said. "I'm getting out of here."

"And just how do you intend to do that?" Sandra asked. "They're not coming to rescue you."

He ejected his AR-15's magazine, checked it, then slapped it back into place. "I'm not staying inside the quarantine," he said. "I don't care if I have to shoot my way out or not, but I'm not staying inside this city. You people can come along if you want. You can stay here if you want. I don't care. Me, I'm getting out."

And with that, he began walking north across the parking lot.

Slowly, silently, the others fell in line behind him.

Chapter 9

Billy Kline stopped at the corner of a pink stucco wall and glanced inside the entrance to the Springfield Adult Living Village. There was a guard shack about twenty feet in with gates on either side. Both gates were hanging open.

So where's the guard? he wondered.

Beside him, Tommy Patmore was almost as far gone as the infected that had just escaped.

"I didn't mean to hurt him. Oh Jesus, oh Jesus, I really didn't. God, there was so much blood. So much of it . . . it got everywhere."

"Shut up," Billy said.

They had seen only a few cars that entire morning. One was going by them now on Tamiami Street. Billy watched it roll by. A moment later, he heard a horn and the sound of skidding tires.

There was a crash.

He heard a woman scream.

When her screams were cut short, Billy made up his mind. "Listen," he said to Tommy. "Hey, you hear me? Tommy."

Tommy made a low groan that was not quite a sign of understanding.

"I killed him, Billy."

"I know you did. But Tommy, listen to me. We are in deep shit, you and me. I need you to stay sharp and keep your eyes open. Follow me."

"Where are we going?"

"Just follow me."

Billy grabbed his bloody garbage spike and made for the gates. Past the guard shack he could see a wild profusion of shrubs and trees and flowers.

"Seems safe enough," Billy said.

He grabbed Tommy by the shoulder of his orange scrubs and pulled him along.

But as they came up even with the guard shack, Billy looked over and saw something that made his guts turn over.

Inside the guard shack, seated on the floor against the wall, was the guard. His Smokey the Bear hat was on the floor beside him. His left shoulder and part of his face were dark with blood. In his other hand he held his pistol. He was watching Billy and Tommy as they went by, his eyes two inscrutable milky clouds.

He started to move.

"Ah, for Christ's sake," Billy said.

He reached for Tommy's shoulder again to pull him back, but Tommy was already walking toward the man.

The man rose to his feet.

"Tommy, what the hell are you doing?"

"I didn't want to," Tommy said. He dropped the shank on the pavement and walked toward the guard with his hands spread wide, a sinner begging forgiveness. "Please, I didn't want to hurt him. I didn't mean to. I'm sorry. You've got to believe me."

"Tommy, for Christ's—"

The guard stepped out of the shack. His head was leaning

to one side. His left arm hung limply. But in his right, he still held his pistol, and this came up with his hand as he reached for Tommy.

Billy saw the guard's fingers clutching for Tommy, and he knew what was going to happen.

A moment later, there was a shot.

The bullet hit the ground between Tommy's feet and glanced off into nowhere with a high-pitched *zing*.

The second shot hit Tommy in the gut.

Tommy dropped to his knees, a look of profound surprise on his face, a startled grunt stuck somewhere in the back of his throat.

Billy backed away.

The guard fell on Tommy and both men tumbled to the pavement. Tommy tried to roll away. He was groaning in agony from the gut shot, and it kept him from regaining his feet.

The guard latched onto him and took a bite of Tommy's calf. Tommy screamed as blood began to darken his pant leg.

Billy turned to run back into the street.

Three of the prisoners from the Sarasota County Jail were coming toward him, all of them freshly turned. Meanwhile, beside him, the guard was tearing into Tommy with his teeth. He turned his bloodstained face to Billy and started to rise again.

Billy just shook his head, spun on his heels, and ran for the cottages inside the Springfield Adult Living Village.

He sprinted across the lawn and reached the nearest of the pink stucco cottages. From the shows he'd seen while frittering away his days in the Sarasota County Jail, Billy knew that loud noises attracted the infected, and once those few infected zeroed in on an uninfected person, they would begin to moan. The moans carried, drawing more of the infected into the area. All the reports of seemingly empty streets suddenly flooding with the infected weren't exaggerations.

Billy kept himself low and out of sight. He got to cover, scanned his surroundings constantly, just like the documentaries about the quarantine zone said to do, and tried not to make any noise. His plan was to reach one of the cottages, get to a phone, call for help, then sit tight and wait for somebody with guns to come and rescue him.

But that plan went out the window when he stepped around the front of the cottage.

Just ahead of him was a narrow hallway, a courtyard farther on. To his left, just before the courtyard, was a gently rising slope of green grass. The courtyard was packed with the infected. More were coming down the grassy slope. They were headed for the doorway to a single cottage, where two old folks were trying to hold their door closed against the infected.

"Ah, for Christ's sake," he said.

He didn't want any part of it. Billy turned away and stepped right into the path of the three prisoners he'd seen from the guard shack. Behind them was the guard. Tommy wasn't with them.

He looked for the gun and was both surprised and frustrated to see that the guard no longer had it with him. He had been a fool for not picking that thing up back at the guard shack.

Billy raised his trash spike and started to run. He was going to flank the three prisoners, sprint around the shambling, slower guard, and take his chances out on the street. But before he could put that simple plan into motion, one of the prisoners broke forward in a furious sprint, crashed into him, and knocked him to the ground, landing on top of him.

Billy landed with his spike across his chest in a port arms position. He jammed it up under the man's chin and twisted, tossing him to the side. Billy scrambled to his feet and jammed the spike into the back of the zombie's head before he had a chance to move. Satisfied the zombie was dead, Billy put his foot on the side of the zombie's head and yanked his spike free from the corpse.

But now he was surrounded.

Some of the zombies coming down the grassy slope had diverted in his direction, and Billy found himself checked everywhere he turned by the mangled arms and faces of the infected.

Billy jabbed his spike into every face he saw and batted at their hands with his pole as he twisted and spun away from their grasp. He rushed into the crowd and ducked away just as a pair of zombies reached for him. At the same time, he brought the pole around in a sweeping path that caught one of the zombies in its upward arc, impaling its left hand. Unable to control his arm, the zombie bobbed on the spike like a balloon on a string.

In the melee, Billy had worked his way halfway up the slope. The zombies were slogging after him in a graceless, clumsy mass, and Billy, still swinging the impaled zombie around by its arm, flung him downward, into the advancing crowd. The zombie flew off and tumbled down to the grass, where it bowled into the others like logs crashing downhill.

Billy ran around the pile and a moment later found himself standing before the old woman and the bent wreck of a man who stood behind her.

"Are you folks okay?"

They just looked at him. The woman's eyes slipped from him to the carnage behind him and then rolled slowly back to Billy.

"Ma'am? You okay?"

She blinked at him.

"They're behind you," she said.

He turned around. At least a dozen of the infected were

rising to their feet. Others had already gained their footing and were closing in fast.

"Can we hide in there?" he said.

"They pulled the door out of the jamb," she said. "It won't close."

Just then he heard a gunshot from the courtyard. He turned that way and saw an old dude in a cowboy hat with a pair of pistols in his hand. He had just shot one of the infected and was motioning two old women and two little kids through a corridor on the opposite side of the courtyard.

The dude in the cowboy hat glanced at Billy, and the two of them made eye contact. Even at a distance, Billy could see the man's face grow momentarily hard with recognition at the orange scrubs Billy wore. But the look faded just as quickly as it formed, and the next instant he was motioning Billy and the two old-timers with him to follow them into the courtyard.

Billy looked behind him again. They weren't going to be able to make it to the street.

To the old woman, he said, "Okay, you two come with me."

"He can't walk fast enough," the woman said.

"I'll carry him. Here, hold this."

He handed his spike to the woman, who took the gore-stained thing like she'd just been handed a pile of dog shit.

Billy picked up the old man, and the next moment, they were all running for the courtyard, a moaning wake of the infected trailing out behind them.

Chapter 10

Jeff Stavers was caught up in the parking lot over LAX for nearly an hour before they landed, and now that they were finally taxiing to their terminal, he was feeling irritable and restless.

The fat lady from Chicago and her even fatter little nine-year-old boy both unbuckled their seat belts at the same time, and the woman groaned as she let her gut relax. The boy's name was Alex. Jeff knew his name was Alex because the fat woman hadn't stopped saying his name since Denver, where Jeff had joined their little family drama already in progress. He'd sat down in the window seat next to the woman because it was the only available seat on the flight, and he was immediately sorry for it. The woman hogged the armrest and her bulging elbow kept oozing into his side. For nearly four hours, he felt like he was crammed into the back corner of an elevator. Plus, the kid wouldn't stop coughing and sneezing. It was a nasty, nostril-clearing sound, and the woman would immediately slap him in the back of the head and say, "Alex, I told you to cover your mouth."

The boy would flinch, then slowly uncoil himself and say, in a high, nasally voice, "Sorry, Mom."

Once, Alex's sleeve had pulled up, exposing a fresh bandage around his elbow. His mother rushed to cover that up, and then whispered something into his ear.

"Sorry, Mom," he said.

Right before they landed, the woman turned to Jeff and said, "Allergies," and rolled her eyes.

He just smiled and nodded and waited for the brown hazy air of Los Angeles to appear on the horizon.

But they were here now, finally, and he could feel the tension headache that had plagued him for the last week slowly going away. When he got back to Littleton . . . Well, he would worry about Littleton when he had to. Right now, all his thoughts were on seeing Colin Wyndham again. Back when they were roommates at Harvard, Jeff would have sworn there wasn't a woman alive who could lasso the irredeemable and profligate Colin Wyndham into marriage, but apparently L.A. had produced such a woman.

This was going to be the bachelor party of the century.

The intercom chimed and the flight attendant spoke up, telling them the local time and temperature and informing them to keep their seat belts fastened and to refrain from using electronic devices until they were stopped at the terminal.

"Will do," Jeff muttered, and took out his cell phone and flipped it open.

He sent a quick text message to Colin.

on the ground finally

A moment later, Colin wrote back:

took you long enough. got a surprise for you. you're not gonna believe it.

Jeff laughed. Typical Colin. He wrote:

what kind of surprise

The flight attendant was looking his way. Jeff put the phone down and tried to look innocent. It was a silly thing to do. He knew that. It wasn't like she was going to call in the air marshals on him. Images flooded his mind of dark-suited men with pistols in their hands boarding the plane, demanding his cell phone, dragging him kicking and screaming and pleading into a bare room for hours of absurd questioning that would make him feel like a character in an Albert Camus novel.

The thought made him laugh. But then he thought of the questions the real police were likely to ask him and the laughter died in his throat.

After all the good times at Harvard, he and Colin had gone their separate ways. Colin was heir to the Mertz family fortune, all $1.3 billion of it. Harvard had been a C-average joke to him. He had no worries, no need to bother with graduate school or law school or medical school or anything, really. There was college, because he had to, and then after that, the world opened up like a sun-dappled delta plain of privilege and pampering.

For Jeff, there were scholarships to keep, which he did. He graduated with a fairly respectable 3.86 GPA, left Cambridge and went to Colorado University for law school, where he did two years before the crack-up that led to flunking out, which in turn led to missing payments on his student loans and racking up $18,000 worth of credit card debt. Now, he was working as a store manager at Blockbuster and waking up everyday in a shabby little efficiency apartment over a garage in Littleton, Colorado, with the constant panicked feeling that he was drowning.

Colin knew the bit about law school, and he knew about the Blockbuster job. He could probably infer the rest. He wasn't stupid, after all. He was a drug-addled party animal, but he wasn't stupid. That was probably why he offered to pay for this whole weeklong party to Vegas. But of course

Jeff couldn't allow that. There was a deep vein of pride in him that would rather deny the truth than let it be said out in the open. And that was why he had steadily, over the last week, taken cash advances from the credit cards his customers used at his store. All told, it was $9,200 in cash, making his wallet feel fat as a brick under his right butt cheek.

Yeah, there was going to be hell to pay when he got back to Littleton.

His phone beeped again. Jeff looked down at it. He had completely forgotten his last text message to Colin. He hit the read button.

greatest surprise of your life. hope you're horny.

"What the . . ."

Jeff closed his phone and looked around.

The fat lady next to him was slapping Alex in the back of the head again. "Stop scratching it," she said, her voice a muffled hiss.

She looked at Jeff and smiled.

"Kids," she said.

They were close enough to the end of their time together that he didn't see any need to be a jerk to her, so he smiled back and said, "Yeah, whatcha gonna do?"

A few minutes later, they were walking through the jetway to the terminal.

Colin was waiting for him, looking cool with his finger-combed brown hair and good tan. He looked smug and well-provided for, with his hands stuffed down into the pockets of his $3,000 Armani suit pants.

Jeff held out his hand to shake and Colin smiled and said, "Fuck that," and hugged him.

"You look good, man," Jeff said.

"I'd say the same about you, but you look like shit."

"Yeah, fuck you, too."

The fat woman and her even fatter kid walked by and the boy coughed, scratching at a part of his arm hidden by his shirtsleeve.

"Take care, Alex," Jeff said.

The boy waved.

For a moment, it looked to Jeff like the boy's fingertips were red.

"Friends of yours?"

"Yeah, you know. We're tight."

"Uh-huh." Colin turned and they walked together to the baggage claim, talking about Colin's new fiancé and his life out here in L.A. He had yet to tell Jeff the girl's name, and Jeff hadn't asked.

"So what's this surprise you were telling me about?"

"Out in the car," Colin said.

They stepped out to the loading zone, and Jeff saw a black limo waiting for them.

"We're taking a limo to Las Vegas?" Jeff said.

"No, we're taking a chartered party bus to Vegas. But before that, we're gonna do a little partying and play catch-up."

Colin reached into his pocket and held out a closed fist to Jeff.

"What's that?"

"Just take it," Colin said. "One for you, one for me."

Jeff looked around. The place was crowded, but nobody was paying any attention to them. He reached out and Colin dropped something into his hand. Jeff glanced at it.

One pink pill, one blue.

"Is that what I think it is?"

"Viagra and the best ecstasy you're ever gonna take. Pop 'em real quick. You're gonna need it."

"For what?"

"Just take it, would you?"

Jeff popped the pills into his mouth and swallowed them dry.

"Cool," Colin said. He opened the back door to the limo and with a sweep of his hand motioned Jeff inside. "Go on," he said. "Check it out."

Jeff put a hand on the roof and peered inside. The first things he saw were two pairs of long, beautifully bare legs. They led up to two tiny black skirts and bare midriffs and halter tops. Above that, smiling at him, were two of the most fantastically sexy women he had ever seen.

Jeff blinked. It took a moment for recognition to set in. There in the backseat before him were Bellamy Blaze and Katrina Cummz, the famous porn stars. He had spent quite a lot of alone time lately with their best scenes.

He glanced at Colin, who just shrugged, a smirk on his face.

When he looked back into the limo, Bellamy Blaze was holding out a martini with three olives skewered on a plastic sword.

"Want a drink?" she said.

Colin gave him a nudge.

"Yeah," Jeff said. "Yeah, as a matter of fact, I do."

Chapter 11

Billy Kline ran for the courtyard, holding the old man in his arms like a baby. The old broad beside him was doing a pretty good job of keeping up. She was gripping the garbage spike tightly in her fists, her eyes wide open and desperately scanning every nook and half-open door they passed for signs of movement.

There was another gunshot up ahead. The old dude in the cowboy hat was popping off a few well-aimed shots at a section of the courtyard off to their right, and as soon as Billy stepped into the sunlight, he saw why. Several of the prisoners from his work detail were there, shambling toward them.

Billy glanced over the buildings behind them and saw a hotel. *That's where they're coming from*, he figured. And that meant there were going to be a lot more of them soon. This part of Sarasota was almost completely made up of hotels and businesses that catered to the tourist crowd. Few of the people stuck here would know the area well enough to get away quickly, which would turn them into sitting ducks.

A shot broke his train of thought. He didn't so much as hear the crack of the report as feel the whistle of air as the bullet passed just inches from his face.

"What the fuck?" he said, and looked at the old dude in the cowboy hat.

The man pointed to the open doorway behind him with a nod of his chin.

Billy looked behind him and saw an old woman whose lower lip and part of her cheek had been chewed off. It looked like the fingers on her right hand had been bitten off, too.

And now, there was a bullet hole in her forehead.

Billy quickly gauged the distance between himself and the old dude who had just fired. It looked to be about forty-five to fifty yards. Billy didn't like guns, but he knew enough about them to respect what they could do. And he knew shooting wasn't as easy as they made it out to be in the movies. Even with a rifle, landing a kill shot at that distance wouldn't be a guarantee. To do it with a revolver was either very lucky or the product of someone who was an extremely gifted shooter.

"Ed, what's happening?" the woman beside Billy yelled.

"We need to make it to the nurse's station," the old dude in the cowboy hat called back.

The woman turned to Billy. "This way, come on."

The old man in his arms was groaning, and Billy was suddenly aware of how roughly he was treating him.

"Sorry, guy," he said. "Hang in there."

The man only groaned.

Zombies were pouring into the courtyard all around them. They were in some kind of central hub for the old-folks' home, Billy figured, and they were starting to attract a pretty big crowd.

For a moment, Billy fought the urge to drop the old man and run for it. There were still large gaps between the zombies, and he was fast enough that he could probably make it through without even coming close to an infected person.

But just as quickly he shot that thought down. He wasn't a coward, and that's what he'd be if he dropped the old man and ran for it. No, that wasn't him at all.

Billy's group and the old cowboy's group came together in the middle of the courtyard.

The cowboy looked at the man in Billy's arms.

"Hey, Art, you okay?"

The old man tried to answer, but it just came out as a slurred mumble.

"I don't think he got bit," Billy said.

The old cowboy nodded. "You're okay, carrying him?"

"I got him."

The squat woman with the two kids came up and whispered to the cowboy, "Ed, what are we gonna do?"

"We're gonna have to shoot our way through. Can everybody move okay?" he said, looking at the others. They all nodded back. "Okay. Let's get going."

A zombie, faster than the others, had made it dangerously close to them. Ed motioned for Billy to stand aside. He raised one of his revolvers and dropped the zombie with an effortless one-handed shot.

As Billy watched, the old man released the catch on the revolver and opened up the cylinder. He depressed the plunger and ejected all six spent shell casings onto the grass. Then he took a speed loader from a leather pouch on his belt, fed it into the cylinder, twisted the knob to release the bullets into their chambers, and then with a flick of his wrist snapped the cylinder closed.

"Where'd you learn to handle a gun like that, old man," Billy said.

"I spent thirty-five years of my life putting men like you into outfits like that."

The little boy who had been standing behind the cowboy was staring at Billy, half frightened, half fascinated.

"What are looking at?" Billy said.

The boy's eyes got even wider. His Adam's apple pistoned up and down.

Just then, Ed Moore pushed his way around Billy and stepped slightly ahead of the group. "Come on, everybody. Nobody stops moving."

Billy was impressed, despite himself. The old cowboy moved with a fluidity that surprised him. He kept up a steady stream of fire, not wasting any bullets, not letting the moans and the horror of all those ruined bodies rush his shots. He fired all the way through both revolvers, then emptied the cylinders and reloaded without losing a step.

In all the reading Billy had done on the subject, and in all the documentaries he'd watched, every single commentator said that the best type of handgun to have in a fight against a large group of the infected was a semi-automatic, preferably a 9mm, as it offered the best compromise between magazine capacity and stopping power and ease of reloading in a combat situation.

But all those commentators had clearly never seen what you could do with a pair of six-shooters if you knew how to use them properly.

Ed cleared the path for them all the way to nurse's station, a large, pink stucco cottage with narrow windows all around it, and they slipped inside the doorway without ever having to break into a trot.

He made it look easy.

"Put him over there," Ed told the kid in the orange prison scrubs, and pointed with the barrel of his pistol to a large overstuffed chair in the middle of the room.

He holstered his guns and looked around. The others were huddled in the middle of the room. The kids were holding on to Margaret's legs like they weren't ever going to let go. Julie Carnes was giving Art Waller the once-over. Barbie Denkins didn't seem to have any idea where she was. She just looked scared and small.

Ed walked over to the door they'd just entered and slid a desk in front of it. The zombies were already pounding on the other side of the door, and the desk wouldn't hold them for long.

He went to one of the windows and looked out over the courtyard. There were bodies crumpled up on the ground in a long, meandering line that roughly paralleled their path across the courtyard. But there were a hundred or more of the infected still on their feet, and the combined sound of all their moans was deafening.

And they were coming toward the nurses' station.

"That was pretty fucking incredible shooting you did out there," said the man in the orange scrubs.

Ed felt a wave of disgust swell up inside him. As a marshal, and an oil field worker before that, he'd been around men who cussed all his life. But he'd never tolerated it. To him, a man who cussed was a man who lacked self-control and respect for others.

A man who cussed around women and children was lower than low.

"Please watch your language around these people," he said.

"Huh?" The smile slid off the prisoner's face, replaced just as quickly by a sneer. "Fuck you, old man."

Ed turned on him. The prisoner was shaking his hands like he was working out the kinks, getting ready to ball them into fists. Ed stood still and waited, watching the man's eyes and his shoulders. If he was going to do something, it would start there, the eyes squinting and the shoulders dropping just a hair to prepare for a punch.

"Ed?" It was Julie Carnes. She came up next to him like

she had no clue what was going on between the two men and said, "Ed, it's Art. He's not doing so good. We need to get him some help."

Ed forced himself to look away from the younger man, and as he did so, he felt a momentary wash of guilt go through him. They were in serious trouble, and here he was posturing with some thug. He didn't have time for this.

"Okay," he said. "Margaret, dial 9-1-1. Tell 'em we're gonna need a bunch of cops out here. Julie, you make Art as comfortable as you can. You two"— he pointed to the kids— "the two of you help Mrs. Denkins onto the couch there and try to make her feel comfortable. Talk to her."

"What do you want me to say?" Randy Hargensen said.

"Just talk to her," Ed said. "You're my deputy now. It's your job to think of something."

Ed turned back to the window.

"How many more bullets you got?" the prisoner said.

Outside, the infected were closing in on the nurses' station and several had already started slapping their hands against the glass, smearing it with blood and dirt. The window was shaking. There were no drapes to close.

"Not nearly enough," Ed said.

He glanced at the prisoner, then back at the courtyard.

"Your name's Ed?" the prisoner said.

"Ed Moore."

"Billy Kline."

Ed nodded. "Good to meet you."

"Yeah, right," Billy said, and laughed.

Just then Margaret came up behind them. "Ed," she said. "The line's busy. I tried a bunch of times but I can't get through. I tried my son's cell phone number, too, and I got a message that the network is busy."

"Okay," Ed said. "Keep trying, Margaret."

He looked behind him. The others were talking quietly

among themselves. Everybody seemed to be doing okay except for Art and Barbie. The two of them looked so frail.

"We're gonna have to do something pretty darn quick," Ed said.

"What'd you have in mind?" Billy said.

"I don't have a clue."

"Well, that makes two of us."

"Where'd they all come from?" Ed said. "I went out for a walk this morning and the streets were empty. All of the sudden, there's hundreds of those things."

He had intended the question rhetorically, but to his surprise, Billy answered him.

"Most of these are probably from the hotel next door. My guess is a boatload of the infected got out of the quarantine zone and made landfall here sometime last night."

"What makes you say that? Did you see a boat?"

"No," Billy said. "It's just a guess."

"Based on what?"

"Well, they're not gonna come by land. I mean, I've seen the quarantine wall on TV. Nothing's getting through that. Coming by sea is the most logical way to do it. There's a lot of ocean, and the Coast Guard's only got so many patrols. Besides, before it all started, I saw a few of the infected that didn't look all that fresh. It was their clothes. They looked like the people I've seen on the news from inside the quarantine zone."

And then he told Ed about the man and the young boy he'd seen tied together at the wrist.

"Yeah, but zombies aren't gonna know how to pilot a boat. That has to be at least a six-hundred-mile trip from here to the closest part of the quarantine zone."

"Well, we don't really know what a Stage Three zombie is capable of. But you're probably right. My guess is it was a boatload of refugees. There were probably one or two who were infected, and they spread it here when they landed late last night or early this morning."

"How do you know when they landed?"

"Jesus fucking Christ, old man, I don't know. I'm just guessing. Late last night makes the most sense, though. Yesterday was the Fourth of July. I saw all the trash left out at Centennial Park from the celebrations. There must have been a bunch of people there last night. If the infected had come ashore any earlier, they would have run into all those crowds and we would have heard about it before now."

Ed nodded. The kid reasoned pretty well.

He pointed at the crowds in the courtyard and said, "Why do you suppose they're all able to move around like that? If the zombies are eating them, don't you think there'd be more of them that are, you know, not able to move? Shouldn't they be dead?"

"I don't think it works like that."

"What do you mean?"

"I don't think the Stage One zombies attack to feed. Not like you mean, anyway. Maybe the Stage Two and Stage Three ones do. The Stage One zombies might even do it, too, if enough of them are attacking an uninfected person at the same time. But I think the Stage One zombies attack just to increase their numbers."

Ed stared at him. He'd never considered that.

"You mean they're like big viruses? They attack just enough to reproduce."

"Exactly."

Ed thought about that, and it explained a lot. "Where'd you hear that?"

"Some of it on TV," Billy said. "Some of it's just stuff I've been thinking about. It explains why the outbreaks spread so fast, you know?"

"Yeah. Huh. That's pretty smart thinking."

"Yeah, well, I may be wearing this thing, but I ain't stupid."

They stood there for maybe half a minute, Ed trying to think of what they were going to do and not coming up with anything, when two things happened more or less at the same time that decided the matter for him.

Margaret O'Brien had managed to get a 911 dispatcher on the phone and she was shouting to send help. Ed started that way. He was going to tell her to calm down, just tell them the address, that they needed help right away. But he didn't make it more than halfway across the room before there was a loud crash and the sound of splintering wood from the doorway. The desk got pushed back a good eighteen inches as the door crashed open. Arms and hands and mutilated faces jutted through the opening.

A moment later, a window broke somewhere in the back of the station.

"Heads up, everybody," Ed said. "We're about to have company."

He crossed to the door, drawing his revolver as he advanced, and fired four shots into the opening. Then he backed up and motioned for the others to get Barbie and Art onto their feet.

"There's too many of them," he said. "We're gonna have to get out of here."

"Ed," Margaret said. "They're coming through the back."

Ed looked around. They were surrounded. The infected stared in at them from every window. They were pushing their way over the desk at the front door. He could hear them breaking more glass somewhere in the back.

He saw a flash of orange in the hallway to his left and looked that way. Billy was pulling the attic access ladder down from the ceiling, unfolding it.

"Come on," he said. "Up here."

Ed ran over to him and looked up into the attic. Then he looked at Billy.

"That's brilliant," he said.

"Not my idea. I got it from *Night of the Living Dead.*"

Ed just laughed. "It's still brilliant," he said.

Ed was the last one up the ladder, covering their retreat with his revolvers.

"We're in," Billy said.

Ed looked up again. Billy was holding a hand out to him.

"Hurry it up, old man."

Ed scrambled up the ladder after him. When he reached the top, the two men turned, folded up the ladder, and pulled it closed just as the first of the zombies reached the space below them.

Billy fished down through the rungs of the ladder and grabbed the pull cord and yanked it up into the attic.

"Can't leave this hanging out," he said.

Ed nodded. *Smart kid*, he thought.

CHAPTER 12

Kyra Talbot stood in the doorway of her trailer in a sleeveless green dress, listening to the little West Texas town of Van Horn, population 987, waking up. A pickup truck was accelerating down Eisenhower, and from the straining note in the exhaust, Kyra guessed it was Mr. Azucena's Chevy. She heard children yelling at each other from somewhere behind her and figured it was the Kirby kids, Jack and Joanna, fighting over something. Off in the distance, she could hear the occasional car passing through on IH-10.

It was a hot, stifling morning. Kyra focused on the heat and the dust against her face and bare arms. There wasn't even a trace of a breeze in the air. She could smell dry grass. She was already starting to sweat and the small of her back and her breasts under her bra were wet.

Next door, Misty Mae Burns let her screen door slam and walked outside, her shoes grating against the cinder path that led down to her curb. Kyra heard bottles clanking together softly, as though in a bag, and guessed Misty Mae was taking out the trash.

"Morning, Misty Mae," she said.

"Morning, Kyra."

Misty Mae's voice sounded rough, scratchy. There had always been a smoky hoarseness to her voice, but this morning she sounded rougher than usual. She almost had a wheeze to her, like there was a ball of phlegm caught in the back of her throat.

"You feelin' okay, Misty Mae?"

"Lousy."

Misty Mae's husband Jake had come home from the oil fields over in Odessa for the Fourth of July weekend and the two of them immediately got after each other like two alley cats in heat. They'd been at it most of the afternoon, started drinking around dinnertime, and didn't quit until long after Kyra had gone off to bed.

There was a muffled clatter of bottles being tossed into a metal trash can and then the sound of the lid being replaced.

"You hungover?" Kyra said.

She had been hungover once, and she hadn't liked it. She hadn't liked being drunk, either. Being blind, Kyra relied heavily on her other senses, and the alcohol had left her with a feeling that she'd had a blanket tossed over her. Everything had seemed muted and washed out, and it scared her.

"Yeah, maybe," Misty Mae said in answer to her question. "Hung over, or maybe I'm coming down with whatever Jake brought back from Odessa."

"What's wrong with Jake?"

"Flu, probably," Misty Mae said. "He come home yesterday complaining his back was hurtin' him. Last night he started throwing up. I thought he'd just drank too much, you know? But this morning he looks like something the dog coughed up."

"You gonna take him over to see Doc Perez?"

"Yeah, I don't know. Maybe. I ain't feelin' so hot myself. Jesus, if that man got me sick, I'm gonna kick his ass. I can't afford to miss no more work."

Kyra could hear Misty Mae's labored breathing.

"Is it hot out here to you?" Misty Mae asked. "I don't mean summertime hot. Good Lord, I think I'm burning up."

She coughed, and it was a deep, rattling sound.

"I'm gonna go inside and take a nap," Misty Mae said. "I'm sorry if we kept you and Reggie up last night."

"You didn't keep us up," Kyra said, though that was a lie. They'd had Tim McGraw's *Greatest Hits* blaring out of the tape player in Jake's truck till at least two.

"Okay. You take care of yourself, you hear, Misty Mae? You let me know if you want me to call Doc Perez for you."

"Yeah, sure. I'll see ya."

"Yeah," Kyra said.

She listened as Misty Mae trudged up her steps and let the screen door slam behind her. Then Kyra turned and felt for the doorknob to her own trailer and went inside.

She was feeling troubled, and it didn't have anything to do with the way sighted people so carelessly said things like, "I'll see ya" or "See you later." Kyra had been blind since she was four, and she had long since gotten over it.

No, it was something else that was bothering her. She was afraid and trying hard not to show it.

She made her way into the kitchen, the fingers of her right hand dancing along the wall, placing her in her mental map of the world she knew. She felt the hard, cool edge of the refrigerator, and she stopped and turned around.

Directly in front of her was the sink.

She reached for the cabinet above it and took down a plastic cup and filled it with water. Growing up, she had developed the habit of putting the tip of her finger down inside the top of the glass and waiting for it to get wet. That's how she knew when to shut off the tap. She no longer needed to do that. These days, she could tell just by how long the water had been running.

She took a few nervous sips and put the cup down.

She let her fingers glance over the counter, over a damp

hand towel, over a few pieces of used silverware her Uncle Reggie had once again neglected to drop into the sink, and finally to the radio.

Kyra touched the baffled cover over the speaker, moved to the right side of the unit, and found the volume knob. She gave it a quick twist and listened as the voices flooded back into the kitchen.

All her life, the radio had been a warm and wonderful friend. She loved music. She loved listening to the high school football games on Friday nights with the cool desert night air blowing in through the open window over the sink, carrying with it the sweet, smoky smells of a nearby barbecue. She even loved the preachers on the AM channels, the way they could give the word "blasphemous" six syllables, the quaking timbre of their voices as they shouted about sin and immorality and turning to Jesus in your desperate hour of need.

She felt the thrill of inclusion when she listened to the radio. But this morning she was not feeling that way at all. None of the regular programs were running. Instead, it was the news. There had been an outbreak of the necrosis filovirus along the east coast of Florida sometime in the last thirty-six hours, and it was spreading out of control. There was talk of moving officers from the Gulf Region Quarantine Authority into the area, of calling in the National Guard and even the military to support local and state police, but no one had any real answers. They talked all morning, and within just a few minutes, Kyra realized the newscasters were talking just to fill up the silence of what they didn't know. It was the same thing over and over again. Breaking developments were just some other person saying the same things that had already been said, and nowhere in there did she hear anything new.

It reminded her of the first outbreak, the one in Houston.

She was nineteen. She could remember everything from that morning, the same way the old-timers in town told her they remembered exactly what they were doing and where they were the day Kennedy was shot. That Tuesday, like every Tuesday back then, she'd stayed home from school till 10 o'clock, when Uncle Reggie would help her into his truck and together they'd make the drive to Fort Stockton, where she and six other blind kids from surrounding towns met for their real-world-skills class. She had been standing right where she was now, listening all morning to the sometimes frantic, sometimes stunned radio announcers babbling the same thing over and over again, and the monotony of it had terrified her even more than the insanity of what they were actually saying.

She heard footsteps from off to her left, Uncle Reggie's heavy tread on the linoleum tile.

"Are you still listening to that?" he asked.

She nodded. She was standing still, arms crossed over her chest, cupping her elbows in her hands, chewing on her lower lip.

"Anything new?"

She shook her head.

A moment later, she felt his hand on her shoulder. He was a big man, with heavy, meaty fingers that could completely envelope her delicate shoulders, but he was also a gentle man, kind.

She put her hand over his.

"The world is so big," she said. "I don't know if I can make you understand that, Uncle Reggie. I don't know if I can make you understand how much it terrifies me."

"It has nothing to do with being blind. You know that, right?" he said. "Everybody feels that way. If the world doesn't seem absurd to you, then you're not alive. At least you're not living a life worth living."

She smiled faintly. Those were pretty words, but they didn't make her feel any better. She thought of telling him so and then reined herself back. It was pointless.

She dropped her hand back down to her side.

"I'm scared," she said.

"I know you are."

"But you're not scared, Reggie?"

He hesitated. She knew he was deep in thought. He always thought before he spoke, and it made her wonder what his face looked like at those moments.

"I lost a lot of people during the first outbreak," he said finally. "A lot of friends. Yeah, it scares me to think of what might happen. I hear this stuff going on in Florida now and all the people who are still inside the quarantine zone trying to bust out and it scares me."

"Will it spread?"

"I don't know," he said. "I hope not."

"The man on the Abilene station said they've already had twenty reported cases."

"Abilene's a good, long way away, Kyra."

"Yeah but, are we . . . okay here?"

"I think so."

"The radio said we should get some supplies. Bottled water, extra gas, stuff like that."

"We're gonna be okay, Kyra."

"Uncle Reggie, please."

She heard him sigh.

"What do you want me to do, Kyra? You want me to go over to the Walmart in Fort Stockton and get some supplies?"

She nodded.

He sighed again.

"You gonna be okay here while I'm gone?"

"I'll be okay."

"You're not gonna let that radio scare you, are you?"

"No, I promise."

She heard his boots scuffing across the floor as he moved to the door. His keys jangled as he took them down from the hook on the wall next to the light switch.

"You sure you're gonna be okay?"

"I'm sure," she said.

"Okay. I'll be back in a little bit."

Kyra nodded. She listened as he fired up his truck and pulled out of the drive and accelerated up 6th Street. A moment later, she was alone again, with the sounds of the newsman on the radio and the sound of dust blowing against the windows and the weight of her fears pushing down on her, making it hard to breathe.

Inside her shell of blindness, she wondered why the world had to be this way.

CHAPTER 13

Aaron Roberts stood with two hundred other members of the Family—Jasper Sewell's affectionate nickname for his congregation members—watching as Jackson, Mississippi, burned to the ground.

The Family stood at the large wall of windows along the south side of the New Life Bible Church's sanctuary, staring out at the crowds fighting in the middle of Manship Street. Faces were lit by wild-eyed desperation and blank, unknowable vacancy. In the distance, towering black columns of greasy smoke rose into a gray, overcast sky like angry tornadoes. There were bodies in the street, and the infected were tearing people apart right in front of the church. Aaron could see wrecked cars and dead cops and rivers of blood flowing into the gutters. The air was full of distant sirens and screams and the roar of buildings on fire.

He thought maybe he was going to be sick.

No one spoke, and that was perhaps the scariest thing of all. He swallowed hard and happened to glance down at his watch. It was thirteen minutes past four. Only an hour had gone by since Jasper brought them all together and warned them this was coming. They had seen it on the news. They had all watched the quarantine collapse and the hordes of the infected spreading across the maps behind the newscaster's head like ripples in a pond. Jasper, in the white choirmaster's robe he always wore when preaching, had climbed down from his pulpit, his microphone in his hand, and sat on the steps.

"The form of the plague is new," he told them, and let his words hang in the air before them like the promise that all would be explained shortly. Surprisingly, it wasn't his pulpit voice he was using. It was the calm, kind voice he used when he talked to you man to man, the two of you sitting next to one another on the couch, talking about church business. Hearing him speak that way, the entire congregation grew silent—not even the babies cried. You could feel it in the air. Jasper was starting to work his spell.

"The form of the plague is new," he said, "but God's message is the same as when he spoke through Jeremiah of the destruction of Jerusalem. 'And I will smite the inhabitants of this city, both man and beast,' he said. 'They shall die of a great pestilence.' Look around you folks. Can any of you doubt the prophecy of those words? Do you not see it right outside your door? We are on the verge of something here, my brothers and my sisters, my children. Things are happening. There is a ring of hatred and conspiracy tightening around us all. There are people out there who want to take away the good thing we have in here. We will not let them do that. We will stand strong in our faith and our love, and we will resist the advances of those who would betray us and make us compromise our faith. I will not let this good thing disappear."

And of course they had all answered with a great and resounding yes that prompted Jasper to close his eyes and hang his head to his chest, nodding slowly.

It had been a powerful moment, and Aaron, sitting there in the front row, had felt his wife, Kate, squeeze his hand in fear. He heard her sobbing.

He squeezed back. Their eyes met. She whispered, "Aaron, I'm so scared."

Aaron was about to tell her that he was too, when suddenly Jasper was there, standing by her side. His hand was on her shoulder, and his fingers were long and slender and delicate, yet undeniably strong.

"What did you say, Kate?"

She looked startled.

"It's okay," he told her. "Tell me what you said just now."

"I said I was scared," she said, though it came out as a muffled whisper spoken into her chest, for she always had a hard time meeting Jasper's gaze.

Jasper didn't speak right away. He cupped her chin in his palm and gently lifted her face to his, holding her with his eyes.

He put the microphone up to her mouth and waited.

She leaned forward into the microphone, the way people do when they're not used to speaking publicly.

"I said I was scared," she repeated.

Jasper smiled at her, then took a few steps back. He scanned the Family, all of them caught up now by the man's dazzling presence and the good feelings that seemed to radiate off him like heat waves off the summer pavement. Then he raised the microphone to his lips and said, "Sister Kate is scared, people. How many of you are scared, too?"

There were murmurs all around.

"It's okay," he said. "We tell nothing but the truth here. How many of you are scared like our Sister Kate?"

The murmurs became voices. A few members of the Family spoke out. Sister LaShawnda, a heavyset black woman in her early sixties who was sitting in the row behind

Aaron, stood up, her right hand raised high over her head as she begged Jasper to save her.

Jasper came to her. He raised his hand to hers, and the old white choir robe sagged down to his elbow, showing the starched and sweat-stained shirtsleeve beneath. It was hot in the church. He locked his fingers together with LaShawnda's and eased her hand down. Then he leaned close to her and kissed her on the cheek.

She melted, and if the pew hadn't been right beneath her, she almost certainly would have fallen to the floor.

He said, "You asked for me to save you."

"Yes," she pleaded.

"I will do that. If you need me to be your friend, I will be your friend. If you need me to be your brother or your father or your husband, I will be those things for you. If you need me to be your Jesus, I will even do that for you. Because I love you. I love all of you."

He took a deep breath and scanned the Family once more, seeming to pause on every face and take the measure of the soul within.

"It is okay to be scared. There is nothing wrong with that. Look outside. These are scary times. But let me tell you something about being afraid. God gave you fear for a reason. He gave you fear to wake up your common sense. It is His way of pressing the button that makes you realize you must act. And act is what we shall do."

He walked back to his pulpit, pausing to touch Kate on the shoulder and give her a reassuring smile.

"In a short while, we will move to the buses Brother Aaron has managed to acquire for us." He nodded to Aaron. Aaron nodded back, the pride of being recognized like this swelling him up inside. "Make yourselves ready. In a short while, we will listen to the warning of Jeremiah. We will leave Jerusalem. Be ready, my brothers and sisters. Be ready."

And with that, Jasper turned and walked back to his office, leaving Aaron to organize the others with a closing prayer and a hymn.

That was an hour ago.

Now, Aaron stood at the church's front windows with the rest of the Family and watched the world consume itself in a fit of fire and the gnashing of infected teeth. He looked down the line of windows. Most of the two hundred people here had been active members of Reverend Jasper Sewell's New Life Bible Church for at least a year. There were a few new faces—some who had come in off the street when things started to get really bad outside—but nobody that Aaron, as Jasper's second in command, didn't recognize, and it grieved him to see the Family so frightened.

Aaron put his hands on his wife's shoulders. Kate touched her cheek to the back of his hand and leaned against him. He felt the warmth of her body where her skin touched his. He felt her full head of brown hair thick against his chin. She was a slender, delicate woman, forty-four years old, and still pretty in an honest, unassuming way. She wore very little makeup. Her clothes were off the rack at Wal-Mart, nothing fancy. She had a high forehead that was lightly dusted with freckles. Her cheekbones were distinct, giving her face an almond-shaped taper down to the point of her chin. It was a feature she had given to their only child, Thomas. Aaron studied her features now, and as he touched her, his hands seemed like clumsy bear paws next to the graceful lines of her face.

She was trembling. When she turned her face up to his, her eyes were shining with tears.

"All of it's gone," she said.

She meant their life together, their house, their two cars, all the material things.

"That stuff can be replaced," he said. "We're here now. Our son is safe. That's all that counts."

She nodded.

"How much longer do you think we'll be here, Aaron?"

"I don't know," he said. "I've been wondering about that myself."

He looked down the row of faces at the window and he wondered why they all kept looking at the destruction. It was so painful to watch. Why then continue to stare at it?

"I'm going back to see Jasper," he said. "I'll ask him how much longer."

Aaron gave her a kiss and went back to Jasper's office.

He knocked on the open door and waited for Jasper to say it was all right for him to come in.

Jasper was sitting with his back to the door, his hands cupped together under his chin, his slender fingers stroking his cheeks. Aaron could see Jasper was sucking his cheeks in and out, his fingers pressing so hard against his face that the skin turned white, and he recognized the gesture. The man carried so much in his mind. He bore so many troubles. On the desk between them was a stack of paperwork. Aaron recognized the word "subpoena" at the heading of one piece of paper, and he understood. The troubles were starting again. Though he couldn't read what was written on those pages, he knew they would contain the same old accusations of tax code violations and deceptive practices that had plagued them back when the church was little more than a cheap storefront on the poor, and almost entirely black, Lee Street.

"The United States government is an enemy of the conscientious religious man," Jasper once told him. "They call us radicals—and maybe we are. We live in a community where all our brothers and sisters are equal. There is no racism here. And they can't stand that about us. They are seeking to destroy this church through their Internal Revenue Service and their tax code violations and their subpoenas."

He'd slammed his fist down on the stack of paperwork on his desk and stared hard at Aaron as the echo of the blow faded away.

Aaron had kept quiet, waiting for guidance.

"You see the truth of it, don't you, Aaron?"

Aaron nodded. He understood a great deal. He and Kate and their son had been with Jasper when he was still a weekend preacher who had to steal time away from his daytime job as a Chevrolet salesman to talk to them about how to live God's life in the real world. They had been with him when he first started to build his congregation among the poor, the blacks, the disaffected college liberals. Even then, his message had been one of hope and power. Things didn't have to stay the same, he said. The world could be changed into something good.

That appealed to Aaron, that message of hope through conviction, peace through political activism. As Jasper's church grew, and the Family got larger and more politically active, Jasper told Aaron his vision for what the church should be. He wanted it to be all-inclusive, something for everybody. If you wanted faith healing, Jasper would give it to you. If you wanted a church that practiced good works in the community, Jasper would give that to you. If you needed a more cerebral church, one that appealed to the intellect, Jasper could do that, too.

Aaron shared that belief all the way down to his toes. He saw why it was necessary for them to collect information cards from people during their first visit to the church. He understood why it was necessary to go to the homes of those visitors and go through their garbage and their mail and even break into their homes and get personal information on them that might be used when they came back for a second visit. When those people did come back, Jasper would call them out, and using the information that Aaron and a few other trusted lieutenants had gathered during their forays, he would preach to them on a personal level that could only be achieved by someone who knew their very soul. Aaron saw no deception in that. There was no malicious intent. Jasper used the information Aaron gathered for him to save people's souls. His was a higher purpose, one with its own morality.

"You do see that, Aaron," Jasper said then, his fist still grinding down on the subpoena on his desk. "I know you do. You understand that we are besieged. The government is like a pack of wild dogs nipping at us from every angle. We are surrounded. We are persecuted. We are plagued by their accusations because they see that we are of one mind and one soul and one glorious purpose. I will not let them dissolve this church, Aaron. I will never let that happen. We will die before that happens."

Aaron stood before him then in much the way as he had stood all those years ago before a much younger but no less committed Jasper, firm in his belief that the man was holding the evil of the world and its governments at bay.

Jasper's white choir robe was hanging on the coatrack just inside the door like always. It seemed to sag tiredly off the hook, as though all the shine and glory had gone out of it now that it no longer covered the shoulders of a great man, a prophet.

"Jasper?" Aaron said.

Jasper swiveled around in his chair. His pale blue eyes seemed tired.

"What is it, Aaron?"

Aaron hated himself then for bringing his worries to Jasper. The man clearly had enough of his own without having to calm the fears of one of his faithful, a man who had seen the genuine miracles done here in the past and should know better than to be afraid. If Jasper said they were going to be fine, they were going to be fine.

"What is it, Aaron?" Jasper said again.

"Nothing, Jasper. I'm sorry to bother you."

"You're not bothering me, Aaron. How are the others doing?"

"They're scared, Jasper. Things are looking bad outside. People are getting torn apart right in front of the church."

Jasper nodded slowly, then rose to his feet.

"Well, come along, Aaron. Let's see how bad things have become."

Aaron stood aside and let Jasper lead the way back to the sanctuary. A few members of the Family turned when they heard Jasper behind them and then the whole room erupted with voices.

Jasper calmed them with a casual wave of his hand.

He didn't respond to the questions thrown at him. Instead, he walked to the windows and looked out. It was a gray afternoon with rain threatening in the west. The sky was full of roiling black smoke. People were running between wrecked cars. A cop with a military rifle was firing into a crowd of the infected. There were bodies in the street and in the grass, and with every shot, the cop added more bodies to the wreckage.

But the cop was surrounded, fighting a losing battle. One of the infected managed to grab him from behind and pull him down. The cop screamed out in pain, a horrible, echoing ululation that sent waves of prickled gooseflesh up Aaron's arms.

The infected swarmed him.

A few moments later, the screaming stopped.

Jasper sighed sadly. He was about to turn away when one of the Family members farther down the row of windows cried out.

Everyone turned and looked where the woman was pointing.

At the edge of the parking lot, near a wrecked Volvo station wagon with its driver's-side door hanging open, was a woman huddled down into a ball, her arms thrown over a little girl, who looked to be maybe two or three years old.

The infected were everywhere around them.

Somebody in the crowd next to Aaron groaned.

Aaron turned to Jasper, but was surprised to see that Jasper was moving away from him, headed for the front doors.

"Jasper?"

Jasper didn't answer, and before any of them could say anything to stop him, he was walking through the doors and out into the parking lot.

"No!" somebody screamed.

The cry was echoed up and down the row of windows as the Family pressed forward to see what was happening.

Outside, Jasper was strolling calmly across the parking lot. An infected man—most of whose right foot had been chewed off and was trailing a thick, clotted trail of blood—was walking toward Jasper.

It seemed they were on a collision course, and yet Jasper made no effort to change direction and go around the infected man, and likewise the infected man made no effort to raise his hands to grab Jasper.

They walked right by each other, passing with less than two feet between them, and suddenly the whole Family fell silent.

A few of them looked noticeably surprised.

Aaron could only shake his head, a smile forming at the corners of his mouth as Jasper casually strode through the crowd of zombies, untouched, and came up right behind the woman and the little girl.

Jasper put his hand on the woman's shoulder. She looked up at him, her face streaked with tears.

Jasper held out his hand to her, palm up, that irresistible smile of his urging her to take his hand.

She did.

He helped her stand. He reached down and picked up the little girl, and she threw her arms around his neck.

Then he led the woman and her child back to the church and through the front doors. For a moment, the Family was too stunned by what they had seen to move or speak. Jasper stood before them, the woman at his side and the child in his arms, and the very air around him seemed to shimmer with a white light that was as pure as a miracle. They all stared at him dumbly, and then, as a body, they all rushed forward, wanting to press against the warmth he was giving off.

He put the little girl down and with another wave of his hand silenced the questions on everybody's lips.

"Sister Kate," he said to Aaron's wife. "I'd like you to help this young woman and her child with their needs."

He turned to Aaron.

"Organize the Family and board the buses. We'll be leaving in a few minutes."

"Absolutely," Aaron said.

Then Jasper spoke to everyone at once, and his voice was the strong, clear, resounding one he reserved for the pulpit.

"Gather your things together," he said. "I want you to follow Brother Aaron's instructions as we move to the buses. Our time has come. God has given us this sign and it is up to us to obey it. We are leaving Jerusalem. Let us not waste the daylight."

And with that, he strode through the crowd, brushing against the hands that reached forward to touch him as he went back to his office.

When he was out of sight, the Family turned to Aaron, waiting for instructions.

Chapter 14

Ben Richardson closed his notebook and slipped it into his pack, which Jerald Stevens had thoroughly rifled twice more since that first time Richardson let him help himself to the Snickers bar and the almonds inside. The poor guy had obviously thought he was doing it on the sly, but of course Richardson had caught him in the act both times. He didn't try to stop him, though. The notebooks were the only thing in the pack Richardson valued, and as long as Jerald didn't touch those, Richardson was willing to let the trespass slide.

But now it was time to get back to business. He zipped up his pack, slid it over his shoulders, and went down the hallway to the sixth-story window where Officer Barnes was watching the quarantine wall.

Barnes hadn't moved since the night before, when heavy zombie traffic in the area had forced them to take shelter up in this office building. He glanced back over his shoulder when he heard Richardson come into the room and then went back to looking out the window without so much as a nod of recognition.

Richardson slid up next to him.

"How's it look?" he asked.

"Pretty fuckin' crappy," Barnes said. "Looks like all the Quarantine Authority folks have given up."

A light rain had fallen earlier that morning and the streets were wet. Here and there, oily puddles reflected the thin shafts of sunlight that managed to penetrate the high, gray cloud cover. The most obvious feature Richardson could see was the quarantine fence, a forty-foot-high monstrosity made of red cedar and barbed wire that cut through the cityscape with all the severity of a prison wall. But now there were no soldiers, no sharp, metallic echo of assault rifles in the distance, only the constant moaning of the infected and the whistling of the wind through the open windows of the building.

Below them, the street was still thick with the infected. They were moving slowly, but steadily, toward the gaping holes in the quarantine wall. Already a great many of them had made it outside and were moving into the cleaner streets on the free side of the wall.

"How does something like this happen?" Richardson asked.

"How the fuck should I know?" Barnes said.

Richardson wasn't put off. He said, "Sandra Tellez was telling me that the uncles have been rioting a lot lately near the walls."

"Yeah. So?"

"Is that true?"

"Why do you keep asking me shit I don't care about?"

"But is it true? Have there been more riots near the walls? I've heard the Coast Guard catches them all the time."

Barnes didn't answer right away. He watched the infected below them and sighed.

"Yeah," he said at last. "It's true."

"Is that what this is, do you think? Did the riots cause those holes in the wall?"

"Doubtful."

"Why?"

"A riot would have been easy to put down. All they would have had to do would be to play some amplified zombie moans to draw the infected into the area, and that would break up any riot before it had a chance to get too big."

"So you think the infected did this?"

Barnes shrugged.

"Wouldn't the Quarantine Authority have been able to stop a wave of the infected? Even if there were a bunch of them?"

"Maybe. If they were here."

"Why wouldn't they be here? I see that building over there. That's a Quarantine Authority outpost. Surely they'd have people here."

"Normally, yeah. But if there was major activity somewhere else down the wall, they would have relocated that way. It's not like we have an unlimited number of people to do this job, you know? We got a shit load of territory to cover and a minimal staff to cover it with. It was only a matter of time before something like this happened."

"How come nobody told me about all the riots? I've been talking to Quarantine Authority people for months now and nobody said anything."

"We're under orders, Mr. Richardson."

"Under orders to mask how bad things are here?"

Barnes didn't answer him. He didn't have to. It was a moot point, and they both knew it. Richardson went back to looking at the scene below them. This part of Houston hadn't flooded like the areas farther south and east, but it had been hit harder by the rioting during the first days of the quarantine, and the area inside the wall looked like a war zone. All of the windows were broken out. Some of the buildings had been damaged by fires. He could see bullet holes in the brick walls. Trash and rubble and abandoned cars were everywhere, choking the street.

Out beyond the wall, the scene was different. The buildings there were in more or less good repair. There were a few broken windows, lots of dead bodies. There was trash in the streets, pieces of paper, soft drink cans, sheets of plywood, a few bloodstained yellow blankets, an amazing proliferation of spent shell casings, but it was all fresh trash, all of it put down in the three days it had taken them to walk across Houston.

Richardson scanned the horizon. He counted the columns of black smoke he saw rising skyward from fires he couldn't see, but he gave it up at thirty.

"Why are there always fires?" he said.

"What do you mean?" Barnes asked.

"In disasters," Richardson said. He turned away from the window and sagged down onto his butt, his back against the wall. "There's always fires. I don't get that. Every time something bad happens on a grand scale . . . it doesn't matter if it's a flood or an earthquake or a tornado, there's always fires. Makes you wonder, doesn't it?"

"About what?"

"About us. If we weren't meant to burn."

"I don't know," Barnes said. "I've never given it much thought."

It rained off and on throughout the afternoon. Eventually, the crowds of infected thinned out, and here and there they saw small groups of the uncles making a break for it.

"I think we should chance it," said Sandra. She and Barnes and Richardson were standing at the window, watching the street.

Richardson thought it was a good idea, too, and said so.

Below them, they heard a young man yelling. They all looked down. He was standing across the street from a trio of the infected, throwing rocks at them and taunting them with a ridiculous string of obscenities. It seemed ridiculous to Richardson, anyway. A zombie didn't care what you called it. It didn't matter what you said his mother sucked in hell, because he wasn't going to get mad. He'd eat you regardless of whether you were kind or profane. You tasted the same either way.

"What's he doing?" Richardson said.

"Distraction." Both Barnes and Sandra Tellez said it at the same time, and they looked at each other in good-humored surprise.

"Distraction?" Richardson said.

"Just watch," Barnes said.

Richardson did. The zombies began shambling after the young man, who was still throwing rocks and yelling. He was slowly backing up, but was careful to keep an eye out for anything moving behind him. He let the zombies get much closer than Richardson would have, and then he turned and trotted off, leading them away from a large hole in the quarantine wall.

He continued to yell. More of the infected stumbled out of the doorways on both sides of the street.

Soon, the street was filled with zombies. It had seemed nearly deserted moments before, but now there had to be at least forty of them staggering after the man.

And then his attitude changed. He stopped waving his arms. The bravado left him. He stopped, looked around, seemed to be gauging the distance between two points that Richardson couldn't see.

"Okay," he yelled. "Do it. Move, move."

Richardson heard running footsteps on the pavement to his right. He glanced that way and saw a small group of people, mostly young women in their late teens and early twenties, a few of them carrying children, running for the hole in the quarantine wall.

The young man watched them go. When the last of them

had made it past the barricades and entered the breach in the wall, the young man grew suddenly animated. He was getting ready to run.

"Oh, no," Sandra said.

She was pointing at the young man, who was yelling now, waving his arms over his head in an exaggerated pantomime of a semaphore flagman.

Behind him, a zombie was pouring out of a wrecked car.

Richardson could see what was going to happen. The man would let the others get too close. He would turn to make his break around the bunched-up crowd, and he would step right into the waiting arms of the zombie behind him.

He had to yell out, warn the man. But it was impossible to speak. The words were frozen in his throat and he couldn't force them out.

And then a rifle went off in Richardson's ear. He fell to one knee, cupping his ringing ear with one hand, looking up at the profile of Officer Barnes, who was standing as still as a sentry, the butt of the smoking AR-15 tucked into the crotch where his shoulder met his cheek.

"What the hell?" Richardson said.

Then he glanced down at the street. The young man was looking at the headless zombie on the ground behind him. Then he turned and scanned the windows of the building above him until he saw Barnes, Sandra Tellez, and Richardson.

He gave Barnes an exaggerated flyboy salute.

Barnes nodded back at him.

A moment later the man was gone.

A few zombies followed after him, but slowly, no real chance of catching him. Others had turned with the sound of the shot and were moving toward the building, their ruined faces directed upward to the window.

"We need to leave now," Barnes said.

"Yeah," Sandra said.

"You ready?"

"We've been ready for a year and a half."

"Well, it's time."

Crossing through the breach was sort of an anticlimax for Richardson. He had expected some kind of celebration from Sandra and her group, but there was none. They stepped through just like they were leaving yet another abandoned building. The guarded edge of weariness never left them.

"It'll be dark soon," Sandra said.

"Yeah. We need to find transportation," Barnes said. "We'll need something that'll give us some temporary protection."

Barnes scanned the area. There were dead bodies everywhere, and the infected were still walking around, though none of them were close enough to be an immediate threat.

He said, "I got it. Come on."

They walked along behind him until they came to the Quarantine Authority outpost. With Barnes taking the point man position, they circled around to the back of the building and came up to a covered carport that Richardson hadn't been able to see from the building.

Under the carport was a large bus with armored sides and armored skirts coming down over the wheels.

"Oh, my God," Richardson said.

"Wow," Sandra said.

"Yeah." Barnes looked around. "It doesn't exactly fill me with confidence though, knowing the guys from this outpost weren't able to use it for their evacuation."

He scanned the vehicle dubiously.

"Well." he said, "We might as well use it, right?"

"I hope they left the keys," Sandra said.

Barnes chuckled.

"No worries there." He reached onto his belt and unclipped a key ring. "All these vehicles are keyed alike," he said.

Sandra smiled. "Beautiful."

The bus made it seven miles before the transmission slipped out of gear and refused to reengage. The mood on the bus had been one of waxing elation, a terrible thing slipping away behind them, a brave new world rolling out before them, but as the bus lost momentum and eventually trundled to a stop, the smiles died away.

Richardson moved forward, the images of the bus ride he had taken into San Antonio in the early days of the quarantine with Dr. Carnes and her UT students suddenly flaring back up in his mind.

He put a hand on the back of Barnes's chair.

"What's going on?"

"Transmission's fucked," Barnes said.

Richardson could hear the engine revving. He could see Barnes's foot pumping the clutch, but the transmission wouldn't engage.

"What does that mean?" Richardson asked.

Barnes looked at him angrily. "You know what? You're starting to piss me off with your fucking questions."

"I'm sorry. It's just . . . I don't understand."

"We're fucking stuck here. You understand that? This bus ain't going nowhere."

CHAPTER 15

Ed Moore hadn't slept for thirty-six hours. He and Julie Carnes and Margaret O'Brien and the others had been up in this attic with no food, no water, no air-conditioning to speak of, all that time, and they were demoralized. Ed could barely keep his eyes open. His eyelids weighed a ton. His back and his legs were stiff and achy. Sleep seemed so deliciously seductive, and yet his forehead burned with a fevered alertness that wouldn't let him relax. He could see the same thing on the faces of the others. Nobody looked up, nobody spoke. They sat, staring, eyes glazed with exhaustion, all eight of them baking away in silence.

And, worst of all, he had to go to the bathroom so badly he wanted to cry. A few of the others had been able to go—by tacit agreement, they were using a low-ceilinged corner that, thankfully, hadn't started to smell yet—but Ed couldn't make himself go in front of the others. Peeing, of course, hadn't been a problem. But pulling down his pants and steaming out a loaf was another matter. Of course, if they were up here much longer that would have to happen, and he was dreading it.

The constant moaning and banging around below them didn't help either.

He scanned the crowd he'd collected, and a wave of pity and helplessness swept over him. Julie Carnes was sitting next to Art Waller, trying to make him comfortable. Barbie Denkins was stretched out on the floor, sleeping fitfully, her face glossy with sweat. Margaret had the kids nuzzled up against her. The boy looked like he was close to falling asleep. The girl was sobbing quietly into Margaret's shirt.

Only the guy in the prison scrubs, Billy Kline, was doing well. He was awake, but he looked bored and angry.

Ed rose to his feet, his knees cracking like pistol shots, and for a moment he wasn't sure he'd be able to straighten out his back. He went over to Julie and nodded at Art. "How's he doing?"

"He's not good, Ed. I think he's dehydrated."

I believe it, Ed thought. Barbie Denkins would probably start showing the same symptoms here in a little bit. He put his palm on Art's forehead. It was hot and damp. His face looked flushed. Not a good sign.

"How about his medication? I know he takes something for his heart."

"He doesn't have it with him." She touched his arm. "Ed, we can't stay up here."

"I don't see where we can go," he said.

She just looked at him. She didn't have to say more. He understood exactly what she meant. The same feeling had been worming its way into his brain within a few minutes of coming up here. It was like they'd painted themselves into a corner and now they were just sitting, waiting on the paint to dry.

And then she surprised him. She said, "Ed, how far do you think this thing has spread?"

"I don't know. I suppose it's possible it could have spread

pretty fast. From what I've read, it depends on the severity of the initial injury, the health of the person infected, and probably a hundred other factors that nobody's really sure about. A person can turn anywhere from a few minutes to several hours after they've been bitten. That leaves a lot of time for the outbreak to spread before anybody really knows what's going on."

Julie glanced over at Margaret holding her two grandchildren. Margaret met her glance and nodded, then squeezed the children tighter.

Julie wiped the back of her hand across her forehead and to Ed it looked like she was trying to conceal her tears.

"Where's your family?" he asked her.

She smiled faintly. "What are you, a mind reader?"

"Body language."

"You get that from interviewing suspects?"

"Something like that," he said.

"I have a daughter in Chicago. She's forty-two."

"What's her name?"

"Gwendolyn."

"That's pretty."

"It was my mother's."

"Ah. Grandkids?"

She nodded, not trying anymore to wipe away the tears. "Three. All girls. The youngest is twelve. How about you?" she said. "You said you'd been on your own for six years."

"No family," he said. "We never had kids."

"You were too busy fighting crime?"

"Too much of a cynic," he said.

"You can't leave me with just that," she said. "Come on, tell me."

He looked down at his hands and picked at a callus on his thumb. "I always told myself I couldn't see bringing a child into a world I didn't trust. I lived through all that crazy stuff you see on the news, you know? The wars, the riots, the sickening things people do to each other because of drugs and racism and religion and just plain meanness. And the more I saw, the easier it got to tell myself I was never going to have a child. It would seem like a betrayal, bringing them into a world like the one we've got."

He held out his hand and made a useless gesture around the room that was meant to include the whole world.

She didn't say anything.

He stood up again, and all at once he felt like an ass. *Nobody wants to hear you rant,* he thought.

"Sorry about that," he said. "Usually, I get to know people a little better before I go off like that."

"It's okay," she said. "Under the circumstances, I understand."

Beside them, Art Waller groaned and bent over, holding his gut in his hands. His skin had turned an ashen white, and sweat was popping out all over his face.

Julie caught him in her arms. "Art? Art? Are you okay?"

He shook his head.

Julie looked up at Ed and her expression was desperate.

"Hold on," he said.

He crossed over to the other side of the attic and knelt down next to Billy Kline. The younger man looked up at him and frowned.

"What the hell do you want?"

"I want to see if we can get out of here."

"You're shitting me, right?" He pointed down at the floor. "You hear that, old man? All that moaning? Tell me you ain't so deaf you can't hear that."

"There's nothing wrong with my hearing," Ed said. Then he leaned forward and whispered, "I'm worried about these people here. They need water and food and medicine. If we stay up here much longer, we're going to be sharing space with some dead people."

"Well, shucks, Mister. How about I jump down there and

let those things tear my ass to pieces? That way you and the fucking Geritol Brigade over there can just waltz on out of here. That what you had in mind?"

"What's wrong with you?" Ed said. "These are human beings. Why do you have to act like a fool?"

Billy was silent, his face inscrutable.

"I just want you to help me," Ed said. "If there's a way to get out of here, and to do it safely, we need to do it."

"Safely? Old man, you are fucking nuts, you know that?"

"Please watch your language while you're up here with us."

"My language? Are you fucking kidding me?"

"No, I'm not. These people are from a different generation. It'll only scare the others."

Billy laughed. "You want to see scared?" he said. "I'll show you scared."

Then he got up and went to a spot where the insulation was exposed. He balled his fist, and before Ed could tell him not to, he punched a hole through the floor.

"Come here, old man. Take a look down there."

Walking in a crouch, Ed stepped over to the hole and looked down. Flakes of Sheetrock and pink cotton candy strands of insulation rained down on the infected below them. The office was packed with zombies. At least a dozen pairs of hands were reaching up for them, bloodstained and snarling faces below those.

"How's that for fucking scared?" Billy said. "You think that'll scare 'em? Because it sure as hell scares me."

Ed sat down on the floor and looked at Billy. He had no idea what they were going to do. All his life, he'd been the one responsible for making decisions. Now he could barely think straight.

"Well?" Billy said.

Ed shook his head. He looked away.

* * *

Later that afternoon they heard muffled voices. At first, Ed wasn't sure he was really hearing what he was hearing. He looked up at the others.

"What was that?" Margaret asked.

"Shhh," Ed said.

He heard more voices, getting louder, turning to shouts. Then the crackle of gunfire.

"What is that?" Billy asked. "Cops?"

"Maybe," Ed said.

The sound of fighting grew suddenly intense, like it was right below them. Ed recognized the sound of fully automatic M16s, fired in well-controlled, short, three-round bursts.

He crawled over to the hole Billy had made in the floor, and the two of them looked down into the office below. The few zombies they could see were turning away from the ceiling and to the front door.

As they watched, three of the infected were knocked backward by head shots.

Another shambled out of a side room and got a full burst of machine-gun fire to the chest.

They heard a man's voice yell, "Clear!"

"Hey!" Billy shouted. "Hey, we're up here!"

The sounds of movement from below came to an abrupt halt. A man's voice, different from the first, said, "Who's there? Show yourself."

"We can't," Billy said. "We're up here. In the attic."

"Stand by," the man's voice said. "Don't move."

A moment later, a man in a SWAT uniform was shining a shotgun-mounted flashlight up at them.

"Easy," Billy said. "Don't shoot."

The man lowered the weapon, and Billy thought he'd never been so glad to see a cop in all his life.

* * *

They were taken to the rounded driveway in front of the office. About twenty soldiers and cops stood by with M16s. Most of them looked tired and bored now that the initial rush of fighting was over. There were dead bodies everywhere, and Ed recognized quite a few of them.

A few other survivors were being led from their cottages to waiting city buses nearby.

"Are we being evacuated?" Ed said to a National Guardsman standing next to them.

The man looked exhausted. His eyes were rimmed with red and his cheeks were dark with dried sweat and dirt. He nodded without really looking at Ed.

"Where are we going?"

"I don't know, Mister. Albany, Georgia's the last I heard."

"Georgia? That far? What's happened?"

"I look like a general to you? How the hell should I know?"

The soldier started to walk off.

"Hey, wait a minute," Ed said. "You can't just expect us to climb on a bus and go to Georgia without being told what's going on."

"Mister, this whole area's under martial law. If you're told to put your wrinkled old butt on a bus, then that's what you're going to do. You can have an opinion about it if you want to, but nobody around here gives a shit what that opinion is."

"You don't need to cuss at me like that," Ed said.

"Mister," he said, "I don't give a shit what you think one way or the other. I've just spent the last thirty-six hours fighting zombies and rescuing crusty old motherfuckers like you, and I ain't even had so much as five minutes to myself to call, my wife and find out how she's doing with my three kids. So if you think I give a shit about you or what you think, you can go—"

"Stanislaw!"

The soldier stopped talking. He stood there for a second,

breathing heavily, his lips squeezed together in a look of barely controlled fury.

Behind him, a man with a major's insignia on his chest stood with his hands on his hips. He was tall, lean, his neck corded with veins. His hair was a deep, unnatural-looking black. It looked like he dyed it.

"Stan," the major said. "Go get Weber. The two of you stand down for a thirty-minute break."

"Yes, sir," the soldier said.

He was gone a moment later.

The major watched him go, then turned to Ed. "My men have been fighting for almost two days straight now. Tempers are strained."

"I can see that."

"Are you folks okay?"

Ed looked over his shoulder. Art Waller was standing on his own, but Julie was right next to him, looking like she expected him to fall over at any second.

He said, "We could use some water and some food." He gestured at Art. "And my friend isn't doing so well. He has a heart condition."

The major nodded. "Food and water is on the way. Once we get you guys settled on the bus, I'll have a doctor come by. We've got a field pharmacy, too. I imagine you folks probably had to leave your medications behind."

"That's right."

The major nodded. "We may not have everything you need, but they should have pharmacy facilities where we're going. In the meantime, if you'll write out your cottage numbers and the names of your medications, I'll have my people go by your rooms and round up what you need."

"Thank you," Ed said. He looked across the courtyard at all the dead bodies in the grass, the blood on the walls and the sidewalks, and the bullet holes everywhere. He said, "That soldier said we were going to Georgia."

"That's right. Albany, Georgia. It's one of six camps that have been set up to help with the evacuation."

"Are things really that bad?"

"Worse than you can imagine," the major said.

The major looked over at the rest of the group and saw Margaret and her two kids. To the boy, he said, "Where'd you get that badge? That looks like a real U.S. Marshals' badge."

"It is," the boy said. He looked at Ed.

"I gave it to him," Ed said. "U.S. Deputy Marshal Ed Moore, retired."

The major nodded. "Outstanding," he said. "We're under martial law right now. You knew that?"

"Yes."

"Well, we need help. Are you fit enough to return to duty?"

"Fit enough?" The question seemed ridiculous. "I don't know, Major. Honestly, I feel like every bone in my body aches right about now, and all I was doing was sitting down."

The major shrugged. "That sounds good enough. You think you can take charge of these people? See them all the way to Albany?"

"You're kidding?"

"Not a bit. They'll need a leader. Can you do it?"

Ed hesitated. There was a streak of vanity in him that ran fairly deep, and that part of him was stirring. He felt an excitement in his gut, like butterflies.

"How many . . . survivors did your men find?" Ed asked.

"Twenty-two."

"Twenty-two," Ed said. He sighed. "There were more than two hundred people living here."

"I'm sorry," the major said. He put a hand on Ed's shoulder and said, "Why don't you get your people ready to move out? Somebody will come by with food and water once you guys are loaded up on the bus."

Ed nodded, and the major turned to leave.

Billy Kline called after him. "Hey," he said. "Hold up."

The major stopped and looked at Billy. He took in Billy's prison scrubs and his bearing stiffened.

Billy said, "You guys are running things now?"

"That's right."

"Well, look. I was part of a work detail from the Sarasota County Jail. I got four months left on my sentence and I don't want to get in any trouble for skipping out. If you're in charge, I'm turning myself over to you. I don't want any trouble."

The major stared at him for a long moment. Then he smiled. "Deputy Moore?"

"Yes, sir."

"Deputy, it looks like you got yourself a prisoner as well."

"No fucking way," Billy said.

The major walked off.

"I don't want to go with this geezer," Billy called after him. "Hey. You gotta take me someplace else."

The major made no answer.

"Hey," Billy said. "Hey!"

Billy turned to Ed and said, "No fucking way, man. It's not gonna happen."

But Ed Moore went right on smiling.

CHAPTER 16

From the helicopter, Major Mark Kellogg looked down on what was undoubtedly the most tragically stupid scene he'd ever witnessed.

And he'd been in San Antonio during the first days of the original outbreak eighteen months ago.

He'd seen stupid.

It was a bleak, gray, drizzly day, and the sky looked like an endless sheet of cooled lead. Below him was a line of vehicles that stretched off into the distance as far as he could see. There were a lot of cars that had broken down and were now abandoned. Most had been pushed off to the side of the road, into the grassy ditch to the right of the roadway. Silvered pools of water gathered in the runoff ditches. It was a three-lane highway, every inch of it covered by cars and trucks and anything else that would move. From a distance of three hundred feet, the vehicles all looked the same color. They all looked the same.

People were riding on the roofs of the cars and in the beds of trucks, but none of them seemed to speak or point or show any kind of emotion at all. The helicopter raced over their heads and only a few of them made any effort to look up.

They seemed morose, waylaid by some awful sense of ennui, like a drenched marching band walking off the parade route.

Every few minutes, they flew over some activity, a fight or group of the infected attacking those stuck in their cars in the frozen stream of traffic.

What seemed so tragically stupid to Mark Kellogg was the herd mentality he saw in the refugees. He'd witnessed scenes just like it in San Antonio, when everyone there was trying their damnedest to get out of town ahead of the riots and the spreading infection. Below him, the freeway ran north–south. There were three northbound lanes and three southbound lanes, divided by a wide grassy median. All that traffic was in the northbound lanes. The southbound lanes were completely empty. All those people had to do was cross over and go the wrong way up the freeway, and they could cover the next thirty miles in a matter of minutes.

But not one of them was doing that.

What's wrong with them, he thought. *Why don't they see what's right in front of their faces?*

We're nothing but lemmings, he thought.

"What highway is this?" he said, calling forward to the pilot.

"This is Eighty-five, sir," answered the pilot. "You look up ahead there, those skyscrapers in the distance, that's Atlanta."

Almost there, Kellogg thought. *Stop off at the CDC, pick up the last member of the team, some civilian doctor with the CDC, then head up to Pennsylvania.*

"What's bugging you, Mark?"

Kellogg looked at the man on the jumpseat across from him, Colonel Jim Budlong, their team leader. He was a lean, fit-looking man in his early fifties, a career military doctor. His cheeks were deeply lined, and when he smiled, as he was doing now, the lines formed wide parentheses around his mouth. His blue eyes were thin slits beneath small blond eyebrows and a high, smooth, intelligent-looking forehead.

Kellogg managed a wan smile in return.

He said, "I was thinking about getting out of San Antonio."

Budlong nodded.

"I remember when I finally got off base," Kellogg said. He started to go on, but found he couldn't. The words caught in his throat.

He'd been trapped inside the hospital at Ft. Sam Houston's Brooke Army Medical Center for nearly fifty hours, the infected everywhere, the hallways covered in blood, dead bodies and those that only looked dead piled knee deep no matter where you turned. Sometimes, when he closed his eyes, he could still hear the screams echoing through the halls.

He let his head fall back against the headrest, then slowly turned to the open side door and looked down.

"Survivor's guilt," Budlong said. "Your job was to save lives, but hundreds of thousands died and you lived. It's natural to feel the way you're feeling now. I'd be worried about you if you didn't feel this way."

"It's not survivor's guilt," Kellogg said.

Budlong waited. The helicopter blades thropped loudly against the air.

Kellogg just shook his head.

"Tell me," Budlong said.

Kellogg took a deep breath. Let it out again. He said, "The image that's burned into my mind is what I saw when I finally made it off base. You know the exit there at George Beach Avenue, over by the helipad?"

"Sure."

"I came out there. I was in this car I'd found running in the parking lot, blood smeared all over the hood. I don't know whose it was. When I finally got through the gate, I was right there at I-35, looking down at the traffic. Jim, there were cars everywhere. Every single one of them was jammed up in the outgoing lanes, nobody moving. Those people, they were being pulled out of their cars by the zombies coming out of the shopping centers along the freeway."

He broke off there, his chin sagging to his chest.

"Mark, I was there when they stabilized the quarantine line. I know you had it bad."

Kellogg shook his head.

"That's not it, Jim. It wasn't the . . . the people dying so much as why they died. That's what got to me. You should have seen them. Everybody just lined up and took it. You know? They stood in line and waited for death to come to them."

He was faltering again, struggling for the words.

"It's the same thing down there. Look at them. They're all packed in there in the northbound lanes. Not one of them has thought to cross over, go up the wrong way."

They were old friends, he and Budlong. They went back to Kellogg's first days at Brooke Army Medical Center in San Antonio, almost seven years ago. Budlong had just made full bird. He'd impressed Kellogg as a conscientious, careful officer, the kind who thrives in the military, and that impression hadn't changed after all the years they'd known each other.

"I'm counting on that to help us," Budlong said.

Kellogg looked at him, confused. "Counting on what?"

"Get yourself back on the clock, Mark." The genial smile had left Budlong's face. He was all military now.

Kellogg nodded. He straightened his spine against the back of the seat.

Budlong said, "I'm counting on your ability to think outside of the box to help us on this. You can see how bad it is down there. My orders are to find a way to stop this. I'm counting on you to help me with that. I need that unconventional thinking you're so famous for to make something good happen."

"Jim, I . . ."

He trailed off. Kellogg had been working on exactly that problem ever since the initial outbreak; how to stop the necrosis filovirus. He had the feeling he was standing at the foot of a cliff, looking up at a smooth stone wall that stretched to the sky and that he was expected to climb. The problem was that huge.

"The medical solution is—"

"The medical solution," Budlong said, "may not be the only solution."

That stopped Kellogg cold. What did that mean?

"You know what it means," Budlong said. "My orders are to stop this plague any way we can. Maybe that doesn't mean finding a cure." He paused there, just for a moment. Then he said, "Think about it."

Kellogg did, and at first the implications made him want to vomit. And then, something happened. The nausea brought on by his offended moral sensibilities dimmed.

Then flickered out, like a guttering candle flame.

The feeling was surprisingly liberating.

For the first time in months his brain felt alive with new ideas.

All options were on the table. A clean slate.

Neither man spoke. Kellogg looked away, out the open door. Off in the distance, the Atlanta skyline loomed.

CHAPTER 17

From the notebooks of Ben Richardson

Conroe, Texas: July 9th, 11:15 P.M.

There was some bad fighting today.

We stayed on that bus all night, not moving, just waiting, trapped on Jackrabbit Road right outside of Bammel, Texas, which up until a few days ago was a tiny little town of about 2,000 people just north of Houston.

When dawn broke, we off-loaded the bus and decided to start walking toward I-45. We hadn't made it very far before Jerald Stevens, the young man who continues to raid my pack for candy bars even though I've told him I don't have any more, stepped into the vegetation growing by the side of the road and shouted out that he had found blackberries. "They're all over the place," he said, and the delight on his face was enough to make anyone smile.

I watched him eat them straight off the vine, making his way down the ditch that paralleled Jackrabbit Road until he was a good hundred feet or so ahead of us. He was facing us, his chin and his cheeks black with pulp and juice, but he heard something and turned around, his back to us.

I heard him shout, "Hey, stop that. Leave her alone."

A second later, there was a shot, and Jerald ducked his head and ran full speed back in our direction, his hands thrown over his head like he actually had a chance of stopping a bullet with them.

"Holy shit," he yelled. "Officer Barnes!"

The street behind him met a smaller side street at a four-way intersection. We could see a gas station over the shrubs to our right. It was from that gas station that our trouble came, for just as Jerald got to where the rest of us stood, three armed men with black bandanas over their faces stepped around the corner and into the street.

Everybody hit the ground, diving for cover.

I heard gunfire, but my mind refused to recognize what was going on. For a crazy second, it seemed like the air had filled with bees around my head. Little white clouds of powdered concrete appeared all around me, and several times, I felt the sharp sting of bits of rock as they flew up from the roadway and peppered my cheeks and my arms.

I thought I'd been stung.

It was only after Barnes yelled at me to, "Get down, you idiot!" that I realized the bees were bullets.

They were shooting at us.

At me.

We all ran for the cover of the ditch at the side of the road, except for Barnes. He ran forward in a crouch, AR-15 up in a shooter's stance. He returned fire, quickly but deliberately, and continued to advance until he was behind the trunk of an abandoned car.

From there, he continued to fire. As I watched, the three men who had rounded the corner with their bandanas and their guns went down. One of them, the last to fall, had gone down to one knee to fire. Barnes shot him with a quick three-round burst and knocked him backward onto his butt. The man sat there, weapon on the ground beside him, his shoul-

ders slumped forward like a marionette with its strings cut, for a long moment. Then Barnes fired at him again, and the man fell onto his back and was still.

Barnes got up and ran for the gas station. I ran after him.

Before I even got to the intersection, I heard lots of shooting. When I rounded the corner, I saw the young man Barnes had saved with his sniper's shot back at the breach in Houston. Behind him were the young women for whom he had created a diversion. All of them were huddled together in the gas station parking lot. Surrounding them on every side were the bodies of more men with bandanas over their faces.

I heard yelling, looked up, and saw Barnes chasing one of the men around the back of the gas station.

I took off after them.

I rounded the corner and saw Barnes had caught his man. The two of them were squared off against each other in the grass next to the men's room door.

Both had knives.

The man lunged at Barnes. Barnes stepped gracefully to one side, and it was obvious from that first moment how the fight was going to end. The other man was clumsy. But Barnes with a knife was like Picasso with a paintbrush. He grabbed the man by his wrist and with his right hand ran the blade all the way up the man's arm. He looked like he was buttering toast. He was that fast, that smooth. Everywhere he went, he cut. The blade licked deep gashes into the exposed skin of the man's arm and sliced his shirt open down the back of his shoulder blade. Barnes came up behind him then and sliced the man across the line of his jaw. The man opened his mouth to scream, but the sound was cut off at the throat. Barnes grabbed him under the chin, forced it up, and before I could even process what he was doing, Barnes had jammed the blade so far into the other man's throat that he nearly decapitated him in one slice.

I stood there, stricken, as Barnes continued to cut. He cut until the man's head snapped back and the torso sank shoulder first into the grass.

A moment later, Barnes was holding the man's head in his hand, grasping it by the hair like some perverse rendering of Perseus with the gorgon's head.

I don't know what I was expecting, but it definitely wasn't what happened next, for Barnes began to scream at the man's head.

He threw it against the men's room door.

He ran forward and kicked it like it was a soccer ball.

He said, "How do you like that, you fuckin' piece of shit? You think you're bad. You think you're fuckin' bad? Motherfucker, I'm your god!"

Then Barnes stepped forward and started smashing the head under his heel. Pounding on it. Grinding it under his foot.

"You hear me?" he screamed. "You ain't shit next to me."

Then he kicked the head some more.

That went on for a long time.

I got sick watching it. I was wiping the vomit from my mouth when he turned away from the battered head and the gore-stained gas station wall.

He wasn't surprised to see me there.

He walked right by me and said, "Time to move out."

I turned and watched him walk back to our group, where Sandra and her people were taking care of the young man and the women our sudden appearance had probably saved.

I am worried about Officer Michael Barnes.

They entered Conroe, Texas, on foot.

Nobody spoke. Nobody said a thing. Their group, which had grown to about thirty as they made their way up I-45, stayed in a cluster in the middle of the road, Officer Michael Barnes walking point about twenty feet ahead of them. They had been walking for hours. Most of the night, in fact. And now that morning had broken, they stared numbly at the pine trees and the well-kept yards and the simple, uninspired architecture of yet another small Texas town, and they were afraid of the emptiness that surrounded them.

They were on a quiet, two-lane residential street. Cars were parked along the side of the street and in driveways. Everything seemed well cared for: the houses, the lawns. Here and there, American and Texas flags still flew from poles in people's front yards, stirring occasionally in the light breeze. And yet there wasn't a soul in sight. The only sound was the constant padded thud of their shoes on the pavement.

Richardson, one of the few members of the group who was armed, walked behind the others, the tail to Barnes's point.

He felt uneasy.

Something was wrong.

They were following the trail of refugees from the Houston quarantine zone and the zombies that had come with them. More of the infected were undoubtedly on the road behind them, pushing outward into new territory. So what was going on here, then? Were they in some sort of eye, the eerily calm center of the storm?

Probably so, he thought. *And that ain't good.*

There was a sudden commotion up front. All at once the quiet that had been eating at Richardson's mind was gone. People were talking excitedly, not yelling, not yet, and pointing off to the left at a fairly large brown brick building that looked like some kind of civic center, maybe a church, though there was no signage that he could see.

And then he saw the girl. She was twelve years old, maybe a year or two younger. The whole left side of her body was the color of iodine.

Dried blood, Richardson thought.

The girl was running toward them. Even at a distance, Richardson recognized the milky white eyes of the infected. She was emitting a noise somewhere between a stuttering moan and an oddly feral barking. Richardson had never heard anything like it.

The group was starting to move backward, toward Richardson's position, and for a moment the crowd thinned enough for him to make out Officer Michael Barnes, standing perfectly still in the point position.

Barnes didn't look around. He raised his AR-15 to his shoulder and squeezed off a round.

The girl's lower jaw exploded in a spray of dark, wet bits and teeth.

Hit in the jaw, Richardson thought. *Sweet Jesus.*

The first shot spun her around and knocked her facedown on the ground. But she got back to her feet and she stumbled forward, trying to run, but managing only a careening sideways roll that made her look like a drunken sailor trying to stay on his feet after getting tossed into the street from some seedy Malaysian bar.

Barnes's next shot put her down for good.

A few people gasped.

At first, Richardson thought they were gasping at what Barnes had just done, and maybe a few of them were, but then he saw the real problem.

From the building, a sickening moan erupted. A few of the infected appeared at one corner of the building. More followed. Richardson's stomach turned at the sight of so many children.

Barnes wasted no time. He raised his rifle once again and, with an easy calm, fired into the approaching crowd.

Richardson turned away. Everyone around him looked stricken.

Richardson heard a woman sobbing. He glanced to his right and was surprised to see Sandra Tellez standing there.

Her cheeks were shiny with tears. She looked like she was trying to make herself swallow the lump in her throat but couldn't quite manage it.

Clint Siefer, silent as ever, put a hand on her shirt and gave it a gentle tug.

Sandra put her arms around Clint and squeezed. Then she looked toward Richardson and seemed as surprised to see him as he had been to see her.

They stared at each other, neither one speaking.

The shots kept coming, one at a time, slow and steady, like a hammer pounding on an anvil, and with each report, Sandra would flinch a little.

Richardson didn't know what to say. He gave her a helpless shrug. There weren't words to describe all that was wrong with the world. It was so terrible, so mean, so pointless.

He shook his head and looked away.

The shooting stopped, eventually.

Richardson looked up as the echo of the last shot died away and a silence once again descended on the world.

The group was zippering apart to let Barnes pass through. He was coming in Richardson's direction, his weapon slung casually over one shoulder, his expression tight but revealing nothing.

Nobody spoke to him. Nobody, it seemed, could even bring themselves to look directly at him.

"There's a Kroger up ahead on the right," Barnes said.

At first, the words made no sense to Richardson.

"A grocery store?" he said, confused. What did a grocery store have to do with anything?

"I want you to take these people up there," Barnes said. "But before you let everybody in, you secure the building. Send two people around the back. Have them check for more infected. If there are vehicles back there, check them to see if we can use them. Once you've got the place locked down, I'll go inside and clear it."

He ejected the magazine from his rifle, checked it, then slid in a fresh one.

"Go on," he said. "Get moving."

"But—"

"What is it?" Barnes said. He wasn't looking at Richardson. He was scanning the surrounding buildings, his eyes reduced to two thin, hard slits in a nest of wrinkles. There was a two-day growth of whiskers on his face.

"I don't understand," Richardson said. "You want me to take them? Where will you be?"

"There are more of those things around here," he said, and indicated the piles of bodies he had just made. "I'm gonna make sure we have a way out of here. I'll see if I can find us some vehicles."

"Okay," Richardson said. That much made sense at least.

"Go on," Barnes told him. "Get moving. We need to make this fast. I'll catch up with you in a second."

They stood in the nearly empty parking lot of a grocery store.

Presently, they heard a noise, a truck lumbering down the street. It was the first vehicle most of them had heard since leaving their homes and joining the trail of refugees and it created a stir among them.

The truck, a white Isuzu two-axle van, lumbered into the parking lot. Barnes was behind the wheel. He got the truck turned around and backed it up near the front doors of the grocery store. Then he got out and approached the crowd.

To Richardson he said, "What's it look like?"

"They've got power in there," Richardson said. "I looked through the windows and didn't see anybody moving."

"Doesn't mean it's clear," Barnes said. "I'll go in and check first. What about the back?"

"Nothing."

"No vehicles?"

Richardson shook his head.

"Okay. Well, I think I've got that taken care of."

Most of the little towns they'd passed through had been cleaned out by other refugees. They had seen nothing but empty shelves and garbage and dead bodies and wrecked cars in the streets. But Conroe seemed different. Hostile as its emptiness was, it was nonetheless relatively intact. Inside the store, at least from what Richardson could see, was an embarrassment of riches. Certainly enough food and supplies for all of them.

Richardson told him as much.

Barnes considered that, then looked at the faces of the others standing behind Richardson, waiting with wide, hollow-looking eyes.

Barnes had left his rifle in the truck. Shortly after killing the masked bandits in Bammel, he and Richardson had gone into a store and found a change of clothes. Now Barnes was dressed in jeans and a blue T-shirt under a thin black windbreaker. He reached inside his windbreaker and removed his .45 semiautomatic pistol.

He ejected the magazine, checked it, then slapped it back into the receiver.

To Richardson he said, "I want you to keep an eye out for any more of the infected. I saw a few a couple of streets over."

Richardson nodded.

To the crowd, Barnes said, "Listen up, everybody. Is there anybody here who knows how to drive a bus?"

A few people raised their hands.

"That's good. I found some transportation for us. I'm gonna go inside here and check to make sure everything is clear. While I'm gone, I want you people who raised your hands to work out who's gonna drive first. We have two buses, so we'll be able to divide ourselves up into two groups. Try to figure out who's going in which bus while I'm in here."

And with that he turned on his heel and disappeared inside the store.

A few minutes later, they heard two shots.

Richardson and Barnes walked side by side up the bread aisle, past packaged tortillas and boxes of crispy taco shells and loaf after endless loaf of bread. Richardson's initial impression of the place was correct. It was largely untouched by the other refugees. But ahead of them, at the end of the aisle, was a thick smear of clotting blood on the floor.

As they got closer, Richardson could see that the trail of blood led through a pair of swinging doors that opened into the store's backroom.

"You put them back there?" he said.

Barnes nodded. He reached out and grabbed a loaf of Jewish rye off the shelf, tore it open, and handed Richardson a slice.

"Thanks."

They ate their bread as they turned in to the refrigerated section of the store, an island of coolers displaying an array of steaks and pork and chicken.

"I want to be organized about this," Barnes said. "I know some of these people have been trapped inside Houston for a long time. They're probably gonna want to get some huge forty-ounce rib eye or something. I can't blame them for that, but we're not gonna have anywhere to cook it either. We need to stick to stuff that can keep while we're on the road."

"That makes sense," Richardson said. But he was surprised. He had worked up an opinion of Barnes as unbalanced, uncompromising, brutal beyond words. He had a genuine fear of him. The others did, too. They sensed something awful about him. And yet here Barnes was, calmly discussing logistics, even showing some empathy for the other refugees.

"Oh," Barnes said, "and find out if anybody in the group is a doctor or a nurse or a pharmacist. Something like that. If so, have 'em go through the pharmacy. I know we're gonna need antibiotics, maybe some painkillers, things like that."

"Okay," Richardson said.

"I'm gonna go grab some of the others and get them to help me with loading supplies onto the truck."

Barnes disappeared down another aisle, leaving Richardson standing there, shaking his head.

Somebody was laughing nearby. It was the reckless, drunken sound of pure joy, and with a half-formed smile on his face, Richardson followed the sound.

It was coming from Jerald Stevens. Earlier, Richardson and Barnes had found him in the candy aisle, sitting on the tiled floor, a five-pound bag of Gummi Bears turned up to his mouth. Now he was sitting on the counter of the deli, holding an enormous turkey breast with both hands and eating it like it was corn on the cob. He had already eaten a good deal of it. On the floor around him were the remains of a package of potato salad, two apple cores, three stones that might have come from some peaches or nectarines, even half of a raw zucchini.

"You eat all this?"

Jerald Stevens looked up at him with a huge grin on his face. There were tears in the man's eyes.

He nodded at Richardson.

"Better slow down, partner. There's plenty for everybody."

Jerald choked down a piece of the turkey. He was breathing hard. "You know how long it's been since I've seen food like this?"

"Too long," Richardson said. He smiled. "Enjoy yourself."

Jerald nodded. He had already taken another bite.

Still smiling, Richardson walked off to find somebody who knew something about prescription medicines.

CHAPTER 18

Nate Royal was sitting on a bench across the street from where he'd parked his van when Jessica Metcalfe pulled up in her shiny new Jag.

He smiled as she climbed out of the car. Somehow, he had a feeling he'd be seeing her today. His knee was throbbing, and in his mind, the girl and the surging pain in his knee always went together.

She was older, like about thirty-five, but the gulf between them was a lot wider than years could measure. She lived with her husband in one of the big white houses on Kansas Street. Martindale, Pennsylvania, was your typical post-industrial town, and it didn't have much in the way of filthy rich, but the Metcalfes came about as close as anyone.

Nate, however, lived with his dad and his dad's girlfriend, Mindy, in a rotting two-bedroom house with the railroad tracks on one side and a drainage ditch mounded with garbage on the other.

Actually, that wasn't totally true. Actually he lived in a converted work shed behind his dad's rotting two-bedroom house. But Jessica Metcalfe didn't need to know that. As far as Nate was concerned, all she needed to do was shake that beautiful ass of hers all the way up the sidewalk, and she was taking care of that just fine.

Nate watched her disappear into the dark, tinted front doors of the Wells Fargo bank, and his mind tumbled back a few years, to the day her husband, the city attorney, had fired him from his job with the Sanitation Department and then turned right around and offered him a completely different job: two hundred dollars to touch up the paint on their pool house.

"Come by this Sunday," he said. "Say, nine o'clock?"

Confused, Nate merely nodded.

Then he arrived at the huge white house on Kansas Street, and he saw the gleaming white marble trim around the pool and the dazzling blue water, and a fantasy was born.

Jessica Metcalfe, wearing an itty-bitty white tennis outfit, had showed him where he'd be working and then gone inside, and as he stood there waiting for her to come back out, he could almost picture her stepping out her back door in a red bikini, peeling it off like Phoebe Cates in *Fast Times at Ridgemont High* as sun-dappled beads of water sprayed over her head.

But of course in real life, she hadn't peeled off anything except a page of unlined paper covered with a loopy, girlish handwriting.

"Here are your instructions. You think you can handle that?"

It was real bitchy the way she said it. He had bristled at that, but he needed the money, so he squinted at the page and tried to make sense of what she had written. Even back in school, when the teachers were working with him in the special classes he took, he'd never been able to pull the sense out of anything more than four or five words long, and she'd written so much stuff down on that paper. He stared at it, feeling lost.

Two hours later, when she came out to check on his progress, she said, "Oh, holy hell! What have you done to my house?" He followed her gaze up to the gutters he had just painted eggshell white and couldn't see what the problem was.

He didn't catch what she said after that, just the part about how he was a stupid retard who couldn't even read, but that was enough to start a trembling rage crawling up the back of his scalp.

He followed her inside the house.

She was sitting at an old-fashioned rolltop desk in the kitchen, doodling little flowers with a pink pen while she talked on the phone. She left him standing there for a full minute before putting a hand over the phone and saying, "Are you still here? You've done enough damage for one day, don't you think?"

"Take it back," he said.

Into the phone she said, "Linda, let me call you back. Uh-huh. No, everything's fine." Then she turned to Nate and said, "You're getting mud on my floor."

He looked at his feet, momentarily derailed.

"I ain't no retard," he said. He heard the high, squeaky register of his voice and puffed up his chest to compensate for it.

"Get out of my house," she said. "You're fired. Leave."

His anger broke then and he took a step toward her, cocking his fist back as he came. What happened next happened all at once, so fast he couldn't really piece it all together. It was like a series of photographs in his mind, arranged in no certain order.

Her eyes got huge.

His elbow bumped something and he felt whatever it was slide off the table next to him.

Some sort of fancy glass crystal vase hit the floor and popped with a hollow and expensive-sounding poof.

The sound stopped him.

He looked at the glass shards on the parquet floor and said, "I . . . didn't mean that. I'm sorry."

"You bastard!" she screamed. "That was from my wedding."

He had been to the county jail once before. In his head, some dim logic worked itself out, telling him that whatever had just happened was about to put him back in county, where he had been beat up four times in three days. He didn't want to go back there, so he ran.

The cops showed up at his house later that day.

He thought they might, and he was ready.

When his dad peeked through the blinds and said, "Oh shit, Nate, what the hell did you do?" Nate didn't stay around to answer. He ran out the back door and jumped the fence. But when he landed on the other side, his left leg curled under him and he went down. All the cops had to do was follow the sounds of his screaming. By the time he made it to county later that night, the knee had swollen up like a watermelon. He didn't get treated till the next day, and by then it was too late. The knee was never the same after that.

A man in a white-and-blue jogging suit ran by, the soles of his shoes slapping on the wet pavement. The whole town seemed to be shaking itself apart getting ready for the refugees they were talking about on the news, but not this guy. He had the calm, faraway look in his eyes that Nate remembered from his own days as a runner.

Nate had run cross-country his freshman and sophomore years in school, before a combination of academic and disciplinary probation got him booted off the team, and he had good memories of running.

Once, they'd gone up to Gatlin to run in a district meet. Gatlin was surrounded by pine forests, and their cross-country course took them through two miles of dense tree cover, the dirt trails beneath them red as baked brick. A senior from Gatlin had managed to stay pretty much even with him for most of the course. Nate could still remember hearing the note of exhaustion in the older boy's breathing as they rounded the last bend two hundred yards from the edge of the trees. It was another half mile after that to the finish, and Nate had been pacing himself, saving his strength for the last hard push to the tape. But when he heard that older boy's breathing start to falter, he began to chant to himself *You've got more than this. Turn it on. Burn him up*. And when he broke through the trees and into daylight, he was running better than he had ever done in his life. It was the one time he could truly say, without question, that he was better at something than anybody else around him.

That had been ten years ago, yet it seemed like another lifetime now.

Now, he was just another of life's losers, sitting on a bench, nowhere to go, nothing to do, no purpose.

And then Jessica Metcalfe came out of the bank. She was holding the strings to about a dozen pink and white balloons in her hand. Watching her, studying her, he realized that she was more than just a nice ass. She was all around smokin' hot, like that girl Bellamy Blaze, whose movies he had in his shoebox back home. He wiped the moisture from his lips as he watched her long black hair, tied back in a ponytail, bouncing playfully between her shoulder blades. She wore a thin white shirt, and even from across the street, he thought he could trace the outline of her bra underneath. His eyes flicked to the hint of bare midriff at the top of her low-rise jeans, then followed the curve of her hips down the length of her legs to where her black high-heel shoes clicked on the pavement. He imagined what it would feel like to peel away the straps of those shoes and stroke her bare feet.

Something flared up inside him, something that felt like

hunger, and before he knew it, he was on his feet and walking across the street toward her.

She was already at her Jaguar, the driver's-side door open. She was bending into the car, her perfect ass pointed at him as she wrestled the balloons into the car.

He grabbed her around the waist and pulled her back from the car. She let out a grunt of surprise—not a scream, but an oddly feminine grunt that almost made him laugh. With his free hand, he threw open the van doors and, before either of them knew what had happened, tossed her inside.

She still had her legs out of the van, but they were off the street, swinging free like a little kid in a big chair. Jessica looked at him, her eyes wide with fright, and said, "Nate, what the hell are you doing?"

She knew his name. That surprised him, and he stopped.

Her question surprised him, too. He didn't really know what he was doing. He hadn't planned on this and didn't know what to do now that he'd done it.

Her eyes darted over his shoulder.

He turned briefly and watched the balloons she had been carrying drift down the street. It was an odd sight, those pink and white balloons floating sluggishly down the wet, dreary length of Brockton Street. They were beautiful, bobbing just above the pavement, trying to take to the sky.

"Help!" Jessica shouted, and the piercing shrill tone of it split Nate's thoughts like a razor.

"Help me!"

"Stop it," he said.

She kicked him, catching his chin with her heel. The blow surprised him, but rather than clear his head it had the opposite effect, and his mind went red.

"Get the fuck away from me, you creep. What the hell do you think you're doing?"

He knocked her foot away, took a step closer, and slapped her across the cheek.

She cried out, not a word, but a weak little yelp. She had her hand on her cheek, cradling it, but gingerly, almost like she didn't dare touch it. Her eyes were wide with fear and panic, and it made him feel really strong, and angry, and somehow vindicated.

He raised his hand again, and she shrank up into a ball, cringing from him, backing up, farther inside the van.

Feeling oddly blank inside, he closed the van door.

He looked around. No one was watching him. No one was looking. He took a small length of baling wire from his pocket and slowly started wrapping the wire around the door handles, murmuring to himself as he worked.

"Oh, Nate, you did it now. You're so fucked. You're so very fucked."

He parked the van behind his dad's house and got out and walked around to the back of the vehicle, staring at it, thinking about the woman inside. What in the hell was he going to do? He couldn't just strip her, look at her, then let her go. Could he? That was all he wanted to do, just look at her. Maybe touch her breasts, pinch the hard little eraser tips of her nipples, maybe get her to turn around in her panties so he could lock that image in his mind along with the daylight at the edge of those trees. Nate Royal's greatest hits.

He undid the baling wire from the door handles.

He was still murmuring to himself, but he felt good, strong. Even the knee felt strong.

He opened the doors, threw them wide, smiling, and got a heel in his teeth.

He staggered backward, his hands over his mouth.

Still doubled over, he took his hands away. They were

bloody. He touched his front teeth with the tip of his tongue, and one of them was loose.

"What the hell did you do that for?" he asked her.

But she was already scrambling out of the back of his van and running past him with everything she had.

He turned, tried to snag her blouse, didn't do it.

He watched her run. She turned back and looked at him for just a moment, her face lit with fear. She whimpered, stumbled, then took off again.

God, she was fast.

The thought thrilled him, and once again the adrenaline was pumping. One more big run, he thought. Catch her. Catch her. Catch her now.

He took off after her, and all the strength, all the grace, all the power that had been his so long ago was back, and he felt great.

She ran over the railroad tracks and across a muddy, weed-choked field before turning up an alley and running parallel to the tracks. He stayed with her the whole way, even gained on her. They were both running for their lives, and he could hear her panting. She was tiring already, and he still had more. *Turn it on*, he thought. *Burn her up.*

Jessica turned one more time to look at him, and in that moment he knew he had her. He was closing fast. Nate reached out a hand, his fingers playing at the fabric of her blouse, and then everything went black. He fell. He tumbled forward, hit the ground, rolled and rolled into a cluster of trash cans and loose garbage and mud.

Something had tripped him up.

Stunned, but unhurt, he looked around.

For a moment, he had no idea what he was looking at. Then it hit him. Jessica was fighting with somebody. The two of them were rolling in the mud. She was screaming. The man beneath her, now on top of her, now side by side, like lovers in a cuddle, was Darnell Sykes. He lived two houses over. Nate had gotten drunk with him about a million times, traded pornos with him. But now he was all fucked up. His face was anyway. His arms, too. His clothes were smeared with blood and dirt and mud.

"What the hell did you do that for, Darnell?" Nate said.

But Darnell did not acknowledge him. He was fighting with Jessica, pulling her arms apart, forcing them down by her side.

He was snarling.

He lunged forward and bit her mouth, caught a corner of it and pulled until her cheek tore open. She screamed, and it was such a hideous, gut-turning sound that it instantly cleared Nate's head.

"Get the fuck away from her," he said.

He put a hand on Darnell's shoulder and tried to pull him back from the writhing woman underneath him.

Darnell turned on him.

Nate's forearm was in front of Darnell's face, and Darnell took a bite of the soft flesh just above the elbow.

Nate screamed. He stepped back, crashed into a trash can, but managed to keep his feet by grabbing ahold of the fence.

He looked down at his arm, and that's when it hit him.

Zombies. The infected. He'd been infected.

He could feel the wound screaming at him, pulsing like somebody had stuck a live electrical cord through it.

"No," he said aloud. "No. Not me."

Darnell rose to his feet. His eyes were milky white and vacant. There was no recognition there. No feeling. No Darnell behind those eyes.

"Dude," Nate said. "You fucked me, man. You fucked me."

Darnell moaned. His hands came up, the fingers opening and closing.

Nate turned and ran.

And that's when the knee went out. He dropped to the ground and screamed.

Behind him, Darnell was lumbering forward, getting closer.

"No," Nate said.

He rose to his feet and hobbled away. Darnell's mother's house was just around the corner. Nate went to it. He limped through the front yard, got close enough to the wooden steps to see blood on the doorway.

Darnell moaned behind him.

"No fucking way," Nate said. "No. No fucking way."

Nate limped on, forcing himself to move.

He managed to get a good amount of distance on Darnell, even with the pain in his knee. He looked behind him, didn't see Darnell, and decided to turn in to a space between two houses.

Another neighbor, Mr. Hartwell, had a lawn mower shed behind his house. Nate could see it from where he stood. He limped toward it, slid inside, and closed the door behind him.

He was in darkness now. He listened for a long time, but heard nothing. There were gaps in the sheet metal. He peered through them, and saw nothing.

The knee was killing him. So, too, was the pain in his arm.

"God, I fucked up so bad," he said. "Oh, God, I don't want to be like that."

He slid down onto his butt, his back against the thin metal siding of the shed, and waited.

What was it the man on the news had said? You get bit, you got four, maybe five hours at the most.

It wasn't much time, Nate thought.

God, not nearly enough.

CHAPTER 19

Kyra Talbot was in her kitchen, one hand on her throat, listening to the news out of Odessa.

". . . been no word as of yet from authorities with the Gulf Region Quarantine Authority as to the extent of the outbreak, but there doesn't seem to be any doubt about earlier reports that the quarantine line has collapsed."

Kyra drew in a sharp breath. She tried to swallow the lump in her throat and couldn't quite do it.

The man on the radio said, "Deputy Director Richard Haskell gave a press conference earlier this morning at the Shreveport Headquarters of the Quarantine Authority in which he said the situation appeared grim."

The voice on the radio changed to that of Deputy Director Richard Haskell. It was a smooth, slow voice, not deep, but very clear, and in her head Kyra pictured a tall, bald, slender man from somewhere in the South, his accent obscured by an Ivy League education, though not completely gone.

He said, "I can confirm that the quarantine line has collapsed around the Houston area. Initially, we directed reinforcements into the area, but it appears that our efforts there have been compromised, at least for now. We already have personnel moving into that area to try to shore up the breach. I spoke with Wade Mitchell, Director of Homeland Security, earlier this morning, and he told me we can expect significant reinforcement from military personnel as early as tomorrow night."

A woman's voice interrupted him. She sounded distant, like she was raising her voice to be heard from the back of a crowded room.

"Is it true, Director, that the outbreak coming up from Florida and Georgia was caused by escapees from the quarantine?"

"That seems obvious," the director said. "Yes."

"But how could that happen? Isn't it your agency's responsibility to stop this kind of thing?"

"It is," he said. "And that's a trust we stake our lives on every day. But the outbreak in Florida seems to have originated from a group of refugees who used a fishing boat to escape along the Gulf Coast. As you know, that is the responsibility of the Coast Guard"—he paused there for the briefest of moments, just long enough to give his next words added weight—"not our agency."

More finger pointing, Kyra thought angrily. *They're so busy shuffling off the blame, they won't tell us what's going on.*

Another reporter asked, "What's being done to stop the spread of the infected?"

"That is the responsibility of the United States military," the director said. "As I understand it, they have been moving troops into the affected areas for the last two days, but what their specific plans are, I can't tell you. You'd have to go to them for that."

"But what are you doing to stop the spread of the infected in the Houston area? We've been getting reports that this latest outbreak has already spread as far as Dallas. And there are reports of cases as far away as Las Vegas, Salt Lake City, Los Angeles, New York, Chicago, and Boston."

Now the director sounded angry, put upon. He said, "I have not heard any confirmed attacks in the Dallas area. The best information we have available—and this is not the rumor mill, mind you, this is confirmed information—is that the outbreak is so far contained within the sparsely populated region just north of Houston. Right now, we are redeploying our command around that area and we hope to have the threat contained within the next twenty-four hours. As for the other cases you mentioned, those again are not confirmed, and I won't comment on unsubstantiated rumors. However, I have been told that the Director of Homeland Security is suspending all commercial airlines until further notice. Should any infected persons be found outside of the quarantine zone, we obviously want to prevent them from flying and spreading the infection to other cities."

"Director," another reporter said. "What do you have to say to those families who, in the meantime, are caught up in the path of these zombies?"

"The infected," the director said, and Kyra could hear the inflection he gave the word, suggesting his distaste for the word zombie, "are extremely dangerous. We saw that in San Antonio two years ago. They can spread at an exponential rate. For that reason, we are asking people to remember their training. Remember the public service announcements we've posted since the quarantine was established. Stay inside your homes. Secure your residence the best way you can. If someone you know has been bitten, isolate that person. Complete depersonalization can occur in minutes, so make them comfortable if you can, and then isolate them. Do not attempt to care for them or transport them to a hospital, as this greatly increases your chances of being infected as well."

"So you're telling people who have been caught up in the outbreak to stay in their homes?" a female reporter asked.

"That's correct."

"What is the incentive for doing that, Mr. Director? If your agency is attempting to re-form the quarantine wall, won't those people who remain in their homes be shut up inside the new quarantine zone the same way residents of the Gulf Coast were two years ago? That would be suicide, wouldn't it?"

A long pause.

Kyra had already heard the director's response four times that morning, but she still found herself leaning forward, holding her breath, waiting for him to say the words.

"Our hopes and prayers go out to everyone caught up in this disaster," he said, carefully controlling the anger he felt for being put so roundly on the spot. "But these are dire circumstances. Some people will have to make terrible sacrifices so that the rest of us can continue to live in safety. I don't expect anybody to like it, but that's the way it's going to have to be."

Kyra gritted her teeth with a gathering rage. *His hopes and prayers*, she thought. *What a ridiculously empty sentiment. The man wouldn't lock himself up behind the quarantine line, and yet he had no trouble doing it to others.* The thought made her face flush with renewed anger, and she snapped off the radio.

Her fingertips glided over the counter to the special clock that Uncle Reggie had bought her for her fourteenth birthday. There was a large spongy button on top. She pressed it, and a vaguely feminine robotic voice told her it was 4:12 P.M. The voice always overaccented the *p* in P.M., the pitch climbing to a sort of mousy squeak, making it sound like there was some kind of bathroom humor there.

It used to make her laugh as a little girl. In the last few

years, it had still managed to make her smile, but today she couldn't even do that. It was getting late, and Uncle Reggie had been gone for a while now, since before noon. She was starting to get worried.

More than worried actually. She was downright terrified. They were a long way from Houston, nearly at the opposite end of the state, but that didn't mean a whole lot when they were dealing with the infected. The infected spread at an alarming rate, and despite what the Deputy Director out of Shreveport was saying, she had already heard plenty of reliable reports of outbreaks as far away as Los Angeles and Seattle and New York. People screaming and dying in the streets made for pretty believable reports, confirmed or otherwise.

Come on, Reggie, she thought. *I need you here.*

She hoped he was taking this seriously. She hoped he was cleaning out the Walmart shelves, loading up the truck.

A noise made her jump.

She let out a small gasp, then froze, listening.

She could hear a scraping noise coming from outside her trailer, like somebody was dragging a stick along the wall.

Her hand went back up to her throat.

The sound stopped.

After a long silence, it started up again, closer to the window now.

Her mental map of the trailer was precise. She knew the exact number of steps it took to get from the kitchen to the front door, how many to get from her bedroom to the bathroom at the end of the hall. She could, with a surprising degree of accuracy, stand at the trailer's front door and point out every piece of furniture in the living room. And she could do the same thing in the kitchen and her bedroom and the bathroom and even Uncle Reggie's room, though she rarely went in there.

Now that mental map of hers was telling her she was

standing right in front of the window that looked out onto the front yard. Whoever was out there would be able to see her through that window.

She stepped back and off to one side.

She waited, barely breathing, listening for the noise to come again.

From somewhere out in the yard she heard a moan, and her sightless eyes instantly went wide. There was no confusing that sound. She had heard it far too many times on the radio, that phlegmy rattling deep in the throat that was the calling card of the infected.

Her mind was humming. What was she going to do? She couldn't go anywhere. She couldn't defend herself. She was trapped inside this trailer. She wouldn't even be able to see them coming. What in the hell was she supposed to do?

Come on, girl, she ordered herself, *think.*

Something thudded against the front door, a heavy, clumsy sound, a drunk stumbling up the stairs.

The door, she thought. *Oh, Christ.*

Moving quickly, she reached out and touched the edge of the counter. Gliding her fingers along the edge, she moved to the door, found the seam, then moved her hand down to the dead bolt.

It was open. *Careless,* she thought. *Stupid.* Stupid could get her killed.

Or worse.

She focused on the dead bolt and turned it as quietly as she could. She closed her eyes and cringed as the bolt creaked out of its seat and fell into place with a final and unavoidably loud click.

The noise outside her door stopped.

For a moment, the world was quiet. She could hear the wind whistling around the corners of the trailer's roof. Outside, she knew, the late-afternoon winds off the desert would be filling the streets with driven dust. She had listened to the soft, gritty movement of that blowing sand against the windows of this trailer all her life, until it became a sort of soundtrack for her quiet, comfortable existence. But now it seemed more like an ominous prelude, the first notes of something terrible.

When the crash hit the door, she was not surprised, though she did jump backward and gasp. Kyra immediately silenced herself, but the damage was done. Whoever it was out there was now beating on the door, throwing their weight against it. She heard moaning and the sound of footsteps on the wooden stairs leading up to the door. A few seconds later, there were more hands beating against the door.

Uncle Reggie kept a pistol in his closet, she remembered. Maybe she could get it and use it, shoot through the door at whoever it was out there.

Yeah, she thought, *and maybe you'll even blow your own head off with it.*

A crash against the door, and this time something gave. She could hear a crunch deep inside the cheap plywood. A moment later, there was another crash. The door burst apart, and Kyra could hear bits of wood falling to the floor.

She heard moaning, too.

She screamed as she turned and ran through the living room, crashing into the coffee table and Uncle Reggie's La-Z-Boy recliner before finally stumbling into the hallway that led back to her bedroom.

Behind her, she could hear bodies clamoring through the doorway, falling all over themselves as they entered her home.

Her own bedroom was to the right, but she turned into Uncle Reggie's room and slammed the door behind her. She tried to move his dresser in front of the door, but it was too heavy for her to do it by herself. Instead, she sat down with her back against the dresser and put her feet up on the door.

Fists beat against the door.

"Go away," she screamed.

She was answered by moaning and a furious pounding on the door.

"Please," she said. "Leave me alone."

Then, from outside, a shotgun blast. The noise was followed by the sound of the shooter racking the spent shell from the breach, and then another blast.

"Kyra? Kyra, where are you, baby?"

Uncle Reggie, she thought.

"In here," she shouted. "I'm in here."

Kyra heard footsteps, Uncle Reggie cussing, then three more blasts from his shotgun.

She waited, her feet still pressed against the door with every bit of strength she had.

"Kyra?"

"In here."

She heard the floor creak on the opposite side of the door.

He said, "Are you okay?"

"I think so." She said it so quickly that the words came out as one syllable.

"Baby, I'm gonna open the door, okay?"

"Okay."

A pause.

"Baby?"

"Yeah?"

"Are you blocking it with something?"

"Oh." She took her feet off the door and crawled into a ball in the corner where the dresser met the wall.

She heard the door open slowly.

"Kyra?" he said.

"Right here."

She felt his hands on hers, and a moment later, she was on her feet, Uncle Reggie's arms around her.

"Don't leave me again," she said. "Please, Uncle Reggie. Oh, my God, I was so scared."

"I know," he said. "I know."

CHAPTER 20

The acid started to work while they were on the road between L.A. and Barstow. Jeff Stavers was sweating. His mouth felt dry. Splotches of heat seemed to move across his face. He was disoriented, but oddly, it wasn't an uncomfortable feeling. He actually felt kind of giddy.

He got up and walked to the rear of the bus, where they had set up a full-service wet bar. The bus was swaying under his feet. He grabbed the headrests on either side of him and closed his eyes and imagined himself floating. This was how he used to feel, walking past Widener Library in the early morning, the only sound the snow crunching beneath his shoes. The whole world had been at his feet in those days, ready for the taking. Now, his skin was tingling with the memory of snow. Colin always bought the best drugs money could buy, and time hadn't changed that.

He passed Colin and Katrina Cummz on his way to the bar. They were both high. Colin was squinting, eyes beet red and drowsy. His clothes and hair somehow managed to combine a look of tousled unconcern with immaculately tailored elegance. Katrina, wearing a flimsy white blouse with a black lacy bra clearly visible through the fabric and a faded and alluringly shredded blue jean skirt, was curled up in the seat next to him, her big blue eyes fixed on Colin. A strappy sandal hung seductively from her toes.

She was asking him what he thought about the riots. When they left L.A., the news was breaking in on all the channels, talking about the street fighting, about how the LAPD was getting overrun and whole areas of the city had devolved into anarchy.

"It's like Rodney King all over again," Jeff heard Colin tell her. "It gets dull, if you ask me." He patted Katrina Cummz on her tan, well-muscled thigh, his fingers lingering at the hem of her skirt. "Don't you let it worry you. It'll be long over by the time we get back."

"You think?" she said. She was responding to his touch, and her own hand was sliding up Colin's thigh to his crotch.

It almost sounded like she was purring, and Jeff thought, *She's perfect for him, completely vacuous.* Or at least she seemed that way. Maybe she wasn't. Maybe she was a freaking rocket scientist. Maybe she had a natural gift for recognizing what men want from a woman, and for giving it to them. Talent was a sort of intelligence, wasn't it? If it was, her intelligence certainly came across in the movies she made.

He continued back to the bar and opened the little personal-sized refrigerator for some ice cubes.

Colin's two other groomsmen let out a whoop. One of them was an investment banker with some big Japanese bank. The other was some kind of executive with Paramount. Jeff couldn't remember which was which.

One of them was sliding a black bra off the shoulders of one of the blonde porno queens they'd brought with them. Another blonde was sitting reverse-cowgirl style in the other guy's lap, her head back and mouth open as his hands moved over her breasts.

Beyond them, toward the back of the bus, was Bellamy

Blaze. She was watching him, stirring her drink with a fingernail that was as red as candy.

She smiled at him and he quickly looked away.

She made him nervous.

There was a sink next to the bar, and Jeff made an exaggerated show of dumping ice into his drink. Anything to keep from meeting her gaze. Then he took a cold can of Coke and mixed it with a heavy shot of Grey Goose.

He took one last look at her, saw she was still smiling at him, and quickly wandered back to his seat. He closed his eyes and let the drugs take over again.

When he opened them again, Bellamy Blaze was French kissing the two naked blondes. Colin's other groomsmen were watching, hooting and hollering like a bunch of frat boys at a strip club. The girls had pretty much been interchangeable during the trip, fucking and sucking at the wink of an eye, all except for Bellamy Blaze. Jeff wasn't sure if Colin had declared her off-limits for the other guys, but it was possible. Colin knew Jeff was infatuated with her. The subject had come up a few times in their e-mails. And it was just like him to spend forty thousand dollars on a week's worth of drugs and reserve a porno star for his old best friend from school.

Now that she wasn't watching him, he was watching her. The warm, sultry chords at the beginning of Gordon Lightfoot's "Sundown" came over the bus speakers, and Bellamy Blaze disentangled herself from the naked blondes and drifted forward, her hands in her hair, eyes closed, lips barely parted in a gesture of obvious arousal. She was wearing a loose pair of faded blue jeans that were barely holding on to her hips. Her white camisole showed a lot of midriff and stretched around the fullness of her breasts.

The drugs were playing with Jeff's senses now, creating an odd sort of visual synesthesia he could feel in his groin. The air became an almost liquid blur around her face. He watched the slow roll of her hips, and it seemed the song had taken physical form. Everything seemed so right about the way she moved, so effortlessly graceful.

His eyes rolled up to her face. She was looking at him again, watching him as she danced.

And then she was standing next to him. He had zoned out, he realized. But now he could smell her, and her scent was like some warm, wonderful blend of sandalwood and cloves and tarragon, only more delicate and distinctly feminine. There was a thin sheen of sweat on her belly.

He swallowed hard. Then he looked up.

"Your friend is quite a bullshitter," she said.

"Huh?"

"Colin," she said, and nodded back over her shoulder toward the rear of the bus. "You should hear him talk."

"I have," Jeff said. He laughed. "All four years we were at Harvard together."

"Oh, God," she said. "Don't tell me you're one of them."

"One of what?"

"You went to Harvard? You're one of those guys?"

"Yeah," he said. He wasn't quite sure why he felt embarrassed about it, but he did. "But don't worry. None of it rubbed off."

She smiled. "You mind if I sit down?"

"No," he said. "That'd be okay. I mean, sure. Yeah. That'd be great."

He winced. He sounded like a jackass.

But she didn't seem to mind. She squeezed around him, her breasts passing only inches from his eyes. Her nipples were erect, and for a moment he thought he could actually see them through her camisole.

Or maybe it's the drugs, he thought.

"I like the way you dance," he said.

"This is one of my favorite songs," she said.

"Really?" Again, he sounded too eager. Jesus, he was

handling this badly. He looked for something to say, something brilliant to keep her attention, but his mind was a blank.

"I love seventies folk rock," she said. "It's cheesy, I know, but I still love it. Always have."

"I don't think it's cheesy."

"Yeah, it's kind of cheesy," she said, and laughed. "Fun, but cheesy."

He started to ask her about music, but stopped himself. It would just end up sounding dumb. Jesus, why was he having such a hard time talking to her? He usually didn't have this problem. Was it the drugs?

"Robin Tharp," she said.

That brought him back into the moment. "What?"

"That's my name," she said. "My *real* name." She rolled her eyes toward the two plastic blondes getting passed between Colin's groomsmen. "I'm not anything like them, Jeff. No more than you and Colin are alike. I get the feeling neither one of us fits in here."

A slow smile formed at the corner of his mouth.

"What do you suppose we do about that?" he said.

"I like to be treated like a real girl, Jeff. I like to hear guys call me by my real name. Will you do that for me?"

"Sure," he said.

"Sundown" faded away. Static took its place. And then, a moment later, he heard a man's voice talking Spanish.

Jeff cocked his head to listen.

"Is something wrong?" she said.

"Listen."

He closed his eyes and tried to focus. The radio was spitting out static again. The man's voice was coming in brokenly, but Jeff was getting enough of it to pull the sense out of the rapid-fire Spanish.

The man was talking about the collapse of the quarantine

zone around the Houston area. Wave after wave of the infected were pouring out of South Texas, but apparently there were other problems farther east. Outbreaks had been reported in Florida, up the Atlantic seaboard, and out West. He said Los Angeles, San Francisco, Santa Barbara, San Diego, Las Vegas, Salt Lake City, and Phoenix, anywhere with a major airport, were reporting devastating outbreaks. The border states in Mexico—Baja, Sonora, Chihuahua, Coahuila, Nuevo Leon, Tamaulipas—were in anarchy, the people there in a mad flight south, away from the infected pouring out of the United States.

Jeff opened his eyes. He looked at Bellamy Blaze—at Robin, he reminded himself. She had a hand over her mouth. Her face was stricken, her eyes wide.

"You speak Spanish?" he said.

She glanced at him and nodded.

"What are we gonna do?" she said.

Jeff looked back down the length of the bus. The others were partying at top volume, rubbing up against each other like alley cats in heat. For two days they had been like this, too high to notice the country was experiencing a full meltdown. Colin and the others still didn't have a clue.

Jeff scrubbed a hand across his face and tried to think clearly. He couldn't focus, and the more he tried, the faster his heart beat. His fingertips were trembling. Robin was saying something, but she sounded like a bird singing, the words pleasant but indistinct. Were they slowing down?

He leaned forward and looked out the window. The desert sands were the color of ripe wheat and dotted with innumerable green balls of sagebrush. Off in the distance, a low line of chalky black hills hunched up to the cloudless sky. Here and there, industrially drab block-shaped buildings shimmered in the heat. Traffic was forming itself into knots. And they were slowing down. He could feel it.

They stopped.

"What's going on, Jeff?" Robin asked.

"I don't know."

"Something's wrong," she said.

All he could do was nod.

Then the driver put the vehicle in reverse and backed up as fast as he could go, sending everything in the bus rolling forward. The bus rocked violently from side to side as the driver struggled to control the wheel. Jeff was thrown from his seat. Robin had to catch herself by grabbing onto his shoulder. There was a stuttering bark of tires. Brakes squealed. They hit something, and the bus lurched violently to a stop.

For a moment, Jeff felt his whole body go limp. Then, after a long, disoriented moment, he looked up at Robin.

"Are you okay?"

She nodded.

"What the goddamn holy fuck is that asshole doing?" Colin shouted from behind them.

Colin's other groomsmen echoed his angry shouts. One of the girls was crying. Jeff couldn't tell which of them it was. Colin, still zipping up his pants, headed for the front.

"What are you going to do?" Jeff asked him.

"I'm about to put my boot up the fucking driver's ass is what I'm going to do."

The bus lurched forward again and there was another impact. Colin fell over the back of one of the chairs. When he straightened himself up, he was insane with rage. He slammed his fist into one of the overhead bins and screamed.

Then he charged forward. The other two groomsmen were right behind him. Jeff watched them go. He turned to Robin. "I got to stop him. He's gonna kill that driver."

She nodded.

A black curtain separated the party area from the driver's

section up front. Jeff pushed his way through the curtain and nearly ran into the back of one of Colin's other groomsmen. Colin had started to scream at the driver, but now he was just standing there, staring out the windows.

Outside, in the distance, was the sparse industrial tedium of downtown Barstow, nothing but one metal warehouse after another. Traffic was snarled up all around them. They could hear tires skidding, the muffled sounds of people yelling, and every few moments there came the sickening crunch of metal and busting glass from somewhere behind them. People were moving between the cars. Some were running, obviously terrified. Others seemed to be injured. They were staggering through the drifting dust clouds and whirling smoke like wraiths coming out of a fog. Moans and screams surrounded them.

A middle-aged woman slapped a bloody hand against the folding glass door to their right. She was screaming at them for help. Jeff couldn't make out what she was saying, but her terror was clear.

Then she disappeared down the length of the bus, still banging against the sides.

"Get us the fuck out of here," Colin said to the driver.

The man looked at Colin and shook his head. "We can't move," he said. "We're stuck."

Then the driver reached under his seat and came up with a black revolver. "You people stay here," he said.

"Where the fuck do you think you're going?" Colin said.

The driver didn't answer him. He threw open the folding doors and stepped down onto the street with his pistol pointed in the air. He looked right, then left, then stalked toward the traffic piled up in front of the bus.

"That fucking idiot," Colin said. "Where the hell is he going?"

Colin stepped off the bus.

"Colin, wait," Jeff said, but it was too late. Things were happening too quickly for his acid-muddled mind to catch up.

A moment later, he and Colin's other two groomsmen were out on the street as well. Jeff felt the desert heat curl his hair, and for a moment the world was swimming around him.

"Colin, wait," he said.

But Colin wasn't listening. He was yelling at the driver, who was leveling his revolver at a man staggering toward them from between a pair of Honda Accords.

Jeff grabbed Colin and caught his shirt. Colin swatted at his hand, but when Jeff wouldn't let go, Colin slid out of the shirt and ran after the bus driver, wearing only his T-shirt and slacks.

Jeff was left holding the shirt. He looked around, momentarily lost, and began to notice all the people. One guy, a kid of perhaps seventeen in torn and blood-soaked clothes, was approaching the bus driver from behind. One part of Jeff's mind was aware that the kid was infected, and Jeff wanted to scream out for the driver to get out of the way, but that part seemed to be struggling through a dense fog, unable to make itself heard.

A man screamed out behind him. Jeff turned to see one of Colin's groomsmen throwing a man in blue coveralls to the ground.

The groomsman landed on top of the man, pinning his shoulders to the pavement.

"Help me!" he said.

Jeff was the first to move. To his left was a pickup truck modified with steeple brackets in order to haul large panes of glass. In the confusion, glass had fallen off the truck and broken into pieces on the asphalt. Jeff saw one that looked like an icicle. He scooped it up, wrapped Colin's shirt around one end to form a handle, and ran back to the two men struggling near the front of the bus.

"Move out of the way," Jeff said. He had the shard of glass in both hands, the tapered point poised over the infected man's face.

The groomsman didn't move.

"Get out of the way," Jeff said.

"I can't," the man shot back. "Just do it. Hurry."

The zombie was clawing at the groomsman's face. The groomsman was doing his best to deflect the zombie's hands with his elbows, but he already had several deep gashes on his jaw and on his neck.

"Hurry," he shouted.

Jeff took a breath and slammed the glass down. The point went deep into the zombie's eye, stopping only when the edges of the glass caught in the orbital bone around the socket and couldn't go any deeper.

Jeff lost his balance and fell over, the glass shard snapping with a brittle crack.

The groomsman climbed off the zombie, and the zombie made no effort to get up. He lay there with his arms spread eagle to the clear blue desert sky, his mouth open. His teeth were black with dried blood.

Jeff was sitting now, his back against a truck tire, watching the zombie. He heard a whimpering sound, and when he looked up, he saw that it was Colin, backing away from the carnage. He was shaking his head, a comma-shaped lock of his rumpled hair moving on his forehead with the motion.

Someone was yelling his name.

He looked to the bus and saw Robin standing there, pointing off to his right.

"Help him," she said. "He's got a gun. Help him."

Jeff saw the driver backing up into the side of a Toyota 4Runner. In front of him was a man whose face was badly burned on one half, as though he'd slept in a puddle of battery acid. One arm hung limply at his side. The other was reaching for the driver. The driver fired at the man, hitting him in the limp arm. The burned zombie twisted away from the hit, but didn't cry out.

"Ah, fuck me," the driver said. "Fuck, fuck, fuck."

He fired again, but this time only managed to hit the side of the car behind the zombie.

Colin's other groomsman was kneeling beside his injured friend. Jeff grabbed him by the collar and pulled him to his feet. "Help me," he said.

"Fuck off," the groomsman said. He swatted Jeff's hand away, then knelt again next to his friend, who was starting to convulse.

"You can't do anything for him," Jeff said.

The other man ignored him.

Jeff stood there, looking around uncertainly. He wasn't sure what to do. His thoughts were so damn foggy. He took a step forward, stopped, then started forward again. Jeff grabbed the uninjured groomsman by the shoulder and pulled him away.

"Help me with the driver," he said.

The man wheeled on Jeff and took a wild swing at his face. The blow missed by a good six inches, but it caused both men to teeter off balance and they stumbled backward. Jeff kept his feet and caught the other man. He pushed him up to his feet and stepped back right as another shot rang out, and this one was so close he heard it whiz past his ear.

In front of him, the groomsman he had just put back on his feet doubled over, punched in the gut by the bullet. A woman screamed. The groomsman swayed for a long moment on wobbly legs, then looked up at Jeff and fell over.

Confused, Jeff turned around. The bus driver was backing away from him. He didn't seem to be aware of what he had just done. His expression was pure panic. The gun in his hand was shaking. He raised it once again, this time pointing it somewhere over Jeff's shoulder.

The driver never saw the man who pulled him down from

behind. Jeff watched him fall between a pickup truck and a Chevy Malibu and heard him screaming as the zombie tore into him.

When the screaming stopped, Jeff heard Robin calling his name. Colin was there, pushing his way past her and onto the bus in a panicked rush. Jeff stood in the middle of the highway, a dashed white line between his feet, and watched in horror as Colin dropped down behind the wheel, put the bus in gear, and hit the gas.

The bus lurched backward, traveled a few feet, and crashed into something.

"What are you doing?" Jeff said. "Wait."

But Colin made no sign he'd heard him. He wrestled with the gearshift, then hit the gas again. He turned the wheel hand over hand, veering just to the right of Jeff.

There was another crash as the bus collided with a row of parked cars, but this time Colin didn't let up. He kept the gas pedal mashed to the floor. Jeff heard the engine straining, the tires starting to slip on the asphalt.

The cars moved sideways. Slowly, inch by inch, the bus pushed its way through the cars.

Jeff glanced up at the windshield. Robin was there, screaming at him. She was waving him inside, toward the door. He jumped over a car's hood just as the bus pushed it to the shoulder. Then he scrambled around the front of the bus and jumped on. He lunged forward and hit the lever to snap the doors shut behind him.

Colin was screaming at the top of his lungs as he piloted the bus forward through the cars. Jeff watched him and thought, *Jesus help us, he's fucking lost it.*

Jeff held onto the railing next to the stairs as the bus bounced off the roadway. Peering over the dashboard, he could see they were headed for a large, and nearly empty, surface street. Colin straightened the bus out and as soon as they were on paved roads again he stopped screaming, though the muscles in his arms were still tightly knotted, his knuckles a bloodless white on the steering wheel.

"Colin," Jeff said. "Colin, slow down."

It took Colin a moment for the sense of what Jeff was saying to sink in, but when it did, he lifted his foot off the gas, and the bus slowed to a stop.

Jeff put a hand on his arm and pulled at it until Colin finally let go of the wheel.

"Come on," he said, and guided Colin out of the driver's seat. With Robin's help, he managed to get Colin into a chair on the other side of the aisle. Then he dropped down behind the wheel and peered out the windshield. They could still hear screams and crunching metal from the freeway behind them, and here and there they saw people running, but the road ahead of them seemed relatively clear. A nearby street sign said they were at the intersection of Barstow Road and Windy Pass.

"What are we going to do?" Robin said.

"Figure out where we are first."

He reached into his pants pocket and pulled out his cell phone. One bar. Good enough. He called up the menu and went to Google Maps. Right away, a map of the city popped up on the tiny screen. Barstow seemed to be laid out precisely along a north–south east–west grid. He zoomed in on their position, and a street name caught his eye.

"Jeff?" Robin said.

He looked over his shoulder at her. "It's okay," he said. "At least, I think it is. Here. Look at this."

He showed her the map. With his thumb, he pointed to a horseshoe-shaped road on the southern edge of town.

"Harvard Street?" she said.

"Yep."

"But it doesn't go anywhere."

There is a joke in there somewhere, he thought. He found

it very funny, and he told himself he'd have to explain it to her sometime.

"It doesn't," he agreed. "But look at this."

He pointed south of the horseshoe to a long, pencil-thin line on the map called Pipeline Road.

"It goes all the way to Interstate Forty, way over here. We bypass all the major population areas and end up here."

She looked out at the desert doubtfully. "You think we can make it? I bet that road's not even paved."

"I don't see that we've got any other choice."

"No," she said. "I guess we don't."

He smiled at her, then put the bus in gear.

Chapter 21

Reggie led Kyra out into the hall, then held her shoulders as he guided her around the corpses on the floor.

She stepped on the side of what felt like the heel of a man's boot and stumbled.

Reggie caught her, steadied her. "You okay?" he asked.

The carpet felt wet, squishy beneath Kyra's sneakers.

"Who were they?"

"That's Jake back there. And there's the Kirby kids up here. I forget their names."

"Ruth and Max," she said.

He grunted and continued to guide her through the living room. She could feel his fingers trembling on her shoulders.

"Misty Mae said Jake was sick last night."

Another grunt.

She said, "Did you see Misty Mae?"

"Yeah. She's outside with the baby."

Kyra brightened. "She's okay?"

He didn't answer right away, and the silence was chilling.

"No," he said. "She was changed. I couldn't even tell at first—you know how you can tell with most of them? She didn't have no bite marks or blood on her or nothing. It was like there was nothing wrong with her. Not till she turned around on me and I saw those eyes. They'd gone all milky, like a dead person's eyes."

"Did you . . ."

They were going down the steps now, out into the yard. It was still bright enough out for the light to show up on her eyes, and she squeezed them shut against it.

"Uncle Reggie?"

"She's dead, Kyra."

"And the baby?"

"You don't want to know about that," he said. "I had to . . ."

But he didn't offer anything else, just trailed off into silence.

Their shoes clattered on the pavement. They slowed, and Uncle Reggie kept a hand on her as he pushed the gate open. The creaking of its hinges seemed deafening.

"Where are we going?" she said.

"Away from here, baby. Things are bad."

"Tell me, Reggie."

He opened the door to his truck and helped her inside. "I want you to stay here," he said. "You hear me? Don't move. This'll just take a second."

"What are—"

But he had closed the door in her face. She leaned back against the cracked vinyl seats, listening to the wind blowing dust against the cab of the truck and the faint grating of the sand against the glass.

She thought back on the night before, listening in her bed to the alley-cat sounds of Jake and Misty Mae having sex in the trailer next door. Misty Mae had said Jake was sick when he came home from Odessa. Had he been infected then? That seemed likely to Kyra. And that made her wonder just how Misty Mae had gotten her infection. Uncle Reggie had mentioned that Misty Mae didn't have any wounds, like you'd get if you were attacked. Had she gotten hers in the bedroom? Were the little swimmers in his baby batter a bunch of zombies, changing her from the inside out?

The thought made her shudder. *God, what a way to go*, she thought.

And then a shotgun blast silenced that line of thinking. She sat bolt upright in the seat, waiting.

A moment later, Uncle Reggie was climbing into the driver's seat. He was out of breath and he had to fight with his keys to get them into the ignition. He tossed the shotgun up against Kyra's left leg. She put her hand around it—the barrel was hot—and waited to see what was going to happen.

"Hold on," he told her.

The transmission made a grinding noise, and he cussed under his breath. Kyra felt a renewed wave of uneasiness wash over her. She'd lived with the man nearly all her life and she had never heard him say a cross word. *He must be scared*, she thought.

They tore away from the curb with a stuttering bark from the tires. Kyra grabbed hold of the door and tried to brace herself.

"Uncle Reggie," she said. "Slow down, please. Uncle Reggie."

"They're everywhere, Kyra," he said.

A car skidded by them, tires shrieking. A horn blared, and kept on blaring as it receded into the distance behind them.

"Uncle Reggie, please. Please stop."

They went around another corner. She heard the engine's exhaust note drop an octave, and soon they were coasting at normal speed.

"What's happening?" she said.

"The whole place, Kyra. Jesus, there's bodies everywhere. And the town's on fire. The propane yard . . . my God, there's so much smoke."

She could smell it. Had smelled it, in fact.

"Where are we?"

"Up near the freeway," he said. "I don't know. Over near Wayne Blessing's place, I think."

West end of town, she thought. A whole lot of empty nothingness stretching out before them, desert all the way to the horizon, and beyond.

"What about Billy Ledlow?" she asked, referring to the town's one and only peace officer, a part-timer who also worked the day shift at the Village Pantry grocery store on Wilma Street.

"Baby, there's nothing. My God. They're all killing each other. I saw ole Ms. Wendy Gruber eatin' on somebody in the alleyway behind her shop. I threw up all over myself."

Maybe that was what she smelled, she thought. They had cleared the smoke now, she guessed, and the air inside the truck was thick with the smell of rot. It was like a package of chicken that had been left out back in the garbage for a few days.

She said, "Uncle Reggie, what are we gonna do?"

"I don't know, baby. I gotta get you outta here. It . . . it ain't safe here."

A silence settled over them, and it stretched on and on.

Uncle Reggie had his window down. She could feel the wind blowing from that direction, and with it came that smell again, that stink of something rotting in the sun.

She said, "Uncle Reggie," and waited.

"Yeah, baby?"

"I don't want you to lie to me," she said.

"I won't ever lie to you, Kyra, you know that."

She waited.

He was silent.

Finally, she said, "Uncle Reggie, tell me the truth. Did you get bit? Is that what I smell?"

He took a long time to answer, but at last he said, "Yeah. On my left shoulder."

"Is it bad?"

"Bad enough. It hurts."

"Did you . . . do anything for it?"

"Like what?" he said. "Can't do nothing for it, you know that. They ain't got no cure."

She nodded, and they were both silent again.

"Damn it," he muttered, a little while later.

"What is it?"

"Kyra, I'm sorry. It's hard for me to focus. This town ain't got more than twenty streets and I keep getting lost. I can't find the fuckin' highway. My head is swimming. I can't stop sweatin'. It's like I got the flu or something. I keep blackin' out."

He coughed, hard, and it sounded like he was bringing something up.

She reached out a hand to touch his shoulder.

"No, don't," he said, and flinched away from her when her fingertips touched his shirtsleeve.

"Reggie?"

"I can't," he began, then broke off into a coughing fit. The coughing went on and on. Then, when it stopped, he said, "I want to find someplace safe for you, Kyra. If I can leave you with somebody we trust, somebody who'll take care of you, that'd be . . ."

"Reggie, please. Pull over. Let me help you."

"I can't pull over, Kyra. They're everywhere. And besides, you can't do nothin' for me. Just sit still a bit and—Holy shit!"

There was a loud crash against Reggie's side of the truck and the vehicle swerved to the right, out of control. They hit a parked car on Kyra's side of the road and she was thrown forward against the dashboard.

"What is it?" she screamed. "What's going on?"

"Fucking zombie," Reggie muttered. "Came out of nowhere. The damn idiot ran right into the truck. Didn't even see him."

Kyra listened as he worked the gearshift between them, grinding the transmission as he tried to get the truck back into gear. She could hear him pumping his foot on the clutch.

"What's wrong?"

"Can't get it in gear. I think it's the clutch or something. It's slipped."

From behind them, Kyra could hear shouts and the sounds of glass breaking. Off in the distance, she heard shots, but just a few. Over all the rest of the rioting, she could hear the moans of the infected, getting closer.

"Reggie."

More grinding gears, more clutch pumping.

"Reggie."

"It's not working," he said.

He threw open his door.

"What are you doing? Where are you going?"

"Give me the gun," he shouted at her.

She fumbled with the shotgun, pushing it awkwardly in his direction. He yanked it out of her hand. She heard his footsteps going away, toward the back of the truck, and then two blasts from the shotgun.

The next moment, he was back at the truck. She listened as he dumped a box of shells onto the seat beside her and worked them into the Mossberg's magazine.

"Reggie, what's going on?"

"We're gonna have to make it on foot," he said. "Can you come on out?"

She scrambled over the seats and he helped her down to the pavement. Kyra heard the moans of the infected all around her.

Reggie put one of her hands on the side of the truck and told her to stand still. He took a few steps from her and fired. He racked the shotgun and fired again. She could smell the gun smoke in the air mixed with the greasy, black smoke of a propane fire nearby.

Something thudded against the driver's-side door and she screamed.

"Motherfucker," Reggie hissed. There was a dull slap, like a hammer hitting a steak, and then the sound of a body falling to the pavement.

A hand gripped her around the bicep.

"Come on," Reggie said.

He pulled her into the street, turned her ninety degrees, and gave her a push.

"Go," he shouted.

She fell forward, but kept her feet.

She turned back, confused. "What? Reggie?"

Once again, he grabbed her by the arm, turned her around, and shoved. "Go," he yelled. "Hurry. I can't hold them off for long."

And then it dawned on her what he expected her to do. "No," she said. "Uncle Reggie, no. I can't. Please. Come with me."

"Go," he said. "Get out of here."

He fired three more times. She could hear him struggling, grunting as he wrestled with one of the infected.

"Go, Kyra. Hurry."

She took three steps, then stopped. She couldn't. Not alone.

Reggie was still fighting. She heard his boots scuffing on the pavement. He grunted as he fought hand to hand with the zombies, pushing them back, buying time for her.

"Kyra!" he shouted. "Go, hurry. Please. Go."

It was the last sound she heard from him. Crying, shaking so badly she thought she might rattle herself to bits, she turned and walked into the desert with only the padded thud of her shoes on the pavement to tell her she was still on the road.

CHAPTER 22

Aaron Roberts stood next to Jasper Sewell on the roof of one of their buses looking out across the wide grassy common area of an abandoned Katrina evacuation village, one of many of FEMA's day-late-and-a-dollar-short approaches to disaster management. There were people everywhere, at least a thousand, possibly more. They had come here, to this vast collection of small, unpainted wood-framed houses, many of them by accident, and found themselves trapped. At least, that had been the case before Jasper saw the confusion from the bus and ordered his driver to pull into the parking lot. Now things were running smoothly.

The first thing he did was to tell Aaron and his other lieutenants to go forth into the mass of people and organize them into stations. Several members of the Family had medical training, and they set up a mobile hospital. The crowd was marched through and inspected for signs of the infection. Once they were cleared, they were asked about their medical needs by several of the registered nurses who were members of the Family. Those with special conditions, such as a need for insulin or antibiotics, were taken care of from the Family's medical stores. All others were moved forward to the next station, where their names were taken down and any special skills they had, like carpentry or plumbing, were recorded.

Aaron was stunned at how easy Jasper made it look.

The greatest moment of the day had come just an hour earlier. Aaron and a few of the other lieutenants had gone to Jasper and asked if he didn't think it was time for them to leave. There was not enough food to feed all these people, they said.

"How much do we have?" Jasper asked Aaron.

"Just what we brought with us," he said. "Five crates of military MREs and two crates of bread. There's barely enough for the Family, much less all these people."

Jasper studied the crowd, his eyes lost behind the dark, rounded lenses of his sunglasses. His broad, strong jawline was beaming with a gracious, easy confidence.

"They are all my family, Aaron," he said. "We are going to provide for them."

And with that, Jasper had taken his cell phone from his pocket and placed a call. Aaron listened to Jasper talking, and he heard the man making arrangements, but he didn't understand what it meant. He felt confused. Jasper was a great man, a good man, and it was in his nature to help anyone he could. He used his pulpit to talk about corruption in politics, about racial injustice, about the homeless, about children dying of hunger right here in Jackson. If there was an issue that needed to be brought to the public's attention, be it something as big as racism in the criminal courts or as small as a school board trying to drop the free breakfast program in an underprivileged elementary school, Jasper would bring five hundred members of his church and pack the meeting hall, every member demanding to be heard. That was the kind of socially conscious message that had attracted Aaron and Kate to the New Life Bible Church in the first place. Jasper was a powerful voice for change in Jackson politics, but did he really believe he could feed a thousand hungry people with five crates of military rations and two crates of bread?

"Where are you?" Jasper said into the phone. He waited. "That close?" Jasper nodded to himself, sunlight flashing off the lenses of his sunglasses. "Fantastic, Mr. Porter. Yes. Okay. We'll see you soon."

He pocketed the phone and put a hand on Aaron's shoulder.

Speaking so that the other lieutenants could hear, he said, "My friends, you are about to witness something wonderful. A miracle. Go through the crowd. Tell them to sit down on the ground and wait, for they shall be fed, each and every one of them."

Aaron wrinkled his brow at Jasper. "But Jasper—"

Jasper held up a slender finger and wagged it in the air. "No questions, my friend. Just do as I ask. Go now. Tell the people they shall be fed."

Aaron and the other lieutenants did as Jasper asked. Using the loudspeakers and their own voices, shouting themselves hoarse, they managed to get the crowd assembled on the ground near the buses.

Within minutes, Jasper appeared before the crowd, and speaking over a bullhorn, said a prayer for them. And as he spoke, reciting from memory Psalm 130, a caravan of mismatched eighteen-wheelers pulled into the lot behind him, each one laden with food collected from the city's grocery stores.

Aaron, with his arm around Kate, had laughed in triumph.

Jasper turned to Aaron and said, "I don't intend for us to stay here."

"But where will we go?"

"North. A long ways."

Aaron nodded.

Jasper said, "I've spent the last thirty minutes in meditation, Aaron, thinking on a place I went to as a boy. Tell me, have you ever been to North Dakota?"

"Jasper, I ain't never left Mississippi."

Jasper smiled at that. "North Dakota's a beautiful place. My parents took me there one summer when I was twelve. I remember we made our campsite in the Cedar River National Grasslands, on the bank of a river. I can still picture it, Aaron. I climbed out of the backseat of my parent's car and I saw grass stretching off into the distance in every direction. The sky was like the color of an old weathered photograph. You know how they get all yellow?"

"It sounds beautiful, Jasper."

"Oh, it was. Very. It was the first place I ever truly felt the presence of God. It changed me."

Jasper paused there, his gaze directed far away, beyond the crowd and the rows of unpainted houses. The sky was still overcast and gray. It hadn't rained at all, though it had certainly seemed like it would. Off in the distance, they could see a few tall columns of black smoke.

Jasper went on. "I knew that one day I would return to that place. God talked to me there for a reason. Now, he's calling me back there. That's where we're going to go, Aaron, the Grasslands."

"Will all these people come with us?" Aaron asked.

Jasper turned his sunglasses on Aaron and regarded him for a long while before answering.

"Would you have us leave them?"

"No, of course not. I just . . . I don't see . . ."

"What?"

"Jasper, I don't see how we're going to transport them all. We have only three buses."

A lemony glare flashed on the lenses of Jasper's sunglasses. His lips pulled down at the corners into a solemn, sad expression.

"Aaron," he said. "You are my most resourceful lieutenant, and yet you have doubted me twice today. Why is that?"

"I . . . I'm sorry, Jasper."

"Haven't you seen what I did for them? Didn't we feed them all, every single one?"

"Yes, of course."

"And have food left over?"

Aaron nodded.

"Then why do you still wonder if it's possible to take these people with us?"

"Jasper," Aaron said. But he faltered and broke off.

"Why do you suppose I brought you up here?"

"I . . . I don't know, Jasper."

"I wanted you to see the people, Aaron. Our Family." He motioned to the crowds below them. "And I wanted you to see where we are going. But most of all, I wanted you to be the first to see that."

He pointed over Aaron's left shoulder.

Aaron turned, and right away he saw the surprise Jasper had coming for them. It was a line of yellow school buses, at least sixty of them, maybe more.

"Oh, my," Aaron said. "How did you . . ."

"Some miracles you create for yourself," Jasper said. "Now, I want to leave here by nightfall. Go down into the crowds and tell them to gather themselves together. Anybody who wishes to join us can come along. All are welcome."

Aaron nodded.

"I'm sorry I doubted you," he said. "It won't happen again. I promise."

Jasper smiled. "I believe you, Aaron. Go now, tell the people to get ready. Spread the word."

CHAPTER 23

They weren't moaning anymore. At least there was that.

In the shed, Nate Royal listened to the low, peaceful sizzle of a light rain falling on the metal roof. He had no idea how long he had been in the shed. Several hours at least. He could still see daylight through the cracks in the door, but it was growing darker, and he didn't want to get stuck in here all night.

He rocked forward onto his knees and put a hand on the shed door, but then the image of Jessica Metcalfe getting torn to bits rose up in his mind, and a shudder went through him.

He sank back against the wall and rubbed his wounded shoulder meditatively.

Surprisingly, it didn't hurt.

He leaned forward again and peeled his shirtsleeve up and studied the wound in the waning light.

It didn't look any worse than the time Georgiana Meyers's dog had tried to chew his hand off when he was six. His shoulder wound was a little white around the edges, like the foam on a glass of beer, and that didn't look right, but it wasn't a scary wound. He'd seen worse.

He thought he remembered something about how the zombie bites were supposed to turn black, and how they were supposed to smell like rotting meat.

He sniffed his shoulder.

Nothing.

And he felt fine. More or less. On TV, they said people who got bit acted like they had the flu. They were dizzy and pale and achy and sweated a lot. He didn't feel any of those things.

"Huh," he said. "Maybe I got a break." God knows he was due for one.

And then he thought, *Well, fuck it. I got lucky once. Maybe I'll get lucky again.*

He stood up, leaned an ear against the crack at the edge of the door, and listened to the rain pattering down on the grass outside.

Nothing.

He pushed the door open, wincing as it creaked, but he kept on pushing.

The sky was washed out and gray, a watercolor smear over the row of houses. Rain puddles dotted the yard. But he was alone. He listened, and when he didn't hear anything, he took off running toward his house. He rounded the corner of the alley and heard somebody shooting.

He ducked behind some bushes.

Lucky thing, too.

Three of those zombie things were shambling down the side street to his right, dragging half-eaten legs, trying to grasp with hands that were too mangled to work.

Nate looked over to his left and saw two guys in white plastic suits, like something out of a science-fiction movie, gas masks over their faces. They had military-looking machine guns.

The lead white suit called out, "Police officers. Stop moving. Put your hands over your head."

The zombies lumbered closer, like they didn't hear.

"Stop where you're at or we'll fire."

The second white suit had a radio in his hand. He said, "Team Seven-Alpha. Evans and Avenue G, three confirmed. Request permission to fire."

Whomever he was talking to must have given him the okay, because a moment later a three-round burst of gunfire slammed into the lead zombie and nearly took his head off. The body went tumbling backward.

The other two zombies kept shambling toward the white suits. They didn't even flinch at the gunfire, just kept right on coming.

Two more bursts took them out.

Nate's eyes went wide.

He jumped to his feet and ran the other way. His feet slid out from under him on the wet road and he probably looked like a tangle of arms and legs, but he didn't care. He just wanted to get away from there.

"Hey," one of the white suits yelled. "Hey, stop. Stop!"

Nate put his head down and ran.

But he didn't even make it across the street before the demon in his knee raised its ugly head and down he went.

He looked back just as the white suits closed on him.

"What the hell are you doing, man?" the first one said. He sounded winded and angry. "We're trying to help you. Didn't you hear the warnings on TV?"

Nate was confused. He looked from one white suit to the other. They knew what he'd done to Jessica Metcalfe. That's why they were here, fucking cops. Why were they fucking with him like this? Just knock his dick in the dirt and be done with it.

"Where have you been all day?" the other white suit said. "The evacuation is mandatory. Everybody's gotta go."

"I—," Nate said, and had nothing beyond that. He shrugged.

"What's wrong with your knee?" one of the suits said. He

wasn't pointing his machine gun at Nate, but he still looked ready to use it.

"I hurt it a few years back," Nate said.

The white suits relaxed a little. The one closest to Nate slung his rifle over his shoulder and held out his hand and said, "Can you stand? You need a hand up?"

"Thanks."

Nate took the man's gloved hand, and the plastic crinkled in his grip. The man started to pull him to his feet, then suddenly let go of Nate's hand and backed away. Both soldiers brought their machine guns up.

"Hey, you've been bit," the first white suit said. "Your shoulder."

"What are you trying to pull?" the second white suit said. "You didn't think we'd notice?"

The first white suit took out his radio and keyed it up. "Team Seven-Alpha, send us the wagon to Evans and Avenue G. We got one injured that hasn't turned yet."

"Team Seven-Alpha, ten-four," came a man's bored voice on the other end. "Is he secured?"

"Ten-four. He's compliant."

Nate covered his face with his hands and groaned at his bad luck. He heard a faint clattering of metal, and then, before he knew what was happening, one of the white suits was slapping him into handcuffs.

Nate looked at the cuffs and then up at the suits.

"What are you going to do to me?" he said.

Neither suit answered.

"Can't you just let me go home? Just let me go home?"

But there was no answer.

A white police van pulled up to the curb.

It had started to rain a few minutes before and Nate was

soaked through to the skin. The world had turned gray and depthless. The white suits got in position beside him and with a wave of their rifles directed him to the rear of the van. Nate offered no resistance. He stood up from the curb and walked where they pointed. They opened the rear of the van and Nate was shocked to see that it already had six other people inside. They were all injured to one degree or another, and they all stared back at Nate with hollow, vacant eyes that were at once tremendously sad and deeply terrifying.

"Get in," one of the white suits said. "Sit there."

"I don't wanna," Nate said.

"Get in or get shot," the other white suit said.

Nate took a look around. This was the neighborhood where he had grown up, where all the fucked-up decisions that were his life had played out in a pathetic tableau. It was all but deserted now, and in the gray sheets of rain that covered everything with a depthless smear, the black, huddled shapes of the houses seemed oddly inviting, as though all of this was a mistake and it wasn't too late to start over.

"Hey, buddy. Come on. Hop up."

The compassion in the white suit's voice shook Nate out of his thoughts. He stared at the man.

"I'll never see it again. Will I?"

The white suit shook his head. It was a barely perceptible gesture behind the gas mask.

Nate nodded, then climbed into the van. He sat down next to a man in a mud-stained business suit. Blood was oozing out from under the man's legs and running in muddy rivulets down the white metal bench upon which he sat.

Nate sat down next to the man.

The man met his gaze, his eyes red-rimmed and haunted looking, and then turned away in silence.

* * *

They were on the road for a long while, but eventually the van pulled into a muddy field and stopped.

The door flew open.

Three white suits were standing there, two of them with machine guns. The suits were standing inside a narrow, muddy lane bordered by tall black fences of metal wire. Behind them was a gate made of the same metal wire, and beyond that a large fenced-in area where several hundred people milled listlessly about.

"Get down. Move it."

"Where are we?" Nate asked.

"Get down here," the white suit said. "Move it."

Nate climbed down. The white suits stepped back along one of the fences and leveled their weapons at him.

"Stand there," the man said, pointing at the opposite fence.

Nate did as he was instructed, then stood by and waited as the others were led down from the back of the van.

The white suit got out a radio and said, "Open the inner gate."

The fence creaked as it slid open.

Nate watched it slide away, then turned back to the white suits.

"Go on," the man said.

Nate looked inside. He saw a lot of sad, vacant faces staring back at him.

Something in him rebelled.

He turned suddenly and said, "No. No fucking way."

He tried to run, but the only place to go was back toward the van.

Under it, he thought.

He dove into the mud and tried to scramble under the rear

axle, but he wasn't fast enough. One of the white suits grabbed him by his ankles and pulled him back out.

Nate turned over, and the last thing he saw before everything went black was the butt of a rifle speeding down toward his face.

CHAPTER 24

They took I-40 from Barstow and stayed with it all the way into Arizona. At Kingman, they turned south onto 93 and started seeing traffic fleeing north from Phoenix, a trickle of headlights going God knows where.

The news on the radio was grim. Along the East Coast, the outbreak was spreading up from Florida at a staggering rate, and people were fleeing west as fast as they could go. Out west, California was in complete chaos, and a military effort to quarantine L.A. had been abandoned when troops there were overrun. Efforts around the Bay Area were more successful, though according to CNN those troops were expected to be withdrawn within the next few hours so that efforts could be focused in defending safe areas in Colorado. He listened to the reports and shook his head. The country was sucking into itself, withdrawing into its breadbasket, abandoning its coasts.

Robin stepped through the partition and took a seat behind him.

"Hey," he said.

She leaned forward and rested her chin on his shoulder.

Despite spending the last eight hours or so on the road, she still smelled nice.

"How is he?" he asked. After Barstow, Colin had raved violently before finally regaining a measure of his composure. But with the calm would come embarrassment over the cowardice he had shown back in Barstow, which he compensated for with more violence. Several times, Jeff had been forced to pull over so he could help to restrain him. Robin had been taking care of him since then, and from what Jeff saw, she had pretty much taken charge of things on the other side of the partition. Katrina Cummz and the other two blondes seemed to be doing everything she told them without question. And there hadn't been any more screaming from Colin in over an hour.

"He's calm now," Robin said. "He's resting. He'd be better if he could get some sleep, though. How about you? You okay?"

"I'm okay," he said.

"You sure? Driving's not a problem?"

"I'm okay," he assured her. "The acid's pretty much gone now. The trick is to keep focused on the road. The trouble is, I'll start thinking about stuff and I'll tune out for a while."

"You want some company?"

Her face was serenely calm, though the red rimming her eyes told a different story. Looking into her face, he got a sense that this woman had her act together, and he was a bit ashamed at himself for being surprised by that. He'd always resented Colin and his friends for their arrogance, the sense of entitlement that came with their money and guaranteed futures. It made him feel like a charity case, like every handshake and introduction was a patronizing pat on the head. He winced inwardly now with the realization that he had looked on Robin in much the same way that Colin and his friends had treated him.

"Jeff?" she said.

"Yeah," he said, and shook himself. "Yeah, some company would be great."

She pointed out the windshield. "The road."

The bus shook as the tires drifted onto the rumble strips.

"Got it," Jeff said. "I'm on it." He got the bus back on the road and put both hands on the wheel and gave her a wink in the rearview mirror. "Got it," he said.

She chuckled. "Great."

She moved over to the edge of the seat so he could see her without having to look in the mirror. The road rolled on beneath them. An occasional headlight beam would light up her face, then slowly slide away, leaving her in darkness again.

She said, "So what does Mr. Jeff Stavers think about while he's up here all alone, drifting off the road?"

"Hmmm?"

"You said you start thinking about stuff and you drift off. I want to know what that stuff is. What goes on in Jeff Stavers's brain?"

"Not much of anything," he said.

"That sounds like a cop-out to me," she said. "Tell me the truth."

He watched the road in the pool of light from the headlamps and he was tempted to tell her that it was complicated. That there was so much it was hard to put into words. But that wasn't the truth. He knew that. What he was thinking was pretty simple.

"I've got this feeling like we've crossed some kind of threshold," he said. "There's the world like it was, and then there's the world like it is now. Or like it's going to be. It's still changing, still evolving. I know that. But I've got this sense that . . . that—"

"That we've been cut free of our pasts."

The frustration he had felt at not being able to find the right words cleared from his face, and he looked at her with renewed surprise.

"Yeah," he said. "That's it exactly."

She smiled at him.

"Why don't you find a place to pull over?" she said. "You could use some sleep. We both could."

CHAPTER 25

Ed Moore rose at dawn and walked out of the tent he shared with the other men from the Springfield Adult Living Village and stretched. He was looking for Billy Kline. All around him, spread out over a five-acre grassy field south of the Marine Corps Logistics Base outside Albany, Georgia, were more than two thousand military-issued tents. They were packed in like bees in a hive. There was trash everywhere. The pathways between the tents were crisscrossed with laundry wires. The ground was worn into muddy troughs after the previous morning's rainstorms, and you couldn't walk more than a few feet from your tent without getting stained with mud up to midcalf. Though it was only a few minutes past sunrise, and much of the landscape was still shrouded in early-morning shadows and haze, the hive was already bustling with refugees trying to get a head start on the crowds that would soon be gathering around the mess halls and the commissary and the medic stations.

Ed frowned at the commotion. This was not at all what he had expected, and he was feeling the vague, unfocused anger of the disillusioned. True, the military had made good on its promise to feed them, clothe them, get them into shelter, but he was appalled at how haphazardly things were being run. Art Waller had yet to receive anything more than a cursory examination by a Marine Corps medic. He was inside the tent now, running a high fever. He'd kept Ed up most of the night with his coughing. There were generators and heaters inside the tents, but no fuel to run them. There were no showers. The only bathrooms in the camp consisted of a row of twenty port-o-pottys that had become disgusting messes by the end of the first day. It was useless to bag your garbage. Field mice and raccoons and feral cats made nightly forays into the camp, and by morning, the bags were gutted and the refuse left to rot all afternoon in the sweltering sun. Everywhere he turned, he saw a reflection of his own frustrated anger staring back at him from other residents of the camp.

They had been here for over a week now. The camp's official military designation was the Pecan City Temporary Relocation Facility, though the residents simply called it the camp.

Ed thought it would be better to call it the sty.

The first day, he'd witnessed the total collapse of military organization, and by that night, the security forces assigned to watch the camp had backed out of the area entirely, letting the residents work out their own law and order.

Ed watched their retreat with bitterness and resentment—but at the same time, he supposed he couldn't blame them. There'd been only a handful of them, none of them older than thirty, and those boys with fully automatic weapons had suddenly found themselves confronted with thousands of screaming, complaining, desperate refugees, every one of them demanding more than an entire division of soldiers and Red Cross volunteers could have possibly delivered.

Their retreat left a leadership vacuum in the camp, and things went downhill rapidly. No provision was made for traffic out on Highway 133, the main road that led along the western edge of the camp, and throughout that first day and well into the night, a steady stream of vehicles poured into the area. The road choked with pedestrians and vehicles till it was impassable. A red, cloying dust hung in the air and made breathing difficult. The new arrivals were uncertain where to go, and nobody seemed to know what they needed or how to get it. People loitered around the camp's facilities, further choking the area.

Few tents were set up at that point, and Ed and the others settled into a sort of temporary encampment a little ways off the road while they waited for somebody to assert some control over the situation. But as the morning wore on and the day grew hotter, the crowd's agitation mounted, and soon it became obvious that order would not be restored anytime soon.

"Atlanta's gone," Ed heard a passerby say.

"Macon, too," answered another man.

All through the day, news filtered in from refugees from the surrounding states, and with every new flood of stunned, staring faces came more dire news.

"We passed through Charlotte two days ago," a woman said. She was with a man, the two of them carrying their few possessions on what looked like the door to a trailer, the door held between them like a stretcher. "Wasn't nobody but dead bodies left in the whole damn town. Every street was deserted."

"What about Knoxville? I have family there."

"Gone, too. Sorry."

"Montgomery? Anybody heard news from Montgomery?"

"They're all gone."

"Columbus?"

"All dead."

A man in a dirty business suit walked by them. His face was vacant, his eyes open but unseeing. He was babbling, clutching at his hair with one hand while he swatted the air with the other. "It's all over," he said. "Fucking gone. Everything's fucking gone."

Streams of people on foot filled the road. Others drove their vehicles, honking to clear the road, leaning out their windows, screaming obscenities while shaking their fists.

"Get out of the fucking way," Ed heard the driver of a battered red Ford pickup shout.

He was answered by vacant stares and pedestrians so dead on their feet they simply showed him their backs and marched on.

Enraged, the man in the truck revved his engine. "Get your asses out of my fucking way," the man shouted again.

Suddenly, the man hit the gas and the truck lurched forward. He tried to leave the road and skirt the knots of people there, but in his haste he lost control and hit a man who was lugging a heavy rucksack along behind him. The man screamed, then fell under the truck. The rear of the truck bounced over the man and threw him some five feet away into the grass. Ed managed to reach the scene in time to see a child, a girl of five or six, staring wide-eyed and stricken at the mangled pile of twisted limbs that lay at her feet. Inevitably, there were infected among the refugees. Shots were fired. People were trampled.

Sometime around eleven that night, reinforcements arrived and the military moved back into the camp to try to assert some kind of order. But the soldiers were so few in number, and the confusion was so great, that they quickly became exhausted and angry. They ended up causing as many beatings as they stopped.

It was only around the morning of the second day that some sort of order settled over the camp. The dead were cleared out, their bodies dumped into military trucks and carted away. Soldiers with bullhorns moved through the camp. They passed out colored cards with numbers on them, lottery cards, and announced times when you could take your lottery card to the scant facilities the camp offered. It was a reasonable system, and might have worked under reasonable conditions. But it didn't work now. There were fights, and stolen cards, and double dipping, and every manner of graft.

But somehow, despite all the fighting and the riots and the confusion, Ed managed to make a niche for his people. They had tents. They had food. They had water and new clothes. They had the basics, thanks to him. He was proud of himself for getting them that much. Looking around, he could see it was more than most had.

But now he needed to find Billy Kline. He had a list of supplies they needed, but he wouldn't be able to carry them alone.

Ed found him a short distance away, coming back to the tents from the toilets. He was dressed in jeans and a red Marine Corps T-shirt that was tight in the sleeves. He hadn't shaved in three, maybe four days, Ed guessed, and his face was dark with patchy stubble.

"I need you to come with me," he said. "We got some stuff to do this morning."

"Fuck off," Billy said.

"Boy, I told you I don't like you cussing at me."

"Seriously? Are you for fucking real? What the fuck do you care if I cuss or not? I'm a grown man."

Billy ducked his head and tried to push his way past Ed. "Get the fuck out of my way."

Ed pushed him back. "Not so fast. I need your help getting supplies."

"I told you to fuck off."

"And I told you to watch your mouth."

"Whatever."

Billy tried to shove Ed out of the way but found his hands

deflected. He rocked backward, off balance, and fell onto his butt. Billy looked up at Ed, uncertain how he had ended up on his ass.

He climbed to his feet. "You stepped in some shit now, old man."

"Really?" Ed said. "Does it have to be like this? Why can't we just do what we gotta do?"

Billy dusted off the seat of his pants, then raised his fists.

Ed let out a weary sigh. "Well, come on then. Give it your best shot."

Billy charged forward and swung a huge, wide-opened right cross at Ed, who sidestepped it easily. Off balance again, Billy spun around on Ed, only to catch a left jab in his mouth. He rocked back, and for a second his legs wobbled beneath him.

Stunned, he touched his fingers to his lips. They came away bloody.

He charged Ed again with another right cross. Ed ducked it, and Billy's punch only managed to knock Ed's cowboy hat from his head. Ed moved back a half step and fired three quick left jabs into Billy's face, following with a quick upper cut to the younger man's solar plexus.

Billy fell to his knees, coughing, gasping, a rope of bloody spit hanging from his busted lips. When he looked up at Ed, Billy's head was swaying on his shoulders like he'd just been hit by a brick.

Ed was standing over him. Though seventy-two, he was still more or less straight up and down in his jeans and flannel shirt, still formidable looking. The muscles stood out like cords on his bare forearms. Only the cap of uncombed white hair on his head belied his age. He stood like an old-time boxer, fists at the ready, but down low, at belt level.

"Get up," he said.

"Fuck you," Billy answered, rubbing his jaw.

"We gonna do this again? I told you to watch your mouth around me. Now get up. I need you."

"You need me?"

"You're the strongest man here, Billy. I need some help."

"Strongest man here," Billy said, and laughed. He moved his jaw with obvious pain. "I think you knocked out one of my teeth."

Ed reached down and scooped up his hat. He dusted it off, then seated it back on his head.

"There ain't no shame in where you're at right now, son. Old age and guile is gonna triumph over youth and raw ability every time. The guile I can teach you, but the old age you're gonna have to get on your own."

Ed held out his hand.

"Now get on your feet, son. I need you."

Billy looked at Ed's hand, then at Ed.

"You're gonna teach me how to fight like that, right?"

"Someday soon," Ed said.

After dark that night, Ed was sitting with Margaret O'Brien and her two grandkids, watching a newscast out of Albany, Georgia, on a portable TV set. He was eating a granola bar. On TV, a young woman in a black pantsuit stood in front of a burning apartment building in western Albany. Riots, she said, were breaking out all over the city. There were fires raging to which the fire department couldn't respond. The infected were everywhere. The streets were littered with bodies, and authorities were ordering evacuations, though no safe areas were suggested.

Ed watched the woman and thought of all those idiot reporters he had seen over the years standing in their rain slickers, desperately trying to stay on their feet as the hurricane rolled ashore, and he wondered how long it would take a band of the infected to come in from off camera and sweep her away.

"Ed?" Margaret said.

Ed turned and looked at her. She wore a light-brown Windbreaker over a white blouse and brown slacks, and she had her arms around her grandkids, Randy and Britney.

Margaret had really blossomed since all this started, dedicating herself entirely to those kids. Ed could see the life coming back into her, the sense of purpose, and in a way, he envied her for that.

She said, "Ed, is this really . . . all over the world?"

He knew what she meant. All day long, the cable news shows had been running images from the Middle East, from China, from Mexico and Europe and Africa and South America. He sighed heavily. "I'm afraid so."

"Can it really be as bad as all that? I just can't believe that everything can fall apart so fast. It's been less than two weeks."

"It's hard to believe," he agreed.

She wrapped her arms more tightly around the kids and squeezed them close. Randy whimpered softly, and she shushed him.

"What will we do, Ed?" she said. "We can't stay here. You know that, right? This place. It's bad."

He put his granola bar down. Maybe it was the lingering depression he felt from watching the news, or maybe it was his own tired body, but the granola bar had lost its flavor, and he had no stomach for it. He rose to his feet and leaned against the edge of the tent. His back and his buttocks hurt from sitting.

"There's been talk around here," he said. "I've heard people speaking about this guy out of Jackson, Mississippi, named Jasper Sewell. Supposedly, he led over a thousand people out of Jackson without anybody getting a scratch on them. He's supposed to be setting up some kind of community in the Cedar River National Grasslands of North Dakota."

"A community?" Margaret looked doubtful. "What does that mean?"

"It's just talk I've heard," Ed said.

He'd heard stories about Jasper around camp. He was supposed to be some kind of preacher, and that had put Ed off.

Though he'd spent nearly his entire life in the South, he'd never felt comfortable with the Southern evangelical spirit. There'd always seemed something desperate, even primitive, about it, and the last thing he wanted to do was throw himself and the people he'd promised to protect into that kind of madness.

But that was where the uncertainty came in. For all the religious fervor that seemed to surround Jasper Sewell and his exploits, the one thing that all the stories agreed on was that the man was saving lives. He had, it seemed, actually led a huge number of people to safety and was gathering more survivors together every day. Compared to the military's failure to provide for them, his community in the Grasslands seemed to offer at least a ray of hope.

He said, "I'm not sure if it's everything people are saying. You know? I mean, it probably isn't."

"But you've already made up your mind, Ed. That's what it sounds like, anyway."

"No," he said. "Well, maybe. Jesus, I don't know." He took his hat off and fingered the bill where a thread was coming loose. "Look, Margaret," he said. "There's a lot going on here, but I think this could be a good thing for us. North Dakota is isolated. There aren't many people up there, and that means fewer infected. Plus, it gets cold there in the winter. We'll be dealing with that soon, the colder weather. If we're somewhere farther north—maybe not North Dakota, but somewhere farther north—we'll have the weather on our side, too. The infected won't be able to deal with that kind of exposure."

"That's true," Margaret said, and nodded. "Yeah, Ed, that makes perfect sense."

"Well," he said, and shrugged good-naturedly. He smoothed his white hair down with his hand and slipped his hat back onto his head. Then he smiled at her. "We'll see," he said.

"Ed?"

He turned, still smiling, and saw Julie Carnes standing in the lane between the tents. Her gray hair was down around her shoulders, coming loose from her ponytail. Her face had an odd, strained quality, and she was trembling.

"What's wrong?" he said.

Margaret rose to her feet, but didn't let go of the kids.

"Ed, I need you to come quick. Please."

"What is it?"

"It's Art," she said. "Ed, he's . . . he died a few minutes ago."

Art Waller's body lay on a cot along the back wall. The others stood a respectful distance off. They were all trying very hard not to look at the body.

Nobody spoke.

Ed stared down at Art. His body looked so frail, so hollow, like spun glass. Ed let out a breath and closed his eyes. Leading these people, surviving, was so much harder than he thought it'd be.

That day they were rescued from the attic, when that army major told him he was back on the clock, it was like his prayers had been answered. Getting reactivated sent a thrill through him. It made him feel like he was getting some long-lost piece of his dignity back. He'd thought it'd be that easy, too. A simple matter of putting his badge back on. God, he'd been such a fool. His shame at his own gullibility actually made him shiver.

When he opened his eyes, Julie Carnes was standing next to him.

Ed took a deep breath, then another. He said, "Did anybody tell the medic station?"

"Yeah, we told them," Billy said.

"Did they send somebody over?"

"They said if he's dead there's nothing for them to do."

"Just like that?"

"Yeah. Just like that."

Ed snarled to himself. "Damn this place," he said. *And damn me, too, for my vanity.*

"Okay," he said. He reached down and pulled the top of a yellowed cotton sheet over Art's face. "Okay. I assume they're not gonna help us bury him, either."

Billy shook his head.

"Okay. We'll do it ourselves. Billy, I'm gonna need your help again. Can you find us some shovels?"

Billy nodded slowly. "Yeah," he said. "I can do that."

While Billy went out into the camp to find some shovels, Ed and Julie Carnes and Margaret O'Brien wrapped Art's body in a sheet and tied it off along the seam. Flies had already started to gather and were buzzing around Art's mouth and eyes. Ed waved them away while they tied off the sheet.

When Billy returned, he offered to carry the body, but Ed refused with a shake of his head. "I'll do it," he said, and picked up the body. Art was light, maybe a hundred and twenty pounds, but it was still more than Ed was ready for. He didn't put the body down, though. He needed to do this, as much for himself as for Art. It wasn't quite a penance, but at least it gave him some way to confront his grief and his anger at himself for his foolishness and his vanity.

"You got it?" Billy said.

Ed nodded.

They chose a spot on the far side of the main road west of the camp. It was a narrow lane of grass at the edge of the pinewoods. Ed and Billy dug in silence for the better part of an hour. Margaret's grandkids, Randy and Britney, slept in the grass a short distance away. Margaret sat near them, stroking Randy's hair while he slept. Julie had her arm around Barbie Denkins. Barbie had gone strangely silent since their arrival in the camp, and Ed wondered how aware she was of what was going on. Despite the fog of Alzheimer's, he figured she was probably aware of more than he gave her credit for.

When it was done, the adults gathered around the grave mound and stood in silence. Ed had a dull headache behind his eyes from the heat and the exertion and the frustration caused by too many days in this place. His gaze wandered from the grave to the camp. Darkness had settled over the land, but there were fires burning in fifty-five-gallon drums all around the camp, and to his blurred vision the orange glow of the fires looked like molten rivers of light snaking through the tents.

"Please be at peace, Art," Julie said. "Please."

The others muttered a quiet amen, then fell silent once more.

Ed felt uneasy. He had, in the back of his mind, assumed they would spend another day or two at least here; but now, looking down at the grave and around the small circle of faces, he felt a renewed sense that they had to leave right away. This was no place for them.

Margaret caught Ed's eye and said, "Will you tell us what you want to do?"

Julie still had her arm around Barbie Denkins. Barbie looked tired and distant, like she was somewhere else.

Julie said, "What are you taking about?"

Billy looked from Julie to Ed. He said, "You want to leave here, don't you?"

Ed nodded. He looked toward the camp and shook his head. "That place is no good. I think we need to go someplace else."

"But where?" Julie said. She sounded suddenly frightened.

"Tell them what you told me, Ed," Margaret said. "About the Grasslands."

"The Grasslands?" Billy said. "I've heard about that. You're talking about that preacher from Mississippi, aren't you? You want to go there?"

Ed nodded.

"What is this place?" Julie asked. "What are you people talking about?"

Ed told her what he had heard of Jasper Sewell.

She listened to it all, and when he was done, she said, "You want us to pick up and travel all the way across the country to follow up on a rumor? Is that really what you're asking us to do, Ed? What about transportation? Did you think about that? We don't have a vehicle. We don't have a way to get one. And what about Barbie, Ed? Did you think about her? How is she going to make the trip?"

Barbie looked up and muttered something Ed couldn't hear.

Julie squeezed her close.

"Well?" she said.

He didn't have an answer for her, only his conviction that this place was a death trap.

"If we stay here, we're going to die," he said.

"You don't know that. There are soldiers here. They can protect us, feed us."

"They couldn't do anything for Art," he said, and he was suddenly angry. His voice rose and he couldn't make himself bring it back down. "Do you think they'll be able to do anything for Barbie? Or for any of us? What happens in the next few weeks, Julie? What happens when the rest of us need help? Huh? What happens?"

Julie looked away from him.

"Please don't yell at her, Ed," Margaret said.

They were silent for a long moment, none of them looking at each other.

Finally, Billy said, "Should we . . . I don't know . . . take a vote?"

Ed sighed. He looked at Margaret, who nodded, and then at Julie. She said nothing. Only frowned and looked away.

"Okay, then," Ed said. "All those who want to leave here . . ."

Slowly, Margaret and Billy raised their hands. Ed raised his.

"I'm sorry, Julie," Margaret said. "I have to think of my grandkids. This is no place for them. It's not safe here."

Julie just shook her head. "Come on, Barbie," she said, and led the older woman away, back toward the camp.

Chapter 26

Nate woke with rain in his face. It came out of a starless night sky, cold and steady. He blinked, disoriented, unable to remember where he was or what had happened to him. Then, all at once, it came back to him—Jessica Metcalfe, the men in the white suits, the van ride. His nose and lips felt tender and swollen, and he could taste fresh blood in his mouth. He was missing a tooth. His tongue kept coming back to the gap it had left behind.

He rolled over onto his hands and knees and spit out a wad of blood and phlegm, then looked around, desperate for something familiar to anchor his mind to his present circumstances. What he saw was a large fenced-in field of trampled grass and mud puddles. It looked a little larger than a football field, though it was difficult to tell for certain because it was dark and the only light came from floodlights pointed down into the enclosure from atop the fences. There were people all around him. Most of the ones he could see were seated, their heads down between their knees, oblivious to the rain pelting the backs of their necks. But quite a few were walking around. They were changing. Some, he could see now, already had.

An older woman, about sixty, was on her back a few feet away. She was looking right at him, her eyes so bloodshot they frightened him. She was mumbling something. Nate tried to look away, but out of the corner of his eye he saw her holding up a mangled, trembling hand. She was trying to say something.

"What do you want?" he said.

Her voice was weak, hoarse. It sounded like she was saying "Please," over and over again.

"Please what?" he asked.

"Please," she said again. "Paul, please."

"Paul? Lady, you're hallucinating."

Nate turned away and tried to block out the sounds of her pleading. Here and there throughout the enclosure, people were rising to their feet and shambling off into the darkness. There were a lot more of them on their feet now.

From behind him, Nate heard the old woman's pleading change to a gurgling, rattling sound.

He looked at her and was shocked that he could actually see her changing. Nate couldn't believe that it could happen so quickly. Her eyes were wide open and unblinking. And they weren't as bloodshot as they had been a few moments before. Now there was a pinkish, milky haze seeping through them. Her body had stopped shaking.

She rolled over awkwardly and at last managed to rise to her feet.

"Oh, fuck," he said.

He looked around the enclosure, and for the first time realized that there wasn't anyplace to hide. Just a muddy field full of zombies and people who were only seconds away from becoming zombies.

There was no way out.

More and more of the zombies were coming toward him, attracted by the old woman's moaning. Nate panicked. He turned and stepped into the arms of a girl of about fifteen whose head was bent to one side, almost all the way to her shoulder. Her teeth were blood soaked.

Nate hit her in the chest and knocked her backward.

A gap opened in the knot of zombies around him. He could see the perimeter fence and the soldiers milling around outside it. He sprinted toward them, and this time, the demon that plagued his knee was no match for the fear in his gut.

He reached the fence and threw himself onto it.

"Get me out of here," he screamed at the soldiers. "Please. Jesus, don't leave me in here."

He took the fence in both hands and shook it.

"Let me out of here."

A few soldiers turned their gas-masked faces toward him, but none made any move to help.

"Please," he shouted. "Please."

Behind him, the moans were growing louder. He turned around and saw a blur of faces closing in on him.

He grabbed the fence again and screamed at the soldiers. "For God's sake, you fucking bastards, get me out of here. Get me out of here."

Someone put a hand on his shoulder and he screamed. He threw an elbow at the man behind him and felt it connect with the man's ribs. The man fell backward, but didn't make a sound.

"Shit oh shit oh shit," Nate said as he started to scramble up the fence. He hadn't climbed a chain-link fence since he was a kid, and he was surprised at how hard it was to pull up his own weight.

But he pulled himself upward. He could feel hands grasping at his feet, tugging at the hems of his jeans, and his fear pushed him higher.

He made it as far as the top of the fence before he touched razor wire.

"Please, help me," he pleaded.

None of the soldiers moved.

Below him, the zombies moaned and shook the fence. The combined volume of so many voices made him tremble. He put his face against the fence and let the rain run into his eyes without blinking it away.

"Please, help me."

Major Mark Kellogg sat in the backseat of a Humvee, watching the figure clinging to the fence. The floodlights were designed to cast light into the enclosure, and so the figure up on the fence was visible only as a silhouette. Below the figure, the infected were clamoring to get at him. He could hear their moaning over the rain pounding on the roof of the vehicle.

He looked over at Colonel Jim Budlong. "All the others have changed," he said. "This is the last one."

Budlong nodded. They had discussed this at length, the time it took a normal person to go from initial infection to full depersonalization. The longest either of them had heard of was a twenty-four-year-old Delta Force operative who had received a fingernail scratch on his calf during a clean-and-sweep operation in Atlanta. The man was in superior physical condition, and he'd been kept nearly motionless from the moment of infection, but had made it only sixteen hours before he changed. And that was the record. Average time to depersonalization was much shorter—anywhere from five minutes to four hours.

The dynamic between severity of infection, location of infection, and physical condition of the victim prior to infection was well documented. It took longer for a physically fit person who was infected through a minor injury in a non-vital area to change than it did for a person with a preexisting health condition, such as hypertension or some form of weakened immune response, who received a substantial bite in a vital area, like the neck or near a major artery. Kellogg's own research over the last year and a half had shown that the necrosis filovirus had a strong affinity for victims with hypertension. In fact, after the degree of physical activity a person undergoes immediately after their initial infection, hypertension seemed to be the leading factor in how fast a person changed. It was such a pronounced factor that an out-of-shape individual with hypertension who received a substantial bite near a major artery could expect to make the change almost immediately—certainly within two or three minutes.

Budlong said, "How long?"

"The last subjects were put in there eighteen hours ago." Kellogg waited, but when Budlong didn't say anything, he said, "Jim, I can tell from here that guy's no swinging dick from Special Forces. Look at him. Beer gut. Mullet haircut."

Budlong sighed. He watched the man hanging on the fence for a moment longer, then sighed again and mopped a hand over his face.

"I don't know," he said.

Kellogg grunted in frustration. He turned, opened his door, and stepped out into the rain.

Surprised, Budlong leaned over the seat.

"Mark, where are you going?"

Kellogg had to nearly yell to be heard over the rain. "You said when you asked me to join your little think tank that you would let me trust my instincts. Time to make good on your promise, Jim."

Kellogg walked over to the enclosure, weaving his way through a maze of vehicles and bored-looking sentries who snapped to attention when they realized who he was. Budlong was at his side by the time he reached the enclosure.

Kellogg found a sentry near the fence and said, "Soldier, how long has that man been up there?"

"Nearly an hour, sir." The sentry hesitated before adding, "You want me to hit the current, sir?"

Electrocute the fence, Kellogg thought. *Jesus Christ.*

"No," he said. "Stand by."

He turned to Budlong. "Well? You heard that. He's been up there nearly an hour. You know how much physical strain that puts on a body to cling to a fence like that?"

"What do you expect me to do?" Budlong said.

"I told you. Make good on your promise."

Budlong stared up at the shadowy figure on the fence, the rain feathering off the hanging man in sheets. Then he looked at Mark Kellogg and he nodded.

"Thank you, Jim."

Kellogg grabbed the sentry and said, "I want that man taken down and put into isolation, you hear?"

The soldier cocked his head at Kellogg. "Sir?"

"You heard me. And make sure no one harms him in the process."

CHAPTER 27

From the vehicles, all they could see were feet sticking out of the grass. Here and there, they could make out the length of somebody's lower leg. It wasn't until they got closer that they saw the rest of the bodies, fourteen in all, the hands and ankles tied together with baling wire, headless necks pushed up against a rail line.

"That's a clever way of killing 'em," Barnes said. "Certainly gets the job done."

Richardson turned away. He wasn't squeamish, not by a long shot, but the bodies had been there a long time, decomposing in the hot summer sun. They were blackened with rot and were badly swollen. A few had burst open beneath their clothes.

They were in a Chevy pickup leading the caravan. Behind them were two buses, six other pickups, and a few cars.

Barnes said, "Probably won't see more of that."

"Thank God," Richardson said.

"Effective, but a little too much effort for what it accomplishes. Somebody's got to hold 'em there, you know, while the train comes. And I bet we're not gonna see too many more trains from here on out."

"No," Richardson said. "Probably not."

The wind shifted and carried with it the smell of burnt things.

Richardson crinkled his nose. "You smell that?"

Richardson knew they were entering the little town of Tobinville, Texas, population 1,458, because there was a sign still dangling from a crazily leaning post on the side of the road. He never would have known otherwise. Everything was burned beyond recognition.

Black snowflakes of ash drifted across the roadway. What had once been pine forests on either side of the road were now smoking, smoldering fields. A few trees, burned to blackened stalagmites, poked up above the black ground. Here and there, wisps of smoke drifted across a surface that looked alien and forbidding. The smell of burnt wood and grass hung heavily in the air, and Richardson coughed quietly into his shoulder as he stared across the remains of the forest.

Soon, the fields gave way to houses, the town proper visible just ahead. They passed a line of cars and fire trucks, all of them burned and sitting on rubberless wheels wrapped in skeins of wire, their windows shattered by the heat, their interiors melted into gooey piles of plastic and twisted metal. The bodies weren't obvious at first because they were as black as the ground upon which they rested, but here and there a charred hand or a knee rose up above the level ground, and once Richardson saw one, it was easier to spot the rest. And there were many.

They entered the town in silence, driving slowly. The buildings were fire-blackened and all but unrecognizable now. They saw the remnants of what might at one time have been a factory up ahead, its charred, crumbling walls towering in jagged lines above the rest of the town.

A line of storefronts along the main street had been reduced to smoking heaps of ashes. A few were made of brick, and those few had partly survived the fire. They also seemed to have acted as a firebreak, because beyond them, the houses and buildings seemed relatively undamaged.

"What happened here?" Richardson said.

"Controlled burn."

"What?"

"This was a controlled burn. My guess is the people in town here started it and it got out of hand. Those zombies we saw at the tracks a ways back, they were probably the first zombies these folks encountered. But when the big waves of them started coming down the road, they probably figured burning 'em would be the way to go. Hasn't rained around these parts in a while. Add a good, strong wind to that, and you've got yourself the recipe for a disaster. The fire probably swept over the town in a matter of minutes."

Richardson looked at him, shocked.

"How in the world do you know that?"

"I'm guessing," Barnes said. "But I saw a couple of drip torches on the side of the road on our way in."

"What's a drip torch?"

"A tool firefighters use to start controlled burns. Think of a metal watering can full of gas and a burning wick at the head of the spout. We used 'em in the early days of the quarantine, when we were trying to force the zombies back inside Houston."

"But the zombies don't react to fire."

"Yeah, I know. But we didn't know that then. The infected just walk right into the flames. Some of 'em walk right back out the other side, like human torches."

Richardson thought of that. These people here in Tobinville—they clearly didn't know that, either. He pictured them, making a last stand behind their vehicles at the edge of town, watching the first wave of burning zombies descending upon them, a wall of out-of-control fire raging behind them.

"Sweet Jesus," he said.

They stopped for fuel at a gas station on the other side of the burn line that divided the town. Barnes got out of the truck and directed vehicles into the stalls. He set up armed guards at either end of the station and told the rest of the people to stay close, nobody wander off.

Richardson, eager to get away from Barnes for even a short while, walked across the parking lot and entered the convenience store adjacent to the pumps. Two men from their group were already behind the counter, forcing open the Plexiglas screens where the cigarettes were stored.

"Want one?" one of the men said. He held up a carton of Marlboros in one hand, Camels in the other.

"No, thanks," Richardson said. "I quit back in college."

The man shrugged, then went back to the cabinet and continued removing carton after carton of smokes. A few women were at the coolers, which had evidently stopped working some few days earlier, and started removing bottles of water. *Smart*, Richardson thought, though the stench of the soured milk in the coolers was enough to make him gag, even over the smell of the burnt buildings.

On the next aisle over, Jerald Stevens was sitting on the ground with a bag of chips open in his lap and a Slim Jim in each hand. He looked up at Richardson and smiled, his mouth full of something.

"How's it going?" Richardson said.

"Awesome," Stevens said. Or at least that's what it sounded like.

Stevens kept on smiling as he ate. His pockets, Richardson could see now, were absolutely stuffed with food. *The man is probably hoarding it*, Richardson thought. But he couldn't blame him for it. Not after what he had been through, two years inside the quarantine zone, living hand to mouth.

Still, it seemed unhealthy.

"Take it easy," Richardson said. "There's plenty of food for everyone."

Stevens's smile wavered a bit but didn't entirely disappear. Richardson did notice him tighten his grip on the Slim Jims, though.

He looked out the window and saw Sandra Tellez walking across the lot with Clint Siefer, her arm around his shoulder. He nodded to Jerald Stevens, then grabbed three bottles of water from the shattered cooler in the back of the store. Outside, he caught up with Sandra Tellez and Clint Siefer and offered them each a water.

"Thank you," she said.

Clint took his without a word, without making eye contact.

Poor damaged kid, Richardson thought.

He said, "Sorry they're not cold."

Sandra shrugged as she opened hers. "What can you do, right?"

"Right," he said.

He'd already gotten a little bit of her story, but he was eager for more. He knew that she had run an in-home day care before Hurricane Mardell drowned Houston. He knew that she had a daughter of her own, the little girl killed along with her husband during the first few days of the quarantine.

She was closely connected to the young man who clung so tightly, and so silently, to her. Clint had been going to Sandra's day care since he was only seven months old. He had grown up in her house, right next to her own daughter. He was fourteen now. His parents were killed by the infected, and somehow, he had managed to wander through the flooded ruins and the hordes of zombies to her house. She had returned to the house merely by chance, she told him. She wanted the three cases of bottled water her husband had stashed in their pantry before he had died, and she entered the house to find Clint curled up in a ball in her living room, crying to himself. The childless mother and the orphaned child had found each other. To Richardson, it seemed there was something very human in that.

The three of them walked toward the buses, Richardson trying to keep the smell of burnt buildings out of his nostrils.

"You must be relieved to be out of Houston," he said.

She nodded.

"What was it like in there?"

She stopped walking and looked at him. "Mr. Richardson," she said. "Are you trying to interview me?"

He shrugged.

"If you don't want to talk," he said.

"I don't mind talking to you. Up to a point, anyway. I won't tell you about my family. And I won't tell you about Clint here or his family. That stuff is private."

"Fair enough," he said.

"But you want to know what life was like inside the quarantine zone?"

He nodded. "Very much."

"We felt abandoned. We felt like our government and our fellow Americans had turned their backs on us."

"That's understandable."

"Is it? Do you really understand? Do you know what I heard on the radio on the way up here?"

He shook his head.

"I heard some man from, I don't know, I think they said he was the Secretary of the Treasury, saying that people had broken through the walls all along the quarantine zone. He said he thought the people who had broken out should be shot as traitors. Can you imagine that? He said we were selfish to endanger everyone else's lives. Can you imagine?"

Richardson shook his head.

He was about to ask her about how they had gathered food in the quarantine zone when they heard Barnes yelling. He was out in the middle of the street, directing traffic in and out of the gas station and yelling at a group of two men and three women who were checking the front doors of houses nearby.

"Stay close," he ordered them. "Stay where we can see each other."

One of the men waved in acknowledgment.

Richardson heard screaming off to his left and saw people running.

Richardson followed where the others were pointing and saw a zombie dragging itself along across a front yard on the other side of the street. The face was blistered and cracked, burned so badly he couldn't tell the person's race or even their sex. There was no hair, only a few wiry strands matted to the scalp with melted gobs of skin. Its clothes were unrecognizable. Not even the moan that escaped its damaged throat was recognizable.

Barnes crossed in front of him from his right, drawing his pistol as he came.

"Back away," he ordered.

The crowd zippered open for him.

He stepped into the grass, leveled his pistol at the burned zombie's head, and fired. The thing collapsed instantly, and to Richardson's mind at least, it almost seemed grateful.

Then Barnes wheeled on the crowd, his anger and his contempt dripping off every syllable. "Listen up, people. I want everybody back in the vehicles, now. Get away from those houses. There's gonna be more of these things around here, I guarantee you, and all you idiots want to do is go on a fucking scavenger hunt."

A few members of the crowd started back toward the vehicles, but most just stood there, gaping at Barnes.

Barnes shoved one man into the street. "I said move it. Go on. Get!"

Sandra Tellez stepped around Richardson and walked right up to Barnes, Clint Siefer trailing along behind her.

"You can't talk that way to them," she said. "You have no right to call them scavengers. You have no idea what these people have been through."

"News flash, lady. That's what they fuckin' are."

"That's what all of us are," Sandra said. "We don't need to be reminded of it. People need dignity as much as they need food and water, Mr. Barnes."

He looked like he wanted to tear her head off. But instead, he lowered his voice and said, "Lady, I am here for one reason, and that is to live. I don't give a damn about your dignity. I do care about surviving. Now, if you care about that, too, help me get these people back into the vehicles so we can get the hell out of here."

Sandra stared back at him for a long time. Then she put her arm around Clint and started gently prodding the crowd back toward the vehicles.

Richardson was watching them cross the street when he happened to spot one of their group running from a backyard fence. "Run," the man shouted. "Ya'll run!"

"What the hell?" Barnes said.

Richardson saw four badly burned zombies staggering out of the yard and into the street. Their skin was red and cracked all up and down their arms and on their faces. One zombie was almost completely nude, and the skin down his right side was blistered and oozing.

More zombies stepped into the street behind the first four, all of them burned, and Richardson had just enough time to think they must have all gotten trapped back there somehow when a woman screamed from the far side of the yard. She was holding a little girl of about seven, hugging her tightly as the zombies changed direction and surrounded her.

Barnes turned away and walked toward the bus.

Sandra said, "Where are you going? You've got to help her."

"Fuck her," he said. "I told you people not to walk too far from the vehicles. She can't do like I tell her, then fuck her."

"Are you insane?"

Barnes ignored her.

The woman screamed again, and this time Sandra ran for her. "Help me," she said to Richardson, passing him up at a sprint.

Richardson pulled his pistol and ran into the fray.

There were four zombies ahead of him. He shot two before they had a chance to turn around. The third was almost to the woman with the little girl when Richardson shot the man in the side of the head, sending him tumbling over sideways into the grass. The fourth zombie turned toward him, but Richardson hesitated. The man looked completely normal, the eyes unfocused and vague, but otherwise the same as anybody's.

He lowered his weapon, uncertain.

"Shoot him," Sandra screamed.

He looked at Sandra, then back at the man in front of him. There was a jagged crescent missing from the top of the man's ear and bits of dried blood along the edges, and seeing it switched something on inside Richardson. He raised his pistol and fired, catching the man right under the nose and sending him sprawling onto his back.

But they were surrounded. Richardson pivoted on one foot, scanning the tightening ring of burned and mangled faces around him, and began firing until the slide of his pistol locked back in the empty position.

"I'm out," he said, and stepped back until he and Sandra and the woman and child were side by side.

The little girl whimpered into her mother's shirt. Richardson reached back and put a hand on her shoulder. Sandra stepped forward and pushed one of the zombies to the ground, but there were just too many of them.

One zombie, a woman in a yellow dress dotted with tiny red flowers, staggered forward over the one Sandra had pushed to the ground. Richardson tensed, his hands up against his chest, ready to sidestep the zombie's grasp and push it down to the ground.

But he didn't get the chance. A shot rang out, and the next moment the zombie's head snapped violently to one side and it sank to the grass, immobile.

Another shot, and another, and another.

They were coming in rapid succession now. Richardson looked up to see Barnes moving across the street in a tactical crouch, his AR-15 tucked up tightly against his cheek as he moved. Barnes fired through his magazine, ejected it, slammed in another, and went on firing. When he was done shooting, and the echoes of his shots faded into silence, there were bodies everywhere. Most of them nearly headless.

The crowd stood watching him.

Barnes surveyed the mess without expression. Watching him, Richardson remembered the reputation the Texas Rangers acquired during their outlaw hunting days in the Old West. Tireless, unforgiving, a law unto themselves.

Barnes used the barrel of his AR-15 to turn over the corpse of a zombie who was facedown in the street. He stared at it, and he seemed to be deep in thought.

Then, suddenly, he stepped over the body and said, "Everybody back in the vehicles. Let's go, people. Move it."

Richardson walked Sandra and Clint back to their bus. Barnes was there, AR-15 cradled in his arm like a baby, watching the crowd as they got on.

Ahead of Sandra, a young man and a woman who was evidently his wife or girlfriend were getting on the bus. The woman climbed on, but as the man was about to follow her, Barnes grabbed the man by the back of his shirt and threw him down onto the pavement.

"What the hell?" the man said. He was on his back, staring up at Barnes.

"You," Barnes said. "Stand up. Move over there."

"What are you doing?" the woman said. "Leave him alone."

Barnes ignored her.

"Get up," he said.

The man didn't move. Barnes reached into his Windbreaker and pulled his pistol. A few people screamed. Others scrambled out of the way.

"Wait!" the man said. "Wait!"

Barnes leveled his weapon at the man and fired three times, twice to the body, once to the head.

The man collapsed onto the pavement, glassy, sightless eyes pointing up at the portico roof above him, and lay still. Blood trickled out of the wound in his forehead and down the side of his face.

"No!" the woman behind Barnes screamed. "No!"

Richardson couldn't believe it. He stared from the corpse to Barnes, too shocked to even ask why.

Barnes holstered his weapon, then took a lock blade knife from his pocket and snapped it open. He knelt by the corpse and cut the man's shirtsleeve open all the way to the shoulder. The fabric fell away, revealing a nasty bite wound just above the elbow. It was already starting to darken to an angry reddish-black.

The crowd gasped.

Barnes looked at Richardson. "You didn't notice he rolled his sleeves down?"

The woman from the bus pushed her way through them and rushed to the fallen man's side. She was crying when Richardson turned away.

"He had his sleeves rolled up when he got off the bus," Barnes said. "They're down now."

"Are you serious?" Sandra said. "You just killed a man for rolling his sleeves down?"

"I just killed a man who was gonna bring that virus onto that bus. He didn't give a damn that he was gonna infect everyone else onboard. I just saved your ass."

"But you weren't sure. You killed him without knowing he was infected."

"I was sure enough."

"Sure enough? Do you hear yourself?"

"Lady, I told you, this is about survival. I told him to stand up and move away from the crowd. He didn't do it."

"You didn't give him a chance."

"Fuck that, lady. You do what you're told the first time or you get fucked. I don't give second chances. I don't play games with my survival. You hear that, lady? All of you, listen up. If you want to survive, you do what I tell you to do. You don't ask questions, and you don't make me tell you twice. I will get you through this. If you're too scared to act, then I'll let you die. If you're too stupid to do what needs to be done to survive, then I'll let you die. There's no place here for sentimentality. If you don't like it, go off on your own. Good fucking riddance to you. But if you want to live, you stay with me, and you do as you're fucking told. That's it."

He looked around the crowd, searching their faces for anybody who would dare to challenge him. Everyone, even Sandra Tellez, stared at the ground.

"Fine," he said. To Richardson he said, "Get them on board. I'll be in the truck."

CHAPTER 28

Every time she wanted to quit, just fall over in the ditch and die, some indefatigable love of life, like an ember deep inside a pile of ashes, made her go on.

Kyra had been walking for two days in the desert heat without water, without shade. The heat from the road was melting the soles of her sneakers. She could hear them peeling away with every step. Her lips had burst open. She felt faint, couldn't concentrate. Very likely, she was going to die out here. She knew that. If one of the infected didn't get her, the heat and the dehydration and the sunstroke would. But either way, she was going to die on her feet, fighting it.

She owed herself that much, at least.

They stopped on the side of IH-10 a few miles east of Allamore, Texas, because the bus was overheating again. They all needed bathroom breaks. Somebody—Jeff was pretty sure it was Colin—had clogged up the toilet beyond repair, and now they couldn't flush it. They couldn't clear the line either, and the inside of the bus had started to take on a sickeningly sweet sewage smell. Driving through the Arizona and New Mexico and West Texas heat with that smell had been unbearable—and that was before the bus's air conditioner started to sputter. He was dreading getting back on board.

"Man," Colin said, "you'd think driving cross-country with a bus full of fuck dolls would be about as much fun as a man could have. I can't believe I'm saying this, but I'm about ready for this trip to be over."

Jeff looked back at the bus, and though he hated to admit it, he agreed with Colin. He found himself wanting to run again, wanting to leave the bus and Robin far behind him, just like he'd left Colorado far behind in the ruins of the not so distant past. He'd never thought of himself as a runner, but it sure as hell looked like that's what he was becoming.

"You think we'll be able to get that air-conditioning working right?" Colin asked.

"Yeah," he said, "if we meet somebody who knows how to fix it. I know I can't, and you can't either."

"That bus is a piece of shit."

Jeff ignored that. It wouldn't do any good to remind Colin that it was in the shape it was in because he had lost his mind back in Barstow. Colin still hadn't owned up to that.

Jeff turned back to the figure coming toward them on the road. It was a girl, staggering, arms and legs lurching out of control, one of the infected. He adjusted his cheek against the rifle.

But he didn't fire.

A long moment went by.

Colin said, "You gonna shoot her or what?"

"Yeah, yeah. Give me a second."

They had set up on a blanket on the shoulder of the road and were on their bellies with a rifle they'd found in a gas station on their way through Arizona. Jeff looked through the scope and sighted the crosshairs on the girl's face, right along the crease between her nose and her upper lip. He had never paid much attention to the public service announcements about the infected, but he'd read the book *One Shot, One Kill: The Story of Marine Scout-Sniper Carlos Hathcock*, and he knew the magic point on the face that snipers called the kill spot—put a bullet dead center right below the nose and the medulla oblongata goes blasting out the back of the head in a pink spray the size of a beach ball. The person dies before their body hits the ground.

Through the scope, her skin looked blistered and cracked, a lifeless gray. Her mouth hung open, her eyes looked milky and empty. He focused on his breathing, thinking about Carlos Hathcock's credo. Control your breathing. Squeeze the trigger, don't pull it. Let the gun surprise you when it goes off.

But he didn't fire.

He looked up, wiped the sweat from his eyes, looked through the scope again.

"What's wrong?" Colin asked.

"I don't know. She doesn't look right."

"What do you mean?"

"You've got the binoculars. Look for yourself."

Colin picked up the binoculars and pointed them at the girl. "Looks like a fucking zombie to me. You want me to shoot her?"

"No, I don't."

Then Jeff stood up and yelled at the girl.

"Hey, what the fuck?" Colin said.

"Shut up," Jeff said.

The girl stopped in her tracks. She turned away, startled, then stopped. She was looking off across the desert. Not anywhere near where they were standing.

"Over here," Jeff said to her.

The girl turned partially in their direction. He waved his

hands over his head, and yet she gave no sign that she saw him. She looked startled, disoriented, even terrified, like she would turn and run the other way if she could.

"Fucking zombie, huh?"

Colin shrugged. "Hey, what can I say? She looked like one to me."

"Yeah, well, she's not. Come on, let's go see if we can help her."

She heard them approaching. She stood very straight, very still, her head and shoulders turned away from them. To Jeff, it looked like she was set to run away, though he doubted she could make it very far in her condition. And besides, if she ran in the direction she was pointed, she'd go straight into a shallow ditch at the edge of the road.

He said, "Miss, are you okay?"

She flinched at the sound of his voice. Stiffened, if that was possible, even more than she already was.

Jeff held out a hand to her.

"It's okay," he said. "We won't hurt you."

She half stepped, half staggered away from him.

"Holy shit," Colin said. "She's fucking blind."

Jeff glanced at Colin. He was shocked he hadn't noticed that. But now that Colin said it, it was obvious.

"Are you hurt?" Jeff asked her.

She shook her head.

"Can you speak?"

She looked indignant. She opened her mouth to speak and tried to speak, but only managed a feeble cough.

"That's all right," Jeff said. He took a step toward her. She took a step back. "It's okay. I won't hurt you, I promise. Are you hurt anywhere?"

"Dude, she's fucking dehydrated."

"Is it . . . okay if I come closer?" Jeff asked her.

She stiffened again but finally nodded.

"I promise I won't hurt you. My name is Jeff Stavers. This is Colin Wyndham. We have a bus over here. We've got food and water."

He held out his hand to her.

"My hand's right in front of you. Is it okay if I help you to the bus?"

She nodded, and slowly, he took her hand and guided her along. He put an arm around her shoulder and he could feel her trembling. It was a hundred and ten degrees out here, and she was trembling.

He looked around. There was nothing but desert around them. He could see to the horizon in every direction, and there wasn't even a tree for shade. Nothing but rocks and blowing sand and a constant wind that whipped about his ears and left his skin dry and chapped.

Jesus, he thought. *What's she been through? Blind. In the desert.*

"What's your name?" he asked.

He heard a mumbled whisper and leaned closer.

"Kyra Talbot," she said.

Jeff got onto the bus first, turned, and took Kyra from Colin. They had to carry her up the stairs, but she was lightly built, and it wasn't hard to lift her. Once they got her steady in the center aisle of the bus, Jeff kept his arm around her, whispering softly to her about what he was doing and where he was taking her. She let him guide her without resistance and without saying another word.

Robin was reading a magazine on one of the couches back near the bar. Katrina—that was Katrina Cummz's real first name, apparently, Katrina Morgan—had filled the sink with water and was washing a shirt. The two blondes, Sarah and Tara, were sitting at an open window in the back, passing a joint back and forth and blowing the smoke out a crack in the window. It reminded Jeff of the way he and Colin had done it in their apartment back in school.

As soon as they came through the partition, Robin and the others looked up. Robin's face went from tired indifference to sudden concern, and she jumped to her feet.

"What happened?" she asked Jeff.

"We found her wandering the road," Jeff said. "Her name's Kyra Talbot."

Robin looked the girl over. Jeff watched her critical eye sweep the girl's features, her blistered and cracked lips, her dirty, mottled skin, her rheumy, vacant eyes, and he knew exactly what she was thinking as she suddenly backed away.

"She's not infected," Jeff said. Then, just mouthing the words, he said, "She's blind."

"I can hear you when you do that," Kyra said. The words came out in a hoarse whisper broken by a ragged, phlegmy cough, but they were clear enough. Robin smiled, and the smile lingered as she caught Jeff's eye. A quick thrill went through him.

"She's dehydrated," Robin said.

"Yeah."

"Kyra?" she said. "Sweetie, my name's Robin. I'm going to sit you down over here and get you some water, okay?"

Kyra nodded, and Robin took the girl by the shoulders and led her away.

CHAPTER 29

Mark Kellogg stood with Jim Budlong on a hastily constructed runway, watching a C-130 taking off for Minot Air Force Base in North Dakota. Over the last two days, the situation in Pennsylvania had gone from bad to just plain catastrophic. It was like San Antonio all over again. Every bit as fucked up. The civilian population was past the point of saving. The federal government's response had been orchestrated with their usual day-late-and-a-dollar-short philosophy toward disaster mitigation. They'd come into the area with the idea that moving real-life people out of harm's way was as simple as moving armies on a Risk board, and now there were thousands dead, and tens of thousands had been infected because they couldn't be evacuated from affected areas in time.

The Department of Homeland Security stepped in and took the lead on the evacuation process, and as usual they completely misjudged what the people on the ground would actually need. They brought in hundreds of work trucks from neighboring towns to help restore electrical power in the area, but they had yet to deliver even one-tenth of the buses they had promised to help get people out of the hot zone. They delivered thousands of cots and tents and bottles of water, but they had assumed a static relocation of the population and made no provision for moving all those supplies a second or a third time when the battle lines changed, and the infected appeared in areas that Homeland Security assumed would remain safe. There were at least fifteen Katrina-style evacuation villages in the area, all of them now crawling with the infected, the supplies dumped there useless. The military was forced to step in and fill Homeland Security's shortcomings, and that had stretched their limited resources way beyond the breaking point. He could see it in the faces of the soldiers standing guard all around them. Some, he guessed, hadn't slept in the last two days.

Kellogg shook his head in disgust and wondered how many times they had to make the same mistakes before they finally grew some sense.

"This is your boy's flight here," Budlong said. He gave him a knock on the shoulder and pointed at a C-130 lumbering down the dirt runway. The plane bounced and kicked up a huge tail of gray dust, and then it was airborne, on its way to Minot with the rest of their team and their test subjects.

Kellogg wasn't thrilled about relocating to Minot. It was the home of the 5th Medical Wing, but it didn't have a medical facility of the sort they were going to need. Everything would have to be flown in and set up right off the C-130s, and if what had happened in San Antonio and again here in Pennsylvania were any indications, they were fighting a losing battle. The only good news about going to Minot was the seclusion it offered. Set in the middle of the North Dakota prairie, it was a thousand miles from nowhere. At least they'd be able to work in peace.

Nate Royal's plane banked hard left and inched across a cloud-filled sky that was still laced with gray from the hard rains of the previous week. He still hadn't shown any signs of depersonalization, and though Kellogg had no idea why that was, he was thrilled.

"That one is gonna be the key to this, Jim."

"I certainly hope you're right," Budlong said. The two watched the plane lumber away until it was just a dark, indistinct speck in the distance. "God, Mark, I'm so worn out."

"I don't doubt it. You haven't slept in, what, the last thirty-six hours?"

"When have I had time? The damn phone won't stop ringing. They scream at me for a cure and then they won't let me off the damn phone long enough to go find it. Everybody's got to make sure I know how committed they are to getting this very important project successfully resolved."

"What they mean is they can't wait to take the credit."

"Probably."

Kellogg sighed. "And you wonder why I hate the military so much."

"I always thought it was that big bowl of hate you eat for breakfast every morning."

"Standard rations for any man who refuses to give up his common sense."

Budlong laughed. "You volunteered to come work for me, Mark. That means you haven't got the common sense God stuck up a mule's ass."

"Thanks, boss."

"You're welcome."

Another C-130 was loading nearby. The rear deck was lowered and a forklift was moving one of the infected containment units toward the cargo area. Guards stood nearby, looking tired and bored, leaning against barricades or just standing around with the hoods of their biosuits thrown back so they could ventilate. Kellogg hated wearing those things, too. With it being as humid and hot as it was out here, he didn't blame the men for the breach in regulations.

The C-130's loadmaster was waving the forklift into the

bay. Kellogg scanned the scene once more, figured they would be in the air themselves in another forty-five minutes, and was about to tell Budlong he was headed for the pisser when he heard a loud crash.

The forklift driver misjudged the ramp. The containment unit was jammed up into the V formed by the lowered rear deck and the plane's fuselage. Even from where he stood, Kellogg could see the door to the containment unit had crumpled, leaving a sizeable opening.

The loadmaster was screaming instructions, waving his arms furiously in the air.

Soldiers were running from every direction.

One soldier jumped onto the ramp near the opening in the containment unit and crouched next to the strut with his rifle pointed down into the unit.

"What the hell?" Budlong said. He took a few steps toward the plane. "What's he doing? No!" Budlong yelled at the soldier to get away, but his voice was lost in the confusion. He waved his hands over his head as he quickened his pace to a trot.

Kellogg ran after him. He caught up with Budlong just as the soldier on the ramp started to fire into the containment unit.

Everybody was shouting now. Men were scrambling up the ramp to join the fray. The loadmaster and a lieutenant Kellogg didn't recognize were screaming what sounded like contradictory orders at the men, and all the while the soldier already on top of the ramp was blasting three-round bursts into the containment unit.

One of the zombies managed to climb over the damaged door and fell onto the loading ramp below. Soldiers coming around the right side of the unit ran right into him.

Kellogg heard a scream, and one of the men went down.

There was a lot of shooting, and at least a few rounds whistled past Kellogg to his right.

The test subjects in the containment unit were lost to them now. He knew that. The soldiers would kill them all and resent anyone who tried to argue with them for doing it. Another shot whistled past his ear and Kellogg ducked belatedly.

He looked around for cover.

He saw a long dirt berm that the bulldozers had pushed into place when they carved the runway out of this farmer's field, and he turned to wave Budlong in that direction.

But Budlong wasn't moving.

He was standing in the middle of the field, looking confused, stiff. There was a dark spot right below his throat.

"Jim?" Kellogg said.

Budlong looked at him and coughed.

"Jim!"

Kellogg broke into a sprint and was at his friend's side a moment later, opening his tunic, carefully pulling the T-shirt down from the neckline, revealing the gunshot wound that was rapidly filling with blood.

"Medic!" Kellogg shouted. "I got a man down over here. I need a medic, damn it."

He put a hand behind Budlong's neck and eased him onto his back.

"Okay, Jim, we got to lay you down."

Budlong put a hand on Kellogg's arm, pushing him away. He tried to speak and managed only a gurgling noise. He gestures became urgent. He slapped Kellogg's arms like he couldn't breathe.

"Gotta open an airway," Kellogg said. "Okay, okay."

He tried to hold Budlong down on the ground, but the man was in a panic, fighting with him.

"Medic!" Kellogg screamed. "I need some fucking help over here."

Kellogg got his legs under Budlong's head to elevate him.

"Okay, okay," Kellogg said. "I got you, Jim."

But Budlong wasn't resisting anymore. He went limp in Kellogg's arms. "Oh, shit, Jim. Jim!" Nothing. Budlong's eyes were glassy. There was no breath, no pulse. "Jim, no, you bastard, don't do this to me."

He started CPR, but gave it up as soon as blood started to spurt out of the wound in Budlong's chest. Kellogg leaned back from the body, shaking his head like he could make it all go away if he just blinked hard enough.

An airman was yelling his name. Kellogg closed his eyes and tried to get some sort of control over the shock and anger and confusion that were swirling through his mind. But it was no use. There was just too much. He put his head in his hands and sat there, gradually growing numb to the sounds of the shouting and the shooting and the fighting going on around him. And the thought that kept going through his head was that it was just like San Antonio all over again.

They were headed into hell.

CHAPTER 30

"Looks like somewhere between one hundred and twenty and one hundred and seventy," said Aaron, handing the binoculars to his son, Thomas. "Must be every zombie in Bismarck down there. What do you think?"

Thomas was nineteen, and he was enjoying playing at soldier, Aaron could tell. The last few weeks had changed him, added a lot of responsibility on his young shoulders. But he seemed up to it. It brought out a seriousness that Aaron always suspected was there, but had yet to see before the outbreak. He was pleased to see it now.

Thomas took the binoculars and scanned the crowd of zombies out in the parking lot below them. Aaron watched the boy's lips move as he counted, his brown hair dancing on his forehead in the light breeze, and he was proud.

"Split the difference," Thomas said. "Call it one-fifty. I see a couple of fast-movers, but nothing we can't handle."

"Okay," Aaron said.

He looked behind him. They had three eighteen-wheelers standing by and twenty men to help load them. The men seemed calm, not at all nervous, almost bored. But then, they wouldn't be the ones down there turning themselves into bait.

To Thomas, he said, "Okay. You and your team move out. Remember, make lots of noise. Keep them engaged. But keep yourselves safe. Got it? No heroics."

"I got it, Dad."

Aaron laughed to hide his nervousness. "Good boy. Now go on. You remember where we're supposed to meet?"

"Dad, I got it."

Aaron nodded. "Okay. Go on."

He watched Thomas and another man get into the bed of a waiting pickup and take up their rifles. The pickup turned down Century Avenue and headed to the Lowe's parking lot. Across the street were a Burger King, a Jack in the Box, and a Taco Bell. Farther along was a grocery store. The infected had no doubt zeroed in on the smell of rotting food, and even if Thomas was successful in his diversion, Aaron and the others would still have to be on the lookout for stragglers coming out of the Dumpsters and from behind the stores.

The pickup moved out slowly, exactly as they'd rehearsed back at the Grasslands.

Aaron held his breath as the pickup turned into the Lowe's parking lot and pulled to a stop at the edge of the crowd of zombies. Thomas and the other man leaned out of the bed and threw Molotov cocktails into the crowd. A few of the zombies caught fire as they moved toward the pickup, made it a few feet, and dropped to the ground.

A fast-mover erupted from the slowly advancing crowd and Thomas dropped it with a well-placed shot from his rifle.

"Good boy," Aaron muttered. The zombie crowd was getting really close to the pickup. "Okay, that's close enough."

After an agonizing wait, the pickup lurched forward, traveling at a crawl.

Walking speed.

The zombie crowd lumbered after them. Those few who managed to close the gap with the pickup were shot. The rest lumbered along, children to the Pied Piper.

It took forty minutes for the crowd to leave the parking lot.

"Okay," Aaron said, waving a hand for the men behind him. "Load up."

Aaron himself climbed into the passenger seat of the nearest eighteen-wheeler and told the driver to move it out.

They had a Lowe's to raid, a village to build.

It was nearly sundown when they rolled into the north gate of the Grasslands. Using preexisting roads had saved them a huge amount of time and effort, and also influenced the shape of the village itself. Most of the buildings were clustered around the intersection of the main road and a small county service road. They had a slab set for the pavilion, which Jasper had dictated would be the communal center of the community. Across from that was the first of three education tents, the radio room, and the office, where Aaron spent most of his day. Farther on were the supply shed, the tool room and vehicle garage, and the woodworking shop. On the west side of the main road were the kitchen, laundry, doctor's office, infirmary, pharmacy, bakery, vegetable stand, and auxiliary dining tent. To the east were the first three of six dormitories for the single men and women, and farther on beyond that, on the far side of a low, rounded ridge they called East Hill, were the cottages where the families lived. They were doubled up now, tripled up in some cases, but that would get better soon.

They approached the intersection, and Aaron held up a hand for his driver to stop.

"Let me out here," he said.

The driver nodded, slowed the rig to a stop, and waited.

"You guys know what to do?"

"We sure do," the man said, and grinned. There was a large gap between his front teeth and Aaron found himself smiling back.

"Good. Get this stuff unloaded tonight so we can make an early go of it in the morning."

"You got it."

With that, Aaron climbed down from the truck and made his way to the West House, where he hoped to find Jasper. It was after dinner, and Jasper always spent at least an hour in his quarters, reading or handling the Grasslands' business. Aaron tried to handle most of the day-to-day operation of the Grasslands village himself, because he knew that Jasper preferred to devote his efforts to the spiritual and intellectual development of the community, but a certain amount of mundane management was unavoidable in a community this size, and like it or not, Jasper was becoming as much an administrator as he was a spiritual focal point.

Aaron arrived at Jasper's quarters and climbed the stairs to the front porch. The front door was open behind the screen door.

"Jasper?" he called into the house.

There was no answer.

Inside, the house was hot and dusty. A white ceiling fan spun slowly in the living room, and the remnants of the late-afternoon sun shone through the windows.

He heard moaning and the sounds of a bed creaking from a back room and turned down the hallway.

"Jasper?"

He rounded the corner and stopped in the doorway of Jasper's bedroom. A young married couple was in bed with Jasper. Aaron tried to remember their names, but couldn't. The man was facedown on the bed, Jasper mounting him from behind, while the wife knelt beside Jasper, licking his chest, her hand running through his black hair.

Aaron nodded and left the room. He went out to the porch and sat in a lawn chair and waited.

Jasper appeared thirty minutes later, his arms around the couple. They exchanged a few pleasantries, then Jasper wished them both a good night and sent them back to their cottages.

Aaron watched them link hands, smiling at each other as they walked back up the hill to the communal center of the Grasslands.

Jasper sat in the lawn chair next to Aaron and sighed.

"I despise engaging in homosexual activity," he said, and sighed. "But, regrettably, it is necessary so that I can connect to our younger male Family members."

Aaron nodded. He knew this. It had been long ago, nearly fifteen years now, since he and Kate had shared Jasper's bed. But there was no latent jealousy there. Aaron understood that it wasn't about sexual gratification. Rather, it was a necessary stage in a Family member's development. All members of the Family had to connect with Jasper symbolically, and sexual activity was an important part of that process. Of course, it was no longer necessary for Aaron and Kate. They were well beyond that phase now.

"How was the trip into Bismarck?" Jasper asked.

"Fine," Aaron said. "Went off without a hitch."

"Got everything on the list?"

"Down to the last bolt. We raided Lowe's and the Ace Hardware. I think they have a few more hardware stores in town, but we've nearly cleaned Bismarck out."

Jasper nodded.

The two men sat in silence for a good long while, comfortable with each other's presence. Out beyond the fence, the prairie stretched into darkness. The sun had turned the sky a stunning flood of crimson and bronze and yellow, and the land beneath it was black. Aaron felt immensely happy.

Jasper said, "And Thomas? How did he do?"

Aaron smiled. "Ah, Jasper, you should have seen him. He made me proud."

"I'm glad. A son should be a father's joy."

"Yes, indeed."

"Tell me," Jasper said, after another long pause. "Has young Thomas found a lady friend among our Family?"

"Not yet," Aaron admitted. "Though Kate has tried to introduce him to a few."

"Well, he's young. Still, it would be nice for him to set an example for the other youngsters in the Family. Nothing says a new beginning quite so well as a wedding."

"I agree," said Aaron. "And I know Kate would agree."

"Yes, I think she would," Jasper said. He breathed in deeply, obviously pleased with the smell of grass in the air. "Tell young Thomas I am looking forward to welcoming him and whatever wife he chooses to the Family."

Aaron smiled.

"I will, Jasper. Thank you. I know he will be honored."

Jasper nodded, and they watched the sun sink into the prairie. Jasper removed a tangerine from his pocket and slowly peeled the rind away, tossing the bits into the grass.

He offered a segment to Aaron and Aaron took it.

"I was listening to the radio today," Jasper said. He was talking slowly, pausing to eat sections of the tangerine as he tore them loose. "There is bad news out of China. They still refuse to acknowledge that they've had any outbreaks within their borders, and yet CNN reported that their military has bombed at least thirty of their own cities."

"Disgusting," Aaron said.

He knew government lying was a sore spot with Jasper. Close as their home in Jackson was to New Orleans, they were able to witness the complete, epic failure of the American government to protect its citizens in the time of a natural disaster.

It was in the wake of Hurricane Katrina that Jasper began using his pulpit to condemn the government's policies on disaster readiness. He studied public documents and FEMA policy and procedures and researched the backgrounds of various leaders within Homeland Security and FEMA, and what he discovered was a dizzying web of corruption and ineptitude that amounted to a racially motivated conspiracy. More and more, his sermons began to zero in on the range of this conspiracy. Hurricanes Rita and Ike only served to reinforce his suspicions and strengthen the arguments he made from the pulpit. People began to take notice. FBI agents showed up at their church and tried to pose as new members. Aaron himself had seen them following him in the grocery store, watching him from cars parked across the street from the church.

And then, when Hurricane Mardell had struck Houston, Jasper's warnings began to receive national media attention. The quarantine zone around the Gulf Coast and South Texas was the final step in the government's campaign against blacks and Hispanics and the southern whites, whom the government considered as tainted because they lived with them. The necrosis filovirus was not a naturally occurring disease, Jasper said. It was bioterrorism. It was the government's final solution.

And now, it seemed, the conspiracy had spread worldwide. China and India were fighting an undeclared war against each other's refugees. The Middle East had retreated completely into Islamic fundamentalism, with the wholesale slaughter of Americans within their various borders hailed as the fulfillment of Allah's will. Europe was reduced to a gigantic street brawl from Madrid to Moscow. Africa, it was said, was already dead. The world was flaming out.

Aaron took another tangerine slice from Jasper and said,

"I heard the same broadcast today on the radio. Things are not looking good. It's no wonder they've made us a target."

"They've had us in their sights for a long time, Aaron. This is nothing new. Only the scope of their attack has changed."

Aaron nodded.

"I've been thinking," Jasper said. He was looking toward the large cluster of vehicles they'd collected since their arrival. All in all, they had roughly three hundred and eighty cars and vans parked in a wide, flat, grassy area west of Jasper's cottage. They'd removed some one hundred and twenty heavy-duty and light trucks from the west lot, and those were parked up along the main road, near the north entrance, where they were being used as work trucks to help build and supply the Grasslands.

"Yes?"

"All those vehicles have radios. My guess is a great many of the people in our community have radios as well. Possibly TVs, too. I want all of that confiscated, Aaron. I want anything that can be used to acquire lies spread by our government confiscated. Can you handle that for me?"

"Absolutely," Aaron said. "I'll have it done tonight."

"Excellent. Shall we go up together? I'd like to address the Family now that we've got our new public address speakers installed."

Aaron nodded happily, and together, they made their way up to the Pavilion.

CHAPTER 31

They were in the back of the bus, all of them huddled around a map of West Texas they'd laid out on a card table.

Kyra and Robin were on Jeff's left. Kyra was looking better. Her lips had some color, and her eyes didn't look as rheumy as they had before, but she had gotten a lot of sun, and the burn was starting to show in her cheeks and on her forehead. To Jeff, it looked like she wasn't out of the woods yet.

Jeff said, "I say we head over here, to Van Horn."

"No," Kyra said quickly. It was the first time she had spoken since they'd all gathered around the map and her voice was little more than a croak. "No," she said again. "You can't go there. That's where I came from. The infected, they were all over the place."

"Well, yeah," Colin said, "but you got out, and you're . . . Well, you know."

The others looked at him.

"I'm just saying," he added quickly, showing them his palms. "I mean, we've got to go somewhere, right? It's here, in this little town, or it's to one of these other places where they have thirty or forty thousand people."

Kyra was quiet for a long time. Colin looked at Robin, then at Jeff, and shrugged.

He said, "I mean, right? If she got out, there can't be that many of them in town."

Robin had her arm over Kyra's shoulder. Kyra shook herself free and turned toward Colin. Only then did they see that she was crying.

"My uncle died getting me out of town," she said. If she'd enough strength to scream she probably would have. As it was, she managed only a harsh-sounding bark before collapsing back in on herself.

Robin put an arm around her and whispered her name.

Kyra let herself be taken in and held.

"You can't," she said from under Robin's arm. "Please. Don't go back there."

Kyra tried to rise to her feet and couldn't. Robin rose and grabbed her under her arms and tried to lift her. Jeff said, "Here, let me help," and took Kyra's other arm.

Together, they walked her to a bed in the back and made her comfortable.

"Is she going to be okay, you think?" Jeff asked.

Robin nodded. She pulled a blanket up under Kyra's chin and waited silently.

Kyra fell asleep almost immediately.

Robin and Jeff stood there side by side, watching her sleep. Jeff could feel the heat coming off Robin next to him. Her arms and face were glistening with sweat, and her bangs were soaked. She had picked up some sun also over the last few days, and her cheeks were glowing with it.

She caught him looking at her and took his hand and held it as they walked back to the map table.

Colin was saying, "I don't see that we've got any other choice. We need supplies. That means groceries, bottled water, medical supplies, even a few more guns and some ammunition. Where else are we gonna get that stuff?"

"He's right," Robin said.

Katrina looked troubled. She had her hand on top of Colin's and she turned and looked at him. "But what about what Kyra said?"

"What else are we going to do?" he countered. "We need those supplies if we're going to wait all this out."

"Maybe we can park the bus outside of town, and one or two of us can go in on foot," Jeff said. "You know, sort of a scouting party."

"That's a good idea," Robin said.

There was a lull in the conversation as they sat and stared at the map. Jeff took a bottled water from one of their coolers and drank from it. They still had water and a decent amount of food, but he knew that it wouldn't last forever.

"Hey, do you hear that?" Robin said.

They all looked up, listening. It was a deep but distant rumbling, and at first Jeff wasn't sure what it was. But as the sound got closer, he knew.

"Motorcycles," Colin said.

"Yeah," Jeff agreed. "Sounds like a lot of them."

He went to the front of the bus and peered out the windshield. A few hundred yards away, but closing fast, was a team of motorcycles and two pickups. They were trailing a long cloud of yellow dust, and it was hard to get an accurate count, but he saw at least eighteen of them.

As the convoy got closer, he could see the men were armed.

He ran back to the others and said, "Okay, we need to hide the girls."

"What?" Robin said.

He told them what he had seen. By the time he was done, the motorcycles had surrounded the bus and they could hear voices outside. Somebody was banging on the door.

"We have to hide them," Jeff said to Colin. He turned to

Robin. "Those guys, if they recognize you . . . I don't want anything bad to happen to you."

He was hoping she wouldn't argue, and she didn't. She seemed to grasp his point immediately, and she turned to find a hiding spot with the others without another word.

More pounding on the door.

They heard voices outside, yelling.

The bus had hidden luggage bins along the driver's side under the seats. The girls climbed into the bins, and Jeff, as an afterthought right before he closed the bin door, tossed in an armful of bottled waters for them.

The riders were kicking open the door now. Another moment and they'd be inside.

Jeff kneeled down and smiled at Robin. "You guys be quiet in there, okay."

Robin didn't speak. She rose up and kissed him on the mouth.

Then she slipped back inside.

When he stood up and turned around, there were men coming through the black partition.

They all had guns.

One of the men pushed his way past Jeff and went back to the bar, where he stopped and looked around.

"Just you guys?" he said.

"That's right," Jeff said.

The biker stared at him. "Bullshit," he said. "What's with all these chick clothes you got?"

"We had our girlfriends with us when we left L.A. They didn't make it."

The biker reached down and picked up a black lacy thong. "Huh, too bad. Where're you guys headed?"

"Van Horn," Jeff answered. "We were gonna get some

supplies and then try to make our way north to the Colorado safe zone."

The biker nodded. "Ain't nothing much left of Van Horn. Pretty much the whole town's been killed or turned into one of them fucking zombies."

He went to the bar and held up a bottle of Grey Goose vodka. He seemed impressed.

"You boys are traveling in style," he said. He poured himself a glass of vodka and took a drink, grimaced, then smiled. "Yes, sir, in style." He put the cap on the bottle and tossed it forward to one of the other bikers. "Me and my friends here, we were down around Acuna when all this shit happened. Man, you should have seen Mexico. We watched it from across the river, and I ain't never seen anarchy like that. Anyway, we made it as far as Van Horn and realized that most normal folks pretty much done bugged out. Ain't nothing around here but them fucking zombies, and we took care of that."

"You got rid of the zombies in Van Horn?" Colin said. "All by yourself?"

The biker laughed. "Wasn't that big of a deal. But yeah, we did it all by ourselves. The town's pretty much quiet now." He looked at the other bikers and a wicked smile passed between them. He said, "Well, it ain't exactly quiet."

Jeff groaned inwardly. This was going downhill fast.

"So you guys are running things there now?" Colin said. "In Van Horn, I mean."

The biker turned to Colin. "Yeah." The word wasn't exactly a question, but even still, he didn't quite seem to know what to make of Colin.

Jeff did, though. Colin the deal maker. He knew what was about to come out of Colin's mouth, and he hoped it wasn't going to get them all killed.

Colin nodded at Jeff and said, "My friend and I were on

our way to Las Vegas when this started. We were planning on heading into the desert and partying with our girls until it blew over."

"Yeah," the biker said. Again the word was not quite a question.

"Well, listen, if you guys are running things in Van Horn, maybe you can help us. Maybe we can help each other."

"How are you gonna help us?"

Colin smiled. He was gaining speed now, in his element. "When was the last time you and your friends did some serious high-grade acid? I'm not talking that bunk shit some idiot cooks up in his basement. I mean the real stuff, pharmaceutical grade."

"I'm listening," the biker said. "But boy, you'd better start getting to your point real fast."

"We've got enough top-shelf dope on this bus to keep you and your friends tripping for the next week. I got fifteen sheets of acid with a hundred tabs apiece. And I've got six hundred hits of X, too. I see you like that Grey Goose. I can even sweeten the deal with four cases of that."

A grin was spreading across the biker's face. He had been carrying a shotgun across his shoulder, but now he swung the gun down and fingered the safety behind the trigger guard.

"And you want to trade me what for all this righteous dope?"

"We need supplies. Enough groceries and water to get us up near the Panhandle." Colin paused for a moment, just long enough to let it sink in. "What do you say?"

The biker stared at him. The smile was gone now. He said, "Where's this dope at?"

"In my bag over there," Colin said. "The red one. Behind the bar." He nodded at a red nylon duffel bag near the biker's feet.

The biker reached down and picked it up, put it on the

bar, and opened it. Inside were several large sheets of acid sandwiched between pages of aluminum foil and a couple of Ziploc baggies of ecstasy. Then he pulled out a pillow-sized baggie of marijuana and whistled.

"You didn't say nothing about this."

"I figured if you guys were down around Acuna, you probably had some of that already."

The biker opened the baggie and stuck his face inside and took a deep, nasally breath.

"Damn," he said. "We'll take this shit, too."

He stuffed everything down inside the duffel bag and walked back to the front of the bus.

"Okay," Colin said. "Sure. Do we have a deal?"

"Possibly," the biker said. "For now. One of you guys get behind the wheel. You can follow us into town."

Jeff drove. Colin sat beside him. Two of the bikers had gotten out of the pickups and were riding behind them. They were both armed with shotguns and pistols.

IH-10 split off just ahead, with the main road continuing to the east while a smaller surface street jogged slightly to the north. They were being caravanned into town, flanked to the front and the rear by the pickups, while the motorcycles swarmed all around them. Jeff slowed the bus to keep time with his escorts, and together they rode into the main part of town.

At first, Van Horn looked just like every other desert town they had passed through. There were a few shabby, dusty buildings huddled into the dirt, and row upon row of worn-down-looking trailers off in the near distance.

But that was where the similarities stopped.

The street was lined with poles that had been jammed into every available patch of dirt. Each of the poles had a severed head impaled on it.

"Oh, Jesus," Jeff said. The bile rose in his throat, but he closed his eyes and forced it back down.

When he opened them again, the impaled heads leered back at him with gaping mouths and wide, surprised eyes.

"What in the hell happened here?" Jeff said.

"I don't like this," Colin said.

Ahead of them, the town opened up into a small square. There were motorcycles parked along the curbs and a bonfire burning on the lawn. Bikers were milling around the square, drinking and laughing. Beyond them, a crowd had gathered around a gazebo, and it looked like that was where they were being led. In a way, it reminded Jeff of the giant keg parties he'd attended at CU Boulder before he'd dropped out of law school.

"Colin, this sucks."

"I know. Just keep going, okay?"

"You don't sound very sure."

"I'm not, Jeff."

One of the bikers was waving them over to the curb. Jeff turned the wheel and coasted into position, the brakes squealing as they came to a stop. Someone else beat a fist against the door, and the bikers behind them spoke for the first time.

"Showtime, fellas. Let's go."

They were led to the gazebo. Someone had secured barbed wire around the outside of it so that it was completely enclosed. Inside was one of the infected, a woman in a blue dress that was shredded on the top so that only a scrap of it still went over her shoulders. The rest draped down over her hips, wet and crusty with dried blood. There were cuts and bite marks all over her chest and face.

The bikers stood around the edges of the gazebo, teasing

her. As she tried to reach for them, they were throwing cigarette butts and beer cans at her.

Somebody had backed a cattle truck up to the far side of the gazebo, and Jeff could see more of the infected inside it.

"What in the hell are you guys doing here?" Colin asked.

The bikers assigned to guard them just laughed.

"Just having a little fun," one of them said.

Suddenly, a cheer went up from the bikers surrounding the gazebo. Jeff and the others turned to see what was going on and saw a man being pulled along a path to the front of the gazebo. He was wearing a cop's uniform, and he had been beaten badly. A thick rope of bloody spit hung from his busted mouth, and his eyes were bruised and puffy. His hands were secured behind his back with handcuffs.

"Oh, no," Jeff said.

One of the bikers opened a door to the gazebo and they threw the cop inside. He tripped and fell, landing on his face.

Another cheer went up from the bikers.

The cop seemed to grasp what was happening, but he was having trouble getting to his feet. Jeff groaned at what he knew was about to happen.

Slowly, the cop rolled over onto his knees.

The zombie in the blue dress turned toward him and moaned. Her hands came up, the fingers clutching at him. The cop seemed to be having a hard time lifting his head, as though the bikers had tied an anchor around his neck. He lifted his blackened eyes up toward the approaching zombie, and the sight of that blood-soaked woman must have been enough to wake up his last bit of strength, for he managed to get one foot under him, and he rose to his feet. Then he ducked his head and rammed his shoulder into the approaching zombie's chest, knocking her backward into the gazebo's wall. They both fell to the ground as a cheer rose from the bikers.

The cop rolled onto his back, his face twisted in pain and rage. But the zombie was unharmed. She flipped herself over onto her stomach and slowly got to her feet again. The cop tried to crawl away from her, but he was too badly hurt, and when she fell on him, his screams didn't last long.

Colin turned and threw up in the grass next to Jeff.

Jeff looked away.

The biker they'd tried to deal with on the bus was standing over by the gazebo crowd. He had Colin's red duffel bag open on a bench in front of him and he was showing the contents off to some of the others. One of them said something and they all laughed. Then the biker turned to Jeff and smiled. One of the others opened the aluminum foil and took out a black perforated gelatin sheet. He tore off a big corner of the sheet and handed it to the biker from the bus.

A moment later, the biker was standing in front of Jeff and Colin. He looked at both of them in turn before finally settling on Jeff. He held up the corner of the gelatin sheet. It looked like about ten hits. "This shit's pretty good, huh?"

Jeff didn't answer.

"Let's see how good it is. Open your mouth."

Jeff didn't move.

Something hard bumped up against the back of Jeff's head. He turned just enough to see that it was the muzzle of a shotgun.

"Open up," the biker said.

Jeff opened his mouth and the biker jammed the sheet inside.

"Close your mouth."

The shotgun bumped Jeff's head again and he closed his mouth around the tabs.

"Swallow it," the biker said.

Jeff forced it down.

"Good boy." Then he pointed to Colin. "I want this one right up front where he can see."

The guards pulled Colin away, and Jeff was left standing on the grass next to the biker.

"Why are you doing this?" Jeff said. "It makes no sense."

"You sound like you're a pretty smart guy," the biker said. "You go to college?"

Jeff nodded.

"Where?"

"Harvard."

"Harvard? No shit?"

"No shit."

"Wow. Hey, that's something. Me, I didn't go to school. I got my GED while I was doing ninety-six months in Huntsville for check washing. You know what that is?"

"No idea."

"It's where you use a chemical solution to wash the ink off people's checks. After that, you change who it's made out to and the next thing you know you got yourself a check made out to whoever your ID says you are. Simple. Course it doesn't really matter now, does it? Nobody's gonna be writing checks anytime soon, right?"

"I guess not."

"Nope. Not for a long while. And that's where I come in. What's your name, anyway?"

"Jeff Stavers."

"Jeff, I'm Randall Gaines."

Cheers erupted from over at the gazebo. Jeff let his gaze slip that way, and through the crowd he saw the cop rise to his feet. Now there were two of them staggering around inside the gazebo, getting beer cans and cigarette butts thrown at them.

Gaines said, "I probably ain't read as many books as you read at Harvard, but I did read this guy named Will Durant. A historian. You ever read him?"

Jeff nodded.

"Yeah, he was cool. You know what he said about anarchy?"

"What?"

"He said, 'As soon as liberty is complete it dies in anarchy.' I'll tell you what. I sat in my cell at Huntsville for nearly a year thinking about that. I'd be interested to hear what you think that means?"

"I have no idea."

"Don't want to play, huh? Well, I'll tell you. See, people talk about liberty, and what they think they mean is the freedom to vote and shit like that. But that's not what real liberty is. Not even a little bit. You see, liberty is the most personal thing a man has got. It's like your soul. It's something that belongs to each man as an individual. Ask any prisoner. He'll tell you the same thing."

Over at the gazebo, a sort of chant had gone up. Jeff could see Colin getting pushed up against the barbed wire, his hands forced inside the cage.

Colin looked like he was crying.

Gaines coughed once. He said, "Now think on this. Think what it would mean if every man achieved true liberty. True freedom. Every man is free to do as he wants, no laws, no religion, no obligations to anyone but his own desires and higher impulses. Can you imagine that? True liberty. That's the root of anarchy right there. And that's what them zombies represent. They are a means for the rest of us to achieve true liberty. They made me, Harvard, not the other way around."

Jeff wanted to tell him that he was insane, but his tongue was feeling as thick as a shoe in his mouth. It was hard to breathe. He blinked, and when he opened his eyes the world seemed to be tilting on him.

"Got nothing to say, Harvard?"

With effort, Jeff shook his head.

"How about that acid? It startin' to work yet?"

Jeff said nothing.

"Here, let me see your eyes."

Gaines grabbed Jeff's face and gave him a clinical once-over.

"Jesus, that's some good shit your friend's got. Look at those pupils. Man, you're tripping hard. Okay, come on."

He pulled Jeff toward the gazebo. Jeff resisted, or tried to, but nothing seemed to work right. He was dizzy, and every step sent a confusing flood of signals to his brain. Gaines let go of his arm for a second and it was enough to send him off balance. He staggered sideways, tried to right himself, but only managed to fall flat on his face.

The biker called out to some of the others and a moment later Jeff was being hauled up to his feet and carried over to the gazebo.

They parked him in front of the gate. Inside, the zombies were staggering around aimlessly. Off to Jeff's right, Colin was trying to say something to him, but his voice was lost in the cheers and laughter of the crowd. The faces all around him were a blur.

Gaines appeared by his side.

"You ready for this, Harvard?"

Jeff grunted. He felt something forced into his hand and looked down and saw a knife there.

He blinked at it, unsure if it was real.

"Good luck, Harvard."

The gate was thrown open in front of Jeff, and a moment later he was pushed inside. He landed face-first on the wooden floor. The knife skittered out of his hand. He reached for it, but his arm wouldn't obey. It tingled, like it had fallen asleep.

A few feet away, the zombies began to moan.

CHAPTER 32

The morning after they buried Art Waller was cloudy and cool. The sun had just broken over the trees to the east and most of the sky was still a golden-gray. Smoke-colored rain clouds were moving in from the north. The breeze smelled vaguely sour, like garbage. People were already gathering outside their tents, getting ready for the day or talking to their neighbors.

There was a restlessness among the tents this morning that hadn't been there before—or at least hadn't been this noticeable. Billy Kline couldn't exactly put his finger on it. He had seen enough fighting during his stays in the Sarasota County Jail to recognize the mute agitation and frustration that could eat up a crowd of people who had been too long contained. It was cabin fever fed by frustration and fear. That was close to what he was feeling now, but not quite.

Margaret O'Brien was by his side. Ed had sent the two of them out to the commissary to bring back supplies, but they never made it that far. Before they got to the clearing in front of the commissary tent, they heard the sounds of people yelling. They saw a commotion up ahead, people rushing forward to get a look.

"Billy," Margaret said. She pointed to a crowd that had surrounded a small group of soldiers, who were blocking the entrance to the commissary. More people were streaming in from all directions. The soldiers looked anxious. Even from a distance, he could see them fingering their rifles nervously.

A large white rock flew from the crowd and struck one of the soldiers in the face.

A moment later, another rock arced through the air, and the crowd surged forward.

For a moment, it looked like they might overwhelm the soldiers at the entrance, but then Billy heard six distinct shots. The crowd stopped its forward surge, and the world seemed to grow perfectly still.

In the sudden silence after the shots, a voice shouted "Gas!" and a metal canister dropped into the crowd with a clank.

A thin jet of dark smoke rose up between the shocked crowd.

More canisters sailed through the air.

Then the people started shouting again. They ran in all directions. Rocks were thrown. More shots rang out.

"Oh, Jesus," Margaret said.

Billy stood still, watching the commotion swirl around him. Already, he could feel the scratch in his throat from the gas.

"Run, Billy. For God's sake, run!"

She grabbed him by the hand, and together they joined the flood of people running from the scene.

Ed and the others were waiting for them outside the tent. When he saw them coming, Ed rushed forward. "What happened?"

Margaret told him everything that had happened to them. "Ed, we have to get out of here."

He turned to Julie Carnes. "Well?" he said.

Julie dropped down heavily onto a lawn chair. She looked much older than she had only a few days before, and though Ed felt for her, he knew there wasn't time to coddle her. They had to do this, and do it quickly.

"Everybody get your things together," he said. "Only what you can carry. Make sure you take all the food you can."

"Ed," Julie said. "How are we going to get out of here? We don't have a car."

"I've got an idea about that," he said. He turned to Billy. "I keep coming back to you, son. You think you can help me steal a truck?"

Billy blinked at him.

Then he nodded.

With Ed in the lead, they made their way south of the camp, through a strip of pinewoods, and out the other side. Before them was a large, open, grassy field and a dirt road leading south. A pair of marines sat on the ground, sharing an orange. Behind them was a Humvee.

"That's our ride," Ed said to the others.

Julie looked at him, mouth open.

Beside him, Billy coughed gently. "Uh, Ed, I don't think they're gonna just let us take that thing."

"I suspect they'll listen to reason," he said.

"Ed, what are you going to do?" Julie said.

He winked at her. "You guys just be ready to go. Billy, as soon as I give you the signal, you load everybody up and get us ready to move out."

"Uh, okay. What's the signal?"

Ed tipped the bill of his hat to Billy and said, "Just be ready, son." Then he got to his feet and walked out of the cover of the trees and onto the grass. He walked straight over to the soldiers, smiling as he advanced.

"Hi, fellas," he said.

The soldiers stared at him, but didn't get up.

Still smiling, Ed reached under his shirt and pulled the pair of revolvers he'd tucked down into the small of his back. Before either soldier could react, he fired a shot right between the legs of one of the soldiers and leveled the weapons at their faces.

"I guess that's the signal," Billy said.

"I think I hate that man," Julie said.

They drove south till they reached Putney Avenue, then headed west to Newton Road and turned north. They passed along the western edge of Albany. The city was dead. They saw a few wrecked cars, and several looked like they'd been burned. And there were bodies in the road. Everywhere they looked, there were bodies. The smell of death was heavy on the air. Margaret pulled her grandchildren away from the windows, and they didn't try to resist.

"Do you think it's like this everywhere?" Julie said.

From the front passenger seat, Ed said, "I don't know. But God, I hope not."

"We ought to dump this thing as soon as we can," Billy said. "They'll be looking for it, and this isn't exactly the most inconspicuous vehicle around."

"Yeah," Ed agreed. "Good point."

"Ed, please," Julie said. "Don't stop here. Get away from this place before you try to find another vehicle."

They passed a badly decomposed body that was swarming with flies.

Ed nodded. "Don't worry. We won't stop."

* * *

They found a large white Ford Econoline van outside Roanoke, Alabama. After dumping the Humvee behind an abandoned gas station, they continued north on nearly deserted roads. By nightfall, they had crossed the border into Missouri and started looking for a place to spend the night.

They were near Marshfield when Billy pulled the van to the side of the road and pointed.

"Look there," he said to Ed.

Off in the distance, some four hundred yards from the roadway, was a large red barn with a sloping metal roof where somebody had written:

GONE TO CEDAR RIVER
NATIONAL GRASSLAND
YOU SHOULD TOO IF YOU CAN

Ed smiled. "Looks like it was meant to be, huh?"

"Yeah, looks that way."

From behind them, Julie said, "Ed?"

"Yeah?"

"Ed, are you really sure? Can we really do this?"

"Yes," he said, and he meant it, too. He felt good about this. Seeing this sign here, it was a shot in the arm when he needed it most. "We can do this," he said. "Absolutely, we can."

They spent the night in an abandoned farmhouse. There was no food left in the pantry, none that hadn't gone bad, anyway, but there was fresh water from a well out back, and they were able to combine that with the ramen noodles they'd taken with them from the camp and turn it into a passable meal.

Later, after everyone else had gone to sleep, Billy Kline walked outside and stood in a field of ripe wheat and looked up at the stars. He watched a meteor shower and took deep breaths of the cool night air. A lot had happened to him in a very short stretch of days, but he felt strangely good, as though he had shuffled off a large weight.

He was starting over, and for the first time in a very long while, he was thankful to be alive.

CHAPTER 33

Nate Royal lay on his bed in his cell and thought about running into daylight. The air conditioner churned noisily behind the walls, and a vent above his bed kept a steady chill blowing down on him. He shivered, drawing himself up into a ball. He tried to remember what it was like that morning in his sophomore year when he left that senior from Gatlin at the edge of the pinewoods and broke loose into the daylight of the homestretch, running like he'd never run before in his life. He thought about all that soft, gold daylight pouring down over him, filling his senses with the smell of pine.

But try as he might, he couldn't hold the good thoughts. His body hurt. The wound on his left shoulder was throbbing constantly. The fingers of his left hand had a tendency to fall asleep if he didn't keep them moving. The insides of his elbows were bruised up from all the injections they'd given him. And they had operated on him, too. That was what was hurting, he decided, not the bite. It was bandaged up now, but he had seen it the night before while one of the nurses was dressing it, and from what he could see, the original bite looked pretty well healed. It was whatever they had done to him that hurt so much.

Nate had lost track of time. The pain was part of it. So, too, was this cell they'd put him. There were no windows, no pictures on the wall. There was nothing but a sink near the foot of his bed and a small bathroom off to his right that didn't have a door. They were careful not to talk around him. They didn't leave magazines for him to look at, no TV, not even a radio to listen to. But the pain and the cell were only part of his hell. The main part was being stuck in his own head.

He forced himself to turn back to the plane ride that had brought him here. It hadn't been a long one. Maybe longer than a movie, but not too much longer than that. They'd landed God knows where, though. It felt colder than in Pennsylvania; he'd been sure of that. The few people he saw had light Windbreakers on. Most were soldiers, though. They hadn't allowed him a chance to look around. He'd been hustled inside a building, stripped, bathed, inspected, injected, interrogated.

"How were you injured?"

"I was bit."

"By an infected individual?"

"A zombie, yeah."

"What were you doing when you were attacked?"

"Just walking. Where am I? Who are you people?"

No answers, but lots more questions.

Later—he tried to remember how much later, but it was so hard to cut through the fog that had settled in his mind—they'd tried again.

"Do you have any allergies?"

"I don't like dickheads in doctor's outfits."

"Tell me about your drug use."

"Tell me if your mother takes it in the ass."

They became less patient with him. He became more sullen, angrier, less cooperative. And the days began to turn to fog. He closed his eyes and opened them. The cell was the same as it always was. Too small. The bed was uncomfortable. Better than the cots at County, but just as small. He thought about taking a dump, but turned over in bed instead and looked away from the toilet. He couldn't flush it himself. There was no handle. It just sort of flushed whenever it felt like it, he guessed. Or maybe they had a remote control somewhere. He'd taken a dump in it during his first day and felt bad about leaving his nasty steamer in there. Later, he woke from a nap and saw a guy in one of those white spacesuits fishing the thing out of the pot. Somehow, it had made him feel even more deeply violated than any of the other things they'd done to him, all the questions and the injections and even the surgery, knowing that they were even digging into his poop. *Jesus*, he had thought.

Behind him, he heard the whoosh of the door and knew they were sending in another spacesuit. More injections. Maybe more questions.

He sighed and rolled over.

A white spacesuited figure set out a small metal plate with a syringe and three empty vials on it, each a different color.

"What are those for?"

"Can I have your left arm, please?"

"Sure. Tell me what those are for first."

Nate was pretty sure he heard the figure inside the spacesuit let out a sigh of his own. But it could have been his imagination.

The spacesuit picked up the syringe and popped in one of the vials, a gray-topped one.

"Your arm, please."

"Go fuck yourself."

"Sir, your arm please. Do it now, or I will have a guard come in here and hold you down."

It was an old threat, but one they'd made good on several times. And the guards were not good-humored about it, either.

Nate held out his arm.

"Your left arm, please."

"Sorry," Nate said.

He put his left arm across his belly, inside of the elbow pointed up. But when the spacesuit leaned in to stick him with the needle, Nate went on the attack. He brought his right hand up and slapped the needle out of the spacesuit's hands. Then he grabbed the loose knob of fabric at the top of the spacesuit's head and tried to yank the damn thing off, though it was taped or Velcroed down tight and didn't budge.

The spacesuit started to shriek like a little girl. He squirmed away from Nate and ran into the wall next to the toilet. He spun around, hands out like he was trying to ward off another blow, and began to back away.

For Nate, it was just like what had happened with Jessica Metcalfe at his van. He felt the same blind snap of rage, followed by the stunned shock as the spacesuit backed away from him. Had he really just done that? Jesus, the guy was really scared.

Nate began to laugh.

But a moment later, two guards came in and the laughter stopped. The spacesuit shrank from the room about as fast as he possibly could. The two guards—even though their faces were obscured behind the gold-tinted lenses of their spacesuits—looked like they wanted nothing more than to drive Nate's head through the wall.

And for a second, he was pretty sure they were about to do it.

Nate rolled out of bed and landed with it between him and the guards. They advanced on him. The little metal plate that spacesuit had brought the syringe and vials in was on the bed, and Nate picked it up and threw it at one of the guards.

It bounced off the guard's forearm and clanged against the wall near the door.

Nate backed up farther, looking around for something to fight with.

The guards advanced on him again.

"Enough!"

The two guards stopped. Nate stopped. Behind them, a man was walking into the room. He didn't wear a spacesuit. He was dressed in green hospital scrubs.

He said, "Enough. You guys wait for me outside."

The guards hesitated.

"It's okay," the man said. He stepped aside and let the guards walk out the door. When they were gone, he pushed the door closed but not all the way. There was no handle, and Nate figured the guy didn't want to be stuck without a way out if he needed one.

"Nate Royal?" the man said.

Nate stiffened, but didn't answer.

"I'm Dr. Mark Kellogg. I'm in charge of things around here."

"Uh-huh."

Nate thought the guy looked a little young to be in charge of things around here. He had a military haircut, military face, all sharp angles and a jaw that looked like somebody had cut it out of rock. But his eyes were kind, and that put Nate off his guard. There was a look there that was definitely not military, and Nate decided that the man probably wasn't a soldier. Or if he was, he wasn't all that serious about being one.

The man was still looking at him, smiling now, just waiting for him to come around.

"So what is this place?" Nate asked.

"You're at Minot Air Force Base. That's in North Dakota."

"North . . . what about my dad? Where is he?"

"I'm sorry, Nate. Your dad and his girlfriend, Mindy Carlson, are not here. We tried to find them right after we learned about you but we haven't been able to locate them. It's been rather confusing in that part of the country, as you can probably imagine. There are a lot of people still wandering around looking for help. A lot of people we still haven't talked to yet."

Nate nodded. Then he frowned. "Why am I here?" he said.

"You mean you don't know?"

"How could I know that? You people won't tell me shit. Every time I ask something, you people stick me with a needle."

"Yeah. Nate, do you want to sit down so we can talk?"

"No, I don't want to sit. I want to stand. I want to go outside."

"I'm sorry," Kellogg said.

"I can't go outside?"

"I'm afraid not."

"That door's open. How about I make a run for it, see how far I get?"

Kellogg shrugged. "You wouldn't get far. Even if you got past the guards—which isn't going to happen, believe me—that knee of yours is going to keep you from running more than twenty or thirty yards."

"How do you know about my knee?"

"Nate," Kellogg said. He sounded tired. His shoulders sagged beneath his scrubs. "I have been over every aspect of your medical record. I have been over every record on you we can find. You used to be a runner. Cross-country, right?"

"That's right."

"A good one, too. At least from what I can tell."

"I was okay. I stopped my junior year."

"Ah," Kellogg said. He stepped around the bed and sat at the foot of it. "Nate, the reason why you're here is because you got bit by a zombie."

"So did lots of other people."

"Yes, and they all became zombies. You didn't. That's why you're here."

"So you can figure out why I didn't change into one of those things?"

Kellogg touched a finger to his nose.

"And what happens when you find that out?"

"Well, hopefully, once I know why you're so special, I'll be able to come up with a cure. That's what this is all about, Nate. A cure. We find that, we could end a world's worth of suffering."

"Yeah, right."

"It's possible," Kellogg said. "Right now, I'm banking on it, in fact. It's about the only hope we have left." He said, "Nate, things are bad out there. You have no idea. There isn't a major population center in this country left untouched by this outbreak. There are millions of the infected now. Millions more are dead. Latin America, South America, all infected. Europe, the Middle East, Africa, Southeast Asia, all those regions are reporting massive outbreaks. Nate, this thing is global. But with your help, maybe we can stop it."

Nate felt sick to his stomach. Kellogg's words were just a muddle. *Jesus, the way some people talk.* But he pulled enough sense out of it to know that Kellogg considered him some kind of medical miracle.

"With my help, you said?"

"That's right."

"Tell me, doc, how long have I been here?"

"We flew you out of Martindale on the ninth of July. Today is the twenty-ninth."

Nate tried to do the math in his head and couldn't. He started to count off the days, but Kellogg interrupted him. "About three weeks," he said.

"And you say a lot's happened?"

"A lot of bad stuff, yeah."

"Can I get a TV in here?"

"There isn't a lot on TV these days, Nate. I can get you a TV, though. The base has a movie library. Maybe you can at least get some movies to watch."

"Okay," Nate said, nodding. "That'd be cool."

"We don't have much in the way of reading material. Some paperbacks. I think we've got some old copies of the *New York Times* and the *Wall Street Journal*—if you're interested?"

"Doc, I . . . I don't read so good."

"Ah."

Nate looked toward the door. Earlier, he had seen some figures walking by, but there didn't seem to be anybody there now.

He leaned forward and whispered, "Doc, you know, I ain't really seen any women in a while. You think maybe the base here has got some pornos in that library of theirs?"

Kellogg smiled, even managed a little laugh. "Nate," he said. "They got cameras built into the walls around here. You probably should, you know, put the brakes on enjoying yourself for a while."

Nate stiffened again. He looked around, studying the walls, wondering how many times they'd watched him in here, jacking off in the dark.

His sense of violation returned, and with it, his anger.

"Nate, you all right?"

"Yeah, fine."

"Is there anything you'd like? Different food, maybe?"

"Can you tell me one thing?"

"Sure."

"I'm never gonna leave this place, am I?"

"Nate—"

"Tell me the truth, doc. I'm stuck here, right? It doesn't

matter that I'm immune to this zombie virus. It's like I got it just the same, right? I may not be one of those things, but I'm sure as hell not gonna be me again either."

"Nate, this may be hard for you to believe, but you're not the only one who's a prisoner here. This outbreak has bound each of us to this place in a very real way. You've got your reasons why you can't leave, and me, well, I've got mine. We're both stuck here, Nate."

Kellogg rose from the bed and chaffed his palms against the thighs of his scrubs.

He laughed. "I'm sweating," he said. "Stress, I guess. I don't get to sleep much these days. Nate, I'm going to send in the nurse again. Are you going to let him take your blood?"

"Why do you want it?"

"Would that help, knowing what we're doing? Would you like us to tell you what it is we're doing before we do it?"

"What good would that do?"

"Well, it wouldn't change our tests any. We've still got to do them. But it would be more than you've got right now. It'd give you some measure of dignity back."

"Dignity? You're kidding."

"It's a start, Nate."

Nate nodded. That was true, it was a start.

"All right, Nate. I'll talk to you soon."

And with that he was gone, and Nate was left staring at the cell.

Chapter 34

From the notebooks of Ben Richardson

Pine Prairie, Texas: July 16th, 1:40 A.M.

We got hit hard today. Four dead. Lost both buses. Now we've only got three trucks and a minivan left.

It happened as we were leaving Huntsville earlier this morning, around 8 o'clock. Jammed-up traffic on I-45 forced us off the freeway and we had to drive through town—something Barnes didn't want to do because Huntsville is home to eight different state prisons, and, as he put it, all them prisoners had to go somewhere when the shit hit the fan. Hindsight is 20/20, of course.

What we saw as we entered town from the south was a mess of traffic on the freeway. A lot of the surface streets were even worse. All except Avenue Q. That was clear, and on the map it connected us back to I-45 north of town, so we took it. We made it past the Huntsville Municipal Airport, swung north again, and got on the connector ramp to I-45.

That's where the trap was.

Barnes and I were in a pickup truck, leading the caravan, as we had done since leaving Houston. He stopped the truck at the base of the connector ramp and just sat there, rubbing the stubble on his chin as he watched the road up ahead.

"What's wrong?" I asked him.

I tried to see what he saw. There were bodies lining the road, but they were obviously dead. You could see it from a hundred and fifty feet away. They were all shot up. On the right shoulder, the back left tire just barely over the lane line, was a broken-down van. Beyond that was a barren stretch of highway.

I didn't see what the problem was.

"Look at the fat white guy on his back up there on the left."

I did. I didn't see anything wrong.

"What is that beneath him?" Barnes said. "See it? Right there under his back? Looks like a paint can."

Somebody behind us honked.

Barnes ignored them. He had been watching the dead guy lying on top of the paint can, but now he was scanning the surrounding countryside. It was flat, green, uninteresting. Nothing moved.

"I don't like it," he said.

He got out, talked to some of the drivers behind us, then climbed back into the truck.

"We're gonna drive through first. If everything's cool, we wave the others through."

I didn't ask what the trouble was. Barnes scares the crap out of me. I think he's a fucking lunatic. But I also think he's a genius when it comes to surviving.

We drove up the ramp without incident. We stopped right where the ramp joins the highway and we got out. I looked back at our caravan. There were a lot of people standing next to their vehicles, watching us, a lot of them with what-the-fuck-is-going-on looks on their faces.

Barnes gave them the okay sign.

The buses started up the ramp. The lead bus got as far as the fat white guy on top of the paint can when the explosion happened. It was the paint can, an IED. The blast was tremendous. Must have been a shaped charge. The road, pavement and all, swelled up in an enormous ball, like a giant was below it blowing up a balloon. I saw it all in the slow-motion sensation that comes with shock and disbelief. The ground exploded upward. The front of the bus dropped down into the hole the charge had just made. People fell forward and I heard screaming.

Then the screams were drowned out by a second explosion. Our other bus had stopped right behind the first bus, right next to the minivan broken down on the right shoulder. Barnes was next to me, yelling, "No, get back. Get that bus out of there." Something inside the van exploded. Our second bus was lost in a gray cloud of pulverized asphalt and car parts. It rocked over onto two wheels, hovered there for a long moment, then fell the rest of the way onto its side. Barnes was still yelling for people to back away, clear out of there, but nobody listened. They got out of their trucks and cars and raced forward to help the injured. They were standing there, confused, scared, unorganized, when our attackers popped up from their hiding holes in the ditches along the road and started firing into the crowd.

Through the clouds of smoke and dust, I saw three men with rifles charging out of the ditch. They were using the gutted and burned skeleton of the minivan for cover. One of the front tires was still burning, sending off a thick black smoke that hid our people from view. I looked for Barnes, intending to follow his lead, but he was already in our pickup, throwing it into reverse.

"What the . . ." I said, watching as Barnes raced toward the men. Two of them never saw it coming. They stood there,

firing from the hip at anyone they could see, right up to the moment that Barnes ran them over.

The third man tried to fire at the truck as it slipped into the smoke, but he lost it.

I watched him turning around, trying to track the noise of the pickup's engine in the smoke and dust around him, but he couldn't get a fix on it. He was looking in a completely different direction when Barnes erupted out of the cloud and sandwiched him between the back end of the pickup and the wrecked bus.

Two other men had come out of the opposite ditch. They ran straight at Barnes, one armed with a shotgun, the other with a pistol. Barnes stepped out of the truck with his AR-15 and lit up the man with the pistol, dropping him at the edge of the pavement. The other man fired once, then, realizing he was outnumbered and outgunned, turned and ran as fast as he could back across the empty field between us and the airport.

Barnes motioned for me to help the others, then chased after the man on foot.

I didn't bother to watch. I knew Barnes could take care of himself. I started helping the injured. A few minutes later, I'm not sure exactly how much later, I heard a single shot.

Barnes showed up a few minutes after that. He studied the scene and gave a disgusted snort at the four dead members of our group we'd laid out on the roadway.

"Anyone else dead?" he asked me.

"None of our people," I said. "We got a bunch of injuries, though. Who the hell were those guys?"

"Prisoners out of the McConnell Unit. They were looking for food."

"Are there more of them around here?"

"Apparently not," Barnes said.

"That one you chased, he told you that?"

Barnes nodded.

"I thought I heard a shot," I said.

"You probably did."

"You executed him," I said.

"Best thing that ever happened to him, trust me." He surveyed the damage once more, our two damaged buses, our people soot-stained and hollow-eyed, some of them crying. "What do we have left, three trucks?"

"And a minivan."

"Let's pack whatever supplies we can salvage. We need to move out of here."

"But these people aren't going to all fit in the vehicles we've got," I said.

"Anybody who doesn't fit walks."

And so, two hours later, our limping, crestfallen caravan made its way out of Huntsville.

Most of us on foot.

Latexo, Texas: July 29th,11:40 P.M.

Tired. Jesus, I think the soles of my sneakers have melted.

We've followed a crazy path the last two weeks, zigzagging all over the map like Cabeza de Vaca on acid. Supplies have been hard to come by, and there aren't many places to scavenge for more. Most of these places have been cleaned out already. So we've been going from one little Texas town to the next, taking whatever we can find. We passed through Staley, Sebastopol, Chita, Pogoda, Cut, and now we're stuck here in Latexo. They all look the same, run-down, a lean-to look about them, like the wind just sort of blew a bunch of lumber into piles and they called them towns. I grew up in a tiny little Texas town, so I understand, up to a point. Sometimes, there's not a lot you can do with the cards you've been dealt. But Christ, who comes up with all these crazy names? Sebastopol, Cut, Latexo? Seriously?

Alto, Texas: August 1st. 2:40 P.M.

Stopped for lunch. I'm eating a Snickers bar, a couple pieces of bread, some beef jerky. Washing it down with a warm can of Coke.

I want to talk about something that happened here in Alto yesterday. A lot of people, Sandra Tellez especially, have been complaining to Barnes about the pace he's keeping us on. We made it into Alto yesterday about 10 o'clock in the morning. The heat was just starting to make the walking unbearable, and most of us were ready to stop, find some place to hole up, and take it easy for a few days. Barnes refused. He wanted to push on. He always wants to push on.

Sandra told him they had a few elderly folks and children. Even a few of the young people in their twenties were getting sick. She demanded they stay in the area for as long as they could, until they could get healthy.

Barnes said, "Sure. Okay. How about food?"

"We have a few trucks. You can take a few men out to gather what you can from the surrounding towns."

"And the zombies? What about them?"

"What zombies?"

He pointed behind her.

I was standing next to Sandra. I looked where he pointed and didn't see anything but a large, grassy field. Here and there, I saw a few dead bodies. At least I thought they were dead.

"They're not dead," he said. "They're sleeping."

I looked again, and sure enough, you could see a few moving here and there. One of them rolled over.

I was shocked.

"Why?" he asked me. "I thought you made a reputation for yourself studying these things. Isn't that what you made that field trip to San Antonio to do? Isn't that what you set out to write your great zombie book about?"

I was too stunned by the field of sleeping zombies to answer.

He said, "You're the one who's been telling me that they're just living people with a disease, like leprosy or something. Well, living people have to eat. They have to shit. And they've got to sleep." He turned to Sandra. "Well, if you want to stay here, what do you want to do about them?"

"I don't know," she said. Then, more quietly, "But these people don't have anything left, Mr. Barnes. They need to rest."

"Fine," he said.

He grabbed me by the shoulder and told me to go to a barn at the edge of the field where the zombies slept and quietly open the front door. It looked to be a good quarter mile away from where we stood. A long way to run when you're standing out in the open, surrounded by flesh-eating ghouls.

He told Sandra to get everyone out of sight and make sure they stayed that way.

"What are you going to do?" I asked.

"Just be ready with that door," he said. "When I tell you to, you slam it shut."

I went off and did what I was told. Sandra did what she was told. Barnes, meanwhile, walked out into the field of sleeping zombies and started whistling, one of those ear-splitters that seems to carry for miles.

Here and there, sleepers sat up and looked around for the source of the whistling. The infected are predictable in some ways; other ways they're not. You can always count on them to go after something living if they spot it. But you can't always count on them spotting it. Or hearing it, either.

Barnes had to whistle himself hoarse before he had a good number of them getting to their feet. Then the moaning started. That did it. I've become convinced their moaning is a trigger, the way certain gestures or sounds from a lead mare will trigger a herd of horses to change direction or suddenly break into an earthshaking gallop. That moaning, I think, is a key means of communication among the infected.

Not the same kind of communication as speech or writing, obviously. More instinctive. Come to where I am. Food here. That sort of thing.

When the moaning started, the zombies—about twenty in all—got to their feet and followed Barnes. Barnes, for his part, calmly walked to the barn where I was waiting. He walked so slowly there were several times I thought he was about to get knocked down, but he never did. He just kept walking into the barn. I heard noises from inside, and I tried to figure out what he was doing, but it was no use. The noises were too indistinct, and I was too scared.

I heard them gathering inside the barn. It took nearly twenty minutes to get them all inside, but I wasn't aware that it had happened. The first notice I had was when Barnes ran up beside me—scared the ever-loving crap out of me, too—and yelled, "Slam it shut, slam it shut." He put his shoulder into the door and together we slammed the thing shut.

He put a bar over the door and that was that. The field was clear, all except for a few that couldn't move well enough to walk.

"We'll take care of them in a bit," he said. "For now, let's go get one of them gas cans from the truck."

"What are gonna do?" I asked.

"Burn 'em," he said, matter-of-factly. "What the hell did you think I was gonna do?"

"That seems inhumane to burn them."

"They'll kill us or turn us if we give 'em a chance. So what's inhumane about burning 'em?"

"Good point," I said.

Most of us hate Officer Barnes. We think he's a tyrant, insane, abnormally cruel. But there's a reason we keep following him.

He does keep us alive.

Dialville, Texas: August 6th, 10:00 P.M.

From Alto over to Elkhart, then north to Palestine, east again over to Rusk. We're all over the place.

I'm hot, thirsty, irritable. If I never see another pine tree in my whole entire life, it'll be too soon.

Christ, will we never make it out of Texas?

Frankston, Texas: August 10th , 7:15 P.M.

We have plenty to eat. It may not all be good stuff, but there's plenty of it, lots of junk food, stuff that doesn't have to be refrigerated. None of us are going hungry.

Sandra Tellez has done a wonderful job getting people organized, keeping them fed. She is, I think, a natural leader. She speaks, and the others fall in line. No discussion, no second-guessing. Maybe they recognize that she survived this way for nearly two years. Who knows? But whatever that elusive quality of leadership is, she has it.

And that's part of the reason why I'm troubled.

I came to Sandra with something I saw the other day. Jerald Stevens is hoarding food. I was suspicious when I first met him in Houston. I was concerned when I saw him eating that ten-pound turkey breast right after we escaped the quarantine zone. Now I know it's true. I've seen him do it. He has pounds and pounds of candy bars and beef jerky and moldy old sandwiches and bags of chips and God knows what else stashed away in his pockets and under his shirt and even inside his pants.

The hoarding I can understand. That's the kind of thing a man can get over—that is, once he sees there's not a need for it anymore. But it's not just the hoarding. He's eating constantly, and it worries me.

The other day, I saw him eat an entire country ham. Have you ever seen a country ham? We're talking fourteen to sixteen pounds of pork. He gnawed it down to the bone during one of our daily marches.

And then he ate dinner with the rest of us, had seconds, and ate a candy bar in his sleeping bag while the rest of us drifted off to sleep.

Sandra didn't think it was that big of a deal. She gave me the line about them surviving off scraps in the quarantine zone. She said he would swing back to normal soon enough. Let him be, she said.

But I disagree. I don't think this is a phase you grow out of, like wetting the bed or chewing your nails. I think this is a bona fide mental illness.

Barnes, of course, had his own opinion. "Fuck him," he said. "If he wants to eat himself to death, more power to him."

Carrell Springs, Texas: August 14th, 8:20 P.M.

Right at dusk—the sky on fire with copper and red and orange, the land a dark purple along the horizon—a miracle happened.

For days we'd been hearing infrequent broadcasts on the AM radio bands about Jasper Sewell and his Grasslands village. Our group was divided. Most wanted to head that way. A few others, Sandra and Officer Barnes among them—the two of them on the same page for once—didn't want to go there. Not to be with some religious nut job, they said.

And then, right outside of Carrell Springs, all of us dripping with sweat, tired, barely able to hold our chins up as we walked the last few miles into another town whose streets stank of human carrion, we saw writing on the road. The letters were huge, painted in white.

They read:

Cedar River National
Grasslands
We are going there
You should too

We all stopped and looked at it. Nobody spoke for a long time. Finally, I walked forward and tugged on Officer Barnes's sleeve.

"What do you think?" I said. "These people. They need a plan, a destination."

I looked at Sandra.

She nodded.

After a long time, Barnes did, too.

CHAPTER 35

The cop was out in front, the zombie in the blue dress right behind him. Jeff grabbed the knife and staggered slowly to his feet. The world was swirling around him in a blur of faces and noise. He swayed drunkenly, unable to control his balance. A beer bottle smacked into the side of his head and caused him to rock back on his heels. A moment later, his arms were pinwheeling out of control as he fell back into the barbed wire.

A hand shoved him roughly back toward the center of the gazebo.

"Get in there and fight, you pussy!"

The floor was undulating beneath him. He stood there watching the approaching zombies, his shoulders slumped, his mouth hanging slack. His hands felt like they weighed a ton.

The cop was on him, but his hands were still handcuffed behind his back and all he could do was snap at Jeff with his teeth.

Jeff stepped to the side and pushed the cop to the wall, where he fell in a clumsy heap.

The zombie in the blue dress stepped around the fallen

cop and reached for Jeff. Her right hand looked like it had been broken at some point after she turned, and the fingers hung uselessly from the hand like locks of hair. The top of her dress was torn away and hung about her waist, her white bra almost black with blood.

Jeff kicked at her and managed to land a blow right behind her knee that sent her to the ground. She grunted as she fell, but showed no signs of pain.

By the time she rose to her feet again, Jeff was scrambling for the cop. He was leaning against the barbed wire and couldn't get back up without his hands. Jeff came up behind him and slammed the knife down into the side of his head with a wet-sounding smack.

The cop stopped moving almost immediately. Jeff still had his hand on the knife. He looked down at the blood seeping around the submerged blade and for a horrible moment he thought he could actually hear it pumping out of the wound. Everything fell away but that sound. Jeff was lost in it, shocked and thrilled and terrified by what he had just done.

The zombie in the blue dress put her ruined hand on his arm and she felt cold.

He yanked his arm back and rolled away from her. She came after him, but the sound of the blood pumping out of the cop's wound had done something to him, energized him. He could feel the drugs surging through him now. He jumped to his feet, ran around the zombie, and grabbed the hilt of the knife sticking from the side of the cop's head.

He pulled at the knife, but it wouldn't budge.

"Come on, damn it. Come on."

He was straining with everything he had, but the knife still wouldn't come loose.

A hand came through the barbed wire and shoved him away from the corpse. Jeff batted the hand away. Through the screen of wire, he could see one of the bikers laughing at him, taunting him. But Jeff couldn't hear him. The man's mouth was moving, his eyes bulging with drunken excitement, flecks of white spit flying off his lips, but there was no noise.

Behind Jeff, the zombie in the blue dress was groping for him.

He turned. He was trapped between her and the corpse and the wall of barbed wire. The biker was still shoving him back away from the wall. Jeff grabbed the man's hand and pulled it inside the gazebo with him as the zombie in the blue dress brought her teeth down on the spot where Jeff's shoulder had just been.

She got a mouthful of the biker's wrist instead.

The man screamed, and the zombie, now focused on the man, slid off Jeff's shoulder.

Jeff stood up just as the man managed to free himself. The zombie tried to force her head through the barbed wire, but somebody kicked her in the face and knocked her backward into the gazebo.

Jeff's chest was heaving. He looked down at the zombie and knew he had to do something. Then his gaze fell on the bra across her back. The clasp was coming loose, held together now by a single hook. Before she had a chance to stand, he reached down and pulled the bra apart. She was struggling to stand up, and as she moved, he managed to get one strap of the bra free from her arm and pull it up sharply, looping it around her neck until it formed a tight garrote. He put his knee in her back and pushed her facedown onto the wooden floor and he held her that way until she stopped squirming. The muscles in his arms were screaming at him by the time he let go of the bra and stood up.

The air was full of shouting. The gazebo was spinning, the faces leering in at him were distorted, alien, and frightening.

Then Gaines was standing in the gazebo with him.

"Harvard," he said. "Holy shit, man. That was awesome. Come on."

Gaines pulled him out of the gazebo and into a roaring crowd. Men were pushing him, congratulating him, slapping him on the back.

The crowd zippered open in front of him. On the ground, looking pale and frightened and angry, was the man who'd been bit by the zombie in the blue dress. He was on his knees, his face wet with sweat, his arms covered in blood. His lips were trembling.

"Here you go," Gaines said.

Once again Jeff felt something forced into his hand.

He looked down and saw a gun. He turned to Gaines, his expression one of complete confusion.

"Kill him," Gaines said. "Ain't got no choice. He's gonna turn."

The man on the ground tried to protest, but the others held him down.

"Do it," Gaines said.

Jeff looked at the gun, then at Gaines. The crowd was shouting for him to do it. Jeff let his gaze sweep over their faces, and in the crowd he found Colin. Colin was a wreck, his eyes puffy with crying, and it occurred to him then that Colin was deathly afraid of the zombies. Everybody was afraid of zombies, but Colin was out of his head with fear. Jeff suddenly felt a rush of sympathy for him. And he understood why Colin had reacted the way he did back in Barstow. It made sense to him now.

"Come on, Harvard. We're waiting."

Jeff turned back to Gaines. "I don't want to."

"You started this, Harvard. Now you got to finish it."

Jeff looked at the gun again. He shook his head. "No," he said. "I don't. That's the thing about liberty, Gaines. Give it to a man, you never know what he's going to do with it. That's what you meant by anarchy, isn't it?"

He raised the gun to Gaines's face and pulled the trigger.

The hammer fell with a click, but there was no shot.

Gaines laughed at him.

Jeff pulled the trigger again, and again, but nothing happened.

Gaines reached out and took the gun from him.

"It's empty, Harvard. I ain't got no college degree, but I ain't a fool. I just like to see my message getting through to a new generation."

He holstered the gun in the waistband of his jeans and motioned to the others. Jeff stepped to one side as the bikers lifted their injured comrade from the grass and threw him into the gazebo with the two corpses.

"Keep an eye on him," Gaines said. "As soon as he turns, throw that one in." He motioned at Colin. "That little pussy's been whimpering the whole time. Let's see how he does."

Colin let out a feeble, sickening cry.

Men pushed their way past Jeff as the bikers moved into position along the walls of the gazebo. Inside, the injured man was pleading with the others to help him, but all he got was a pelting of beer cans.

Jeff staggered toward Colin. He was guarded by three bikers, but as Jeff got close, two others stepped in front of him and held him back.

"Colin," Jeff said.

He was about to tell him he knew what had happened back in Barstow. Somehow, it felt absolutely critical that he say his piece, that he told Colin he understood and didn't blame him for it, that it wasn't his fault.

But he never had the chance.

From somewhere behind him there was the sound of an explosion.

Jeff turned and saw a fireball rising into the darkening sky. A pickup truck was on fire, and men were rolling in the street next to it. Some of them were on fire.

A figure was running from the burning truck toward the bus.

Jeff squinted, and all at once he realized it was Robin. She ran for the bus, and he expected her to keep running, but she stopped at the door and took something from Katrina.

It was a bottle of Grey Goose with a rag hanging from the neck. Even from a distance, Jeff could see her lighting the rag on fire and he thought, *My God. A Molotov cocktail. Robin, you crazy, wonderful, beautiful woman.*

She threw the burning bottle at a crowd of men who had advanced on the bus and it exploded at their feet. Two men caught the main part of the splash of broken glass and burning alcohol, and they caught fire instantly. One of the men ran a few steps, fell, and rolled in the street, trying to put out the flames. The other was beating at his pant legs as he staggered toward the curb. Their screaming filled the square.

Robin threw another burning bottle, then slipped inside the bus with Katrina just as the rest of the bikers seemed to grasp what was happening. Like a wave, they ran for the bus.

One of the men guarding Jeff ran with them. Jeff wanted to throw a punch at the man holding him by the shoulder, but that tingling feeling was spreading down his arms again, and it felt like his hands were a million miles away. The world was moving around him in slow motion.

But he wasn't frozen. He recognized the opportunity and threw an elbow into the crotch of the guard standing next to him.

The man doubled over with a gut-clearing rush of air, but before his partner could move in to help, Jeff scooped up the fallen guard's gun from the ground, turned, and put a round into the second guard's face.

The sound of the gunshot was lost in the larger roll of gunfire that had erupted at the bus. The bikers had tried to force their way into the door and found it jammed with something. Frustrated there, they had taken to shooting the vehicle with their shotguns and their pistols, and already a thick cloud of smoke was drifting into the square from that direction.

Jeff was lost in the swirl of noise and movement. It was all happening so fast. Somewhere in the back of his head, he thought to himself that this was battle; he was in the midst of a battle. He saw men running, saw their faces distorted into howling masks of teeth and bulging eyes and rippling veins, and it just seemed so insane, so useless.

One of the bikers fired at him. Jeff dropped to a crouch and ran around the gazebo to the cattle truck where the bikers had locked up most of the zombies they'd captured. He scrambled up the ramp, pulled the truck's back doors open, and jumped down into the grass. Glancing over his shoulder, he saw a flash of blood-soaked, rotting faces leering out from inside the truck.

He got to his feet and ran.

Colin was leaning against the gazebo, his face fear stricken. A man with a huge black wound on the side of his face was staggering toward him, his hands outstretched, his eyes milky and vacant.

"Colin," he shouted. "Come on. Move it."

But Colin couldn't move. His will was gone. He just stood there staring at the shambling wreck moving closer. Jeff ran for him. He shoved the zombie and knocked him to the ground, then grabbed Colin by the front of his oxford shirt and pulled him away from the gazebo. There was a black Chevy truck, one of the ones that had guided them into town, parked along the curb on the opposite side of the street, and they ran for it. No one bothered to stop them. Those who weren't shooting up the bus had seen the advancing zombies and were rushing that way to fight them.

Gunfire rolled through the square. Men were running in every direction. Some were injured and screaming for help.

Others were hollering for more ammunition. A few had taken off between the buildings and were running north into the residential part of town.

Jeff managed to get Colin into the cab of the truck and then climbed in after him. The keys were in the ignition, and Jeff thanked God for at least that one small mercy. The truck started up the first time, and Jeff wrestled with the stick shift to get it into gear. His little Honda Accord back home was a stick, but the truck was a more cantankerous vehicle and he had to grind the gears before it finally seated into first.

They started off with a lurch. The wheel was big and hard to control. Plus, Jeff was starting to hallucinate, and the road ahead looked like a writhing carpet of ants where men ran like lunatics through a fog of gun smoke.

But the truck picked up speed. Twenty miles an hour. Thirty.

Beside him, Colin braced against the door. "What the hell are you doing?"

"Keep your head down," Jeff ordered.

He braced himself for impact. The knot of bikers ahead of them was thick, all of them shooting into the sides of the bus. Jeff pointed the truck into the heart of the crowd and mashed down on the gas.

A few of the men turned and saw them coming and managed to jump out of the way, but most never even saw it coming. The truck hit the crowd and it was like suddenly driving off-road as the bodies got sucked down under the front of the truck, the engine straining furiously against the sudden resistance. The wheel turned in Jeff's hand and the truck started to drift sideways. Jeff struggled to regain control but the vehicle was already spinning. They hit the rear of the bus and glanced off, the back end of the truck racing to get ahead of the front as they spun completely out of control.

The truck slid to a stop with the hood pointed back in the

direction they had come from. Bikers were looking at them in shock. Men were on the ground, some dead, some still moving.

The windshield exploded, and glass rained down into Jeff's face and into his lap.

The bikers were shooting at them now.

Jeff got the truck back into gear, popped the clutch, and peeled out, heading right back into the crowd.

This time they were ready for it, and all but two of the bikers were able to get out of the way. Jeff didn't give them a chance to get organized, though. He backed the truck up and hit a biker who was running for the cover of a parked car. Then he pulled forward and drove down another one who was running for the sidewalk.

At the same time, the zombies from the gazebo were entering the street. A few of the bikers had run that way and straight into the arms of the infected.

Their fighting line was broken. Even in his drugged state, Jeff could see most of the remaining bikers were running for the shelter of nearby buildings. He used the confusion to back the truck into the front bumper of the bus.

To Colin, he said, "Go inside and get the girls."

"What?"

"Break out the windshield and get the girls. Hurry, Colin."

Then Jeff climbed out and scanned the bodies on the ground. A few of them had dropped their weapons in the street, and he ran over and picked up a pistol. A bullet hit the pavement next to him and sent up a tiny umbrella of powdered rock and dust, but he couldn't see where the shot had come from.

He turned to Colin and yelled, "Move it, Colin. Hurry."

Colin climbed into the bed of the truck and then through the broken windshield. Jeff could hear him yelling inside. A shot whizzed past his head and this time he could trace it. Gaines was across the street, surrounded by zombies. His men were fighting them, but Gaines was ignoring them, focusing his shots in Jeff's direction instead.

Jeff fired back at him, but missed. It was hard to hold the gun steady. Aiming was impossible. The front sight kept floating off the gun.

"Jeff!"

He turned and saw Colin and the girls climbing through the windshield. Colin was carrying Kyra in his arms like she was a child. Robin had an arm around Katrina's waist and looked like she was supporting most of her weight.

Jeff ran to help them. Colin handed Kyra down to him and Jeff took her weight. Then Colin was beside him, taking Kyra back into his arms. The girl was like a rag doll, no resistance. She could barely hold her head up.

"Is she okay?" Jeff asked. He had to yell to be heard over the gunshots and the screams that were filling the square.

"Unconscious," Colin said. "I don't see any wounds."

"Where are Sarah and Tara?"

"Dead," Colin said.

"What?"

"Shot. Both of them."

Colin steadied Kyra in his arms, then carried her to the passenger seat and helped her inside.

"Jeff!" It was Robin, calling to him from inside the bus. "Behind you."

A man in denim coveralls, his white, chest-length beard crusted and stiff with dried blood, was staggering along the length of the truck. Jeff pulled the revolver from his waist and fired point-blank at the man, hitting him in the chest right below the nape of his throat.

The man fell back against the truck and coughed and gagged, but he didn't go down.

Jeff took aim again, sighting the weapon this time squarely on the man's forehead, and fired. The bullet hit its mark with a loud, wet smack, like a raw steak slapped on the kitchen counter. The man's head jerked back and he tumbled to the street in a motionless heap.

Jeff looked over to the square and tried to find Gaines in the throng of bikers fighting with the zombies, but he couldn't make him out.

He turned back to Robin and took Katrina from her.

"Careful," Robin said. "Her stomach."

The inside of Katrina's shirt was soaked with blood. He could feel it as soon as he touched her. She groaned with the pressure of his hands on her midsection, but she didn't cry out. *In shock, probably,* he thought.

Her head lolled onto his shoulder and he could hear her breathing, a wet, raspy sound mixed with whimpers of pain.

"Easy," he said. "I got you."

"Here," Robin said, jumping down into the bed of the truck beside him. "I'll take her."

Robin put her arms around Katrina and slowly lowered her down to the bed. She turned so her back was against the cab wall and pulled Katrina into her lap, cradling her as best she could.

"Get us out of here, Jeff," she said.

Jeff jumped out of the bed and climbed behind the wheel.

"Everybody hold on," he yelled.

He got the truck in gear and mashed down on the gas. The back tires chirped on the asphalt and the truck leaped forward. In front of them was a knot of people, both bikers and infected. Those bikers lucky enough to find an opening through the infected were running for their lives, while others not so lucky had resorted to hand-to-hand fighting, using anything they could to fend off the zombies.

Jeff scanned the crowd as they accelerated, looking for Gaines. He saw him running toward the street from the gazebo, on an intercept course with Jeff and the others.

Jeff jogged the wheel to the right and went up on the curb.

He was aiming right for Gaines, mowing down bikers and zombies alike when they couldn't get out of the way.

Gaines stopped running and pulled his pistol.

He took slow, measured aim at the approaching truck and fired.

The rear windshield behind Jeff's head exploded, and Jeff instinctively veered to his left. More bodies disappeared beneath the front of the truck and the vehicle bounced over them before landing back in the street and straightening out.

As they sped away, Jeff looked back at Gaines. Gaines was standing in the middle of the crowd, zombies all around him, though he didn't give them even a passing glance. Instead, he leveled his pistol again and fired at the truck.

Robin screamed.

Jeff immediately hit the brakes and looked back. Robin's face was splattered with blood. Beside her, Katrina's head was blasted open on one side, a yellowish-gray mass of tissue visible through the huge hole in her skull.

Another shot hit the roof next to Jeff's face.

Colin said, "Go, go, go!"

Jeff took one last look behind him, saw Gaines standing there with the gun in his hand, and stepped on the gas.

Three hours later, Jeff pulled to the side of the road. Colin was still holding Kyra as tightly as ever, and Jeff wasn't sure who was comforting whom. But he couldn't drive anymore. The acid was coursing through him stronger than ever, and the road was moving like a living thing. He got out of the truck and went to the back. Robin was still there, holding Katrina in her arms, stroking the corpse's blood-matted hair. She hadn't wiped the blood from her own face, and when she rolled her eyes in Jeff's direction, the whites stood out in stark contrast to the rest of her face.

"We should bury her," he said.

Robin pulled Katrina closer to her and stared at him.

"I can do it," he said. "If you want me to."

"No," she said. Her voice was a hoarse whisper. "No, I'll help."

Together, working silently, they lowered Katrina's body from the truck, took a shovel from behind the driver's seat, and headed off into the brush. They followed a trail to the top of a small rise and stood, side by side, looking down over a desert landscape silvered with moonlight.

"Do you like this place?" he asked.

She nodded. He could hear her sniffling.

Two hours later, the grave was finished. It wasn't deep, but it would do.

Jeff took off his shoelaces and used them to lash two sticks together into a cross. Then he hammered it into the ground at the head of the grave and stepped back.

Robin muttered, "I love you, baby," and knelt forward and kissed the cross.

Then she took Jeff's hand and together they walked back to the truck.

Colin and Kyra were waiting there, standing outside the truck. Colin turned when he heard them coming down from the trail and he motioned them over.

He was staring up at a green highway sign that announced the Guadalupe Mountains National Park thirty miles ahead. Somebody had written over the sign in white paint.

WE ARE GOING TO THE CEDAR RIVERS
NATIONAL GRASSLANDS NORTH DAKOTA
JOIN US

"What do you think?" Colin said.

He turned to the others. Jeff turned away from the sign. Something about those letters, the strong, confident brushstrokes, tugged at him. Finding them out here in the middle of nowhere, and at a point when he stopped because he couldn't make himself drive any farther—it felt like some kind of sign. A shot in the arm when they needed it most. Like it was meant to be. He raised an eyebrow at Robin.

She closed her eyes, lowered her head, and nodded.

And just like that, it was decided.

"Let's find a map," Jeff said.

CHAPTER 36

Athens, Texas, was just like all the other small towns they'd gone through. Lots of trees. Lots of sun-baked asphalt. Not a hill in sight.

Ben Richardson was tired. His eyes hurt from the sun reflecting off the road. He'd been walking all morning, dragging himself along, keeping a weary eye on the little houses and buildings they passed, and trying not to breathe too deeply whenever they passed the dead rotting in the sun on the side of the road. Ahead of them, about a quarter mile down Garrison Street from where he stood, was a shabby, redbrick building with a sign out front advertising it as Lewis & Sons Mercantile. Garrison Street curved right around the other side of that building, and Barnes, who was walking point as usual, had already turned the corner.

Richardson stopped, cradling his rifle in his arms like a baby, and drank most of a bottled water in one gulp. Every stitch of clothing he owned was crusty from dried sweat, and he was pretty sure he was developing shin splints. There was a pain in his legs that ran from the bottom of his kneecaps all the way to his toes. He put the cap back on the water and found it difficult to muster the will to keep walking.

And then he heard yelling coming from the front of the caravan. He groaned inwardly. He was tired of zombies, tired of fighting. That part inside him that used to hum with fear at the sight of them had gone numb. But he knew his job. As rear guard, it was his responsibility to make sure they had a place to retreat to if they needed it. He spun around and scanned the street, already considering the buildings for the shelter they might offer and the streets for the easy, fast getaway.

But something was different this time. It took him a moment to realize it, but when he did, he looked back over his shoulder and saw people running toward the redbrick building. They were jumping up and down, waving their arms in the air. He saw people laughing.

"What in the hell?" he said.

Sandra Tellez and Clint Siefer were in the bed of a truck up ahead, tending to a woman who had broken her ankle the week before.

Sandra stood up and watched the scene over the cab of the truck, then looked back at Richardson.

"What's going on?" she asked.

He shrugged.

Tired as he was, he broke into a trot. He rounded the corner next to Lewis & Sons Mercantile and stopped. He lowered his rifle and stood there with his mouth agape.

"Can you believe it?" a man next to him said. He was laughing, and he gave Richardson a playful push.

Richardson smiled.

Ahead of them, five, maybe six hundred feet up the road, was an immense parking lot full of brightly painted recreational vehicles.

"Are those Winnebagos?" a woman asked.

"No way," said the man who had pushed Richardson. "Those are Fleetwoods, top of the line. Even the cheap ones cost more than our house did."

Excited people pushed their way past Richardson. He stood there, letting himself get jostled.

He said, "Sweet Jesus. No more walking."

Then he let out a yell and started running.

Richardson was thumbing through a brochure for the Fleetwood Revolution LE, the stripped-down, no-frills edition starting at $289,600, when he stepped onboard one of the demo models.

The brochure slipped from his fingers.

"Holy hell," he said.

Sandra Tellez was sitting next to Clint on a white leather couch, giggling like a six-year-old little girl. Barnes was seated in the driver's seat, checking out the exterior cameras and nodding with grudging admiration.

"Pretty respectable," he said.

Richardson thought the living room looked like a cross between a luxury private jet and the Playboy mansion. The floors were tiled. The leather furniture looked like fluffy white clouds. Recessed lighting ran the length of the ceiling. The kitchenette, directly across from where Sandra was sitting, was done up with stainless-steel Viking appliances. There was rich mahogany wood trim everywhere.

"You gotta see the shower," Sandra said.

"There's a shower?"

She nodded toward the back. Curious, he walked that way, slipped through a doorway, and nearly cried. In front of him was a bedroom the likes of which he had only seen in television shows about the rich and famous. The shower that Sandra had referred to was to his right, and it did bring tears to his eyes. Oh God, how he yearned for a shower.

From the brochure, he knew this thing had a washer and dryer, too. What a joy that would be. Clean clothes, a hot shower, a meal cooked on a real stove.

He dropped down into a chair in the corner and just stared at the room.

"Well," said Barnes from behind him. "What do you think?"

Richardson looked up at him.

"You want to know what I think?" he said. "I think I can't wait to brush my teeth."

From the notebooks of Ben Richardson

Waurika, Oklahoma: August 22nd, 4:38 P.M.

Thank the lord, we finally made it out of Texas. Thank the lord. I could hear the cheering from the other RVs even as we were driving down the road . . .

Chickasha, Oklahoma: August 23rd, 3:50 A.M.

Drunker than Cooter Brown tonight and feeling pretty damn good about it.

We pulled into Chickasha earlier today and found a liquor store. These RVs have got ice makers on board, so, yeah, I made vodka martinis for everybody on our RV.

I don't know how many I had. A bunch.

So, something a little lighter for the old notebooks tonight.

We've been on the road for a couple of weeks now, and we've seen a lot of infected wandering the roadways. One of the things I've seen quite a bit of is something I call the walking epitaph, people clipping little signs to their chest to let the rest of us know who they are, and maybe to give us a little glimpse of who they were in their uninfected life.

I suppose the epitaphs were inevitable, really. Nobody wants to be forgotten. We've all seen how the necrosis filovirus robs its victims of their sense of self. It only seems natural to want to hold on to a piece of who we are for as long as possible. I can't blame anybody for that.

The quality of the poetry—and I've noticed that it's almost always poetry of some sort—is fairly uneven. But the humor is consistent, and I think that our need to poke fun at death speaks volumes about us as a species. I guess I'm not the only one who does his best work with a deadline.

Here are just a few of the epitaphs I've seen. They're not the best. Not by any means. But they all struck me as special when I saw them, and that's why I'm recording them here.

This walking corpse is Marvin Reece's.
Have mercy on my soul, dear Jesus,
Just like I'd do if I was you, Jesus,
And you was this corpse of Reece's.

* * *

Poor Jamie O'Dell, she's gone away,
Got sick and rose that very same day.
She had a fever and a hacking cough,
But her legs still managed to carry her off.

* * *

This is the body of Margaret Pound
Whose mind went missing and was never found.

And then there is a subset of these epitaphs that almost read like permission slips to the reader to kill the wearer.

Burn me up or cut me down,
Either way is fine;
Just make it quick
And make it stick.
Fuck you, World,
Signing off, Alex Mentick.

* * *

This is the body of William Bunn
Who would like to be killed by a gun.
Really, his name was not Bunn, but Hood,
But Hood wouldn't rhyme with gun, and Bunn would.

* * *

I'm the dentist John Hannity
And it seems I've met with calamity.
Please dispatch me with some gravity
As I'm eager to die and fill my last cavity.

* * *

Take your best shot at Mrs. Annabelle Bostich.
She was my landlady and a mean old witch.
Go ahead—
I asked around; they won't miss the bitch.

* * *

I tried to die in bed.
I got up and walked around instead.
Kill me or I'll kill you
Before this mess is through.
Love always, Debbie Shue.

Well, that's it for tonight. God, I'm gonna have a head-splitter in the morning.

Nearly five hundred miles away, just outside Dalhart, Texas, a man on a motorcycle pulled to the side of the road and stared at a pickup parked under the awning of a Valero gas station. The truck's back windshield had been shot out. There were bullet holes in the tailgate. The Harley burbled noisily in the hot, dusty night air. Randall Gaines killed the motor and stepped from the bike.

There was no other sound save for the echo of his worn boot heels clicking on the asphalt.

He looked into the bed of the truck and saw blood everywhere.

“Hello,” Gaines said.

He walked around the truck to the hood and put his hand on it. It was warmer than the night air, but no longer hot. No more than an hour gone, he guessed.

“But where did you go, Harvard? That’s the question I want answered.”

He opened the driver’s door and looked inside. He saw candy bar wrappers and cigarettes and crumpled pieces of paper.

And something else.

A map.

He opened it and saw the United States. His gaze drifted over the states until he came to a thin penciled circle around the Cedar River National Grasslands in North Dakota.

A straight shot up Highway 83, he realized.

He folded the map and slid it into the back pocket of his jeans. Then, whistling, he slowly made his way back to his bike.

Chapter 37

"There's nothing on the radio."

Billy Kline hit the radio's Seek button and watched the numbers speed all the way through the FM band without stopping.

"I can't believe this. You'd think we'd at least be able to find one of those automated BOB or JACK stations. There's fucking nothing on."

Billy caught himself.

"Sorry, Ed."

Ed shook his head. "You're not gonna find anything. Except maybe one of those radio preachers on the AM stations, and I don't want to listen to that. Might do you some good, though."

"You think so, huh?"

Ed shrugged, smiled.

"You're a funny guy, you know that?"

"Yeah, I've been told that."

Outside the car, the Kansas prairie went on forever, flat and gray. They'd been driving the entire day, stopping only for bathroom breaks (Randy and Billy both had to go nearly every thirty minutes, it seemed) and to raid the occasional gas station for candy bars and bottled waters. They went through town after town, all of them dead, bodies in the streets, the infected wandering around houses that were empty and ominous in their desolation. But now, after thirty hours of driving across the prairie, the emptiness was starting to give way to farmhouses and outbuildings again. They saw chickens pecking the dirt in machinery-choked yards. They saw swings on rusted jungle gyms dangling listlessly in the breeze. Here and there, they passed faded billboards advertising colas and gas stations.

"We're gonna need to find a place to rest for the night here pretty soon," Ed said. He pushed the brim of his cowboy hat up with his thumb and pinched the bridge of his nose.

"You okay to drive?" Billy asked. "I can take over."

"No, I got it. It's the road. Straight and flat and monotonous, you know? Gets you exhausted."

"Yeah. Emporia's up here another ten miles or so. Maybe we can find a place there."

They entered Emporia a few minutes later. A 30-mile-per-hour speed limit sign marked the change from highway to Main Street. They crossed Elm Street, then Oaklawn Street, and pulled up on the town square. Houses lined Main Street on either side. They were plain, wooden structures with covered front porches and small lawns that looked untrimmed and shaggy. There were bodies here and there, faceup in the street. They passed an infected man near the corner of Main and Birch wearing nothing but a bloody T-shirt and soiled boxer shorts. He turned on his heel and stumbled toward them, but he was too far away to be a threat and Ed didn't even bother to accelerate.

"Man, you could smell that guy from here," Billy said.

"Yeah, they don't have the ability to take care of themselves, you know? They still have to do all the things anybody else has got to do, like going to the bathroom and stuff, but they're not aware enough to take care of it. They just sort of go whenever. It's a wonder to me that more of them don't get sick and die from some kind of disease."

"A lot of 'em do," Billy said. "I read about it in *Discover Magazine*. They did some studies in San Antonio and found that most of them have got worms and all kinds of nasty stuff. The article said the average life span for an infected person is about two weeks."

"Really? They die that fast?"

"Most do. Some'll live for years, of course. But most die pretty fast."

Ed turned the van onto Chestnut Street and headed west. He said, "You've done a lot of reading on the infected, haven't you?"

"There isn't a whole lot else to do when your ass is rotting in jail."

Ed raised an eyebrow at him.

"What? I can't say ass? Come on."

Ed slowed the van to a stop.

"What's up?" Billy asked. "You're not gonna beat me up again, are you?"

"No." Ed turned to the others and said, "Who here wants to go shopping?"

"Shopping?" Billy said. "Where?"

Ed pointed out the windshield at Costco down the block. "Right there."

"Badass," Billy said, and flinched. "Sorry. But man, I love Costco."

Randall Gaines had been riding all day, too. His clothes were matted with sweat and filthy from the dust blowing off the Kansas prairies. He was sitting in a barber's chair at the corner of Chestnut and 3rd Street, a cooler full of Budweiser on the ground at his feet, watching a white Ford Econoline pull into the Costco parking lot across the street. It was the first vehicle he'd seen driving around in a day and a half, and he felt a momentary thrill of anticipation as it stopped and the doors opened.

He leaned forward in his chair, eager as a kid at Christmas, waiting to see if Harvard would step out of the van.

But when an old man in a cowboy hat, a couple of old women, some kids, and a young, Jewish-looking guy stepped out of the van, he fell back into the chair and muttered, "Well, shit."

He watched them as they stretched and milled about the van. The young Jewish-looking guy carried himself like a swinging dick, might even have done some time. And the dude in the cowboy hat looked like he thought he was Paul Newman or something, but the others were nothing.

Randall Gaines lost interest in them fast. He took another big gulp of his Budweiser and got comfortable. Maybe he could even take a nap before he got going again.

He was about to drift off when another vehicle pulled into the lot.

"Hello," he said, perking up immediately.

It was a glistening, maroon F-350 pickup. A crewcab, four-door model. Dark tinted windows. Oversized, off-road tires. The King Ranch Edition.

"Traveling in style," Gaines said. "Nice."

The pickup coasted up to the front of the store and parked about fifty feet from the white van. The old folks from the van watched it, the young guy and the clown in the cowboy hat trading apprehensive looks.

The doors opened, and Gaines leaned forward again without even realizing he was doing it.

"Come on. Who are you?"

Four people got out, two men and two women. One of the women was a brunette with a body that could have made a dead man stand at attention, but Gaines wasn't looking at her.

He was looking at Harvard.

"Holy shit," he said, and drained the rest of his beer. "Looks like we gonna have us a party after all."

He reached down into the cooler and pulled out a .45 semi-automatic pistol.

"Colin?"

A woman's voice. To Billy's ears, she sounded young, pretty. He rounded the corner, hoping to see the hot brunette that looked so familiar—though he still couldn't place her, an actress maybe—and instead saw the slender, dark-haired girl. The blind one.

She was standing in the middle of the aisle, looking lost.

She stiffened when she heard his feet clicking on the linoleum. "Colin?"

"Uh, no," he said. "My name's Billy Kline. I'm with that group you met out front."

She half turned from him, like she might take off running if he so much as breathed wrong.

"I'm sorry if I frightened you," he said.

"You didn't frighten me."

He heard the West Texas drawl in her voice and liked it right away. It fit her, a country girl. But he didn't believe her when she said he hadn't frightened her. The way she hugged her arms around her chest made him feel like a monster.

"Glad to hear it," he said.

"I was looking for Colin. Have you seen him? He's the one with the real short hair."

"No, sorry, I haven't seen him. Is he your boyfriend?"

"He's a friend."

"Oh, well, that's good."

She frowned. "What's that supposed to mean?"

"Uh, nothing," he said. "I'm sorry. I just, you know, when you meet a pretty girl and, well, you find out she doesn't have a boyfriend, it's . . ."

She unfolded her arms from around her chest and put a hand on her hip and cocked the hip to one side.

"It's what?"

One of the guys from the fancy pickup truck trotted around the corner and stopped when he saw the two of them together.

Billy nodded at him.

He said, "I think this is Colin behind you."

The girl turned and said, "Colin?"

"Yeah, Kyra, I'm here." He came up next to her and took her hand in his. He said, "Everything okay?"

"Everything's fine," Billy said.

Kyra didn't say anything.

"Kyra, you okay?"

She nodded. "Colin, where'd you go?"

"I was looking at the canned chili, and when I turned around, you weren't there." He put a hand on the small of her back like he meant to lead her away. "Come on, we found some good stuff over here."

"Okay."

She let Colin turn her around, but then she stopped and turned back to Billy. "It was nice to meet you, Billy." And then she smiled. It was a nice smile.

He gave one back to her, making it a point to avoid the glare from Colin standing beside her.

"Here, zombie zombie. Come here, girl."

Randall Gaines was standing on the edge of a loading dock behind the local high school. In his hands he held a pool skimmer that he'd fitted with a length of rope that looped out at the far end into a makeshift dog handler's pole.

The zombie shambled closer. She was barefoot, leaving a path of mud and blood on the white concrete. Her clothes were little more than rags now. She had the look of starvation about her, her skin saggy on her bones from recent, dramatic weight loss. There were open sores on her face and arms and a huge gash across her right cheek that might have been caused by fingernails. She smelled of rotting meat and defecation.

"Thatta girl," Gaines said. "Come to daddy. You know you want it."

The zombie raised her arms and let out a stuttering moan. She staggered closer, closer, and Gaines extended the pole, waiting to drop the loop of rope around her neck.

"Closer now. Come on, come on."

Gaines swatted her hand out of the way with the pole, then gave the pole a quick flick to open up the loop of rope. It slid over the woman's head and fell down around her shoulders.

He yanked on the pole and the rope tightened.

"Gotcha," he said.

The woman started to choke, but she never stopped reaching for him. Slowly, careful to keep her on her feet, Gaines walked to the bottom of the ramp upon which he stood and began the slow, tedious process of turning the zombie around and guiding her onto the ramp. At the far end was the three-axle produce truck he'd found on a farm just outside town. It had taken some doing, but eventually he'd managed to lure eight zombies into his trap. Stinky girl here was his final catch of the day.

She was trying to turn around and grab him, but Gaines wouldn't let her. She snarled and snapped at him, but for all her fighting, he managed to get her to the end of the ramp without too much effort. Then he positioned her at the edge of the ramp, just above the open bed of the produce truck where the other seven zombies waited, moaning and reaching skyward for him, and pushed her over.

She fell face-first into the bed of the truck, not even aware enough to try to break her fall. She crashed into three other zombies and sent them all tumbling into the railing. The woman caught her chin on the slat and Gaines heard something crunch.

"Ouch," he said.

While she was down, he released the loop from around her neck. A moment later, with her jaw askew in a nasty break, she was on her feet, reaching for him.

"Okay," he said. "That's it. Time to go, folks."

He jumped down from the edge of the ramp and climbed behind the wheel of the truck.

Fifteen minutes later he was pulling into a spot near a farmhouse at the edge of town. He could see the white van and the pickup parked in the driveway near the front door. The windows were lit from the inside with the soft orange glow of candlelight.

It looked so sweet and peaceful he wanted to vomit.

"Okay, Harvard," he said. "Time to party."

CHAPTER 38

There wasn't a table big enough for all of them to sit down, so some of them had to eat standing up, their plates on the kitchen counter. Nobody seemed to mind, though. It was a party, and they were all feeling good.

The wine helped, Billy thought.

They'd found the good stuff at Costco and brought home three cases of it. He'd never cared for wine, but then, he reminded himself, he'd never had wine like this. The stuff in a box was no match for this fancy French shit he couldn't even pronounce.

They'd also brought back a ton of food—and Margaret O'Brien and Jeff Stavers immediately found in each other kindred spirits of the kitchen. They made a huge meal of buttermilk fried chicken and biscuits with sweet cream butter and honey, oven-roasted rosemary fingerling potatoes, and steamed broccoli with a butter, white wine, and shallot reduction. They had loads of potato chips and pretzels and bread. And for dessert there was a raspberry-chocolate-and whipped-cream swirl.

Their plates were piled high, their faces shining with the promise of the first real meal any of them had had in over a week. Billy and Ed both had pieces of chicken halfway to their mouths when Kyra suddenly stood up and bowed her head.

"Dear Lord," she said, and though she spoke quietly, her opening words managed to make everyone go silent. "There is so much we do not understand. So much has happened, and so many good people have died. Everyone here has wondered why these things had to happen. We mourn for the lives we had and the comforts that are gone. We wonder if we are lost forever. But in your mercy you have given us each other. We give thanks, Lord, for bringing us together with these fellow travelers who share our destination. We give thanks, Lord, for their company and the strength they bring us and for the bounty you have set before us tonight. Please, bless this food, and bless each of us in the time to come. In your name we pray. Amen."

A very sober round of Amen answered her.

It was at that point, while looking around the kitchen at the others, that Billy realized he was in the middle of his first real Thanksgiving dinner.

They even had a kids' table. Robin Tharp, the incredibly beautiful brunette who Billy was certain he recognized from somewhere, had taken an instant shine to the two kids, and they to her. She was sitting at their table now, making them giggle over something.

The sound of their laughter was contagious, and it spread smiles around the room.

The wine started flowing.

But it wasn't the food or the good spirits or even the sense of security he had here with these people that convinced him he was having his first real Thanksgiving dinner. He looked across the kitchen at Kyra and saw her cover her mouth with her hand as she laughed at something Colin had said, and he realized that this dinner was different because it was the first time in his life that he was truly thankful for the skin he lived in.

"So what do you think of the old-timers?" Colin asked.

Kyra said, "I like Ed. And Margaret's sweet."

"Yeah, Ed's cool. Did you hear him say he used to be a federal marshal? Those guys are hardcore."

"I like the way he tips his hat at me when he says hello."

That stopped Colin. "Wait a minute," he said. "How did you know he wears a hat? And how did you know he tips it when he says hello?"

She laughed, a bubbly sound.

"You forget where I grew up," she said. "He's a West Texas cowboy. I've known men like him all my life. They're all a bunch of crazy rednecks, but they'll always tip their hats to the ladies."

He shook his head in admiration. "Yeah, well," he said. "I don't know much about West Texas, but I do know it gave you the cutest accent I think I've ever heard."

She blushed. "I think I'm a little drunk," she admitted.

"You're doing fine," he said.

They stumbled. He caught her, and her giggling dried up.

Colin leaned against the wall, his arm around her waist. She felt good in his arms, like she belonged there, and he didn't want to let her go. She turned her hips in his arm so that her belly was against his. He could feel her breasts pushing against him, small, but firm, the nipples erect.

He leaned in to kiss her. She backed away with a gasp, but then slowly came back and touched her lips to his.

She was trembling.

He said, "Where are you gonna spend the night?"

Her breath was sweet from the wine. "Colin, I've never—It's always been so scary for me."

"I want you to come to my room," he said.

"Colin, I—"

He silenced her with a kiss. "Come to my room with me."

She nodded, her hair falling over her face. He brushed it aside with his fingertips and kissed her again. Then, leading her by the hand, he took her down the hallway to his room. The house was old, and they could hear the wind howling outside and the sounds of the others coming from different parts of the house. Kyra was still trembling. Colin found it incredibly exciting. He was sweating. He could feel it under his shirt and on his face.

But when they reached his door he stopped and let her hand go.

"Colin?" she said.

"What the hell?"

"Colin, what's wrong?"

He stood there, looking at the wall. There had been an old black-and-white picture of the family who used to live here on the wall. It was smashed now on the hardwood floor. In its place, in large white letters, somebody had written AS SOON AS LIBERTY IS COMPLETE IT DIES IN ANARCHY.

"Colin?"

"Hold on," he said. He went down to the next door, Jeff's door. He pounded on it with the side of his fist until Jeff opened. He was wearing a white T-shirt and boxers. Behind him, in a long white T-shirt, was Robin.

"Colin, what's going on?"

Colin grabbed him by the shirt and pulled him out into the hallway.

"Hey, what the hell?" Jeff said, slapping Colin's hand away. But he didn't say anything else. He saw the writing on the wall and stared at it.

"What does that mean?" Colin said.

Jeff leaned back against the wall and wiped a hand over his face.

"Jeff?"

"It means we're fucked, Colin."

Downstairs, Ed Moore finished off the last of his wine and started back to his bedroom. He had a three-week-old copy of the *Chicago Tribune* under his arm, and he was looking forward to reading in bed.

A door thudded closed from somewhere down the hall. It was dark and he couldn't see very far into the gloom, but the sound stirred something inside him.

It was probably one of the others, he told himself. Margaret and the kids had taken the master bedroom at the far end of the hall. Julie and Barbie had taken a smaller bedroom that shared a bathroom with the master, while he and Billy were sharing the office across the hall from the master. But something didn't feel right. The alarms in his head were ringing full tilt.

He set the paper down on the edge of the couch and started walking down the hall. In the dim light, he saw the outline of a man rounding the corner that led to the bedrooms.

"Billy?"

The man disappeared around the corner without saying a word.

A moment later, Ed heard a scream.

Ed rounded the corner at a full sprint and ran right into the back of a zombie. The impact sent the zombie sprawling face-first onto the floor of the master bedroom. Beyond him, deeper in the room, Margaret O'Brien was standing in front of her grandkids, trying to shelter them from another zombie that was already in the room. Margaret had a wooden chair in her hands and she was brandishing it like one of P. T. Barnum's lion tamers.

Off to his right, Julie and Barbie were dealing with trouble of their own. A female zombie in ragged clothes was staggering toward them, pushing them back toward the far corner of the room. Barbie was standing in the middle of the room, babbling happily at the approaching zombie, while Julie was pulling on her arm, trying to get her to move.

"Ed," she shouted. "For God's sake, help us."

He was stuck. His guns were in his room, locked up. Without them, he knew he could save one set of friends, but not the other.

"Ed!"

"Would somebody please tell me what's going on?" Kyra said.

Colin took her hand and looked at Jeff. Robin came out of the bedroom. She was wearing her jeans now. She looked at the writing on the wall and her eyes grew large.

"Jeff, what is that?"

"It's Gaines," he said.

"Gaines? You mean the biker from Van Horn? The one who killed . . ."

He nodded.

"But that's impossible. How could he have found us?"

"I don't know," Jeff said. "This is him, though. That's what he said to me right before he threw me into the cage."

"What does it mean?" Colin asked.

"Yeah, Harvard, why don't you tell him? I've come a long way to hear your answer to that question."

Jeff turned around and saw Gaines leaning against the wall, a toothpick in his mouth. The man was covered head to foot in dust. It rained down off his clothes with every movement, however slight. There were dark, damp circles around his eyes.

"What's wrong, Harvard?" he said. "No witty retort?"

Colin was backing up, away from Gaines. He let out a

high-pitched, almost girlish squeak of a scream. At the same time, a chorus of groans erupted from around the corner. The smell hit Jeff right afterward. So did the sound of feet dragging across the wooden floor.

Colin dropped Kyra's hand. Fear gripped him instantly, and he fell backward against the wall.

"No," he said. "No, please, stay away."

And the next instant, he scrambled past Kyra, pushed his way past Jeff, and ran screaming into his room.

The zombies rounded the corner.

Kyra moved her head from side to side, like she was trying to locate the source of the moaning—but in the narrow confines of the hallway, that was impossible.

A zombie closed on her.

Jeff lunged forward, caught her by the arm, and pulled her back from the corner just as the zombie collapsed against the wall where she had been standing.

He turned, expecting to see Gaines blocking the hallway, but instead saw nothing but a clear shot to the stairs. Still holding onto Kyra's hand, he motioned to Robin, and together they pulled Kyra toward the stairs.

"What about Colin?" Kyra said.

Jeff looked behind them. There were four zombies in the hallway now, moving past Colin's door.

"There isn't time," he said. "Come on."

She fought them. She screamed that she wouldn't leave without Colin. Jeff caught her fingernails across his cheek and gasped in pain. But he didn't let go of her. With her fingers clawing for his eyes, he managed to get an arm around her and he half pushed, half carried her down the stairs.

Ed made his decision in a snap.

The zombie he'd pushed to the floor was still trying to get up. He didn't give it a chance to do so. He hustled forward, stopping next to the zombie's shoulder, and brought his boot heel down on the back of the zombie's neck. There was a fierce snap, and the zombie lay still.

Margaret swung the chair she'd been holding and hit the second zombie in the shoulder, knocking him off balance, but not to the ground.

Ed grabbed the zombie by the back of his soiled shirt and slung him toward the bed. The zombie went tumbling over the bed and landed head-first in the gap between the bed and the wall.

"Come on," he said, holding out his hand to Margaret.

They ran out into the hallway. Ed turned off at Julie and Barbie's room and saw the zombie had already pulled Barbie to the ground. He was on top of her, his fingernails digging into her arms, his teeth snapping at the wrinkled folds of her neck.

He saw Barbie rolling with terror. Alzheimer's or not, she was aware enough to know the thing on top of her was trying to kill her. The zombie got his teeth on her neck and she let out a terrible scream that seemed to shake the whole house.

Ed could feel his blood run cold.

He stepped forward and grabbed the zombie by the hair on the back of its head and yanked it away from Barbie. The zombie felt as stiff as a piece of furniture in his hands. He reached forward and cupped a hand under the zombie's jaw. Then, before the thing had a chance to scratch at him, he twisted as hard as he could, snapping the zombie's neck.

Instantly, the body went limp, and he threw it to the side.

Barbie was on the ground, looking up at him, gasping and coughing. Dark blood filled her mouth and stained her teeth.

Beyond her, Julie was staring at Barbie in horror. Slowly, her eyes came up and she met Ed's gaze.

He looked away.

* * *

Jeff and Robin managed to get Kyra to the bottom of the stairs. She was screaming for Colin, still fighting them with everything she had, completely unwilling to listen to what they were telling her.

There was a moaning at the top of the stairs.

Jeff glanced up and saw the first zombie step off the top stair. She lost her balance and rolled halfway down the stairs, then rose and extended a gray and freshly broken hand toward them.

Jeff grabbed Kyra by the shoulders and shook her. "Stop fighting me," he said. "They're coming down the stairs, Kyra. We can't go up there."

"What about Colin?"

"We can't go up there." He turned to Robin. "We need to get to the truck," he said. "We've got to get out of here."

She nodded.

Kyra started to object again, but Gaines's voice cut her off.

"Jesus, Harvard. You're some friend, ain't you? Leaving a man behind like that. Of course I don't think less of you for it. I'm just pleased you're coming around to my point of view."

"What view is that?" Jeff said.

Gaines smiled graciously. "You mean to tell me you don't know by now? Harvard, how come you can be such a dumb-ass? It's what I've been trying to tell you all along. There ain't no man, and there ain't no institution or religion or idea that's worth a man's loyalty. You give something or some-body loyalty, and you give up your liberty. And you know me, Harvard. Liberty's everything to me."

Then he turned to Robin and put a hand on her chin.

"Of course, right about now, my dick's thinking it's pretty damn excited to be sharing the end of the world with the hottest porn star of all time. Ms. Blaze, I've seen what that pretty mouth of yours can do. If there's a person anywhere who could make me give up a little liberty, I bet it might be you."

She pulled away from his grip. "You're trash, Gaines."

"Maybe so. But hey, you've fucked worse, right?"

Jeff threw a huge right-handed haymaker at Gaines's face. Gaines ducked it, came up fast with a hard right jab to Jeff's gut, doubling him over—then brought his knee up to meet Jeff's mouth and nose on their way down.

Jeff's head snapped back and for a moment he couldn't see. The world was a swimming blur of purple. He tried to keep his feet, but everything was spinning, and he tilted to the side and fell over the edge of the couch.

Gaines laughed as Jeff fell.

Jeff rolled over onto his back. Gaines stood over him, a blurry mass. He barely saw the fist coming down on his nose. There was an intensely bright explosion of pain, and a moment later, he was out.

Gaines watched Harvard slump to the floor like a wet towel. Then he turned to the blind girl and Bellamy Blaze. But mostly Bellamy Blaze. *Imagine that*, he thought. *Of all the fucking luck!* Who'd have thought he'd have this for a reward? He was getting hard just thinking of the things he was gonna do with that girl.

But first things first. The zombies were nearly at the bottom of the stairs, and he still had the other folks to deal with. After that, after the others were out of the way, then he'd have some fun with Ms. Bellamy Blaze here.

Still, there was time for a little feel.

"Do that look you do for me," he said. "You know that one where you put your finger to your mouth and look all innocent, like you don't know if you're gonna be able to take the whole thing. I love that look."

"Fuck you."

"Oh, you're gonna do plenty of that, girl. Don't you worry about—"

Something hit him hard from behind and sent him sprawling into the banister. He felt a man wrapping him up, trying to get a grip on the back of his head. Gaines ducked down and grabbed the man's foot and yanked it up as hard as he could. The female zombie was right above him now, the others a few steps above her, but he ignored them. He wheeled around and saw the young Jewish-looking kid who had rode in with the old folks.

"You wanna play, too, huh? Okay, come on."

He advanced on Billy, who scrambled to his feet just as Gaines closed on him. Billy threw a hard left jab and managed to connect with Gaines's chin.

Gaines's head snapped back, but he wasn't hurt.

He looked at Billy and smiled.

"That all you got?"

He came at Billy and feinted with a left jab. Billy put up an arm to block the punch—but it never came. Instead, Gaines swept Billy's feet out from under him, dropping him onto his butt on the hardwood floor.

The next instant, Gaines was on him. There was no time to react. One after another, Gaines pounded short, hammer-like right jabs into Billy's face. Blood flew in the air, splattering the floor and the walls. Billy fell limp under the blows, but they continued just the same.

When Gaines stopped and looked up, he saw Bellamy Blaze pushing two of the zombies away from Harvard.

So that was the score, was it? Bellamy Blaze was giving it away for free to Harvard.

Well, fuck. We'll just have to see about that.

And he was right about to do just that when the old dude in the cowboy hat walked in.

* * *

Ed took in the scene right away.

Billy Kline beat to shit on the floor, blood everywhere.

Jeff Stavers and Robin were over by the couch, the girl trying to pull her boyfriend to safety from the zombies coming down the stairs.

Then he saw Gaines.

He reached for his gun, but Gaines was on his feet already and coming at him with a left hook.

Ed moved back, stepped right. The left hook went wide, and Ed came up behind Gaines.

Ed slapped him in the ear.

Gaines, his head ringing from the slap, turned around in time to get four hard left jabs in the mouth. He fell back against the wall, stunned. His head lolled on his shoulders. He sagged noticeably, like his legs had grown suddenly weak.

Gaines touched his fingers to his pulverized lips and said, "Holy shit, old man."

He leaped forward then, leading with his right.

Ed ducked under the punch and hit Gaines in the solar plexus. Gaines fell to one knee. He reached up and tried to grab at Ed's shirt, but Ed hit him again, dropping him to the floor.

Behind him, Robin screamed.

She had a zombie on either side of her, closing fast. Jeff Stavers was nearly comatose in her arms. She was bent under his weight, trying to move out of the way, but running out of room fast.

Ed closed the distance between them, pulled his pistols, and fired. The zombies on either side of Robin were knocked backward with two perfect head shots, and she was left standing there, panting in fear but untouched.

"You okay?" he said.

Robin nodded.

Ed turned and fired left-handed at the two remaining zombies. One of them flipped backward over the stair rail. The other staggered forward and landed facedown on the floor.

"Ed, behind you!" Robin shouted.

Gaines was getting to his feet. There was a nickel-plated .45 semiautomatic in his hand. Ed saw the flash of it coming up and behind it Gaines's wild eyes, and he reacted. He fired both guns, emptying them into Gaines, then went over and kicked the nickel-plated pimp gun from Gaines's lifeless hand.

"Anybody see anymore zombies," he said, as he opened the cylinders on his pistols and emptied the shell casings onto the floor.

"Colin's upstairs," Kyra said.

Ed turned to the blind girl as he fed a speed loader into each pistol. "Was he bit?"

"I don't think so," Robin said. "He went into his bedroom."

"Okay," Ed said. "I'll go check on him."

Ed made his way upstairs. He saw the writing on the wall, frowned at it, then went into Colin's room.

"Colin, you in here? It's Ed."

Silence.

He looked around the room and figured a teenage boy had lived here once. Probably went off to college a year or two before. It had that look, like it'd been empty for a while.

"Colin?"

No answer.

Ed had done this kind of thing before, plenty of times, searched the house of somebody who didn't want to be found. He closed his eyes and listened. Heard frightened breathing coming from under the bed.

He lifted up the sheets and looked under the bed. Colin was back there, huddled into a ball as far away as he could get.

"You can come out now."

Colin was shaking badly. He looked at Ed, and there were tears in eyes.

"I can't," he said.

"Why not?"

"Those things . . . they scare me so bad. I can't . . ."

"They'll all gone, son. Now come on out of there."

"No. You don't understand."

Ed sighed. "I understand there ain't no shame in being scared. Hell, we're all scared. The only shame's in how you handle it. Now come on out of there."

Sobbing, wiping the tears from his face with the back of his hand, Colin slowly pulled himself out from under the bed.

Ed helped him to his feet.

"You won't tell them how you found me, will you? Promise me you won't."

Ed looked at him. "Sure," he said. "I promise. Now clean your face up and let's go downstairs. Blow your nose while you're at it."

Margaret was holding a wet towel to Billy's face when Ed and Colin came downstairs. Billy and the others were in the living room now, waiting for them.

Ed looked at Billy. "How you feeling, kid?"

Billy tried to smile, but his lips felt like two busted peaches. Everything hurt. All he could manage was a painful grunt.

"Everybody else okay?" Ed said.

He looked around the room. Julie was sitting on a

barstool at the far end of the living room, crying quietly to herself.

Billy watched Ed go over to her and put a hand on her shoulder. She looked up at Ed, and Billy couldn't quite decipher the look on her face. Was she pissed at him? Was it something else? He wasn't sure.

She said, "What about Barbie, Ed? You can't leave her back there like that. You have to make sure she doesn't come back."

He nodded.

Billy and the others watched him slowly pull a pistol from his waistband and open the cylinder and check the rounds he had left there. Then he snapped the cylinder shut and made his way back down the hallway toward the master bedroom.

Robin looked at Billy. "What's going on?" she said.

He shook his head, then took the towel from Margaret and looked down at his lap, waiting for the sound.

It came a moment later, a single pistol shot. They all flinched.

CHAPTER 39

It was August 6, three days after the death of Randall Gaines and Barbie Denkins in Emporia, Kansas, about 11:30 in the morning, when Billy Kline pulled the van to the side of the road and put it in park.

"Hey, Ed," he said over his shoulder. "Ed, you awake?"

In the backseat, Ed pushed the brim of his Stetson up his forehead with his thumb and looked up. He'd been driving most of the night, the group deciding they were so close now it was best to drive on through until they reached the Grasslands, and he felt worn down, tired almost beyond sleep.

"Come here and look at this."

Ed leaned forward in his seat, expecting to see more of the infected wandering the road. Over the last few days, they'd seen a bunch scattered in the roadside debris of abandoned cars and abandoned tent cities.

But there were no zombies. They were surrounded by green, rolling land all the way to the horizon in every direction. Had been for the last day and a half. Billy pointed up the road and Ed looked that way. He could see metal roofs and wooden structures in the distance, the roofs glistening like pools of motor oil in the sun. Off to one side, outside the camp's perimeter fence, he could see a pair of yellow earth-movers cutting into the ground.

He opened the side door and climbed out. Billy got out, too. Jeff Stavers and the others pulled up alongside them. Soon, they were all standing in the middle of the road, looking north at the buildings of Jasper Sewell's village. Up ahead was an old wooden billboard. Whatever it had once advertised was completely effaced now. The white paint was peeling off in large flakes. But in bold, red letters, the paint still fresh, were the words WELCOME TO THE GRASSLANDS. HERE THERE IS PEACE.

"We did it, Ed," Billy said. "We got here."

Ed looked at him and smiled. He couldn't help it. The smile spread across his face and he could barely hold the wind in his lungs. He felt good. They had really made it.

Beside him, Jeff Stavers was shielding his eyes from the sun with his hand. He held Robin's hand with the other.

"What are you thinking?" she said.

"That it's real. I think a part of me just didn't believe that it would be real."

That was it, Ed thought. *He's put his finger on it.*

He took a deep breath and let it out. He closed his eyes and opened them again. The village was still there, its roofs dappled with sunlight.

It was real. Good lord, it was real.

From the top of a mounded earthen dome near the kitchen, Aaron Roberts stood watching the pair of vehicles as they approached the main gate. His gaze drifted to the earth-movers to his right. Zombies had gathered at the perimeter fence during the night and had to be put down. The earth-movers were almost done burying the bodies. On the loud-speakers, Jasper was praising the work they'd all been doing recently.

"We are becoming a self-sufficient island of God's love," Jasper said. "We are building the world anew here in the Grasslands, and each of you is a vital part of that rebirth. Each of you matters. People, people, people, don't you see the wisdom of this? The United States government has abandoned its charge to the people it was formed to protect. The check that Martin Luther King Jr. was so determined to cash has bounced after all. The government has turned its back on you and on me and on God himself. Why, just the other day I was listening to them talking about us. Us, people, you and me. They were talking about us. And do you know what they had to say? They called us communists. They called us deserters. Do you hear those words, people? Do they make you mad? Well, let them call us what they will. Let them say whatever they want to say about us, for you and I know the truth, don't we? We know we are building this community from solid rock. We have built our house on the best soil, and it will soon feed us the same way God's love feeds our souls. Bless you all for your hard work. God loves you. I love you. Each and every one of you."

Well spoken, Aaron thought. He personally had not heard the broadcast Jasper was talking about, but that didn't matter. If Jasper said it, it was real. And Jasper had said the Family was doing well. Aaron felt proud of that. They'd organized effectively when the zombies appeared, and they'd fought like trained soldiers. Yes, indeed, let the government say what it would. They were taking care of themselves.

Aaron saw a boy of about fourteen coming out of the bakery with an armload of metal sheet pans. He called out to him.

The boy put down the sheet pans and came running.

"Yes, sir?" he said.

"Look there," Aaron said, and pointed at the vehicles coming down the road. "Go tell Jasper we have some new arrivals."

"Me?" The boy sounded amazed—and a little frightened.

Aaron ruffled his hair. "Yes, you. Don't worry, he doesn't bite. Go on now."

"Yes, sir."

The exterior wall surrounding the village was a hurricane fence some fifteen feet high, strung together between large, rectangular cedar posts, like enormously long railroad ties. Ed sat in the passenger seat of the van, watching a group of workers who were repairing a section of the fence, and whistled.

"Looks pretty well fortified," he said.

"That's good, right?" Billy said.

"Yeah, I guess so." He nodded ahead. "Looks like they're letting us in."

Billy put the van in gear and they slowly rolled forward. On their right, they saw two large sheds, and next to those, a well house. Farther up the road, they saw a number of buildings. A few looked unfinished, but quite a few were impressively well situated.

"They've done a lot in a month," Billy said.

"Yeah."

A man in a worn, floppy farmer's hat stepped into the road and held up a hand in greeting.

"The welcoming committee?" Billy said.

Ed nodded.

The man waved them off to the right, where two rows of vehicles already were. They parked and got out.

"Hello," the man said. "Welcome to the Grasslands."

Ed tipped his hat to the man. "I'm Ed Moore," he said, shaking hands with the man.

"Aaron Roberts," the man in the farmer's hat said. "You folks look tired. Have you come a long way?"

"Sarasota, Florida, for me and these folks here," Ed said,

indicating his group. "These folks here we met on the way up. They're from California."

Aaron nodded at Jeff Stavers and his group.

"Well, it's good to have you."

"Thanks."

"Ed," Aaron said, and then stopped himself. "May I call you Ed? We are very informal here."

"Ed is fine."

"Wonderful. Ed, I suppose you folks have heard stories about us. And about Jasper Sewell, our leader. That's why you are here, right?"

"We've heard stories, yes. Quite a few, in fact."

"I heard," Kyra said, "that he can walk among the infected without them attacking him."

Ed laughed. "Yeah, that's the kind of stories I've heard, too."

Aaron nodded. "That particular story is true."

Ed frowned.

"It's true. I saw it myself. It happened right in front of our church back in Jackson, Mississippi. Jasper walked right out into a crowd of the infected, scooped up a mother and daughter, and brought them safely inside our church. And he did it as calmly as you or I would order a cheeseburger. Just went out and got 'em."

Ed nodded dubiously.

"Jasper will be meeting with you shortly," Aaron said. "He likes to greet all new arrivals personally. Understand, though, please, that we have a quarantine rule here. Before you are allowed to mingle with the rest of the Family, we need to make sure that you are not infected or sick in any way."

Ed looked at him. "The Family?"

"An affectionate term for our community here. The quarantine is only for a few hours, but I hope you can understand why it's necessary."

"Yeah," Ed said. "Sure."

There was a commotion from the direction of the buildings and Aaron turned that way.

"Ah," he said. "Here comes Jasper now."

Ed and the others followed his gaze up the road. There was a large pavilion just to the left of the main road, the largest building they could see, and a crowd was coming out of it, headed their way. And in the middle of the crowd, in a white suit over a gray shirt and wearing white shoes, was a man with unnaturally dark hair and a square, oddly plastic-looking face. He wore large, round sunglasses that, to Ed, seemed almost comical.

"Good Lord," Ed said.

Later that evening, just before six, they were released from their quarantine.

"You must be hungry," Jasper said to them.

"Yes, actually," said Kyra. "Very much."

"How very odd," Jasper said. "There are times when I can hear the West Texas twang in your speech very clearly, and other times I can't. Why do you suppose that is, child?"

"I . . . I don't know. Uh, sir."

"Jasper, please. Child, call me Jasper."

Beside her, Colin took her hand. She turned slightly and smiled in his direction.

"Kyra," Jasper said. "Would you permit me to ask you a personal question?"

"Uh, of course," she said.

"Have you been blind since birth?"

"No," she said. "It happened when I was four. I was in a car crash."

"Ah," he said. "How very dreadful. I'm so sorry. But tell me, do you enjoy listening to the radio?"

That stopped her. She stopped so suddenly, in fact, that Colin turned and looked at her.

"How did you know that?" she said.

"A hunch," he said. "Repeat these numbers back to me. 67459089 and 14258463 and 78546338. Can you do that for me?"

Kyra smiled at him. "Of course." And then she repeated the sequence back to him without hesitation.

Jasper laughed and clapped his hands together.

"Wonderful," he said. "Exactly as I thought. Child, your ability for recall is impressive, but I bet you can do a lot more than that, can't you? Your eyes are gone, but your mind compensates in other ways."

Kyra blushed.

"I . . . maybe."

"Of course you can," he said. He turned to Aaron, who had been walking along behind them, silently observing the tour, and said, "Brother Aaron, I do believe we have found a radio room messenger."

"A what?" Kyra said.

"Child," Jasper said. "I think I have just the job for you. Yes, indeed, just the job."

When the tour was done, they met in the pavilion for dinner. There was a prayer and singing, and Jasper spoke to them over the loudspeaker. Later, they were led through the line where they were served cafeteria style. Billy had a double portion of macaroni and cheese, pot roast, two chocolate milks, and a peach cobbler.

He sat down between Ed and Julie Carnes. Both were eating lightly.

"You're not hungry?" he asked Ed.

"Not really, no."

"What's up?" Billy asked. "You've been acting weird since before our tour. Something wrong?"

Ed didn't answer.

"Ed?"

"Yeah, I'm here. I was just thinking." He looked around the pavilion, noticing the loudspeakers that carried Jasper's voice across the village, but it troubled him that he hadn't seen a single radio or TV or cell phone anywhere in the entire camp.

"Thinking about what?" Billy asked.

Ed let out a breath and slapped Billy on the shoulder. "Nothing," he said. "My nerves are still a little raw from the road. Enjoy your dinner."

CHAPTER 40

Four days after their arrival at the Grasslands, Jeff Stavers was leaning in the doorway of a classroom and watching Robin Tharp finish up her classes for the day. Jasper had seen the way Margaret O'Brien's grandkids took to Robin during their quarantine, and he'd asked her to lead one of their classes for the village's elementary-aged kids.

She glanced up from the book she was reading and smiled. He nodded back and slipped outside. Though it was early August, midafternoon, there was still a slight chill in the air, and it felt good. The sky above them was a limitless blue, broken only by a high, thin band of white cirrus clouds far off to the west. *Jasper and his people did an amazing job of planning this place out*, Jeff thought. They had fresh water from the Cedar River to the south and plenty of land for farming and cattle and development. He breathed deeply, and realized that he felt wonderful. He could really, finally, breathe.

"Hey there, handsome."

Jeff turned. Robin was standing there, a copy of *The Celery Stalks at Midnight* clutched over her breasts. Kids ran around her on the way to the playground. One of them stopped to hug her, then ran off after the others.

"You sounded really good in there. I'd never be able to manage all those kids."

She reached down and took his hand in hers. "I'm enjoying this. The teaching. It's wonderful."

"It shows," he said. "What were you reading them anyway?"

She showed him the book.

"*The Celery Stalks at Midnight*. Cute. What's that about?"

"It's about a vampire bunny named Bunnicula who drains the juice from vegetables. There's a cat named Chester and a dog named Harold who try to stop him but never quite manage it."

"Bunnicula, huh? You know, I'd have thought that kids these days would have had enough of being scared."

"It's actually a pretty funny book. But you know, I don't think kids will ever really get tired of scary stuff. It's part of growing up, you know? You can read a scary story and compartmentalize it, own it, in a way, because it's a bite-sized chunk of terror. Sort of like a vaccine against an illness. Once you master your fear of the scary stuff in the story, you can approach the larger world, growing up and stuff like that, with a little more self-assurance."

They had been walking down a dirt lane toward the pavilion, but he stopped and looked at her. Really looked at her. "Robin," he said. "That's brilliant."

She huffed.

"No, really. I mean it. You've really given this a lot of thought, haven't you?"

"I have a lot of life experience to back it up," she said.

He nodded to that.

They started walking again, and he said, "So, you're happy? You think we made the right choice coming here?"

"I think so," she said. "Jeff, I love being a teacher. It's wonderful. And Jasper's great, too."

"Yeah?"

"Jeff, you're wonderful. Don't take what I'm about to say the wrong way. You really are a wonderful man. Smart, caring, even a little sexy—in a dopey kind of way."

"Thanks."

"But you've got to understand something, Jeff. Even you, when you met me that first time—remember, in Colin's limo?"

"I remember."

"Well, even you, sweet as you turned out to be, when you looked at me that first time, you recognized me. You had this impression of me that was based on what I did. But Jasper, when he first saw me, he didn't see a . . . Well, you know. He saw somebody who could teach children to read. He looked at me in a way I've never been looked at before. Do you have any idea how that feels?"

"I bet it feels great," he said.

She gave him a sexy pout. "I knew you'd take it the wrong way. I wasn't criticizing you."

"How am I supposed to take it? You just lumped me in with every pervert who ever watched a porno."

"You are a pervert." She smiled at him, the tip of her tongue just visible between her lips. There was mischief in her eyes. "You're a cute pervert, though."

"Yeah, right."

She took his hand as they walked past a group of squealing kids in the middle of a game of tag.

"So how about you?" she asked. "How's life on the farm?"

He grunted. She meant the farming work he'd been doing in the vegetable fields. That first day, in quarantine, while Robin was discovering the teacher within, he'd gone through a rather embarrassing question-and-answer session with Aaron. After answering "None" to a whole string of questions about his experience with the practical survival skills of carpentry, plumbing, brick making, and animal husbandry, he'd been assigned to work in the fields. But it wasn't all bad, the farming. He'd met another Harvard alumnus, a real-estate attorney from Maryland, and the two of them had had a pretty heated discussion about the recurrence of the True Thomas folktale in Keats's poetry while they shoveled manure from the bed of a pickup.

Jeff didn't tell Robin about that, though.

She said, "So what are you going to do now?"

"I don't know. I was going to get some lunch. You hungry?"

"A little." She glanced around, like she was making sure they were alone. Then she said, "Of course, we don't have to go get lunch. I mean, if you don't want to."

"What else would we do?" he said.

He looked at her. She smiled back.

The dormitories weren't that far away.

Later that afternoon, Jeff was walking around, exploring the area around the new adult-education building to the south of the common area, when he bumped into a heavyset black woman in her early sixties named LaShawnda Johnson. He recognized her as one of the original Family members, the people who had come with Jasper from his church in Jackson. Jeff had met her that first day, after dinner, when he was trying to get settled in the dormitory. At the time, she'd acted like a den mother, smiling and laughing and telling jokes like she was determined to fill the day with sunshine. But she wasn't acting friendly now. She seemed stiff, almost cold, like she'd caught him doing something dirty with a girl way too young for him.

"I'm sorry," he said, thoroughly mystified. "Did I do something wrong? I was just looking around."

"You just go on back to the pavilion till suppertime. Don't come round here without permission, you hear?"

"Sure," he said. "I hear you."

"Go on," she said.

He excused himself and walked away. But when he looked back, just before he turned the corner between the kitchen and the pharmacy, he saw she was still watching him, her expression hard and forbidding.

Confused and a little rattled, he made his way back across the main road, past the tool room and the vehicle garage, and past the education buildings. Most everybody seemed to be indoors, and the public areas were quiet.

LaShawnda Johnson was out of sight, but the feeling of unease he'd gotten after speaking with her remained. What had done? Why did she get so defensive? Unable to hold back his curiosity, he doubled back to the adult-education building, where classes in subjects as varied as soap making and canning and carpentry were held each night, and he started looking around. A moment later, he heard the sounds of a struggle coming from within the building. A body hit the floor. He heard men and women grunting, muffled snarls.

Swallowing hard, Jeff headed toward the front of the building and stopped at the doorway. Inside, he saw Jasper standing on the riser of a small stage on the far side of the rectangular building. Aaron stood beside him. A dozen or so members of the original family were on the floor, formed in a loose circle around a tall, lanky, brown-haired man in a blue T-shirt and brown corduroy pants. They were hitting him, kicking him, forcing him back into the center of their circle each time he tried to make a break through their line.

One man landed a hard right punch to the man's face and knocked him backward, onto his knees. Then he stepped forward and kicked the tall man in the belly. The tall man collapsed to the ground and several others closed in on him, throwing punches and kicking him.

The tall man on the floor lurched with the blows, but offered no resistance. Jeff stood wide-eyed, not quite able to make himself believe what he was seeing. The tall man on the floor made a feeble, defeated sound, and Jasper raised a hand in the air.

Instantly, the family backed away.

"A moment, friends. Let him speak."

Jasper kneeled down next to the man's bruised face. "Tell me, friend. Why have you forsaken me?"

"I haven't," the man said. "Please."

"But you have, friend. Don't you see that? You were trusted with the safety of our people, and you betrayed them when you tried to flee."

"No," the man said.

"Yes," Jasper answered. "When I send you on a gathering detail, that's a sign of my trust. Why, then, friend, would someone so much in my confidence see fit to run the first chance he gets?"

The man made a feeble, inaudible reply.

Jasper rose, shaking his oddly square head. His sunglasses glinted in the sunlight that streamed in through the windows.

Jeff heard the crunch of gravel around the left side of the building. From the right side, he heard the sound of someone breathing hard. He looked around for someplace to hide, but there was no place to go, no cover.

He heard LaShawnda's voice. "I'm telling you, I saw him going this way."

Oh shit, Jeff thought. He looked around him again.

Then he looked down.

When LaShawnda and the other four members of the Family rounded the corner, they found the porch empty.

Aaron stepped out of the front door. "What's wrong?" he said.

"I saw that Jeff Stavers boy come this way."

From beneath the porch, Jeff looked up through the slats. In the thin sliver of daylight that filtered down to him, he could see them gesturing toward the outhouses on the far side of the building. Jeff held his breath and waited, listening as Aaron told LaShawnda to keep looking around.

She stood, looking at the buildings around her, then left the porch and followed after the others. Aaron went back inside the education building.

Jeff waited, listening.

A few minutes later, he heard Jasper order the Family to resume their beating of the tall man.

And while the Family punched and kicked, and the tall man whimpered beneath the blows, Jasper laughed.

CHAPTER 41

Lemmon, South Dakota.

From the driver's seat of the RV, Michael Barnes stared out over an enormous ocean of grass. They were almost there.

"Why don't you go back and sleep, Mr. Barnes," said Sandra. "Send Jerald up here. He's slept long enough."

"I'm all right," Barnes said.

"You're exhausted," Sandra said. "Look at you. You can barely keep your eyes open."

She was right, of course. Last night, they had seemed so close, and he made the decision to keep going. They had seen a lot of the infected on the road—a lot more than he had expected to see this far from major cities—and he didn't think it was safe to stop. But it was almost dawn now. The sky was turning a luminous gray to the east, and they still had so many more miles to go.

A nap would do you good, he thought. He'd given up his turn at the bed and let Jerald Stevens have it all night so he could be the one to drive them into the Grasslands, but that was before he'd had to deal with the monotonous prairies of South Dakota. He got the feeling a man who spent too much time looking out across those limitless waves of grass would go quietly insane. There was an immensity there that was so spectacular it left a man no choice but to turn his eye inward and look upon himself. And, Barnes knew, that way led to demons.

"You'll wake me before we get there?" he said.

"Of course," Richardson answered.

Barnes nodded slowly, his mind already drifting toward sleep. He got up and let Richardson climb into the driver's seat.

He walked back to the bedroom at the rear of the RV. Clint Siefer, the kid who never seemed to say anything, was sleeping on the couch. He'd fallen asleep with the TV on, the original *Star Wars* playing in an endless loop on the big-screen TV across from him. Irritated, Barnes scooped up the remote and turned off the set. Then he dropped the remote on the couch at Clint's feet and dragged himself back to the bedroom.

The light was off and he didn't bother to turn it on. Instead, he pulled off his boots and said, "Jerald, get up."

No answer.

"Come on, man. Get up. They want you up front."

Again there was no answer. Barnes felt anger flare up inside him. He could see Jerald's outline on the bed, his face turned away, one arm tossed absently over his forehead. Barnes put a hand on the bed and the other on Jerald's shoulder, intending to push him out of bed, but he stood up suddenly when he felt something thick and squishy under his right hand.

He stared at the thing he'd just touched, and as his eyes adjusted to the darkness, he saw it was a thick slice of deli turkey. The rest of the turkey breast, the size of a football and covered with bite marks, was cradled up against Jerald's hip.

"Oh, man," Barnes said. "Jerald, get the fuck up, man. That's fucking disgusting."

He shoved Jerald a little harder, and the man's body felt as stiff as the legs of a table.

Barnes straightened.

He turned around, hit the lights, and went back to the bed. Jerald was pale in the face, his lips blue, his eyes open and staring blankly off at a corner of the room. A small puddle of vomit was on the bed below his mouth.

Barnes couldn't believe it. The stupid fuck had actually eaten himself to death.

"Idiot," Barnes said. The anger took over. "Goddamn fucking idiot," he yelled. "Goddamn son of a bitch."

He grabbed Jerald's body and yanked it out of the bed.

The RV slowed and stopped, and Barnes nearly fell. He put his hand on the wall to steady himself. Then he grabbed the corpse by the shirt at the back of the neck and dragged it one-handed out to the living room.

The others were running back to him as he was coming out. He tossed the body at their feet.

Richardson stared at the body. Sandra clamped a hand over her mouth. Clint Siefer sat up on the couch and stared at them sleepily, not sure what was going on. Then he saw the dead body, and his eyes went wide with fright.

"What . . ." Richardson tried to say.

"The dumb fucker finally did it," Barnes snapped. "He ate himself to death. Rigor mortis has set in. Probably been dead three or four hours."

"Oh, my God," Sandra said.

"Fucking idiot," Barnes said. Then he gave the body a savage kick.

CHAPTER 42

"Where do you suppose they're coming from?" Billy asked.

Ed and Billy were on top of the perimeter fence near the main entrance, making repairs. So far, Jasper and his cronies hadn't made a big deal of it, but every morning, when the work crews went into the fields or worked on the buildings near the perimeter, they saw more and more zombies gathering at the fence, trying to claw their way inside.

"I don't know," Ed said. "Maybe they were on their way for the same reason we were. They saw the signs Jasper's people put up, same as we did. They just didn't make it."

From where they sat atop the fence, they could see dead bodies out in the grass. And there were two more zombies staggering toward the main entrance out on the road. Ed could see them dragging themselves along on ruined legs.

Billy scanned the prairie and shook his head.

"But there's so many."

"There's gonna be more still, is my guess," Ed said. "All those people on the road, headed here. It's like leaving a trail of bread crumbs."

"You think they're following the garbage on the road, the abandoned cars, stuff like that?"

"Could be."

Billy looked down at the damage they'd been tasked with repairing and sighed. Ed knew what he was thinking. They were in for an all-day job. Last night, about twenty zombies had beat on the fence, and they'd done a fairly respectable job of breaking it down. There was a large section that had been pulled away from the posts, and it would have to be reinforced with new wire mesh and bolstered by razor wire. What neither of them said was that it would only get harder from here. A few weeks ago, there had been only a few zombies. Now, it was every night. They woke up to the crack of rifle shots echoing across the prairie. And sometimes, when the wind shifted, they caught the foul odor of burning bodies from the disposal pits to the north of the compound. If things continued the way they were, eventually they'd reach a point where the fences wouldn't hold the infected at bay. It was only a matter of time, he knew.

"You okay, Ed?"

He'd been daydreaming, Ed realized. Not a smart thing to do while they were fifteen feet above the ground. He smiled and slapped Billy in the shoulder.

"Great," he said. He heaved a skein of razor wire up onto the top rail and picked out the loose end. "Here, grab the skein," he said.

Billy took it from him and pulled it back and out of the way, so that he could feed it out to Ed as needed. They'd spent a lot of time together up here, and they'd gotten good at this. Ed enjoyed his time up on the fences with Billy. He'd actually grown really fond of the boy, despite their rough start. Julie Carnes had joked with him that he'd finally found the son he never had, and while he didn't think it was as much as all that, he still liked talking to the boy.

And now they were up here again, working easily together, and their conversation turned, as it usually did, back to Kyra Talbot.

Lately, she was all Billy thought of.

"She's working in the radio room," Billy said. "The way she explained it to me, she sits in this little room outside of where Jasper monitors the radio. When he needs her, he calls her in, tells her a message to take over to the office, and she delivers it."

"That's it?"

"Yeah, that's it. She probably gets him coffee and stuff like that, but I think that's about it."

"I guess it beats freezing up here, doesn't it?"

"Or being one of those poor bastards out there."

Ed nodded. They were silent for a time, and Ed noticed Billy's attention drifting back to the center of the compound. "Hey," he said.

"Hmm." Billy looked at him. "What'd you say?"

"I didn't say nothing. I didn't have to. You got it bad for her, don't you?" Billy didn't answer. "You ought to be careful there."

"Careful?"

"I'm old, Billy, but I was your age once. You don't seriously think you're the first guy to go nuts over a girl, do you?"

Billy smiled. "Doesn't do any good to try to lie to you, does it?"

"Not really. But I'm wondering if you've thought this thing through. She's tight with that guy from California, from what I can see. What's his name? Colin?"

"Yeah, Colin. He's an asshole."

Ed cleared his throat.

"Sorry," Billy said. "But he is."

"It's okay. I happen to agree with you, actually."

"Really?" Billy looked up at Ed, and the expression on his face was hopeful, like he'd found an unexpected ally.

Ed recognized the look. It wasn't the message he'd meant to deliver. "I think he's desperate, Billy. That's never a good thing. All of us are dealing with a world that has completely fallen apart, but some of us aren't handling it as well as others."

"So, what are you saying?"

"I'm saying I don't think he's stable," Ed said. "I'm saying he's holding on to Kyra because he sees her as an element of this new world that he can control. You take that away from him, there's no telling how he'll react. Just be careful, okay?"

Billy didn't answer.

"What does she think about life here in the Grasslands?"

"She likes Jasper a lot."

The way he said it, the enthusiasm, the sudden brightening of the eyes, bothered Ed. Billy was smart about so many things, and yet there were times when he just didn't think a thing through. First the girl, then this place. Damn, it was frustrating.

Ed put a nail in his mouth and clenched it while he hammered another into the section of wire on which he was working.

"Easy there, partner," Billy said. "Pounding on that thing a little hard, aren't you?"

Ed just grunted.

Billy put his hammer down and pushed himself up to a sitting position, his legs dangling over the side of the fence.

"What's up, Ed. You all right?"

"Happy as a pig in slop." He took the nail from his mouth and set his own hammer down. No, it wouldn't do any good to lie. "I thought this place would be safe, Billy. That's why I brought us here."

Billy looked at him strangely. "What are you talking about, the zombies?"

Ed started to speak, then stopped himself. There was a lot he felt he needed to say, but couldn't. He hated feeling so helpless. He tried to smile but couldn't make himself do it.

He turned away and scanned the surroundings instead, the green prairie that stretched off to the horizon everywhere he looked.

Finally, he said, "I don't know, Billy. This place . . ."

"What about it? You don't like it here?"

"Do you?"

"Well, yeah," said Billy. "I mean, sure. What's not to like?"

They had Billy working in the kitchen most mornings, and in the laundry in the afternoons, both jobs he'd held as a trustee in the Sarasota County Jail. He seemed to enjoy the work, at least as far as Ed could tell, but Ed wondered how much longer that would go on.

"Jasper's good at making people feel useful," Billy said. "You got to give him that."

"Yeah, that's true," Ed said. And it was. He had built schools for the kids and organized activities for those too old or feeble to work. There was plenty to eat. Medical care was more than adequate. But still, Ed felt uneasy.

"So what's the problem?" Billy said.

"What do we know about the world outside these walls, Billy? Answer me that."

Billy thought for a moment. "Well," he said. "Jasper says that—"

"Stop there," Ed said. "We've been here, what, about three weeks? In all that time, have you seen a radio? A TV? A cell phone? Nobody gets word from the outside but Jasper. Doesn't that concern you?"

"Well . . ."

"It concerns me. Billy, I want to find out what we're missing."

"I don't follow you. You think he's lying to us?"

"I don't know one way or the other," Ed said. "But I'd like to know that for myself. Wouldn't you?"

Now it was Billy's turn to look troubled. He fidgeted on

the fence for a moment, suddenly uncomfortable, like new thoughts were just now occurring to him.

Ed said, "Hey, look there."

He was pointing off to the horizon, down the main road. Far off in the distance, the sun was dancing off the roofs of three large brown RVs.

"Looks like newcomers," Billy said.

"Yeah," Ed said. "Wonder where they're from."

CHAPTER 43

There were two zombies in the middle of the road. Barnes was behind the wheel again, and he didn't even bother to slow down. One of the zombies turned at the sound of the approaching vehicles and he was the first one hit.

The other was sucked under the RV a moment later.

In the passenger seat, Richardson glanced at Barnes. Barnes exhaled through his nose and tightened his grip on the steering wheel, ignoring the apprehension in Richardson's expression.

They drove through the main gate and stopped. Barnes studied the perimeter fence and liked what he saw. It was a good twelve to fifteen feet high and sturdy, solid wood beams framing heavy-duty hurricane fencing, and they even had crews up on top attaching razor wire. *Excellent*, he thought. Farther in, he could see a number of well-built wooden structures with metal roofs that looked like pools of molten light beneath the late-morning sun.

The main road leading up to the buildings was thick with mud from a recent rain. Two men trotted down it and pulled the gate open.

Then one of the men waved them through.

"The welcoming committee?" Richardson asked.

"I doubt it," Barnes said. He rubbed his chin, smooth for the first time in weeks. "Look at that fence. These people are too well organized for these jack-offs to be the security. Keep your eye out for buildings along this main road here. I bet you'll see guys with rifles."

"Rifles? You mean in case we have any infected on board."

"It's what I'd do."

Barnes put the RV in gear and drove forward. They passed a pair of buildings and what looked like a concrete water reservoir on their right.

"There," Richardson said, pointing at the rear shed where a man with a rifle ducked out of sight. "You were right."

"There's another over there," Barnes said. "Beneath that truck in the parking lot."

Richardson squinted at the truck, then nodded slowly.

"I wonder where the others are," Barnes said, scanning the spaces on either side of the road.

They reached the turn-off to the parking lot and stopped. Up ahead, there were people walking from what had to be a kitchen to a large covered structure. They were carrying food on white Styrofoam plates. On their left, they saw a middle-aged balding man in a brown shirt and jeans walking toward them.

"This is our welcoming committee," Barnes said. "Part of it, anyway."

Aaron Roberts approached the lead RV. The vehicles were brand new and painted with flamboyant splashes of color. *Traveling in style*, he thought.

A door opened on the lead RV and a man stepped out. He walked around to the front and stood watching Aaron, his arms akimbo. He was white, somewhere between thirty-five and forty, and carried himself like a soldier or a policeman.

Aaron stepped forward with his hand outstretched. "Hello," he said. "Welcome to the Grasslands. I'm Aaron Roberts."

The man shook his hand, then dropped it.

"Thank you," he said. "Michael Barnes."

Barnes was a good six inches taller than Aaron and built solidly. His face was clean shaven and severe, and when he met Aaron's gaze, he didn't blink. His eyes were dark brown, but they glinted with a hardness that spoke of self-confidence and resiliency.

"Are you folks looking for a place to stay?" Aaron said.

"We are."

"How many are you?"

"Thirty-one."

"Where are you from?"

"Originally from Houston. Some of us are refugees from inside the quarantine zone. Others we met along the way up here."

Aaron looked down the line of RVs. "Not bad for refugees."

"A lucky find along the way," Barnes said. His voice was flat, emotionless. "It's been a hard road."

Aaron hesitated. He didn't like this man, he could tell that already. "You should know we have a mandatory temporary quarantine here. You and your people are welcome here, but they will need to spend several hours under observation before they're allowed to mingle with our community."

"I expected as much," Barnes answered. And then, as an afterthought, he added, "Your security is admirable."

"We get very few zombies this far north. And what few we do get never make it past the fence."

"I don't think that's true," Barnes said. His bluntness surprised Aaron. "Not if what I saw on the road up here is any indication. But I was talking about your snipers. The one behind that building behind us. The two in the parking lot there. And the two in that field over there."

So, Aaron thought, *knows his stuff, this one. Jasper will want to know that.*

"You spotted the two in the field," he said. "I'm impressed. Those are our aces in the hole."

"They're not as dirty as the others working the field," Barnes said. His tone suggested they weren't that well hidden, and when he turned away from the fields and faced Aaron, it was clear he'd dismissed them as unimportant. "Where is this Jasper Sewell I've heard so much about? He's all over the radio. What little there is of it."

Aaron stiffened. He wasn't used to being treated as an errand boy around the compound, but that was exactly what was happening. This man had been inside the walls for less than ten minutes and already he was asserting himself like he was doing them all a favor with his presence.

Self-consciously, Aaron straightened himself up before he spoke. "Jasper tries to greet all our new arrivals personally, but today that isn't possible. You'll have to wait for that honor. He tends to stay very busy. But I'm sure you will see him very soon."

"Fine," Barnes said. "My people have been on the road for a long while, Mr. Roberts."

"Why don't you call me Aaron? We are informal around here. If you are allowed to stay, you will come to see that."

Barnes didn't react to the needles in Aaron's voice. He simply said, "Aaron, okay, that's fine. What do you say we get this quarantine thing out of the way as soon as we can?"

"Fine," Aaron said stiffly. "I'll lead the way."

"That one is the leader of their group," Aaron said.

He and Jasper were standing outside the quarantine cells,

looking in at Michael Barnes through one-way glass. Barnes was standing, one of the only ones who had yet to take advantage of the chairs and couches offered to the group. Instead, he stood near the back wall in a black Windbreaker over a white T-shirt and jeans, watching the people he'd brought with him. He reminded Aaron of a sheepdog watching a flock.

"Really?" Jasper said. "That's what you see, a sheepdog?"

"That or a hawk."

"Do you want to know what I see?" Jasper asked.

"No, what?"

"I see exhaustion," Jasper said. "That is a man who has been pushed beyond what he was meant to endure. What do we know about him?"

Aaron consulted the clipboard he carried. He had asked each of Barnes's people to complete a personal history questionnaire, and they had used that to do a more detailed background check through LexisNexis and Accurint. This was a bigger party than usual, and luckily Aaron didn't have any trouble with the Internet today. Part of the reason the quarantine took so long was that, most of the time, they had difficulty getting online. Not today, though.

"His name is Michael Barnes," Aaron said. "He's a former Houston Police Officer and Gulf Region Quarantine Authority Agent. He's a helicopter pilot and SWAT officer. He served six years as a warrant officer in the army, fought in Afghanistan, where he earned the Bronze Star."

Aaron knew how Jasper felt about the Gulf Region Quarantine Authority, and he expected to see derision on Jasper's face. But instead Jasper smiled.

"I think I can make something of that man," Jasper said.

Then he pointed to a woman who was making her way around the cell, talking with each of the group in turn. Aaron noticed the way they smiled at her.

"And what about this one?" Jasper said.

"Sandra Tellez," Aaron said. "She's from Houston. Lost a daughter and her husband right after the quarantine was established. She worked as a registered nurse before getting married, then got certified as a day-care provider and worked out of her home. See that skinny young man with the shaggy black hair? His name's Clint Siefer. Apparently, he's been going to her day care since he was a baby. He found his way back to her after his family was killed by the infected and he's been with her ever since. Hasn't spoken since then, though."

They needed more teachers and more infant and toddler care, and Aaron expected Jasper to fit her there, but he didn't.

Instead, he frowned. "There are two leaders in that room, Aaron. Officer Barnes over there. And that woman." Jasper stared at Sandra Tellez for a long time before speaking again. Finally, he said, "Separate her from the others as soon as possible. Assign her to the infirmary."

Aaron raised an eyebrow. They were actually lousy with trained medical personnel and didn't need any more, but if that's what Jasper wanted. He waited for Jasper to go on.

"What about that one," Jasper said at last. "The one writing in the notebook over there."

"That's Ben Richardson," Aaron said. "He's a—"

"A reporter," Jasper said. "Yes, I know."

"Yes," Aaron said. "He's written quite a bit about the outbreak since it started."

"I read about his trip into San Antonio with those college kids from Austin in *The Atlantic*. My guess is he's still writing about the outbreak."

"And probably his trip up here," Aaron said.

"Exactly what I was thinking."

He turned away.

"Is that it?" Aaron asked.

As he walked away, Jasper said, "Get me that notebook he's writing in. I want to read it."

* * *

When they released him from the quarantine cell and told him he was free to go wherever he liked, Michael Barnes wandered through the village until he came to the pavilion. It was early afternoon, still a good two hours before dinner, and the large, open structure was empty. There was a stage at one end with steps leading up to it. He sat down on the top step, took a tennis ball from his jacket pocket, and laid down on his back so that he could throw the ball up into the air. It'd been so long since he was by himself that he'd almost forgotten how restful it was to just take his mind off-line and focus on the ball going up, coming down, going up, coming down.

It landed in his left palm with a smack, and the sound was a trigger. Instantly, his mind was back online, but somewhere else, looking back at Houston.

Images rose up like snapshots.

He saw a flooded street and hurricane-damaged houses in the sepia light of a Houston summer evening, the air still strangely alive with the echoes of the recent storm. He saw himself from above, like he was a spectator in his own memory, wading through the flooded ruins, his pistol in his hand, scared, searching for movement. A shot rang out to his right, coming from a storm-damaged, crumbling house that many years ago had been a mansion but was now carved into seven separate, ratty apartments. Jack's apartment. His brother Jack.

He saw himself peering into the building's bottom floor, completely flooded and filled with floating trash. Zombies everywhere. He heard shouting from upstairs and went inside, and he shot his way through the bottom floor till he reached the stairs. A voice called to him for help. At the top of the stairs, he saw a wounded man sitting against the wall, an infected woman with ruined legs pulling herself along the floor to reach him. He shot the woman in the back of the head and asked the man if he'd been bitten. When he nodded, Michael stopped talking and simply walked away. He pounded on Jack's door while the wounded man pleaded at his back for help. "I'm sorry," he said over his shoulder, and then kicked in Jack's door.

Jack was there, on his knees, crying over his wife's body on the couch. The back of her head had been smashed in, and there was a nasty bite wound on her wrist. A bloody crowbar was on the floor next to Jack. The two brothers shared a look. Michael swallowed hard. "Come on," he said. "It's time to go."

The vision flashed away. In its place, he saw the two of them, him and Jack, at the bass boat where Michael's team had been ambushed. Officers Waters and Parker were still in the boat, dead. Waters had one hand cupped in his lap and was holding his intestines. Parker's face was gone and his shirt was torn open. The infected had fed on him, devoured his torso. The inside of the boat was filled with blood. Michael, who despite having seen combat and having made countless high-risk entries in his career as a SWAT officer, had no idea the human body could hold so much blood.

Michael waited for Jack to finish throwing up before handing him Parker's AR-15.

They roamed the wasted city throughout the night. Michael tried to radio in for air evac, but got only empty promises that help was on the way.

Near dawn, they'd found a group of survivors, volunteers from the Red Cross who had managed to evade the infected throughout the previous day. There had been sixty of them, but now they were down to just twelve. They had two wounded, and they were out of food and water and medical supplies. None of them were armed.

Morning found them pinned down, the infected swarming all around them, the moaning so loud it felt like a jumbo jet was continuously flying overhead at treetop level. They had to shout at each other to hear, and sometimes not even that was good enough.

The infected were pouring out of the buildings all around them. From his position atop an abandoned car he was using as a platform to get a better view, Barnes could see west along Westheimer Boulevard and north along Dairy-Ashford Parkway. Both streets were filling with the infected. There were thousands of them. To the south and east, the streets were flooded, and the crowds of infected were not as thick.

Barnes turned his group east down Westheimer, thinking they could skirt the crowds moving down from the Town & Country Mall area and come out somewhere north of where he'd originally planned. He had given up on an evacuation. The radio had gone silent. Huge columns of smoke rose from fires all across the city, and he could hear gunfire coming from all around him. Screaming, too. They were on their own.

One of the Red Cross volunteers next to him was suddenly pulled under the water. The woman let out a startled, panicked cry before she went under. Barnes stared at the empty spot where she had just stood, blinking.

The woman popped up a few feet away, but she wasn't moving. The water was turning a greenish-red around her.

"They're in the water," he shouted.

He could see faces in the water, their noses and mouths just above the surface. They were closing in. Red Cross volunteers were toppling over all around him. The moaning was growing louder again, and Michael jumped onto the hood of another submerged vehicle and did the only thing he knew how to do. He started firing.

He burned through an entire magazine before he was able to slow down and get a grip on his fear and start placing his shots. The roar of activity around him was deafening. The infected just kept coming, pouring out of every building, every alleyway, rising from the water. People were falling all around him, screaming at him for help. He was firing as fast as he could, but it was like trying to spear fire ants with the head of a pin as they rushed out of the mound.

All that noise and movement and violence dropped around him like a curtain. His heart was pounding in his ears. Someone was screaming his name. He turned and saw Jack, one of the last of his group standing, backing toward the hood of the car. Three zombies were on him, clawing at his face, pulling him down. He looked back at Michael and his eyes were wide with fear.

Michael fired at the zombies, putting them down in fast order, but the damage was done. It was too late. Jack's face was a mess of bleeding fingernail scratches. He was missing the tops of two fingers.

He fell face-first onto the hood of the car, and his rifle skittered out of his hand and landed at Michael's feet.

"Jack!"

He held out a hand to his brother, but Jack didn't take it. He stepped back from the car.

"Jack!" Michael screamed.

A zombie popped up from the water and grabbed Jack by the throat, pulling him down. A moment later, Jack was gone. Vanished.

Stunned, Barnes looked around. Everything was falling apart. Jack was dead. The world was dead, and so too was something inside Michael. What was left was as hard as a rock, and every bit as cold.

He took up Jack's rifle along with his own, and holding both of them over his head, he jumped down into the water and ran for his life.

He emerged from the wreckage later that evening, only a few hundred yards from where work crews were assembling the wall that would seal up the city forever. Soldiers looked at him as he walked away from the city, a tired policeman, dripping wet, holding a rifle, head down in a world of his own, and they let him pass.

As that image faded, Barnes tossed the tennis ball into the air, caught it, threw it up again.

"Michael Bar—"

The man hadn't even finished saying his name before Barnes rolled off the stairs and pulled his pistol from inside his Windbreaker. But the man didn't flinch. He looked at the big black hole at the business end of Barnes's .45 and simply smiled.

"My guess is you're an expert with that," he said.

Barnes just stared at him over the front sight. He was trembling and unable to stop himself. His mind felt like it was teetering for balance on a high wire.

"You probably shoot a rifle with surgical precision, but my guess is that pistol there might as well be an extension of your hand. Am I right?"

"What do you want?"

"To talk," the man said, spreading his hands apart as if to suggest there was nothing else he could want.

"Just leave me alone, guy."

"Ah," the man said. He moved to the stairs and sat down. He looked at Barnes and patted the spot next to him. "No? Well, okay. Stand there with your pistol if you must."

"You got a lot of nerve, talking down to a man who's got a gun pointed at your head."

The man smiled. "Two things," he said. "First of all, Michael, I'm not talking down to you. I will never do that. My promises don't mean anything to you now, but they will someday, and I'm making you a promise now. I will never talk down to you."

Barnes was not impressed. "And the second thing?"

"Just this. I know you won't shoot me."

"How's that?"

"Michael, I've thought a lot about death over the years. I've thought about the death of our self-respect, the death of our country, the death of the world. I've also thought about my own death, and I know I wasn't meant to die like this. Not from a gun."

Barnes started to speak, then stopped. He kept the gun pointed at the man's oddly square face. The man's skin had a grotesque, plastic look about it, like an aging actress with a bad face-lift. He wore large sunglasses that hid his eyes from view. The combination of his features should have made him look ridiculous, but for some reason, Barnes found him oddly compelling.

"How can you be so sure about your own death?" Barnes asked at last.

"Mmm. Well, that takes some explaining, doesn't it? Let's just say that I've found a purpose for my life. I've found that thing that makes a life worth living."

"You've found the meaning of life? Tell me, please, I'm dying to know."

"You're being sarcastic, Michael. But you've touched on something. Let's talk about you."

"Not interested."

"But I am, Michael. I am, very much."

"Why?"

"Because I know you. I know the demon that drives you."

"You know jack shit."

The man's smile didn't waver.

"Always on guard, aren't you? Ever ready. Always set to take on the fight. You've been fighting a long time, haven't you, Michael? You've seen more death and meaningless suffering than most men could ever imagine. You've come to see the world as a mean and brutal and selfishly nasty place. And you've met that world head-on, with your fists and your courage and your skill. Everything they heaped on you, you gave it right back to them. With interest."

Barnes nodded. He lowered the gun an inch.

"You know what I see? I see exhaustion, Michael. You're tired because no matter how hard you fight, you can't make the world make sense."

Barnes nodded again, more slowly.

"You've been going at it all wrong, Michael. You've been fighting the wrong battles. I can show you the right path. But you have to trust me."

Barnes looked at him.

"You're Jasper Sewell, aren't you?"

Jasper smiled broadly, confidently. "Guilty as charged."

Barnes looked at the gun in his hand. His body was still trembling. He said, "Can you really help me?"

Jasper nodded. "I can. I will. But you must trust me completely, Michael. If you don't, this will just be another wrong battle. Like all the others you've fought before."

"What do I have to do?"

Jasper clasped his hands together above his knees. He said, "I want you to put that gun on the step between my feet."

Barnes lowered the weapon. The man's expression never changed, but Barnes could feel the confidence, the positive energy flowing out of this man. He put the gun on the steps and backed away.

"Now sit here beside me."

Again, Barnes did as he was told. Already, he was feeling better. He was releasing a burden, giving up the need to be in command that had kept him going for so very long now.

It felt good, not being in control.

Then Jasper did something that surprised him. He reached over and put his arms around Barnes's shoulders and pulled Barnes's face to his chest.

Barnes surprised himself by letting Jasper pull him tight.

And he surprised himself again by crying.

"Do you promise to trust in me entirely?" Jasper said.

Barnes nodded, still crying.

"You're no pansy, Michael Barnes. Don't give me a pansy's answer."

"I do," he said, his voice muffled by Jasper's chest. "I will."

CHAPTER 44

When Mark Kellogg came into the control room, the group of three enlisted men at the monitors turned and stared. *Word of the phone call has spread already*, he thought. They knew. He ignored their looks and stared instead at the bank of monitors in front of them, lost in his own thoughts. They'd know the truth soon enough. The whole base would.

He shook himself. It was getting hard to think straight. The pills he'd been surviving on for the last few days had made things soupy in his head, and there was a crash coming. He could feel it looming on his horizon.

Gradually, the three enlisted men turned back to the monitors.

Behind him, the door closed softly. It was Jane Robeson, one of the civilian doctors they'd picked up from the CDC down in Atlanta. Her team was working on mapping the antigenic shift of the population strains of the infected taken out of the Pennsylvania area by comparing them to the original samples recorded along the Gulf Coast. Kellogg ran down the latest progress reports from her team in his head. They were doing good work, though he was doubtful they were going to turn up any usable leads in the next few weeks. The kind of work they were doing was the stuff of years, and that was time they just didn't have.

"How's it going, Jane?"

"Good as can be expected, I guess." She was a gray, bedraggled woman in her late fifties, with a frizzled mess of hair pulled back in a loose bun behind her head. She seemed anxious. "I was wondering . . ."

"Yes?"

"Well, we all heard about the call. We were wondering, was it really him?"

In front of him, the three enlisted men stiffened without trying to make it obvious they were listening. Kellogg sighed. It was going to come out sooner or later. This might as well be the time. "Yeah," he said. "It was him. The president. The slippery bastard said we have the hopes and prayers of a desperate nation riding on our efforts. He said he has the firmest confidence that we will see this thing through to a successful conclusion. He actually talks like that in real life, Jane. Did you know that? The bastard can't have a simple phone conversation without making it sound like a proclamation."

"But what about reinforcing us? Additional supplies. Mark, I'm having to share computer time with three other teams. We've got equipment here that would be considered inadequate even for a high school chem lab. We can't be expected to keep up any sort of pace like this."

"I know what you're up against, Jane."

"But did you tell him that? Does he know how bad things are here?"

"He knows."

"And what did he say?"

Kellogg laced his hands together behind his back. A tension headache was building behind his eyes. He wanted one of his pills, but that would have to wait. On the monitor in front of him, he saw Nate Royal sitting at the edge of his bed, watching TV, a remote control in his hand. The man looked bored out of his head. He hadn't moved in two days, and the nurses reported that he hadn't slept, either. He just kept watching *Top Gun* over and over again. He was depressed. You didn't need to be a psychiatrist to see that. But what were they going to do about it? They were all prisoners here, of one sort or another. Rosetta stone to this pandemic though he may be, Nate Royal didn't have a monopoly on depression.

"Mark? What did he say?"

"He quoted Abraham Lincoln to me, Jane. Can you believe that? 'Endeavor to persevere,' he said. Lincoln said that to the Indians as he was preparing to send them out to the reservations. Do you get the implication, Jane? Do you know what that means for us?"

"But surely he can't mean we're not getting any help at all. Mark, is that what he said?"

Kellogg's gaze shifted once again over the monitors in front of him. One screen was split into six sections, each section showing a different part of the base's perimeter. The infected were swarming against the fence. A week earlier, they'd seen a few stragglers from the town of Minot, and the guards had amused themselves with popping off headshots from their Humvees during their patrols. Kellogg had watched them and winced at their sport, but ultimately decided that he didn't care enough to order them to stop.

Somehow word had spread to Minneapolis that Minot was doing research on the virus. If there was going to be a cure, the rumor went, it was going to come out of Minot. Soon there were streams of refugees descending on the base, and the results were predictable enough. A hundred thousand people had brought their infected friends and family with them, hoping for some kind of miracle cure. They had tried to storm the base and had been repulsed. Now that flood of humanity was essentially an army of the infected, beating on the gates. The guards were no longer shooting them for sport. That had stopped shortly after the first incursions and a sort of besieged mentality had set in among the base's population. It was just a matter of time now, like it had been in San Antonio and Pennsylvania.

The truth was they were dealing with a global pandemic. There were reports coming out of every corner of the globe. Nuclear weapons had been used on refugees along the India-Pakistan border. China was in chaos. U.S. troops in Europe and the Middle East were collapsing as soldiers abandoned their posts and tried to find ways to make it home to their families stateside. Globally, they were past the tipping point. The great crash was already a part of history. Armageddon had come and gone. Now they were just witnessing the wreckage.

"Mark?"

Kellogg started. For a moment, the room had disappeared, but the sound of Jane Robeson's voice brought him back.

Kellogg's gaze drifted back to Nate Royal. "That one is our best hope right now," he said, nodding at the screen.

Standing beside him, she watched Nate sitting at the edge of his bed.

"He's a tough nut to crack," she said. "We've tried everything."

"But we're going to have to crack him. There is an answer there, Jane."

"I hope you're right," she said.

"Me too. God help us, me too."

Nate Royal sat on the edge of his bed, watching *Top Gun*. Again. The same scene. Over and over. Maverick and Goose are in Stinger's office. They've just saved Cougar. Stinger is offering Maverick his dream shot, telling him, "Son, your ego is writing checks your body can't cash."

Stop.

Backtrack.

Play it again.

Like Kellogg, Nate was looking for answers. The absurdity of his position hit him a week ago. He was sitting here in his bed, eating raspberry Jell-O with his fingers, listening to Tom Cruise saying "I was inverted," and it struck him. His life was a waste. He was a waste. He had burst into daylight one day during his sophomore year and rather than finding a world that made sense, he had found this world.

Now they were telling him that he was some kind of cure. It was absurd. He had never mattered to anybody, and now they were telling him he mattered to everybody. Nate found it hard to believe, and even harder to stomach. That wasn't the kind of responsibility he wanted. He remembered Jessica Metcalfe's husband, the big-shot city attorney who had offered him the job painting his pool house, telling him that he had to take some responsibility and put his life back on the rails. That had seemed like an empty load of shit at the time. How could he really be expected to do that? He was just one man, and the world was so huge. It didn't make sense.

And that was the problem, really. Nothing made sense. Dr. Kellogg had promised that the lab people would start telling him what tests they were doing on him and why, and they had. They'd been good to their word. But it didn't help Nate any. He still didn't understand why it had to be him and not somebody else.

Nate stopped the DVD. Made it go back a track. *Son, your ego's writing checks your body can't cash.*

He didn't know about his ego, wasn't even really sure what that was, but he did know his body wasn't up for cashing any more checks. He'd reached the end of his rope, and he didn't have anything left. So, really, it boiled down to one simple question: Did he want to go on living? He decided that he didn't, and it surprised him how easy the decision was to make. Screw what everybody else wanted. It was his life. He wrecked it, so it was up to him to fix it. Maybe Jessica Metcalfe's husband was right. Maybe it was his responsibility. Running into daylight hadn't worked. Maybe he'd find better luck with darkness.

Son, your ego's writing checks your body can't cash.

He stopped the disk. Looking down at the remote, he found the Eject button and hit it. The disk slid out. Nate took it from the carriage and watched the light dapple off its surface before snapping it cleanly in half. He studied the edge he'd made and decided it would do. It was going to hurt, but that'd be over soon enough.

He pushed himself up to the head of the bed and climbed under the sheets. The cameras Kellogg had told him about picked up the whole room, and it wouldn't do him any good to get caught before he could make good on this.

Nate spread his legs butterfly fashion, his hands on the bed between his knees, the sheets pulled up around his elbows. Just below the surface of his wrist he could see two green lightning-bolt-shaped veins. Using the corner of the broken disc, he picked at the skin there. He winced at the pain.

He eyes were shut and he couldn't remember closing them. He forced them open.

His wrists were marked by a pair of deep scratches. There was a smear of blood on the white sheets. The wound was stinging, but it didn't hurt as bad as he thought it would.

Son, your ego's writing checks your body can't cash.

Not this time, he thought.

Nate took a deep breath. And another. Then he put the disk to his wrist and began to cut.

Chapter 45

Ed Moore found that he wasn't alone with his feelings of unease. A few others had noticed that something was wrong with life in the Grasslands, and they came to him with their concerns.

It is funny, he thought, *how like-minded people tend to find each other*.

Now it was late, dark outside, and cold, and Ed stood before a group of six young men and two women. Among the group were Billy Kline and Jeff Stavers. Ed looked at Jeff now and thought of the beating the young man had witnessed, and how he'd been forced to hide to avoid a confrontation with Jasper's most loyal followers. Ed figured they would be watching Jeff closely, just as they were no doubt watching anybody he associated with, and that meant they were all going to have to be extremely careful.

"I have no idea what they will do if they find us out," he told the group. "Maybe nothing. Maybe kick us out."

"Yeah, or maybe worse," said Jeff.

The room echoed with mutters of agreement.

"Yes," Ed said. "Maybe worse."

He shivered. Unlike the others, he wasn't wearing a coat.

He was dressed in a black flannel shirt and jeans. He'd been issued a heavy winter coat, but it was as white as a show pony, and they were going to have to maintain a low profile if this was going to work. That meant dark clothes worn under the cover of darkness.

He said, "That's why I can't ask any of you to go along with us if you're not serious about this. If we get caught, you can bet they'll try to find out who else is with us. So please, if you're not committed to this, back out now. I only ask for your silence."

He looked around the room. Nobody stirred. He saw eight stalwart faces staring back at him.

"Okay," he said. Outside, the wind howled, and Ed stopped to listen. The constant roar of the wind made it hard to hear the guards who patrolled the camp at night. "Tonight," he said, "what I want to do is get inside that supply shed and see if there are any radios. After that, we'll distribute what we find and see what happens. Just remember. Keep a low profile, okay? I don't want anybody getting discovered."

Ed took a small, dark beanie cap from his back pocket and slipped it over his white hair.

He looked to Billy and Jeff and said, "You guys ready?"

Both men nodded.

"Okay," he said. "Let's roll."

The three of them knelt under the eaves of dormitory number two and glanced across the common area of the village. A narrow sliver of a moon cast a faint bluish tinge over the grass. Buttery yellow sodium vapor lamps lit the road at even intervals from the pavilion all the way down to the cottages. An armed patrol walked along the road. They looked bored, but still attentive. Ed, Billy, and Jeff waited for the patrol to crest the small hill that led down to the cottages, and when the guards were out of sight, they ran for the education tents.

Once there, they had to wait for another patrol to cross the space between the radio room and the office. The two armed men wandered slowly toward the pavilion, where they stopped and talked for a few moments before continuing their way down to the dormitories.

"How many of them are there?" Jeff asked, indicating the patrols with a nod of his chin.

"No telling," Ed said.

He looked across the grassy courtyard to the supply shed. The door was padlocked, but they knew that already, and Billy had said it wouldn't be a problem. The problem was the door itself. It was facing the main courtyard, and there was absolutely nothing around it in the way of cover.

"I don't like it," Ed said.

Billy shook his head. "Don't worry about it. I got it." He took a screwdriver out of his pocket and smiled.

"You can use that to open the lock?" Ed said.

"Not exactly," Billy said. "I looked at the thing the other day. It's a heavy-duty Yale. There's no way in hell you're popping one of those things open unless you have a bump key, which we ain't got."

"So how are we getting in?" Jeff said.

"People don't think when they put locks on doors," Billy said. "They buy nice shit—sorry, Ed—they buy nice stuff, but they don't think about installation. The plate that holds the lock on the door is secured to the jamb with four regular screws. All you got to do is screw the plate off the doorjamb and you're in."

"Nice," Ed said.

"Yeah, I thought you'd appreciate that."

They sprinted across the field to the door. Ed and Jeff took up lookout positions while Billy went to work on the door.

From where he stood, Ed could see Jasper's private quarters through a gap between the supply shed and the vehicle garage. There was a light on, and two figures stood talking in the faint moonlight. Off to his left, he could see the cottages. They were all dark except for the occasional sodium vapor lamp. He could see one patrol moving between the cottages and another coming up the dirt path that led to the communal areas.

"How much longer?" he said to Billy.

"Ten seconds."

Ed turned and watched the patrol coming up the path. They were still a long way away, but getting closer.

"Billy?"

"We're in," Billy said. "Come on."

A few minutes later, Ed leaned against the inside of the shed's door and called out to Jeff, who was supposed to be standing lookout outside.

"Jeff, we clear?"

No answer.

Ed got low to the ground and tried to look out onto the courtyard from beneath the door. He couldn't see much, but what he could see was clear.

"Come on, let's go," he said.

"Hope you know what you're doing," Billy said.

"Yeah, me too."

Ed pushed the door open and they slipped outside.

"How long will it take you to replace the screws?" Ed asked.

"Just a second," Billy answered. He took the screwdriver from his pocket and started working.

Meanwhile, Ed scanned the darkened buildings for any sign of Jeff. He couldn't see a thing, and that worried him. Where was he?

A sound from the right side of the building brought him back into the moment.

He looked at Billy, who redoubled his efforts on the screws.

"Hurry it up," Ed said.

"I am hurrying," Billy hissed back.

Ed listened carefully. He had four radios in his hands, and there was no way he was going to be able to lie his way out of this if they got caught. He watched Billy twist the screws back into the faceplate. *Come on. Come on.* They had three in now, and Billy was starting on the forth and final one.

The tip of the screwdriver slid off the screw and struck the faceplate with an audible crack.

"Shit," Billy muttered.

Ed and Billy looked at each other, listening. From somewhere behind the shed, they could hear the sound of footsteps getting closer, as though a pair of men were suddenly picking up their pace to a trot.

"Oh, no," Ed whispered. "Billy, hurry up."

"Almost done."

Ed watched him put the last screw in and quickly work it into place.

"Done," he said.

"Good. Sounds like they're coming up behind us."

Ed could hear footsteps in the grass just around the corner. The nearest building was sixty feet away at least, and there was no way they could reach it without being seen.

But he didn't see any other way. "You ready to run?"

Billy nodded.

"Okay, let's do it."

But before they could break into a sprint, they heard glass breaking off to their right. The footsteps stopped. He heard frantic whispers from the patrols.

"The warehouse!"

"There he is!" a second guard said.

Ed scanned the darkness over by the warehouse. The patrols were sprinting into the clearing, chasing after a dark figure that looked like Jeff Stavers.

Ed let out a long sigh of relief.

"That's one brave dude," Billy said.

"You're right about that," Ed said, and together they slipped off into the night.

CHAPTER 46

The next morning was intensely cold. It was mid-September, and the sky was a roiling mass of dark gray clouds. A front was rolling in from the north. There was a thin crust of ice on the ground, and the promise of a wet, cold sleet to come in the midafternoon.

Jeff Stavers was scraping ice from the windshield of the pickup he was sometimes allowed to use to cart manure from the cattle fields to the gardens along the northern edge of the village. Though his hands were numb and the cold air hurt his chest when he breathed, he was able to turn off his mind and lose himself in the simplicity of scraping ice. It comforted him.

Colin was on the other side of the hood, doing the same thing to his side of the windshield.

He said, "Hey, Jeff."

"Yeah."

"What's up, man? You look tired."

Jeff nodded. "Yeah, I was up most of the night."

"Oh yeah?"

"Couldn't sleep."

"Something wrong?"

"No, not really," Jeff lied. After losing the patrols down in the cottages, he'd spent most of the night curled up beneath the sewage pipes leading out of the communal bathrooms. The smell had been horrible. He kept scraping ice from the windshield, but gradually he noticed that Colin was still looking at him, waiting for him to look up.

"Aren't you happy here, Jeff?"

"Sure," he said. "Yeah, of course."

"That doesn't sound very convincing. Seriously, is everything okay?"

Jeff looked at him. "Colin, you know what I miss? I miss driving my car down an empty country road, the windows down, a cool March breeze in my hair, my favorite song on the radio. I miss books and movies and being able to go to a bar anytime I want. I miss the world."

"Jasper says the world outside of the Grasslands is evil."

"Yeah, I heard the lecture, too." Jeff stopped scraping and with a snap of his wrist flung the shaved ice from his scraper. It landed with a wet-sounding plop in the hard dirt next to his feet. When he looked up at Colin, his old roommate was looking at him. The expression on his face was an odd mixture of pity and contentment, like one of the faithful staring at a bum on a park bench.

You don't have to have this conversation, Jeff told himself. He knew the smart thing to do would be to walk away, but he couldn't help himself. He was angry at himself and angry at this place and angry at Colin, and he couldn't leave it alone.

He said, "Remember reading Hermann Hesse, Colin? Siddhartha said the same thing right before he had his awakening and rejoined the world."

"Siddhartha was just a character in a book, Jeff. This is real life. This is our life, our future. What's outside those walls is not worth having. Jasper says most of it is gone, and what's left just wants to tear us down because we've found happiness and they haven't."

Jeff went back to scraping ice.

"Jeff?"

"Yeah, Colin?"

"I wanted to ask you about something."

"Shoot."

"Can you stop doing that a second and look at me, please?"

Jeff stopped. He put the scraper on the hood and looked at Colin. Really looked at him. He'd lost weight since all this started, gotten leaner. He didn't look so soft. He'd gotten a tan from spending so much time in the fields, and he looked more focused. Jeff wondered if it was because Colin was sober for the first time in his life.

"Kyra and I have been talking, and we've got something we want to ask you and Robin about."

Jeff thought, *Oh shit, tell me he didn't ask her to marry him. Please don't let it be that.*

"Sure," Jeff said. "What is it?"

"We want to join the Family. We talked it over, and we want to take the oath. We were thinking today at lunch. And we wanted you and Robin to take it with us. What do you say, Jeff? We could make a home here. Together, with Jasper's guidance, we can take what's left of the world and make it good again."

Straight out of Jasper's mouth, Jeff thought. It was depressing, seeing Colin this way. The man was never a deep thinker, but he had a natural intelligence that had always allowed him to squeak by. Still, that aside, Colin was not the kind of person to completely subjugate his will to somebody else, especially some country-fried Mississippi preacher. Something had snapped inside Colin's mind, Jeff decided. That was the only explanation.

Jeff said, "I can't speak for Robin, you know that. But me personally, I think you're fucking nuts."

Colin looked stunned.

"What did you say?"

"Colin, do you have any idea what you're getting yourself into? What you're getting Kyra into? This place, Colin, there's something terribly wrong going on here."

Colin stepped around the front of the truck.

"I know exactly what I'm doing," he said. "And so does Kyra. Jeff, we've found something good here. Can't you see that? The things Jasper has done for us"—he motioned around him with a wave of his hand—"can you deny how good this is? Jeff, it's a paradise. We've got all the food and clothes and supplies we need. We're becoming self-sufficient. We're happy."

Jeff started to argue, but Colin put up his hands and shook his head.

"Jasper took us in when the rest of the world was falling apart. Our government failed us. Our military failed us. The only person who hasn't failed us is Jasper. How can you stand there and tell me that something is wrong here? How do you do that?"

Walk away, he thought. *You're not going to make him see. Jasper's pulled the wool over his eyes.*

But a moment later, he was talking again, unable to make himself stop. "Colin, look, I don't think you're seeing what's going on here. I think you lost more than anybody. You had it all. You had wealth beyond measure. You had beautiful women and booze and drugs and everything you could have ever wanted at the snap of your fingers. But you lost all that. I think it left a vacuum in you, Colin. And I think Jasper stepped into that vacuum and he filled it up with a lot of pseudoreligious, pseudopolitical crap. None of this is as it seems, Colin. The Family, Colin, they're not sane."

Colin thumped him in the chest with his finger.

Jeff took a step back, his palms up to make it clear he didn't want to fight. "Colin, please."

"Take it back."

"I know it's not what you want to hear, Colin."

"You're telling lies. It's just like Jasper said. People tell lies."

Colin turned away from him. Unwilling and unable to let it go, Jeff put a hand on his shoulder and tried to turn him around.

"Colin, wait—"

Colin spun around and punched him. Jeff never saw it coming. One moment he was standing, and the next he was on his butt, looking up at Colin, who was standing over him with his fists balled so tightly that the color had drained from his knuckles.

"You don't want to join the Family. Okay, that's fine. But Jeff, don't you ever tell lies around me again." He jabbed a finger at Jeff. "Don't you ever."

Then, as though he were lost, he turned and walked away.

Jeff watched him go, feeling like something important had just ended.

Chapter 47

There was a knock at the door.

"Ah," said Jasper. "That's my eleven-thirty appointment."

Aaron put his iced tea down on the table and Barnes followed his lead. When Aaron rose from the table, Barnes did, too.

Barnes said, "You keep appointments this late?"

"Even later sometimes," Jasper admitted. "There are a good many folks here who need my guidance."

Barnes nodded. He could believe it. It had been a few weeks since his arrival, and in that time, Jasper had done wonders for him. He felt as though he had shrugged off a heavy weight, and not just the weight of command, but also of loss. Sitting here, drinking tea with Jasper, talking to him, it was the first time in a very long time that he hadn't thought of Jack and the senselessness of all that death. Things were coming together for him here.

He followed Aaron to the door.

"Aaron," Jasper said. "Will you see Misty and Carla in, please?"

"Of course," Aaron said.

"Good night, Michael."

"Good night, Jasper."

Aaron opened the screen door and he and Barnes stood aside to allow two young girls to come inside. One looked about sixteen, a brown-haired beauty. The other was a little older, chunky, but still pretty. They smiled at Aaron, but didn't meet his eyes.

"Come on in," he said. "Jasper's in the kitchen."

The girls mumbled their thanks and went in.

Aaron pointed Barnes to the door and said, "Come on, I'll see you out."

They stepped out into the night air, and the sudden chill felt good against Barnes's face. He breathed deeply. A constant, howling wind moved over the prairie, sending waves through the grass that moved off into the darkness. The sky was alive with stars.

"I've never seen so many," Barnes said, his head craned back to admire the view.

"Yes," Aaron said. "It's beautiful here."

Barnes looked at him, a middle-aged man who should have been radiating the joy of being one of Jasper's privileged lieutenants but instead seemed distant, preoccupied, troubled.

"You've been with Jasper how long? Nearly twenty years, isn't that what he said in there?"

"Yes."

"I wish I'd found him twenty years ago," Barnes said. "It would have saved me an awful lot of wandering."

Aaron didn't respond right away. He looked back at Jasper's quarters. Inside, they could hear one of the teenage girls talking.

"Listen," Aaron said. "I'm sorry, but I'm not feeling well tonight. My stomach. If you'll excuse me."

"Sure," Barnes said. "Good night."

Aaron nodded, and walked away.

Alone once more, Barnes leaned his head back and watched the stars. One of the girls inside giggled, and it brought Barnes out of his reverie. He put his hands down into the pocket of his Windbreaker and started up the trail that would lead him back to his dormitory.

He saw one of the patrols heading from the vehicle storage lot behind Jasper's quarters over to the utility well and smokehouse, and he waved. The two men waved back. Though the curfew was in effect, Jasper had given him permission to wander the camp whenever he wished, and the patrols knew to let him be.

He reached the main road and walked toward the pavilion. The wind coming in off the prairie moved the swings on the playground and sent a chill through him. Soon, it was going to get extremely cold. He'd already seen ice on the grass in the mornings and small snowflakes in the air on cloudy days, and he realized he wouldn't be able to enjoy these nightly walks much longer. He'd have to find some other way to meditate about the changes he was going through, which was a shame. His midnight walks were so calming, a chance to reflect on all Jasper had taught him so far.

He heard a faint crack to his right and stopped. In the darkness, he could see the outlines of the supply room and the vehicle garage on the other side of the office. In the starlight, their roofs looked touched with silver. He stood still and watched and listened. Nothing moved. He couldn't hear anything but the wind and the faint creaking of the swings behind him. But his cop instincts had gone on alert, and he glanced at his watch to note the time. Then, as quietly as he could, he walked that way.

* * *

There were three of them. They were trying to remove the screws where the dead bolt fastened to the door frame. Besides the one screwdriver, he didn't see anything else that could be used as a weapon.

Barnes stepped around the corner and came up behind them before they had a chance to react. One of the men noticed him when it was too late and tried to make a break for it, but Barnes was too quick for him. He shoved the guy into the wall, and the man hit it hard enough to shake the building.

By that point, the other two had turned to face him. They watched their friend hit the wall, then slump to the ground, rubbing the back of his head.

The guy with the screwdriver stepped forward, wielding it like a knife. He said, "All you gotta do is step aside, man. It ain't worth your life."

Barnes just stared at him.

"I mean it, man. I'll fucking run you through."

"Put your weapon down and get facedown on the ground," Barnes said. "Or I'll kill you."

The man Barnes had knocked against the wall stood up. The other three seemed to take that as some kind of cue, and the man with the screwdriver lunged forward like he was going to stab Barnes in the belly.

Barnes stepped outside the man's thrust, grabbing his wrist with his right hand and pulling the arm straight while at the same time pivoting his body so that he could strike the back of the man's elbow with his left hand. The man's arm broke with an audible crack and he screamed. At the same time, Barnes bent the wrist back to the man's shoulder and kept downward pressure on his doubled-up arm, walking him around in a circle until his momentum forced him to fall face forward on the grass.

When the man rolled over onto his back, Barnes slammed his heel down on the man's mouth.

He turned back to the other two just as one of them threw a clumsy roundhouse punch. Barnes dodged it easily, then closed the distance with a flurry of left jabs and a hard right to the solar plexus. The man doubled over, unable to breathe. Barnes grabbed him by the back of the head and pulled his face down to meet his knee.

The man fell back on his ass, his face covered in blood, trying to gulp air through his shattered nose and mouth.

One of the patrols had been alerted by the noise and was running up from the cottages. The third man saw them coming, looked at Barnes, and took off running in the opposite direction. Barnes motioned for the patrol to cover the two injured men and ran after the third man.

He caught him just as they entered the playground. Barnes pushed him forward and the man tumbled to the ground, landing beneath the swings.

Barnes was on him before he could get to his feet. He wrapped one of the swing's chains around the man's neck and yanked on it. The man was gagging and turning blue by the time the patrol got there.

Jasper emerged from his quarters, still buttoning his shirt.

Aaron and Barnes were standing off to one side. The three men Barnes had caught breaking into the supply room were on their knees, their hands secured behind their backs with plastic flex ties. The patrol stood behind them, rifles at the ready.

"What in the hell is going on here?" Jasper said, storming across the lawn.

Aaron wasn't surprised at Jasper's anger. Jasper could handle government agents and criticism in the press with barely restrained contempt and maybe a temper tantrum or two. But betrayal from within, by those he considered *his* children, *his* people, was enough to send him into a paroxysm of rage that might take days to die down. And he was definitely in a rage now.

"I asked, what in the hell was going on?" he said.

One of the patrol guards looked at Aaron for help, but Aaron simply nodded at the man.

Jasper was breathing hard, opening and closing his fists.

"Answer me," he screamed.

The guard who had looked to Aaron for help blurted out an explanation, glossing over in a few words what Barnes had done to capture the men.

"Is that true?" Jasper asked Barnes.

Barnes nodded.

Jasper stared at the prisoners. "You're Tom Wilder," he said to the first man, the one who had tried to attack Barnes with the screwdriver.

The man looked away.

"And you," Jasper said to the second man. "Your name is Reggie Waites, from Norman, Oklahoma."

Jasper went to the next man and said, "Harold Morrison. You work in the kitchen."

None of the men spoke.

Jasper motioned for the two-man patrol to get back to their route. When they were gone, he pulled a .45 pistol from his waistband and handed it to Barnes.

"This is yours," he said. Barnes took the gun with a smile. "I cannot abide a traitor," he said to Barnes. "When you first came here, I told you to trust me."

"Yes."

"I told you that you would grow strong if you did."

"Yes."

"These men have betrayed that trust I extended to them." Jasper paused. "Do you know what I want you to do?"

Barnes adjusted his grip on the pistol and nodded.

As Barnes stepped behind the prisoners, raised his pistol to the back of the first man's head, and fired, Aaron heard Jasper begin to laugh. It was a high-pitched tattoo that Aaron had heard many times over the years. But this was the first time it ever made him sick to his stomach to hear.

CHAPTER 48

Ed had warned him not to do this in the daylight, but Billy Kline needed a better look at that door to the supply room. After their last midnight raid on the supply room, the Yale lock had been bolstered with two additional locks, one of them a dead bolt. It was going to be much harder to get in there now. Not impossible, but certainly harder.

He scanned the communal area. A cold front had rolled in during the early-morning hours and an icy sleet had started to fall. Already, the ground was slushy and the air bitingly cold. Most of the people moving through the communal area were more interested in getting inside as fast as they could than in milling around and talking, and that was a good thing.

With his hands in his pockets, walking as slowly and as casually as he could, Billy approached the supply room door. He stopped in front of it and glanced around. Aaron, Jasper's number-one guy, was coming out of the radio room off to Billy's right, not sixty feet away. Billy knelt down and started pretending to tie his bootlaces as Aaron walked by.

But Aaron seemed preoccupied, maybe even troubled. He didn't look up at Billy as he walked by. He was muttering to himself, the words indistinct, and a moment later, he was gone.

Billy looked around, didn't see anybody else, and went back to examining the locks. He would need tools, he realized. He could get in and out without making it look like the locks had been tampered with, but it would take time.

A few days earlier, he'd met a guy named Tom Wilder from Bowling Green, Ohio. The guy had done some time for burglary and forgery before the outbreak, and like Billy and Ed, he'd also been on edge about some of the things that were happening around the Grasslands. He'd become part of their growing group at the midnight meetings and, the night before, he'd volunteered to go get additional radios and maybe a TV if he could from the supply shed.

Now, looking at the added security, the freshly installed locks, Billy wondered if Wilder's group hadn't screwed up somehow. They must have done something to tip off Jasper's people, something careless.

They both had the early dinner. He'd ask him then.

"Hello? Is somebody there?"

Billy nearly jumped out of his boots. He spun around, half ready to fight, half ready to run away, and saw Kyra Talbot standing there.

He let out a sigh of relief.

Then he smiled. Kyra was wearing a white heavy coat over blue jeans and brown snow boots with blond fur around the tops. Her brown hair was tied back with a black velvet band and it hung between her shoulder blades in a ponytail. She was smiling, her sightless eyes looking in his general direction, but not at him.

He said, "Kyra, here. It's me, Billy Kline."

She straightened. The smile wavered a bit.

"Oh," she said. "Hello, Billy."

He stepped away from the door and walked over to her. "You delivering a message?" he asked.

She nodded. "What are you doing?"

"Oh, I just stopped to tie my shoes. I'm on my way down to the laundry."

She nodded again. For a moment, he thought she was about to turn away and head off to the office without saying anything else, but then she surprised him.

"Is that what you're doing, working in the laundry?"

He smiled, thinking of something Jeff Stavers had told him. *What have they got you working at?* was the question on everyone's lips around the camp. It was a conversation starter.

"In the mornings, I work in the kitchen. After lunch, I work in the laundry."

"Oh," she said, brightening a little more. "Do you know how to cook?"

"Sort of," he said. "Not like you're thinking of, though." He hesitated here, because he hadn't really wanted to admit this, not to her. "I was in jail for a while before the outbreak. That's where I learned to work in a big kitchen. That first day, while we were in quarantine, Jasper came up to me and asked me if I'd ever been in jail. The way he looked at me, I couldn't lie to him. He asked me if I'd ever worked in the kitchen or the laundry and I told him yeah, I'd done both. He just clapped his hands and said he had a job for me."

"He's pretty good at reading people that way."

He'd frightened her with his talk of jail, and he mentally kicked himself. Her lips were pressed tightly together and she looked nervous, like she wanted to leave.

"Look," he said. "Don't let the whole jail thing frighten you about me. I mean, yeah, I've been in jail. Several times, actually. Oh, man, that sounds bad. But I'm not a bad guy. That sounds stupid, I know, but I'm really not a bad guy."

"I don't think you're a bad guy," she said.

"You don't?" The way she said it, he wasn't sure if she

was being honest with him, or merely appeasing him so that he wouldn't hurt her.

And then she smiled, and it was a beautiful smile. An honest smile. "I believe you because of Ed Moore."

"Because of Ed?" He shook his head. "Why Ed?"

"Ed likes you. He's taken you under his wing. Billy, I grew up around men like Ed Moore. Cowboys like him, I know the importance they place on a man's character. If he thought you were bad news, he would have dropped you already."

Billy liked that. He liked talking to this girl, too. There was something about her, the twang in her voice, the mixture of vulnerability and solid, inner strength, that turned him on.

She said, "Billy, what's prison like?"

He was caught off guard. "Uh," he said. "Well, I was never in prison. I was in the county jail. Prison is for state or federal prisoners. Those are the guys who go in for the big-time felonies. Me, I was strictly small-time."

"Oh," she said. "That's reassuring, I guess."

He chuckled. "One jail is pretty much like another. There's a lot of waiting around for nothing to happen. There's this feeling that your life is slipping away, like you're stuck in the weeds in the side of a river while the rest of the world floats on by you, and you're powerless to stop it. It drives some men crazy."

"I've heard stories from the guys in the town where I grew up. A few of them have been in prison. Or jail. Actually, I don't really know which they were in. But none of them described it like you did. They were just angry, you know? Kind of mean about it. You, though, you don't sound angry."

"Jail will make you angry," he said. "It's easy to be that way. You can't help it when you're locked up like that. Part of you resents the system for controlling everything you do, but another part of you kind of likes not having to take responsibility for yourself. I think those guys who let the anger eat them up are aware of that, at least on some level. They can't decide who they hate more, the system or themselves. That's a hard nut to crack. But then, you already know that, don't you?"

"I've never been in jail, Billy."

"No, I know that. But you've been blind most of your life. You're asking me about jail because you're wondering if feels the same way as being blind. That's it, isn't it?"

She didn't answer him, but she didn't look away, either. *That's it*, he thought. *I put my finger on it.*

Neither of them spoke. A gust of wind shook the awning roof over their heads and Billy felt a chill across his skin. He'd already felt several wet, icy raindrops fall on his face.

He said, "Are you cold? I'm cold."

"A little."

"Would you like me to walk you to the office? It's on my way."

Colin watched them slip into the office.

He felt so incredibly angry. He'd been betrayed by a skinny, blind, dark-haired fashion victim. What in the hell was she thinking being with him? He'd heard only the end of their conversation, but that was enough. That piece of shit was trying to use his time in jail to hit on his girlfriend. And the disgusting little whore had bought it, hook, line, and sinker.

Jeff's words echoed in his mind. *You've lost more than anybody. You lost all that, and it left a vacuum inside you.*

"Yeah, well, fuck that," he said aloud. "Fuck that."

Sure, he'd lost a lot, but fuck it all. Fuck them. Yeah, that was it. Fuck all of them. Jeff had thought he'd lost it all.

Well, he was wrong. He hadn't lost it all. He still had Kyra, no matter what that piece of shit Billy Kline thought. He had her, and he wasn't going to lose her. She was his, damn it. She was his right now, his alone, and nobody was going to take her away from him.

Nobody.

CHAPTER 49

Ed Moore woke to a siren blaring.

He sat up in bed quickly and tried to focus in the dark. The other men he shared this section of the dormitory with were sitting up as well, all of them looking around for an explanation.

Ed and Billy traded looks from across the aisle.

Ed got out of his cot and forced his feet into his boots. His toes were numb with the cold, and pressing them down into the leather sent pulses of pain through his feet.

"What's going on?" Billy asked.

"Perimeter alarm," Ed said. "Get your coat. Come on."

A moment later, the two of them ran out into the biting cold of the North Dakota predawn morning. The ground glittered with a fine crystalline layer of ice. Everywhere they looked, the Grasslands seemed empty, almost pristine. Only the insistent blaring of the siren and the distant sound of men yelling broke the calm.

"Ed?"

"Sounds like it's coming from the north gate." He let out a frustrated breath that misted before his eyes. "Damn, I wish I hadn't given up my guns."

"What are we supposed to do?"

The community had drilled for fires, and most of the folks in the Grasslands had taken basic CPR, but they had no public zombie contingency plans. Jasper's only public statement on the matter was that the perimeter fence would protect them from the small number of zombies likely to make it this far north. When pressed why non-Family members weren't allowed to keep their weapons, he said only that the Family would protect them from any zombie danger. Now, Ed was kicking himself for not squirreling away one of his guns.

Floodlights came on to their right. Ed and Billy both turned that way and saw bright white light spreading across the icy ground.

Behind them, and to their left, more and more people were coming out of their dormitories. They looked confused and frightened. Ed could hear the low murmur of their confused voices.

"Come on," he said, grabbing Billy by the sleeve.

"Where are we going?"

"Weapons," Ed said.

He guided Billy over to the still-unfinished dormitory number six building and the two of them chose cast-off pieces of lumber to use as cudgels. Then they were sprinting toward the main gate, the ice crunching beneath their feet. The siren continued to blare. Others were following them.

As they got close to the dirt road where the community's trucks were parked, they could see some of the armed patrols forming skirmish lines. Up ahead, in the bright glow of the floodlights, they saw the main gate hanging open and folded over at the top as though the supports that held it upright had been shattered. And beyond the gate, moving with agonizing slowness, were the infected.

Ed saw several hundred ruined faces, more than he had seen in one place since coming to the Grasslands. They were funneling toward the open gate. Several bodies already lay within.

As the patrols formed their lines, the sounds of yelling gradually died off, replaced by the rattle of sporadic gunfire.

One man was trying to yell orders to the patrols. Ed saw him waving wildly to somebody, but his features were lost in shadow and his voice drowned out by the roll of rifle fire.

Ed turned again toward the approaching zombies, but his gaze lingered on three of the corpses just inside the gate. There clothes were different from the other infected, newer, not soiled.

And then Ed was able to make out the face from the shadows, and he recognized Tom Wilder.

"Billy," Ed said.

Billy was staring at the zombies pouring through the gate, but at the sound of Ed's voice, he looked where Ed was pointing.

"What?" he said. And then he saw it. "Oh, shit."

The gunfire was growing steadier.

Billy turned to Ed. "Ed, that's Tom. What's going on?"

Ed didn't get to answer him.

The man who had been yelling and waving at them suddenly appeared in front of them. "What the hell are you doing?" he demanded. "You think you can do anything with sticks? Get back!"

And before Ed could protest, the man was pushing him back behind a makeshift cordon with the other members of the Grasslands.

Amid the sound of gunfire and people shouting and the constant, low vibrating moan of the infected came the sound of a truck approaching. Ed turned as the crowd of people around him zippered apart to let one of Jasper's black Chevy Tahoes glide past.

The Tahoe stopped, and Jasper and Michael Barnes got out.

Barnes had an AR-15 slung over his shoulder. He wore a light black jacket and jeans over brown work boots, and he moved casually, like one accustomed to this sort of thing.

Immediately, Barnes took charge. He took up a point position and motioned for six other members of the patrol to form up in a V behind him.

Ed raised an eyebrow as they advanced. He had worked crowd control in the wake of the L.A. riots back in 1992 and he knew that a unit didn't just fall into a fighting echelon position. It took lots of practice, lots of dress rehearsals. And even then it was hard to get right.

But Barnes and his team moved out silently, effortlessly. Barnes himself did most of the shooting. They advanced into the knot of zombies coming through the gate, their shots measured and precise. They made it look easy, and a moment later they had cleared the gate and were standing outside it, shooting at their leisure at every zombie that came within range.

Less than ten minutes later, with the echo of gunfire still sounding across the prairie, Barnes stepped back in through the gate. His AR-15 was slung over his shoulder again. There was a look of unflappable calm on his face.

Jasper was clapping, and a moment later, he was leading the crowd in cheers as he slapped Barnes on the back.

Ed watched it all with a growing sense of unease. Things were definitely not right. Not at all.

CHAPTER 50

Later that afternoon, after lunch, Billy Kline was making his way through a crowd of people returning to their work when he saw Kyra Talbot slipping around the corner of the office building. He hustled after her.

But when he rounded the corner, she was gone.

He stood there, confused, looking around.

He saw her again as she came around the far side of the office. She was wearing a red blouse and blue jeans, her hair down over her face, not her usual ponytail. It looked like she was in a hurry not to be seen.

"Kyra," he called after her.

She ducked her head and walked faster, feeling the wall with her fingertips for guidance.

"Kyra?"

Their last conversation had left him eager for more, and he broke into a trot and went after her.

"Kyra, wait up," he said. He was coming up behind her now. "It's me, Billy."

She wouldn't let him see her face.

"Kyra?"

He put a hand on her shoulder and she flinched.

"Sorry," he said, pulling his hand away. "Kyra, it's me, Billy. I didn't mean to scare you."

"I've got to go, Billy."

"Hey, wait," he said. He put his hand on her shoulder, and though she flinched again, he left it there. He turned her gently around to face him. "What's wrong?"

But he could see what was wrong. She had her hair down over her left eye and cheek, but he could still the shiner and the busted lip. The wounds stood out on her pale and slender face.

"What happened?"

"Nothing," she said. She touched the wall and turned away.

"Wait," he said. "Who did this to you?"

"Nobody. I fell."

"Bullshit," he said. She flinched again, this time at the anger in his voice. "I'm sorry," he said. "Kyra, please, who did this to you?"

Then it came to him.

"It was Colin, wasn't it?"

She didn't speak, but she gave a quick, almost imperceptible nod of her head.

"That bastard. Where is he?"

"Billy, please, you've done enough."

"Me?"

"He heard us talking. I told him it wasn't nothing, but he got so mad. The more I tried to make him understand, the madder he got."

"Oh, God," Billy said. "When did this happen?"

"This morning."

He closed his eyes and took a deep breath. When he opened them again, Kyra's sightless eyes were pointed right at him. They were shining, but no tears had fallen.

She was scared. He could tell that. Surviving Van Horn had brought her out of her shell. That was what he had seen in her that first night in Emporia, Kansas, and that had attracted him to her. But her first attempt to trust somebody had gotten her this, and the injustice of it made him want to kick something.

"I think your eye's gonna be okay," he said. "But we need to put something on that lip. If I go get some ice, will you let me help you?"

She nodded her head slightly, and her hair fell down over her face again.

"I'll be right back," he said. "Will you wait for me here? I promise I'll be right back."

She nodded.

Kyra listened to his footsteps fading away in the grass and thought of running. She could probably make it back to her dormitory before he caught up with her, and she could spend the rest of the day in bed. If Aaron came looking for her, she could tell him she wasn't feeling well. She had a stomachache. Her eyes were hurting. Hell, she could tell him any damn thing, just so long as they would leave her alone.

She hadn't felt this helpless in a long time. It was worse than walking the highway after escaping Van Horn. Even, in a way, worse than losing Uncle Reggie. Since coming to the Grasslands, the world had grown brighter. She was contributing to the effort. She was making a difference. And then this, two hard slaps from someone she had trusted, from someone she had given her virginity to, and suddenly she was that scared and isolated four-year-old little girl all over again, alone in her head and alone in the world.

"It went smoothly," she heard a man say. "Just like I said it would."

The voice came from around the corner to her right. As quickly as she could, she ducked back around the corner to her left and pressed her back into the wall.

"That's good, Michael. Very good. You did good work, getting the bodies out of here."

Jasper's voice! Kyra sucked in a breath.

"It wasn't hard. We put 'em with the zombies we shot this morning and burned them."

"Good."

"But Jasper, our house isn't clean yet."

"Yes, I know. Those men had help."

"That seems pretty plain, yeah."

"Do you know who?" Jasper asked.

"Not yet."

"But you'll find them out."

"Yes."

"I cannot abide a traitor, Michael. Even that man who sins in his mind against me has betrayed me, and I will not abide a traitor."

"No, of course not."

"You'll begin searching the village for the missing radios?"

"Immediately."

"Very good," Jasper said. "I'll see you this afternoon then."

Kyra heard the door to the office creak open, then slam shut. The second man's footsteps faded away in the opposite direction. She stood absolutely still against the wall, listening, unable to catch her breath. She felt like the ground beneath her feet was shaking.

The whole world, it seemed, was shaking.

CHAPTER 51

"Nate."

A distant gunshot, somewhere down the hall.

"Nate, damn it, get up."

More gunfire, three or four shots. Closer now.

From Nate, a mutter: *"Get off me."*

Kellogg gave him a hard shake. He pulled the blankets away and saw the blood pooled under Nate's thighs and under his buttocks. He saw the deep, ragged cuts up Nate's left wrist.

"Nate, Jesus. Oh, Jesus. What did you do?"

"Fuck off. Lemme die."

"Oh, crap, Nate."

Kellogg threw the covers off the bed and scooped up one of the sheets. He tried to tear it with his fingers and couldn't. He used his teeth until he felt the fabric give, and then he tore it into strips. "Here, give me your hand," he said, and yanked Nate's wrist into his lap. Working fast, he wrapped the strips around the wound, keeping up the pressure.

"Christ, you lost a lot of blood. What the hell were you thinking, Nate?"

"Lemme alone." Nate was listless, his voice slurred and

faraway. He resisted, but he was as weak as a kitten, and Kellogg was able to pull him off the bed without any trouble.

"You're gonna have to stand on your own, Nate. Can you do that?"

"Lemme alone. I don't want to go with you."

"You have to, Nate. They're inside the hospital. Christ, they're everywhere."

"Huh? Lemme go."

"Not on your life."

Kellogg got his shoulder under Nate's uninjured arm and hoisted him upward. Outside in the hall, he could hear a woman screaming and the sound of something heavy being dragged along the linoleum floor.

"I don't know how they got inside, but they're everywhere. Nate, can you walk?"

A mutter. A grunt.

Kellogg pulled his pistol at the door. As they stepped into the hallway, a soldier with a big chunk of his face missing shambled forward, a moan gurgling up from his throat.

Kellogg raised his pistol and fired, laying the soldier out on his back.

"Come on," he said. "This way."

"Where are you taking me? Lemme go."

The main lights were down, and only the dim red glow of the emergency lights lit the hallway. In the shadows ahead, Kellogg saw an infected soldier kneeling over a civilian. The body was twitching as the soldier tore into it with his teeth. There was a long, gory trail of blood on the ground, and it looked like the civilian had been dragged to her current spot from a side hallway.

The zombie rose to his feet as Kellogg and Nate approached. Kellogg shot him without even looking at his face, then turned down a side hallway and started to pick up speed.

"Where are you taking me?"

"Cafeteria on two. Gotta take the back stairs, though. The whole first floor is overrun."

"Just lemme die here, doc. I don't want to go."

Kellogg looked Nate in the face. His skin was ashen, the lips tinged blue. There was a dull, glassy torpor in his eyes.

"You're not gonna die, Nate. I won't let that happen."

To his left, Kellogg saw a stairwell. It was dark, but in the darkness he could see a faint red glow and tendrils of smoke rising up to the landing. From somewhere down below, he could hear the sound of fighting mixed with the moans of the infected. Off to his right was a long, empty hallway, also dark, and as he stared down its length he had a sudden flashback to San Antonio and the five days he'd spent wandering the hallways of Brooke Army Medical Center, fighting the infected and praying for rescue.

Their first cases had come in late in the afternoon by EMS. Kellogg's specialty was blood-borne pathogens, and he had no idea why they were calling him into the ER. The scant description they gave him made it sound like the San Antonio Police Department had beat the shit out of a handful of meth freaks, and now they expected him to . . . do what exactly? Triage wasn't his thing.

And then he stepped into the ER, and everything changed. There were bodies everywhere. People were screaming. Doctors and nurses were moving from bed to bed like ants on a mound. Nobody seemed to have any idea what was going on. Kellogg saw terrible wounds on every bed he passed. He saw firefighters and cops with blood all over their uniforms, some of them slumped on their butts on the floor, heads hanging in exhaustion. A woman was tied down to an EMS gurney. Her lips had been torn off. She was straining against her bonds to reach him, her face bright with fever, eyes milky and bloodshot, every vein and piece of connective tissue in her neck standing out like electrical cords beneath her skin. Kellogg stared at her in shock. A nurse pushed by him and nearly knocked him down. "Excuse me," he said angrily. But the nurse didn't even pause to acknowledge the contact. Kellogg turned back to the woman on the gurney, and only then did he see the blackened necrotic tissue in the wounds around her mouth. Only then did he smell the unmistakable odor of rotting flesh. In that moment, he knew this was no typical San Antonio Saturday-night street brawl gone bad. This was something else entirely.

He turned to find the officer in charge. He wasn't sure what they had yet, but he was already sure they were dealing with something highly virulent, and in his head, Kellogg was running down his list of containment options. It was difficult to pick apart the exact moment that things got out of hand. Perhaps it was already too late before Kellogg even stepped foot in the ER. But what he remembered of that first afternoon was the shooting. Three shots, high and hollow-sounding pops. He turned to see a wounded cop shooting at two men in a hallway to his left. Everyone hit the deck. Then they watched as the men lumbered forward, one of them already shot twice in the abdomen, and collapsed on the cop.

It was chaos after that. Any pretense at organized triage broke down. The infected—though at the time he still wasn't thinking of them as such—rose more or less en masse and fell on the staff. People were yanked off their feet. Kellogg watched a friend of his get his throat torn out by an overweight woman in a bloodstained black miniskirt. A man with deep, infected scratches along the side of his face grabbed Kellogg by the shoulders and tried to throw him to the ground. Kellogg twisted in the man's arms and swept his legs out from under him. The man went down easily, clumsily, like a drunk, and though he hit his head on a corner of the wall, he rolled over and got back to his feet without acknowledging the pain. He stumbled forward, and for the first time, Kellogg heard the moaning that would forever afterward haunt his sleep. "Back off," he said to the man. But the man kept coming. Kellogg backed up and hit a chair. He pulled it around and raised it between him and the man. When the man held out his hands to grab, Kellogg caught him up in the legs of the chair and twisted, throwing him to the ground once more.

He was left on his feet, staring across the confusion on the ER floor, looking at the open exterior doors. Outside, dusk was just starting to settle over the parking lot. The sky was pink, and the lights of San Antonio's skyline were just visible in the distance above the thicket of oak trees that lined the southern perimeter of the base. That had been his moment. He could have run for it right then and made it outside. Maybe escaped into the city itself and saved himself five days of hell. But he didn't take it. He waited just a moment too long, and a moment later the gap closed and the daylight was gone. Only the nightmare remained.

Behind him, he heard the sound of a body hitting the floor, and it roused him from his thoughts. Kellogg looked around him, at the damaged hospital and Nate Royal hanging on his arm, his breath sour and rancid against his cheeks, and Kellogg's head felt clearer than it had in days. He turned and saw the infected coming up the stairs. Four of them. Now six, then nine more. He could hear more on the stairs below.

"Nate," he said.

A weak mutter.

"Come on, buddy, time to go."

So the back stairs were out. Ahead of them, at the end of the hallway, was a waiting room that overlooked the lobby. There might be a way down to the second floor from there, but Kellogg wasn't sure.

With the infected behind them, filling up the hallway with

their moans, Kellogg pulled Nate toward the doors on their right. Nate wasn't resisting, but he was nearly deadweight on Kellogg's shoulder and it made moving difficult. By the time they reached the end of the hallway, three of the infected had managed to close the gap between them. Kellogg turned and shot the lead zombie in the chin, blowing the bottom of the zombie's face off in two large bloody chunks. The zombie went down and flailed against the ground, trying to get back up, but Kellogg didn't bother with a follow-up shot. There wasn't time. Another zombie was on him. Kellogg fired and managed only a glancing blow to the thing's shoulder. The bullet's impact spun the zombie around but didn't put it down.

Kellogg reached for the door and tried to push it open, realizing too late that it was controlled by a panel button along the wall of the hallway.

There was another zombie between him and the panel button, and more coming down the hall. He threw his shoulder into the door, but couldn't get any leverage against it while still holding Nate's weight.

Nate groaned, then slipped off Kellogg's arm.

At first, Kellogg thought Nate was falling and he tried to catch him, but Nate pushed him away. "I'm okay," he said. "Get the door open."

Kellogg threw his shoulder into the door and felt it give a little, but it still wouldn't open.

"The button on the wall," he said to Nate.

Kellogg raised his pistol and shot the zombie in front of the button, this time landing a solid head shot. The zombie fell back against the wall and sagged to the ground, spreading a smeared line of gore down to the floor.

But before Kellogg could step into the gap to hit the button, Nate was there. A zombie lunged at him from his left and took a bite of Nate's forearm, causing Nate to erupt in a scream so raw it seemed almost feral. The two of them wrestled awkwardly as Kellogg, momentarily frozen, stood there watching.

"Hit the fucking button," Nate said.

Kellogg shook himself. He jumped forward and slapped the button on the wall. Behind him, the doors swung open, revealing a wide, carpeted, comfortable-looking waiting room with couches and chairs arranged around a TV set mounted on the far wall. Beyond the furniture was a row of cubicles separated by thick round columns that rose to a height of about ten feet off the floor but didn't go all the way to the ceiling, the tops festooned with ferns.

He grabbed the back of Nate's shirt and pulled him away from the zombie. A moment later, they were rushing across the waiting room toward the cubicles and climbing up the walls to the top of the nearest column. Kellogg pushed Nate onto the column, then scrambled up after him. He dropped down next to Nate and kicked the plants down on top of the zombies reaching up for him.

"That was close," he said.

Beside him, Nate was clutching his arm, his eyes tightly shut against the pain.

Below them, the room filled up with zombies.

"They sure got on us fast enough."

Kellogg pulled his knees up to his chest. He was breathing hard from the climb up the column, and sweat had dampened his scrubs so that they stuck to his chest. He glanced over the side, into a ring of snarling, mangled faces, and said, "Yeah, they tend to do that. You hear that in every survivor's description, how fast they swarm. We still haven't figured out how they do that."

"How come they don't kill each other?"

"What do you mean?"

"When they attack somebody who's not infected. I've seen how sometimes they kill people—eat them, you know—but most of the time they don't. I mean, they're still in good enough shape to get up and chase other people around after they turn. Why is that?"

Kellogg was still winded. "Nobody really knows why they stop attacking a victim when they do. I don't think it's a conscious decision. It can't be, actually. They don't have any capacity for conscious thought, so it can't be that."

A dead body was propping the door open, and more and more zombies were coming into the waiting room, attracted by the moaning.

Kellogg said, "I think the important thing to remember is that these people are basically human-sized viruses after they turn, and a virus is like any living thing, up to a point. Its goal is to reproduce itself, to survive. That's what the infected are doing. They're spreading the virus. Propagating the species."

"You mean the viruses are the ones telling people how much they can hurt somebody?"

Kellogg frowned. "Well, no. Not in so many words."

"How can viruses do that?" Nate asked.

Kellogg looked at him. "They can't, Nate. Not really. It's more of an expression. A handy way to look at the problem, you know?"

"Yeah, I guess," Nate said doubtfully. He turned his arm over in his lap and inspected the bite he'd just received.

To Kellogg, the wound didn't look too bad. It had already stopped bleeding. In his mind, he reviewed rates of infection, all the various factors that went into motion as soon as a person became infected. By all rights, Nate should have been showing at least a few of the early signs of infection, like labored breathing, sweating, irritability. It was too early still for confusion and unfocused aggression, or for the rank odor of necrotic flesh, but regardless, any normal person would have been showing some signs of the change.

"You did a brave thing back there," Kellogg said. "Thanks."

Nate grunted. "They can't hurt me. I'm immune."

True, Kellogg thought. "No courage without consequences, I guess."

"I don't know what that means," Nate said.

"It means you're only brave if there's a chance you can actually get killed."

"You're making fun of me."

"No, Nate, I'm not."

"Whatever."

Kellogg picked at a loose part of the carpet near the edge of the column. He said, "Nate, you mind if I ask you something?"

Silence.

"Why did you try to hurt yourself?"

"I didn't try to hurt myself. I was trying to fucking kill myself. There's a difference."

Kellogg shrugged. "Yeah, I guess that's true."

He flicked a bit of the carpet down into the face of one of the zombies. It landed on the man's bottom lip and hung there amid a spray of white spit.

"I told you the world needed you, Nate. Didn't you believe me?"

"Fuck the world," Nate said. "The worthless scum-sucking bastards never did shit for me."

"So you won't do shit for them. Is that about the size of it?"

"Yeah, sure."

"You think that's fair?"

For the first time, Nate looked him in the eye. "Who gives a fuck if it's fair or not? You ask me, they all deserve to die."

Kellogg raised an eyebrow at that. "Nate," he said. "You're a nihilist, aren't you?"

"You're making fun of me again."

Kellogg laughed. "No, Nate, I'm not."

"Then stop calling me things that I don't know what they are."

Kellogg paused.

"You're right, Nate. That's not fair." He straightened himself up and turned as much as he could to face Nate. He said, "A nihilist is a person who believes in nothing. I mean nothing. He believes in nothing the way other men believe in liberty or God. They don't see any reason to be loyal to anyone or anything because none of it matters. There's no point to anything we do. In fact, a true nihilist has one guiding notion, and that is to destroy, to make all things nothing."

Nate rubbed his arm. "I don't want to destroy anything."

"Yes, Nate, you do. You want to destroy the one thing in this world that has any value. You want to destroy yourself."

Nate seemed to consider that. Then he said, "I told you. I don't owe anybody shit."

"Okay, I'll grant you that. But have you stopped to think why that's true?"

"Why what's true? Stop trying to confuse me."

"Nate, I'm not—Look, I'm not trying to make fun of you, Nate. I see you struggling with this, and I want to help."

"Why?"

"Because I get it, Nate. I understand where the hatred of the world comes from. I used to work in a hospital. I've seen the disgusting things people do to each other. I get it, Nate. I know the world is a mean and nasty place filled with people who don't deserve to go on living another minute. I understand where the impulse to nihilism comes from. But the thing is, Nate, I just don't buy it."

"You don't?"

"No, I don't."

"Why not?"

"Well, some people have God to fall back on. They say that nihilism is indefensible because ultimately there is God behind it all to give life meaning."

"I don't believe in God."

"No, me neither."

From somewhere below them, the sound of gunfire was increasing. They could hear shouting, somebody giving orders.

"Sounds like they've almost got to us," Kellogg said. "Hopefully, we won't be up here much longer."

Nate was silent for a long moment. Kellogg sensed that he was turning thoughts over in his head, questions that suddenly demanded answers.

"So why don't you buy it then?" Nate said. "If you don't believe in God, why bother? Why don't you just kill yourself?"

"You're not the first person to ask that, Nate. About seventy years ago, a man named Albert Camus asked the same question. He said that there is but one truly serious philosophical problem, and that is suicide. He said that life itself was—"

"I don't care what he said. I want to know what you think. Why don't you kill yourself?"

Kellogg sighed. "I don't think there has to be a reason, Nate. Not a good one, anyway. We are put into this hostile, alien world as isolated individuals. We can learn to like other people, even love them, but we can't ever truly know them, and so we remain isolated. We're not allowed to know why life has meaning, not for sure anyway, and yet we feel compelled to create some sort of answer. It's an absurd downward spiral of impossible things, and yet it's our lives."

"So what does that mean?" Nate asked. "Are you saying that a world based on bad reasons is enough?"

Kellogg thought about that. "Yeah, I guess I am. To me, there doesn't have to be a right answer. The questioning, the searching for an answer is enough in and of itself. I find that liberating."

"Like . . . running into daylight?"

"You lost me, Nate. I'm not sure what that means."

"You know, like, running into daylight. When the whole world goes white. It's like it goes on forever. It doesn't matter how fast or how hard you run. The world goes on forever."

"Okay," Kellogg said. He wasn't following Nate's reasoning, but he saw that Nate was onto something, in his own head at least, and that had been the point he was trying to get across in the first place, that we find meaning in our personal struggles to understand.

Kellogg picked at the scrubs stuck to his thighs. He was sweating fiercely, and feeling a little dehydrated.

He said, "God, it's hot. Are you hot?"

Nate shrugged. "I'm okay."

"Seriously? You're not hot?"

"I'm okay."

That stopped Kellogg. He looked at Nate and realized that was true. In all the tests they'd run on him, the only thing that stood out at all was his temperature. Always low. They'd injected him with both live and dead necrosis filovirus doses, and Nate's body had never raised its core temperature to infection-fighting levels. That got Kellogg thinking. Fever was the body's way of fighting infection. But what if that reaction was what the necrosis filovirus thrived on? What would happen to a body that didn't give the virus what it wanted, like Nate's?

There was gunfire out in the hallway. Somebody was barking orders, calling out if anybody was alive down here.

"In here," Kellogg shouted.

Soldiers burst through the door. The zombies clustered

around the column turned and stumbled for the soldiers advancing across the floor.

It was over in seconds.

Then a security forces lieutenant was standing at the base of the column, surrounded by dead bodies.

He said, "Major, you guys okay up there?"

"Yep, we're good." Kellogg and Nate traded smiles.

CHAPTER 52

Dinner was barbecued chicken and creamed corn and green beans, all dishes Kyra had loved growing up. But now the food tasted like ash in her mouth. Nothing had been right for the last two days, not since Colin had gotten so angry with her. Even eating was a chore.

She put her fork down. She felt so confused, so irritable. Nothing made sense. She'd put so much trust in Colin and look what it had got her. She was feeling sorry for herself and lying to everyone else around her. *No, I'm okay. No, no one hit me. I fell down the stairs. It happens to blind people all the time.* Jesus, had it really come to this?

She remembered a girl she'd known in her real-world-skills class, blind like her, who was something of a wonder to the other girls because she dated a sighted boy, went out on real dates. The girl told Kyra one day how she'd made out with the boy on her parent's couch, letting him take off her shirt, bra, and jeans, but stopping him at her panties. The boy hadn't stopped, though. He got her panties off and stuck two fingers inside her. But the girl refused to call it rape. She said it was her fault, that she'd been wrong to lead the guy on like that. Kyra had gotten so disgusted at the girl's self-deception that she refused to talk to her ever again. And at that moment, she'd promised herself she would live without her sight, but never without her self-respect, not like that girl. That really was blind.

And yet, here she was, dodging a boyfriend who had beaten her up. She was running scared instead of taking back her self-respect and doing something about it. Was she any different? She hadn't told anybody. Well, nobody except Billy, of course, and look what that had gotten her. She hadn't done anything about it. Instead, she ate when the pavilion was empty. She told them she was too sick to work. She'd started wearing sunglasses when she had to appear in public. Anything to avoid the truth.

But she had no idea what else to do. After what she'd heard the other day behind the office, she couldn't even go to Jasper.

Why didn't anything make sense?

She heard Colin's voice behind her and stiffened.

"Where?" he asked. His voice sounded strained, urgent.

A voice she didn't recognize said, "I don't know. I saw her go that way."

Kyra got up from the table and felt her way to the main aisle that divided the rows of picnic tables. From there, she walked as fast as she could toward the back of the pavilion. She stumbled on the first step, but didn't fall. The lawn sloped downward toward the playground. She had a vague mental map of it, but she didn't know this part of the camp very well, and the uncertainty of every step terrified her.

"Please," she said, whimpering with every step.

"Kyra!"

"No. Oh, God, no!" For the first time in her adult life, she broke into a run.

The voice behind her turned from a shout to an angry hiss. "Kyra, Goddamn it. Stop!"

Her right foot collided painfully with a wooden log and

she pitched forward into playground gravel. She threw her hands out reflexively and clutched fistfuls of small, rounded pebbles. Her foot was pulsing with pain, but she didn't stop moving.

"Kyra, get back here."

She rolled over onto her back and couldn't stop gasping.

"Colin, no. Please." She heard his footsteps coming closer. "Please, Colin. Leave me alone."

"Where the hell have you been?"

She braced for the worst. In her mind, she had an image of him grabbing her hair and dragging her across the lawn. She thought, *He's gonna hurt me. Oh, Jesus, he's gonna kill me.*

Her body tensed in anticipation of the worst.

The blood was roaring in Colin's head. His peripheral vision disappeared. The air around Kyra was sizzling, diffuse, like it was shot through with heat shimmers. There was only Kyra on her back, hands up in the air like she had a chance in hell of stopping this, her chest heaving.

The little bitch deserved a beating for putting him through this. Didn't she know how good he could make things for her? Damn it, all he asked in return was a little respect.

"Colin, please," she said.

But her whining only served to send him deeper into his rage. "Get up," he said.

"Colin, no."

"I said get up. Now. Get your ass up."

His whole body was trembling with rage. He reached for her, but just as he was about to put his hands on her, he felt a hammer blow to the back of his knees that dropped him onto his ass.

He looked up and saw Billy Kline staring down at him.

"What in the fuck do you think you're doing?" Colin said.

Billy ignored him. "Kyra, you okay?"

"Get the fuck out of here," Colin said. "This isn't any of your business, asshole."

"Dude, you cuss a lot, man. You should watch your mouth."

Colin jumped to his feet. His heart was beating like a wild bird in a cage. The skin of his face was tingling. There was no fear. There was only a red veil that had dropped over his vision and a terrible urge to tear Billy Kline's eyes from the sockets. He ran at Billy and pushed him.

Billy grabbed his hands and twisted, and the next thing Colin knew, he was on his ass again.

"Motherfucker," he said.

"Better stay down."

Colin rushed him again. He swung wildly and the punch missed. Billy just disappeared, only to pop up far enough to Colin's right that he couldn't get turned around in time. Billy pumped his left twice to Colin's face, knocking him backward and off balance. His legs felt like sand beneath him and the world went purple as he fell to the ground.

When he looked up, Billy was standing over Kyra, helping her to her feet.

Colin tried to stand and couldn't.

"Goddamn it," he yelled. "Motherfucker."

Billy glanced back at him, but didn't say anything. He put his arm around Kyra and the two of them walked away.

"No," Colin shouted. "No!"

But there was nothing he could do. He couldn't make his legs work, and the girl was gone. *Fucking little bitch*, he thought, sagging to the ground. *You can't do this to me.*

CHAPTER 53

Colin went back to his bunk in dormitory number two and put his head down gently on the pillow. There was a ringing in his ears that wouldn't go away. His jaw and his knees and tailbone were all sore, but it was his pride that hurt the most. He let his gaze wander around the large, open barracks. Sunlight slanted in through the windows on the north wall, touching the white sheets on the empty beds around him, lending the room a sepulchral aspect. How could this have happened to him? He looked back over the events of the last few months and it was a complete mystery to him. He'd been on the verge of inheriting one of the largest fortunes in America. Now, he'd lost one of his oldest friends and had been reduced to fighting a two-bit Florida peckerwood over a damn blind girl. It just didn't seem possible that he could have fallen so far.

He rolled over and slept fitfully for the remainder of the day. When he awoke, the sky was plum-colored and there was a faint odor of wood smoke in the air from the barbecue pits down in the common area around the pavilion.

His anger had subsided a little, but it still grated on his nerves the way he'd been outplayed and abused by Billy

Kline. The barrack's wooden floors were cold, and so he slipped on his shoes before he went to the bathroom at the end of the hall to wash his face. There were bruises at the corner of his mouth and on the point of his cheek and around his right eye. He tried to think of a way to hide the injuries but knew it was pointless. Even an idiot would be able to tell that he'd had his ass handed to him in a fistfight.

He stared at his reflection in the mirror and a thought that had been going around in his head since he lay down came back to him.

Michael Barnes. He was the solution to this.

In very little time at all, the man had become one of Jasper Sewell's favorites, and though nothing was ever said officially in front of the whole Grasslands community, it was generally acknowledged that Michael Barnes was the head of internal security at the compound. Ever since the morning that the infected had broken through the main gate, he'd had Jasper's ear. If there was some way, through Barnes, to heap Jasper's asperity onto Billy Kline, then he could remove his rival without lifting a finger. It would be the best kind of revenge.

Yes, indeed, the best kind.

Later that night, after most of the compound had retired indoors to get out of the cold, Colin knocked softly on Michael Barnes's office door and poked his head inside.

Barnes sat behind his desk, reading some kind of report and making notes.

Colin said, "Uh, excuse me—" He was uncertain how to address Barnes, and so he added, "Sir?"

Barnes didn't look up.

"Uh, is it okay if I talk to you for a second? It's kind of important."

"I'm busy," Barnes said. He didn't bother to look up.

"I know you are, sir. But this is important."

Barnes put down his pen and looked at Colin. Barnes was lean, severe, all hard angles. The ligature of his neck stood out like cables beneath his skin. Everything about him suggested a wild animal waiting to strike.

"What's your name?"

"Colin Wyndham, sir."

Barnes seemed to be searching his mental Rolodex. "Oh, yeah," he said. "You're from Los Angeles."

"Yes, sir."

"You came here with a group from Florida."

"Well, yes, sir. But we only hooked up with them as we were heading through Kansas. I'm not *with* them."

Barnes just looked at him.

"It's actually them I wanted to talk to you about. Can I sit down, please?"

He made a gesture toward the chair opposite Barnes.

Barnes didn't answer, and Colin didn't push it. He suddenly felt very small, very afraid. This wasn't going to be as easy as he thought it would be.

"I think a couple of the people in the Florida group are spreading lies about Jasper."

Barnes's eyes narrowed. "What kind of lies?"

Colin thought of Billy Kline with his girl, and the words came pouring out.

Michael Barnes spent the next two days keeping an eye on Ed Moore and Billy Kline. His experience as a cop had taught him that people never change. Reformation was a pipe dream. You start out as a piece of shit, you'll remain a piece of shit no matter what the rest of the world tries to do on your behalf. Billy Kline was a car burglar, a thief, and in

Barnes's estimation, thieves were like sex offenders and drug addicts. They were broken on a fundamental level. The only cure was a bullet.

But he was surprised about Ed Moore, the retired U.S. Deputy Marshal. The man had been a cop for thirty-five years, a marine before that. If anybody could appreciate the way Jasper had stamped a sense of order onto a world that made absolutely no sense, it should have been Ed Moore. Didn't he have everything he needed here? What was wrong with him that he couldn't see that?

The screen door opened behind him and a young man of about seventeen came out. Jasper had his arm around the boy's shoulder. They both looked disheveled, the hair on their brows matted with sweat. Jasper was wearing an enormous grin, and as he stepped outside, he breathed deeply of the cool morning air.

The boy looked docile, and he wouldn't look Barnes in the eye.

"You're doing well, Thomas," Jasper said. "Very well. What did you think of today?"

The boy mumbled something that sounded like he said that he liked it very much.

"Fine, fine," Jasper said, squeezing the boy's shoulders tightly. "Very fine. I'm looking forward to sharing another session with you soon, Thomas. Can you come by tomorrow morning, say, just before breakfast?"

"I don't know if—"

"You come by tomorrow morning, Thomas. I'll see you here at seven, okay?"

The boy nodded. Then he slipped out of Jasper's embrace and trotted back toward the center of the village, limping slightly.

"Fine boy," Jasper said. He stared out over the prairie and breathed deeply again. "I've hardly seen you the last two days, Michael. What have you been doing?"

"I've been looking into some things."

"I see," he said. "You've found out something?"

Barnes nodded.

"Well, I guess you better come in, then. Let's hear what you've got."

Chapter 54

Later that week, on a cold, gray October morning, Aaron Roberts walked with his wife, Kate, and his son, Thomas, across the narrow stretch of ground that separated his cottage from Jasper's, marveling to himself how quickly the seasons changed here in North Dakota.

A fine powdery layer of snow lay upon the compound, and the dark wood of the cottages around Jasper's private quarters stood out in stark relief from the whiteness of the snow and the depthless gray of the sky. The cold had been upon them for nearly a month, but not the biting cold that now stung his cheeks and turned his hands to claws. That had come upon them almost overnight. As a boy, he'd read stories of Indian fighters who passed this way during the 1870s and 1880s, men whose pants had frozen to their saddles and whose spit had turned to ice with an explosive crackle before it hit the ground. He'd known that the coming winter was going to be a hard one, but until this very morning, he hadn't quite realized just how hard it was going to be.

Out of the corner of his eye he caught Kate looking at him. There were creases around her mouth and a sadness in her eyes that suggested the years were catching up with her.

How much of that, he wondered, had happened in just the last few months?

Behind them, Thomas followed along with his head down, eyes on his shoes.

Aaron and Kate both slowed so their son could catch up. Aaron watched Thomas trudge through the snow, and a wave of grief washed over him. The boy—hadn't he been calling him a man just a couple of weeks ago?—had grown increasingly despondent since his first visit to Jasper, and seeing it stirred up familiar feelings of anger and pity and self-loathing for the way it had happened.

The feelings were unexpected, too. Aaron himself had shared Jasper's bed numerous times over the years. As had Kate. For them, sexual congress with Jasper had been an act of faith, a form of communion with the man whose brilliance and spiritual guidance had made it so that their world made sense. Watching Thomas grow, he'd looked forward to the day when Thomas, too, could find the same sense of oneness that he'd found. But now, as he watched the transformation that had come over his son, he felt hollow inside, and he was aware that what had started out as an act of fatherly kindness had been transmuted through some horrible alchemy into sin and betrayal.

Thomas would not look him in the eye any longer—hadn't since that first visit to Jasper's bed. He complained of fatigue and nausea in the mornings. He seemed to have lost his appetite completely. And, worst of all, when Aaron put his hand on his son's shoulder, he felt Thomas's back constrict and a shudder move through the boy's body. During those moments, he could picture once again the morning Jasper had asked Aaron to send Thomas to him. He could hear Thomas pleading with him, the tears streaming down his cheeks as he begged not to go.

They'd fought. For the first time in years, they'd fought. Screaming had filled their small cabin. And Aaron had responded with renewed anger, his self-doubt turning into a rigid demand for obedience. Aaron had not cried since he was a teenager, but he had cried that morning.

But what could he do? Really, honestly, what could he do? His whole world was here, in this place. He had devoted everything to Jasper. More than half his life had been steered by that man. The structure of his family, his worldview, his relationship with God, all of that had been shaped by Jasper, guided by his wisdom. Could he really divorce himself from that now, with the rest of the world in ashes?

"Aaron," Kate said. "Baby, you okay?"

He looked at her. Between them, his eyes cast down at his shoes, Thomas seemed like a shell of the person he had once been.

"I don't know, Kate. I just don't know."

They entered Jasper's quarters and found Barnes and several of Jasper's lieutenants seated around the coffee table, waiting for them. Jasper stood next to the small dining room table in the back right corner of the house. A tray of paper Dixie cups was next to him on the table, each one containing what looked like wine.

"Thomas," Jasper said to Aaron's son. "Come here and take this for me."

He gestured toward the tray. With barely concealed reluctance, Thomas crossed the room and took the tray to the coffee table without a word, while Aaron and Kate took their places on the couch.

"I want each of you to pick up a cup," Jasper said.

Everyone leaned forward and picked up a cup. A few of the younger lieutenants traded looks around. Aaron didn't bother to meet anyone else's gaze.

"The wine is mixed with potassium cyanide. Drink this and you will die within two minutes." Jasper's southern twang gave the words a chilly resonance. "Now raise your cups. Go on, each of you. Let's see 'em."

The group each raised their cups. Aaron could feel the nervous tension in the room, and yet he also felt strangely dead to it.

"Now drink," Jasper commanded them.

Nobody moved.

A few cups wavered in the air as people traded anxious looks. The man across the table from Aaron swallowed, his Adam's apple pumping in his throat like a piston.

One of the younger lieutenants, a black man named Lucius Johnson, said, "Jasper, I don't wanna drink it."

Aaron glanced up. He expected Jasper to fly into a rage and start screaming at the man. This was the kind of thing that set him off, direct disobedience to a command. But Jasper surprised him. He spoke quietly, softly, to the man. "Lucius, you drink that up, you hear? I got my reasons. If you love me, if you believe in me, you'll drink."

Barnes drank his down in one gulp. Then he leaned forward and dropped his empty cup on the tray.

Kate and Thomas and a few other lieutenants drank theirs as well. Without raising his head, Aaron raised his cup and slowly sipped it down. The wine was overly fruity, with a cheap boozy aftertaste. He hadn't had a drink since he was seventeen, not out of a sense of decorum or religious conviction, but because he didn't like the taste, and he found age hadn't changed him in that direction. It was still a foul substance.

He put his cup on the table next to the others.

Lucius was crying. He said, "Jasper . . ."

"Don't be afraid," Jasper said. "There's no pain. You'll just fall asleep."

The man had tears in his eyes as he raised the cup to his lips and swallowed it down in a hurry. He sat there for a moment longer with the cup to his lips, his eyes closed, his fingers trembling. After a while, he put the cup down and waited, the dark skin of his cheeks looking flushed.

"Excellent," Jasper said. "Excellent. Each and every one of you." He pulled out a chair from the dining room table and sat down with them in the circle. "I believe in each of you, just as you believe in me. This is our covenant, and it will not be broken. Now listen. None of you will die today." He looked at Michael Barnes. "Some of you, perhaps, have already figured that out. What you did just now was prove yourself to me. And that proof will be important in the days ahead."

He leaned forward and laced his fingers together, pointing at the family members with his doubled index fingers.

"Something terrible happened this morning, and I need to tell you about it."

Aaron glanced up. He expected to hear about the zombies they'd been seeing more and more of. Aaron had heard Barnes's reports from the field, and they were not encouraging. The hard, cold weather hadn't done a thing to slow the zombie advance. If anything, their numbers were increasing, and each morning, Michael Barnes had to lead teams out through the gate to clear the roads.

But then Jasper surprised him. He took off his sunglasses and broke into the deep, resonant voice he reserved for the pulpit.

"For months now, I have been telling you that the American government has betrayed us. They have set their sights upon us because we dared to speak up against their injustices. While they sought to preserve the privilege of the rich, we preached to the poor. While they sought to contain the nonwhite races, we held out our hands to all the races. They created a pressure cooker in the form of the Gulf Coast Quarantine, and when it exploded, we dared to survive. We set up this outpost of progress here on the prairie in open defiance to their ways, and it has driven them to distraction.

"I listen to them on the radio, talking about us. Spreading lies about us. Ah, if you only heard the filth they talked about us. Well, it seems they have finally decided to test us directly."

Aaron took Kate's hand.

"Yesterday morning I was contacted by the United States Air Force Base in Minot. They want to send a delegation here. They told me they've heard of the wonderful things we are doing, and they're looking to see why we're doing so well."

Lucius Johnson said, "It's a trick. They want to take our homes away."

The others murmured in assent.

"A moment," said Jasper. "Brother Lucius, you're absolutely correct. I know it's a trick." He turned to Barnes. "Go ahead, Brother Michael."

Barnes looked around the room, making sure the others were all looking at him.

"I went to Minot last night," he said. "It's a large base, well supplied, but they are surrounded by the infected."

"Surrounded?" Lucius said.

"Far worse than we've seen here. Our worst days have brought us four or five hundred at a time. Last night, I saw tens of thousands of the infected around the base. Another three to five thousand were dead, piled up against the fence. They're under siege. From what I saw, it's only a matter of time before their defenses collapse under the weight."

"But how could they be surrounded?" Lucius said.

"I killed a few of the infected along the road leading into Minot," Barnes said. "I checked the IDs in their pockets. Most are from Minneapolis. What they're doing there I couldn't say. But almost all of them have come from Minneapolis."

"Perhaps they're looking to the government for help," Jasper said. "But ultimately, it doesn't matter. The one thing that does matter is that all those government troops will surely be looking for a place to relocate, and you know what that means. They will try to come here. They will try to destroy the way of life we've created. They will parachute in here and kill us if they have to. Imagine a whole battalion of soldiers, coming in here, guns blazing. They haven't seen a woman in months. They will rape our women. They will spear our babies on their bayonets. Do you see it, people? Please, listen to what I am telling you. The end of this good thing is near. There will come a day very soon when we will have to make a decision. Do we let them take our lives away, or do we end our lives with dignity and purpose? My soul is prepared for that day, and you've just proven to me that yours are as well."

He stopped there, looking at each of them in turn, a barrel-chested, gimlet-eyed man with lips pulled back over rows of large white teeth.

He said, "Go now. But be prepared. The day will come very soon when we must exercise the one option left to us. I know you'll be ready."

The group filed out into the gray, cold day in solemn silence. Aaron held the door open for his wife as she stepped out. He glanced back and saw that Michael Barnes had not moved. He still sat on the couch, Jasper standing next to him with his hand on his shoulder.

Aaron nodded to them both and closed the door. Then he stood there, lost in thought, watching the limitless vista of white waves that stretched out before him.

From behind him, he heard Jasper say, "Tonight, Michael, I have something I need you to do."

Aaron had a pretty good idea what that was, just as he was also pretty sure that he had just been bumped as Jasper's personal confidant.

* * *

As Aaron closed the door, Michael Barnes let his gaze turn on Jasper.

"You're gonna have a busy night ahead of you, Michael. I'm sorry. I hope you're up for it."

"Whatever you need, Jasper."

"Those troops are coming here because their base is overrun with the infected. When they get here, I want them to see that things aren't any better here."

"A few hundred zombies won't deter them, Jasper."

"No. But a couple thousand would."

Barnes looked at him for a long time.

"Our fences wouldn't be able to hold against that many."

"They won't have to, Michael. Because there's something else I need you to do, too."

Chapter 55

Sirens echoed through the building.

They were inside the hospital again. Over the sirens, Nate could hear shouting and gunfire and people running down the hallway outside his room. Kellogg had made sure Nate knew what to do when the infected got inside the hospital, and Nate didn't waste any time. He threw a heavy flannel shirt over his T-shirt and jeans, laced up the boots they'd given him, and slipped into a thick gray jacket with a fur collar. Then he went out into the hallway. Soldiers were running down the stairs to his left. A faint odor of electrical smoke hung in the air. There were bodies on the ground and blood splattered on the walls. One of the bodies off to Nate's right was still moving, trying to claw his way toward him.

Nate turned to his left and headed for the stairs. The building was a large, ten-story cube built around an oval-shaped central hub. Nate's room was on the fourth floor. In order to reach the cafeteria, where Kellogg had told him to go in case the hospital was overrun, he had to take the south stairwell down to the second floor and then come back toward the hub. He and Kellogg had walked it several times after that day on the column, and he knew the way even through the thickening smoke and the darkness and the wailing of the sirens.

He didn't get scared until he stepped off the landing on the second floor. There were bodies everywhere. Not just people in regular civilian clothes, either. Dead soldiers, too. In the darkness it was hard to tell who was still moving and who was dead. He could hear moaning. A hand grabbed his ankle and he jumped.

"Get off," he said, and kicked at the hand until the grip slackened and he was free.

He started to move, watching his step through the mangled bodies and the still-writhing fingertips clutching for a grip on the bloodstained floor.

There were spent shell casings all over the floor. They skidded out from beneath his boots and made it hard to walk. Somebody spoke to him from the floor, but he couldn't understand what the man was saying and he kept walking.

Farther down the hall from where the double doors to the cafeteria hung open was the entrance to the building's central hub. Nate knew that from there he could look down onto the first floor and the main entrance to the hospital. The walls around the entrance were glass, and Kellogg had said that if the zombies were going to enter the hospital, it would almost certainly be through there. There was no practical way to defend against it. Now, listening to the moaning coming from behind the doors that led to the building's central hub, Nate figured the big one had already happened. The volume was tremendous. It sounded like a train was going through the downstairs lobby.

He turned toward the cafeteria's double doors. There was a thick puddle of blood just inside the doorway, and a long blackish smear leading off into the darkness.

"Doc?" he called out.

A groan from the back of the room.

"Doc?"

"Nate. Back here."

Nate followed the sound through a jumble of overturned tables and chairs. After a few steps, he could smell something bad, like shit and rot mixed together. He gagged on the smell, but didn't vomit. The black smear on the floor glistened like oil.

He found Kellogg propped up against a collapsed display of hoagie sandwiches. There was blood on the counter above him, and sandwiches were strewn about on the floor. Kellogg was sitting in a puddle of blood, one arm draped over a nasty-looking wound that curved from the left side of his chest down across his stomach. Most of his shirt was gone. What Nate could see of the wound was a crusty yellow rimmed with blackened flesh. Pus oozed up from the deepest part of the wound.

"Doc, holy shit."

Kellogg managed a faint laugh. "Looks bad, huh?"

"What happened?"

Kellogg held up a pistol that he'd had tucked under his thigh. "One bullet left," he said.

"You saved it?"

The doctor coughed, spraying black wads of phlegm onto his chest. He looked up at Nate with rheumy, glassy eyes.

"So you're gonna do it then?" Nate said.

Kellogg nodded. "I'm sorry," he said, and his voice was so faint Nate had to lean in to hear the words. "It's hard to talk."

Nate knelt down next to Kellogg, cursing his own stupidity. He knew he was supposed to say something. The man was dying, for God's sake. This really smart man was dying, and here the guy was stuck with an idiot who couldn't think of anything beyond "Sorry, dude" to say.

"Nate."

"Yeah, doc?"

"Listen." Kellogg coughed again. When the coughing

stopped, he was winded. It took him a long time to start again. "Listen," he said. "This is important." He put the pistol down. There was a lanyard around his neck with a flash drive hanging from it. He took it off and held it out to Nate. "I want you to take this," he said.

"What is it?"

"It's all the work we've done on you. I think"—he stopped there and caught his breath—"I think we're done."

"You mean you found it? A cure? Doc, that's huge. I mean, right? That's huge, right? It's what all this was for."

Kellogg nodded.

"But what am I supposed to do with it?"

Kellogg closed his eyes. His breathing was ragged, labored. Nate could hear something rattling around inside his chest, like beans in a can.

"Doc?"

Kellogg opened his eyes again. They were bloodshot and starting to turn milky.

He said, "Nate, you need to escape this place."

"How? Where am I supposed to go?"

Kellogg shifted impatiently. He was breathing hard. "Listen," he said. "Colonel James Briggs is leaving here tonight with his command staff. There's a civilian compound not far from here that seems to be doing pretty well. I told Briggs about you and how important it is that you get away from here. He's going to try to get that civilian compound to take our people in. I want you with him." Kellogg's eyes swung heavily toward the flash drive in Nate's hand. "You need to get that to somebody who can do something with it."

"Doc," Nate said. He felt helpless. "I can't."

Kellogg shook his head. "No, Nate, listen to me. Remember when I called you a true nihilist?"

"I remember."

"Nate, we come to nihilism because we feel like the world is empty. The Buddhists call it samsara. It means disgust with the world. It doesn't matter what we do. We'll never change the fact that the universe is a sterile landscape without any meaning."

"But you said we can make our own meaning. Like running into daylight."

"Yeah, I did. I still believe that, Nate." Kellogg paused and tried to catch his breath. "Jesus, it hurts to talk. Hold on, give me a second." He reached for the pistol but couldn't grip it. "Nate, I don't have much time. There's still so much I want to tell you."

"Just tell me what I'm supposed to do, doc."

"I can't, Nate. That's the point I'm trying to make. There's only one answer to the absurdity of living in this world, but I can't tell you what it is. It's a different answer for everybody. It's confusing, I know. I can't simplify it for you. I want to, but I can't. All I can tell you is that the search for an answer is an answer in itself."

"Even a world filled with bad answers is still a world you can understand."

Kellogg nodded weakly. "That's right. But Nate, I trust you. I think, if you look, you'll find an answer that makes sense to you. You'll find a reason to get this cure to where it needs to be."

"So you really think the world is worth saving?"

"I don't know, Nate. You're the one running into daylight. You're the one who's gonna fill it with meaning. Or not. It all depends on what you do."

"But I don't want that responsibility."

"It doesn't matter, Nate. Living creates that responsibility. If you don't choose to die, you have to choose to live. It's the only question in philosophy that has a yes-or-no answer."

Nate lowered his head. Kellogg was shaking badly now, about to turn.

"Help me with this, Nate."

Kellogg was fumbling for the gun at his side. His fingers couldn't wrap around the receiver.

Nate sniffled, then helped Kellogg grip the gun. "It's heavy," Kellogg said.

"I don't want to do this, doc."

"It's okay, Nate. I can do it. Go on now."

Nate rose to his feet and backed away.

"Doc, I'm sorry. I don't know what to say to you."

Kellogg rested the pistol across his chest. His eyes rolled in his head, but he managed to lock his gaze on Nate's.

"Put that thing around your neck."

Nate slid it over his head.

"Just tell me yes or no. What's your answer?"

"Yes. My answer's yes."

Kellogg nodded. "That's courage, Nate."

"Because there are consequences?"

"That's right. That's good, Nate. Now go. This'll take care of itself."

Nate watched him for a moment, still feeling stupid and inadequate, then turned and headed out to the hallway.

He stopped there and waited for the shot.

Chapter 56

Not everything about life in the Grasslands was bad. There were some bright spots. And, for Ed, one of those bright spots was Sandra Tellez.

They'd met a few days before, while she was helping out in the med clinic. Ed had spent that entire morning on top of the east fence, repairing the damage from the last time the infected had broken through. Overnight, the wind had piled snowdrifts along the base of the fence, and from his perch he could look north and east across a vast, pillowed range of white where the earthmovers pushed the zombies that had been shot that morning into burn piles. But the fires hadn't started yet and the air still smelled clean. The sky was a huddled gray mass sitting low on the plains, like fog, giving the surrounding countryside a sheltering look. It was intensely cold up there on the fence, so cold that not only did his hands refuse to work but so did his mind. He found himself drifting, thinking about people he had known and lost, and before he knew it, his jeans had frozen to the wooden rail on which he was sitting.

Two men had to peel him from the fence. He couldn't bend his legs, so they had to carry him to the clinic. It was a simple wooden cabin with a portable sink in one corner and a foam-top table they'd salvaged from a real medical clinic over in New Salem. Ed was facedown on the table.

Sandra Tellez had come in like a breath of fresh air. He'd seen her around the compound and thought she was pretty. He'd always had a thing for Latinas. He liked the way they could hold on to their youthful appearance well into their forties and fifties.

"Well, this ought to be interesting," she said. "How you feeling?"

"You asking me if this hurts?"

"Does it?"

"Kind of, yeah."

"What happened?"

"I froze it to a fence post."

She blinked. And then she started to laugh.

"It's not funny," he said.

"Mr. Moore, you nearly froze your ass off. And I mean that literally. You gotta admit, that's funny."

She laughed again, and this time he couldn't help but smile. "I like what it does to your face when you laugh," he said.

The smile wavered on her face, but didn't go away. "Are you hitting on me, Mr. Moore?"

"Just making conversation," he said. "That's okay, isn't it?"

Her smile became a smirk. "The way I see it, you got two choices."

"Oh? What are they?"

"You can either lay there and wait for your pants to unfreeze or you can let me pour some hot water over your butt."

"How long do you think it'll take my pants to melt?"

"Don't know. An hour maybe."

He shrugged. "Might not be so bad, with a little company."

"You're a sly old devil, Mr. Moore. You are hitting on me."

"Call me Ed," he said.

Later that afternoon, she joined him for lunch. She told him about living inside the quarantine walls in Houston, and it was the first time he'd heard anybody talk with any authority on the way the infected changed over time.

"They're excellent scavengers," she said. "That's one of the biggest changes. The new ones, the ones they call Stage One zombies, those exist by killing and eating whatever they can catch. That's why so many of them die off. They either can't catch enough to live on or they die from eating whatever they catch."

They were sharing roasted turkey legs and spaghetti squash and mashed potatoes with a weak brown gravy. Ed watched Sandra cut off a pat of butter from the serving dish on the table between them and mix it into her squash.

"What about the other kinds of zombies, the later-stage ones?"

"The Stage Three zombies, they're scary good at finding food. Whenever we'd see them, we'd tail along, waiting to see what they'd find. More often than not, they'd lead us to something good. The trick was to take them out before they had a chance to taint whatever they found. I remember this one time they led us to somebody's stockpile of canned goods and fresh water. We ate good for about a week on that."

"Would they have been able to open the cans?" Ed asked.

"I don't know, maybe. The Stage Three zombies can do some pretty weird stuff. I've heard stories about them answering to their names, stuff like that. They can open doors and climb ladders and even play dead."

Ed shook his head. "That's amazing that you survived all that time."

"Survival was never a question with me. I never once doubted that I was going to live. When I saw my daughter die, I think that was it for me. That was the moment I knew I was going to live. That sounds weird, right? I mean, you always hear people say that if their child died, they wouldn't be able to live another second. I used to think that, too. But then, when it happened"—she shrugged—"I don't know. It was strange. I just couldn't let her memory go. Does that make sense? It's like I could keep her alive, at least some part of her, by remembering her. I couldn't give up. Does that make sense?"

"What was her name?"

"Maria. People used to say she looked just like me, but when I looked at her, all I could see were her father's eyes."

"I bet she was beautiful."

"She was." Sandra smiled at him. "But then, after that, Clint came back into my life, and it became that much more important to live. It was tough going, but we made it, living hand to mouth, until that day we saw Officer Barnes's helicopter crash."

"And he brought you guys here."

"That's right."

Ed chewed on his bottom lip, thinking. He said, "I don't know if I've got Michael Barnes figured out yet. He seems, I don't know, dangerous somehow."

Her eyes shifted left, then right, like she was checking to see who was within listening range. "Ed," she said, her voice a hoarse whisper. "He's more dangerous than you know. He's not sane."

"He seems to have Jasper's ear."

"I know." She pushed her plate away and looked at him. "Ed, tell me the truth. Is this a good place? Are we safe here?"

* * *

That night they caught a movie, *Butch Cassidy and the Sundance Kid*, one of Ed's favorites. Afterward, he walked Sandra back to the cabin she shared with Clint. It was a cold, cloudless night, and most of the village had already turned in, even though curfew was still a good twenty minutes off.

They stopped at the door to her cabin and she turned to face him. "I had fun today," she said.

"Me, too." He was about to ask her if she'd like to join him for breakfast in the morning when he heard the sound of a truck shifting gears. Sandra's cabin faced the compound's southern fence and Ed turned toward the road in the distance. He saw a pair of trucks moving along the road that led around to the west entrance of the compound. They were struggling with the thick snow on the road, the headlights bobbing in the air like fireflies.

She said, "Ed, what's that?"

"They're pulling trailers," he said.

They watched the trucks swing around to the west entrance, near Jasper's quarters. Several men ran out from the sheds behind Jasper's quarters and opened the gates.

"What are they doing?" Sandra asked.

The men who rushed out to open the gates were unloading barrels from the trailers now, stacking them into piles down near the fence. Ed recognized a few faces in the glare of the headlights, most of them members of the security patrols.

"Ed, look there."

"Where?"

"By the truck. That's Michael Barnes."

Ed studied the figures. His eyesight wasn't what it once was, but it was still good enough to make out Michael Barnes talking with Jasper.

And Jasper looked as pleased as punch.

CHAPTER 57

The military delegation from Minot arrived the next morning. It was late October and intensely cold. The sky was a gray, leaden swirl above Aaron's head. Snow was heavy in the air and thick on the ground. The wind was a constant roar. Aaron, who was standing on the downhill slope in front of his cottage, didn't see or even hear the helicopter until it was right over top of him, coming down in the open area west of the cottages.

Michael Barnes and a small group of security personnel were out there with trucks to meet them. From his front porch, Aaron watched the helicopter touch down in a blast of disturbed snow. As it powered down, soldiers in winter gear climbed out and approached Barnes and his group. None of the soldiers looked to be armed from what Aaron could tell. And yet, they were here.

Ever since Jasper had started taking Thomas to his bed, Aaron had been plagued with questions. Over the years, he'd burglarized the homes of new members, looking for information for Jasper to use during prayer services. He'd helped slander elected officials who were critical of Jasper, and he'd sabotaged their election campaign functions. He'd overseen the beatings of Family members who tried to leave the church. He'd lied to federal prosecutors under oath. He'd even delivered his own son up for a ritualized rape, all because Jasper had asked him to. And over the past few months, during their time at the Grasslands compound, he'd heard Jasper deliver his dire warnings of governmental conspiracy to the people during mealtimes. He'd listened as Jasper told them of the military's plans to kill their children and rape their women, and he'd shouted and prayed for Jasper to protect them, even though Aaron was one of the few who knew that the military had made no such announcements.

But watching as Thomas sank a little more each day into his own private hell had made him doubt all of that. It was like somebody had suddenly wiped the cobwebs from his face, and he was only now realizing that he was standing in the midst of corruption so vile and complete there was no way to pull himself out. He had come to question everything, to react with nausea and distrust to everything Jasper said.

And then the military arrived.

Their presence here was a powerful confirmation of the things Jasper had been telling them. Aaron shivered, though not entirely from the cold.

Kate brought him a cup of coffee, black with a touch of sugar, just enough to take off the bitterness. "Thank you," he said, holding it close to his chin to let the radiant heat warm his face.

Together, they watched Barnes and the military delegation trade greetings. Then Barnes led them to the waiting trucks and a moment later the whole procession was headed for the west gate. One of the officers pointed out into the prairie beyond the fences, where the infected had knotted along the fence line and were banging on the wire. Farther out, long dark caravans of the infected were approaching, and Aaron wondered where they had all come from. There had been hundreds before. Now, there were literally a thousand, maybe more.

Aaron looked over at Jasper's quarters. He had yet to make an appearance, but Aaron was certain he was ready for them. He only wished he'd been invited to listen in.

"Things are changing pretty fast," he said.

"Should I be scared, Aaron?"

He looked at his wife. She was still an attractive woman, though her age was beginning to tell in the crow's-feet wrinkles at the corners of her eyes and the wisps of gray in her hair. It was the soft glow of her smile that had won him over more than two decades before and he hadn't seen that in a long while. He missed it.

"I think—" he said, and stopped himself. This was important. Too important to lie to her. He said, "Kate, I'm worried." He nodded out toward the approaching vehicles, a gesture that included the approaching zombies beyond. "I'm worried about that. And I'm worried about what's going on here. I think, maybe, we might have made a mistake."

There, he said it. For better or for worse, the cat was out of the bag.

She didn't say anything for a long while, simply stared out at the prairie, at the approaching crowds of zombies. She had been his faithful companion now for twenty-two years of marriage. She'd borne him a fine son. Together, they'd lived in the shelter of Jasper's church, their love for each other growing as the church grew and prospered. Now, he'd thrown down a gauntlet. Would she follow him? Would she turn away from the man who had been at the core of their life together for so long, or would she turn him over to that man? He waited on tenterhooks for her reply.

At last she looked at him. She moved her hand to rest on top of his, and she said, "Do you want to leave here?"

He nodded.

"Can we survive out there?"

"I don't know," he said. "But I know we won't survive in here."

She brushed the hair from his forehead with her fingertips.

"I'm with you, Aaron. You, me, and your son. We'll make it together."

The vehicles were pulling up to the front of Jasper's quarters now. Aaron turned and watched the soldiers, four older air force officers and one young, long-haired man who had obviously not spent a day of his life in the military, climb out of the trucks. They looked around, taking in the size of the village, before being ushered up to Jasper's quarters by Michael Barnes.

The younger man's head was on swivel. He kept turning every which way, like a country bumpkin dropped into the heart of the big city, and Aaron could see right away that the kid didn't belong. It made him curious.

Aaron took another sip of his coffee.

It was definitely time to leave the Grasslands.

From the notebooks of Ben Richardson

The Grasslands, North Dakota: October 18th, 3:30 P.M.

The military delegation arrived today. They're down in the pavilion now, interviewing Jasper, I think.

Like the rest of the non-Family members, I had to stay out of the way during their tour. Barnes's security people told us to make sure we avoided all contact with them, but there was never any real danger of us getting close enough for that to happen. They kept us pretty well corralled. The only time I got a really good look at them was when they filed past our dormitories at a double-time march. I stood there with Ed Moore, Sandra and Clint, Jeff Stavers, and some others while the delegation was hustled through their tour. Looking at Jasper, I got the feeling the tour was not going well. He was angry. He kept running his hands over his face. He waved and gestured and once, after they'd got about twenty yards up the road from where we stood, I even heard him raise his voice at one of the officers. Wish I had heard what he said.

But then something really interesting happened. Billy Kline came up behind us with the blind girl, Kyra Talbot, holding his hand.

"They gone?" he asked.

Ed nodded. Then he tipped his cowboy hat to the blind girl and said, "Ma'am."

"I want you to listen to what she's got to say, Ed," said Billy. "The rest of you too." He squeezed her hand. "Go ahead, Kyra. It's okay."

I hadn't talked to Kyra at all before that moment. I'd heard from Jeff Stavers that she was good people, but that she was totally enamored of Jasper. Supposedly, she loved it here.

And that made what she told us seem even more incredible.

She told us how she had overheard Jasper and Barnes talking about killing Tom Wilder and his two friends. Ed had told us what he'd seen that morning the zombies broke through the main gate, but I don't think any of us had really wanted to believe that they'd been murdered.

But now, we couldn't deny it.

By the time Kyra finished speaking, Ed was leaning against the side of the building, eyes closed, trembling as he tried to catch his breath.

And then Kyra really dropped another bomb on us.

She said, "They want me to be at the office in ten minutes to meet the military guys. I want to give them this."

She held out a piece of tightly folded paper for one of us to take.

Sandra took it from here and unfolded it. It read:

SOME OF US WANT TO LEAVE
AND HE WON'T LET US
GET US OUT OF HERE PLEASE

I was stunned. This was it, then. As soon as the military saw that, they would know something bad was happening here. Something beyond the sudden increase in the number of zombies we've seen at our gates lately. They would press the issue. The country was still technically under martial law, after all, even if the military was powerless to enforce it on large population centers. They could do it here in the Grasslands, though. They had resources close by.

"There's no turning back once they see this," Sandra said.

"You're right," I agreed. "Ed, what do you think?"

I could see him steeling himself for the task ahead. Old as he was, there was a singular strength about him that I found reassuring.

"Okay," he said. "Do it."

Later that afternoon, Aaron sat at a picnic table in the pavilion with about four hundred other Family members, attending a reception for the military delegation. At one point, the military leader, an air force colonel named James Briggs, stood up to say a few words.

He was a tall, fit-looking man in his forties, nearly bald except for a thin cottony donut of hair at his temples. His cheeks were bright red from the cold.

He said, "When we first planned to come down here, we

had no idea what we'd find. We half expected you folks to be starving or freezing or living out of holes in the ground."

This brought a few well-orchestrated chuckles from Family members.

"But now that we've seen the Grasslands for ourselves, I have to say that there are a lot of folks here who think this is about the best thing that has ever happened to them."

His next sentence was cut off by a torrent of applause. He dutifully stopped talking and smiled at the cheers. But the cheers went on a little too long. They seemed a little too enthusiastic. Aaron watched the colonel watching the crowd, and he realized that Briggs had picked up on it, too.

Not everything was as it seemed in the Grasslands compound.

An hour later, Aaron was standing next to a table where Jasper was talking with Colonel Briggs and his delegation. The conversation was not going well. In all the time they'd known each other, Aaron had never seen Jasper so rattled. He was sweating, disoriented. He kept touching his face, dragging his fingers down his cheeks, almost as if he could pull his black hair down over his head like a hood and block out the interview. One minute, he was nearly screaming. The next, he was pleading with Briggs to understand what he was trying to achieve here. Briggs, for his part, seemed more and more alarmed.

At one point during the interview, Briggs said, "Do you think everybody's happy here?"

The question seemed to take Jasper by surprise. "Of course they are. We're a family."

"Not all families are happy families," Briggs said. "What if I told you that some of your family wants to leave here? Would you let them go with us?"

"Who wants to leave?" Jasper countered.

"I don't know," said Briggs. He held up a tightly folded piece of white paper. "This note was passed to me anonymously. I look around, and I see a lot of smiling people. But I'm also a trained observer, Mr. Sewell. I've seen the people watching us from the cottages and the dormitories. We haven't spoken to them yet. What if there are people here who want to leave? I'm told you won't let them."

Jasper shook his head. He seemed to be holding on to his temper with both hands.

"What can I do about lies, friend? People tell lies."

"Will you let them leave?" Briggs repeated. "If I come back here tomorrow with enough trucks to get them away from here, will you let them leave?"

Jasper threw up his hands.

"Leave us, friend. I beg you. Leave us. We're not hurting anybody. We just want to be left alone. There's no racism here, no hatred. It's not like it is out there in your world. We just want to be left alone."

Briggs sat back in his chair and crossed his arms over his chest.

"That's a nice sentiment, Mr. Sewell, but it doesn't answer my question. Will you let them leave? Yes or no?"

Jasper dragged his fingers over his face.

He said, "Anybody who wants to go can go. Just go now, please. Leave us in peace."

Briggs looked at the others in his delegation, then scanned the rapidly dwindling crowd of Family members at the surrounding tables.

"Okay. We'll be back tomorrow at oh-nine-hundred."

"Fine," Jasper said, and waved them away without looking at them. "Just go, please."

Briggs and the others stood and walked out. Jasper remained at the table, his face in his hands. Aaron was shocked to see Jasper so deflated. But as Briggs and the others left the pavilion, Jasper suddenly sat up again, and his face was grim.

He motioned for Michael Barnes, and though Aaron couldn't hear what he whispered to Barnes, he was pretty sure he knew what was being said.

And it made his stomach turn.

Aaron was standing on his porch again when Barnes and his men drove the delegation out to their helicopter. Thick gray snow clouds were hanging low in the sky, though the air was, for the moment, clear. It would be dark in another hour, and the night promised to be a cold one.

He was leaning against a wooden post, thinking of all the ways his world had changed, when he thought he saw a bright flash from inside one of the trucks.

He stood up straight, straining his eyes to see.

Three more flashes erupted inside the lead truck, followed by a few more in the back truck. Aaron listened, but there was no sound save for the wailing of the wind coming off the prairie and the faint mechanical whine of the helicopter's rotors.

The trucks pulled up to the helicopter and two soldiers came forward to greet them. Both had rifles, but the rifles were slung over the shoulders.

Barnes stepped out of the lead truck and shot them point-blank with his pistol; they never had a chance.

Aaron could almost picture the pilot's reaction. He heard the whine of the engines growing louder, higher in pitch, and he knew the man was trying to power up fast.

It did little good, though.

Barnes jumped aboard, and a moment later, two bright flashes finished the matter.

Then Barnes turned to the lead truck and motioned for his patrols. They climbed out with the young man from Briggs's delegation in tow. The kid looked scared. The patrols dragged him up in front of Barnes. Behind the kid, other members of the patrol pulled the dead bodies from the vehicles and put them on board the helicopter.

When it was done, they climbed back into the vehicles with the terrified long-haired kid and sped back toward the quarantine room.

From the notebooks of Ben Richardson

The Grasslands, North Dakota: October 18th, 8:40 P.M.

We were called to curfew early tonight. Jasper got on the PA and told us the military delegation was dead, that they had attacked without warning, but that Michael Barnes and his security forces had managed to put them down.

"I didn't plan this," Jasper said, "but I know that it happened. We didn't want this, but now we've got to deal with it. People, people, people, don't you see? It's only a matter of time now. We're gonna get more soldiers in here now. They'll parachute in here and burn our houses and bayonet our children and all because they cannot abide the life we've made here."

There was more, but there's no point in recording it here. He talked in circles. He said the same thing over and over again. I could tell he was becoming unhinged. One minute, he'd be ranting, full of paranoid conspiracy theories. The next, he'd be pleading with us to understand that he'd done all he could to save us.

But I think Sandra Tellez said it best. She was sitting between Ed Moore and Clint Siefer, holding Clint's hand, as Jasper's speech came to an end. She looked around the room and said, "That man, he's about to kill us all."

Not get us killed.

Kill us all.

None of us bothered to contest it.

P.S.: Ed says we need to make a break for it as soon as possible. Like, maybe, tomorrow morning. Minot will almost certainly send a party out looking for their missing delegation. He says that when they do, we need to be ready to flag them down. We need some way to separate ourselves from the rest of the Family.

Poor guy. I've gotten to spend some quality time with Ed these last few days. He blames himself for not getting these people out of here sooner. But from what I've heard and seen, I can't imagine he could have handled the situation any differently.

It was nearly dawn, and neither Jasper nor Michael Barnes had slept.

Barnes was coming out of the quarantine room, rubbing his bloody knuckles. There was blood splattered on his face and on his clothes and smeared along the toes of his boots. Behind him, inside the room, the kid from the Minot delegation was on his side, curled into a fetal ball, whimpering.

Jasper studied the young man for a long time. His name was Nate Royal, and it was much as Jasper suspected. Things at Minot were bad. They'd been overrun, and Briggs and his delegation had been bluffing. They'd had nowhere to go back to. But Jasper had already suspected that from what Barnes had told him earlier. What he really wanted to know was what a senior group of military officers was doing with a mullet-headed peckerwood in tow.

Barnes had stripped the man out of his heavy winter gear before beating him, revealing a blue air force utility uniform underneath that was completely devoid of insignia. It only reinforced Jasper's hunch that the man was not a soldier.

He had nodded to Barnes from outside the glass and the beating went into high gear. Moments later, Nate Royal was babbling something about a cure for the necrosis filovirus the military had distilled from his body. Barnes had stopped then and looked at Jasper. Jasper took in the news and was furious. It was a lie. An awful, insidious lie.

"Where is this cure?" Barnes asked.

He kicked Nate in the gut and Nate vomited blood on the floor.

"At Minot," Nate said. "The doctor who developed it died yesterday. His research is there."

Jasper motioned to Barnes to come out.

He said, "It's time. Go tell your men to get started."

CHAPTER 58

"Thomas."

The boy groaned and rolled over.

"Thomas, come on, son. Wake up."

The boy groaned.

Aaron gave his son a hard shake.

"Thomas," he hissed. "Wake up. Come on, we gotta move."

The boy's eyes fluttered open. He looked up at Aaron as though he hoped all this was a dream, like they were still back in Jackson, Mississippi, living a normal life. But the look faded, and Aaron could almost see the light bleed away from his face.

"We don't have much time, okay? We gotta move."

Thomas nodded. There was no fear in him. No emotion of any kind. Not really. His expression was dead. He got up from his cot and grabbed his small duffel bag and stood in the middle of his small room, waiting patiently for instructions.

"Your mother's waiting on us," Aaron said. "Did you wear your long johns like I asked you to?"

Thomas nodded.

"How about a gun?"

Thomas nodded.

"Okay. Might as well get it out. I don't think we'll have any trouble, but just in case."

They walked to the living room where Kate stood waiting. Husband and wife traded looks. Then Kate's gaze shifted to Thomas coming out of his room, stuffing the pistol into his belt, and she gasped.

"So this is it," she said. "This is where it ends."

Aaron nodded. He held out both hands and his wife took one and Thomas took the other and they formed a circle.

They each bowed their heads and quietly Aaron prayed for their safe deliverance.

Aaron had planned their escape in haste, but he thought his plan was a good one. During one of his many forays into the deserted towns that surrounded the Grasslands compound, Barnes and his men had brought two trailer loads of chemicals into the camp. Those chemicals were now hidden down near the west fence, just south of the auxiliary-vehicle storage lot. The barrels were placed into two separate piles, so that they didn't accidentally mix before Jasper was ready for them to, and then each pile was covered with several layers of heavy-duty tarp. Snowdrifts had covered the piles during the previous night, and the twin mounds created a perfect break for his family to hide behind while Aaron cut the fence. From there, they'd have to cross a few hundred yards of open, snow-covered grassland, dodging the infected as best they could, before coming to the old county road. Aaron had used his ability to move in and out of the gates to leave a fully gassed Chevy pickup about a quarter mile up the road beyond that. With any luck, they'd reach it in less than forty-five minutes.

The moon was nearly full, but the sky was full of heavy

gray clouds and falling snow. Aaron put his family into the hollow behind the mounds and went to work on the fence with a pair of wire cutters, hoping that the bad weather would offer them a little extra cover from the roving patrols and the zombies.

"Dad," Thomas said, his voice barely a whisper.

Aaron turned around, his eyes scanning the village for movement.

"Dad, what is this stuff?"

Aaron saw where Thomas had cleared some of the snow away with his hand and lifted the tarp, exposing several barrels of Bonide.

"A sulfur spray," Aaron said. "They use it as an insecticide." He nodded at the other mound. "That one over there is muriatic acid. The muriatic acid is used to clean pools."

"We don't have any pools here, Dad," Thomas said.

"No, we don't. But if you mix the two together, you get a noxious gas. Makes you pass out."

"And then?"

"And then," Aaron said, "the heart stops."

"You mean it kills you."

Aaron nodded. He clipped the last of the fence and started peeling it out of the way.

"But there's enough here to kill everyone in the village," Thomas said.

"Leave it be, son," Aaron said. "We have to go."

"Dad, you knew about this?"

Reluctantly, Aaron nodded. "Come on now. We need to go."

The boy's eyes went wide.

"Thomas?"

The boy stiffened. He shook his head and Aaron's stomach dropped. He turned slowly, and saw Michael Barnes standing behind him, two of his security guards flanking him with rifles at the ready.

"Evening, folks," Barnes said. He scanned their faces, smiling.

Aaron hung his head. Above and all around him, the prairie wind howled. A moment later, rifle fire split the night.

At the sound of the shots, heads popped up from the snow outside the fence. Michael Barnes watched the infected moving toward the hole Aaron had made in the fence, the volume of their moans building. They were going to be a problem, but not a big one.

To his patrols Barnes said, "Keep this secure. Hold it as long as you can, but when you hear the call to come up, you come running. Understand? It won't matter if they get in at that point."

The two men nodded. Barnes took a last look at the dead bodies of Aaron and his wife and son, shook his head, and then headed back to the pavilion.

Chapter 59

Ed Moore walked out of the auxiliary dining tent and into the cutting chill of the morning air. A fine, powdery snow covered the fields and the roofs of the nearby buildings. Here and there, patches of brown grass protruded from the white sheets of snow and ice. An old-fashioned analog thermostat hanging from a nail on the side of the tent read twenty-two degrees. There was ice hanging from the face of it like a beard, and to Ed the twenty-two degrees seemed a little like wishful thinking. In the distance, the north fence was like a ghostly black arm protruding from a gray fog of low clouds. He could hear the infected moaning outside the gate, and he wondered how long it would take Barnes and his patrol to clear them.

Something was going on near the pavilion. People were moving up the road from the dormitories, and he could hear their voices, loud but indistinct, over the wind.

"What's going on?" Billy asked. He had just come from the dining tent and was dressed in a red flannel shirt and jeans over thick layers of long underwear. His hair was getting long, but his beard was still spotty.

"Don't know," Ed said.

Jeff Stavers came out of the dining tent and stood next to Billy.

On the far side of the pavilion, children were breaking off from their parents and getting shepherded toward the education tents. A four-wheel-drive pickup with oversized tires was chugging up the frozen hillside from down near Jasper's quarters, several white fifty-five-gallon drums in the bed.

"Ed," Billy said. "Look at that."

"I see it."

"What do you think Jasper's planning?" Jeff asked.

"No idea. I don't think it's gonna be good, though."

A few of Barnes's men came by with rifles slung over their shoulders. They seemed agitated and impatient. One went inside the dining tent and called everybody outside while the other one told everybody to head toward the pavilion.

"What's going on?" Ed asked them.

"Just get to the pavilion," the guard said.

Ed nodded, and when the patrol moved off toward the kitchen, he turned to Billy and Jeff and said, "I think we just ran out of time, guys. Start getting everybody together in one spot."

"What have you got planned, Ed?" Jeff asked.

"I don't know yet."

"You don't know? What about the military? Where are they?"

"I don't know," Ed said. There was a sense of urgency in his tone. "Just move. Quickly now."

Ed watched them go.

Billy went off to the office while Jeff broke off toward the education tents. When they were gone, Ed drifted up toward the pavilion, looking for anybody he had seen at the midnight meetings.

More and more people were massing into the pavilion area. At the same time, Barnes's men were positioning the chemical containers along the edge of the crowd. People watched them hooking the fifty-five-gallon drums up to sprayers, but incredibly, to Ed's mind at least, nobody seemed concerned. Nobody questioned them.

Ed entered the pavilion floor, pushed on by a wave of people. He spotted Julie Carnes up near the stage. Looking at her now, he couldn't believe she was the same woman he'd flirted with back at Springfield. She'd seemed so like him then, angry at growing old and refusing to be cowed by it. He had gravitated to that spark in her. But now, as she waved her hands over her head in a ridiculous display of devotion to Jasper and sang along to a rocked-up version of "Shall We Gather at the River," all he felt for her was a deep and abiding disgust.

On the stage, Jasper gripped the podium with both hands, staring grimly over the crowd. Barnes was at his side.

Off to the east, Ed heard the sound of the fence cracking. A few of the others heard it, too, and soon there were people pointing, shouting.

From behind them, down near Jasper's quarters, came a few isolated gunshots.

The crowds turned anxious. People were panicking, trying to round up children, asking confused questions.

Onstage, Jasper raised his hands. Some people were still singing, but that stopped when Jasper motioned to them. The sudden silence caught people's attention and heads turned toward the pavilion.

"People, people, people," he said. "Listen to me now. You've got to hear me. You must come closer. We've been betrayed. So terribly betrayed. You all know how hard I've worked to make this the best life you could have. But in spite of everything I've done, and all the work we did together, some of the people here have told the military lies about us.

And in doing that, they've made our lives impossible. We have to confront this now, people. There is no way to live with what has happened in the last twenty-four hours."

A murmur rose from the crowd, but Jasper silenced them.

"We are all joined by what we tried to do here in the Grasslands. We belong to each other. But we've been betrayed. The wrath of the U.S. military's war machine is on its way. It will swoop down upon us, people, but I have a plan. They will not murder us. The infected that even now are swarming inside our gates will not murder us. We will be own masters. Here, in a few minutes, we will take control."

He stared at the silent crowd. Hardly anyone moved, even though the moaning of the infected could be heard on the main road now.

Jasper went on. "I don't think this is what we wanted to happen to our children, but it is what must happen. We will not lie here like cowards and let the military kill us. The infected will not kill us. It's just like I've been trying to tell you all this time. The outside world wants to stop what we've achieved here, which is happiness. It is good and peaceful. We will not let them take our lives from us. We are going to lay our lives down ourselves. We have been terribly betrayed people, but we are not beaten."

Ed listened in horror as the people all around him erupted in applause. Here and there, people would shout out some asinine bit of praise for Jasper, and he would respond with a smiling "Thank you, thank you," and a nod of his head. Did none of them see what Jasper had planned for them? Ed pivoted in a circle, watching the crowds, listening to their chants, and his mouth dropped open in stupefied shock. The madman was up there talking about mass suicide, and these people were ready to follow him.

Gunfire erupted from his left. The patrols there were shooting the infected as they reached the center of the village. Ed glanced behind him and saw more zombies coming up the hill from Jasper's quarters. There was no one there to stop them.

Jasper pointed at the Family members around the perimeter of the gathering and motioned for them to turn on their machines.

Across the crowd, Ed saw Sandra Tellez. He took off his cowboy hat and waved it over his head. It caught her eye and she waved back.

Ed pushed through the crowd to reach her.

Over the PA, Jasper said, "Be brave in the face of what's about to happen, all of you. The world is a violent, terrible place filled with terrible people who will hurt us if we let them. Well, that's what we're putting a stop to today. We're stopping the violence of the world. Even if this is the only day this works, then it'll be worth it. This one act of defiance will be our legacy. So think about your children. Think about our seniors. Do you want them to suffer in that world? Do you want them to be raped and killed by the soldiers who have vowed to destroy them? Bring them forward, people. Bring them into the pavilion near the sprayers. This is not suicide we're doing, people. This is a revolutionary act of defiance. Things'll be better on the other side, people. You'll see. Now bring them forward. That's it, that's it. There's no pain. It's just like falling asleep."

Ed quickened his pace through the crowd. He could see people moving forward in a slow wave. People coughed and gagged as the sprayers hummed to life. A dirty white cloud spread through the crowd nearest the stage, and still the people moved forward, heads down, right into the jaws of death.

The sound of gunfire had stopped now, and over the low, resonant roll of the moaning zombies, Ed could hear children crying.

Jasper said, "They're not crying because it hurts. They're

scared. Mothers, take your children. Hold them. Help them come forward. If you don't, you'll see soldiers landing out there in the fields. They'll torture your babies."

Ed couldn't listen. He blocked out everything but the sight of Sandra Tellez working her way toward him through the crowd. She had Clint Siefer with her. Behind her, Ben Richardson was helping some of the others from the midnight meetings.

They met near the back of the pavilion. Sandra said, "Ed, we have to go now."

One of the people behind Richardson said, "What about the military? Where are they? Jasper said—"

"I don't know," Ed said.

"Ed, what are we going to do?" Sandra asked.

He scanned the pavilion area. People were staggering away from the sprayers, some falling right into the arms of the infected. People were screaming and coughing, children were crying. Adults were wandering the clearing with tears running unabashedly down their faces, their mouths twisted into grimaces of fear and confusion. And the zombies were on them now, staggering through the spreading fog of chemical death.

"You and Richardson move everybody that way," he said, pointing east toward the vehicle storage lot. "Those RVs are still over there. Try to get everybody you can on board."

"But where are you gonna be?" Sandra asked.

"Bringing up the rear. Hurry it up, now."

Sandra and Richardson led the group away from the pavilion. Ed was waving the others after them when he heard Jasper's voice again.

"What's that? What's that, sister?"

Ed followed Jasper's gaze, and he saw Robin Tharp standing in front of a group of about thirty children. Here and there, a few parents stood among the kids.

He saw Margaret O'Brien there, too, her grandchildren standing close by her side.

Robin said something that Ed couldn't hear.

Jasper said, "No, no, that's not right, Robin. It's the people who go on living after this who are cursed. This world is wrong. Do you really think it's fair they have to go on living in it?"

The crowd, those who were still able, applauded.

People were collapsing all around them. Ed saw people staggering drunkenly out of the pavilion, the gas still swirling around them as they fell into heaps on the ground, and in the fog it was impossible to tell who was the poisoned and who was the infected.

A man stood up on one of the tables and said, "This ain't nothin' to cry for. We should be cheering this on. For me,"—and he turned to Jasper—"for me, Jasper, you brought us all this ways and my vote is to go with you."

"Thank you, thank you," Jasper said. "Please, people, let's get moving. Let's do this. Breathe deeply everyone. This isn't self destruction you're breathing in. This is defiance."

"But all these children," Robin said, and this time her voice rang out loudly and clearly above the others. "There's no reason they should have to die. What did they do wrong that they should have to die? They didn't make this world."

Jasper said, "Sister, they deserve a whole lot more than to die the way that's coming. Maybe you can't see what's gonna happen here in a little while, but I can. Those babies deserve some peace. Let 'em have it. Don't do this. Don't create fear. Let them die with dignity. Everyone, stop the drama. Death is better than what life is gonna be like in the days ahead. Defy that and die with dignity."

Jasper motioned for his patrols to move on Robin. One of the guards grabbed her by the arm and pulled her toward the pavilion. A little girl behind her grabbed her shirt and tried to pull Robin back. One of the guards grabbed the little girl and threw her to the ground. The girl screamed, and it was that scream that tapped something inside Ed.

With a wet handkerchief over his face, his eyes burning with chemical-induced tears, he ran into the gas.

Billy Kline started to choke with the first burn of chemicals in his lungs. All around him people were staggering away from the pavilion, falling on the ground, their muscles jerking in uncontrollable fits. Here and there, he recognized the infected by their soiled clothes and steered clear of them. His nose was running uncontrollably. His eyes burned, and he couldn't stop blinking. Everything was blurry, and he needed to vomit.

He staggered forward, stepping over bodies as he made his way toward the office on the far side of the pavilion. The gas was spreading over the lawn. Billy made it to a clear spot, and his visibility opened up. He caught a glimpse of Kyra standing under the eaves of the radio room and he called out to her.

"Billy?" she said.

He was still too far away and she couldn't get a fix on where he was. She kept saying his name, turning this way and that, looking helpless and confused.

He pulled his shirt over his burning nose and mouth and ran for her.

"Kyra," he said as he reached her. "Oh, my God. I've been looking all over for you. Are you okay?"

"Billy—"

"We're gonna get out of here," he said. "Come on."

"I didn't know which way to go, Billy. I heard Jasper talking over the PA. Oh, God, tell me it's not really happening."

He put an arm around her and led her around the back side of the radio room.

But then he stopped.

"Billy?" she said. "What's wrong?"

Colin Wyndham was blocking the path ahead of them. He was wearing a gray T-shirt and jeans. The skin on his arms and face was bright red from the intense cold, but he didn't seem to notice it. He was holding a wooden baseball bat, his eyes wide open and staring with the dark malignancy of insanity.

"Colin, let us by."

"You're going back to the pavilion," Colin said. "We're all going back. We're part of the Family."

"That's not gonna happen, Colin. Put the bat down, okay? You don't have to do this."

But Colin was as unreachable as the zombies swarming into the pavilion. Billy could see that, and when he ran at Billy, Billy was ready.

Colin swung wildly at Billy's hip and Billy jumped backward, landing off balance and falling back against the side of the building.

Colin rushed him. He swung again, and this time there was no jumping out of the way. Instead, Billy stepped into the swing, catching Colin's wrists and twisting his whole body around so that Colin went tumbling over his leg.

Colin snarled at him. The bat lay on the ground between them.

"Don't," Billy said. "Just let us—"

But the rest was lost as Colin ran for him. Before getting lessons from Ed Moore, Billy would have wrapped him up and wrestled him down to the ground, relying on his superior strength to come up on top. Now, he knew the key to winning a fight like this was to always stay on the offensive, never miss an opportunity to hit the other guy. When Colin ducked his head for the charge, Billy slammed his elbow down onto the bridge of Colin's nose, the bone breaking with an audible crack.

Colin went down on his knees and groaned. He swayed, then fell over forward.

Billy watched him fall. Colin was down, but not out. He tried to get up but only managed to raise his bloodied face a few inches off the ground before falling back down into the thin layer of snow on the grass.

A zombie staggered around the corner of the building behind Colin, his ratty clothes still trailing a wisp of chemical fog.

Billy scooped up the bat, grabbed Kyra by the hand, and led her around the building just as the zombie fell on Colin. There was a short, muffled scream that was almost lost against the sound of so many others screaming and coughing and crying.

He guided her away, but she stopped him after a few hurried steps.

"What is it?" he asked. "Kyra, we gotta go."

"Thank you," she said. "God, I would have died."

They were very close at that moment, their lips only inches apart. He could taste the wintergreen coolness of her breath. In a movie, he'd have kissed her then. But this was really happening, and he could taste the sting of chemicals on his lips and feel it gathering in his chest. The best he could manage to get out was a strangled "You're welcome," as he pulled away from the pavilion.

Jeff Stavers heard Robin's voice above the crowd and ran to it. He saw her standing in front of a large group of children and a few adults, the only voice in the crowd to challenge Jasper's insanity.

The patrols moved on her before Jeff could push his way through the crowd. He saw one of the guards grab her by the arm and pull her away while her children screamed. Jasper was still talking over the PA, trying to get everyone to calm down and just get on with it. Jeff ran at a dead sprint for Robin and threw his shoulder into the guard who was pulling her toward the pavilion.

They both went down, but Jeff got up first. He had the man's rifle in his hands.

"Get them going toward the RVs," he told her.

Two guards advanced on them, but Jeff got his rifle up before they did and fired, hitting one man in the neck and the other in the gut. Both went down without firing a shot in return.

"Jeff!"

He turned and saw Robin pointing toward the pavilion. The dead and the dying and the zombies were everywhere. Jasper was yelling hysterically into the microphone and pointing at Jeff and Robin and the children they had with them, gesturing his patrols to go after them.

"Jeff, please."

"Right," he said. "Let's move."

CHAPTER 60

Ed felt the gas burning his eyes and lips, the snot running from his nose as he stepped through the field of corpses, and he pressed his handkerchief tightly over his face as he fought his way through to where he'd seen Robin Tharp fighting with the guards. He'd lost sight of them in the confusion and the drifting clouds of gas.

Jasper's voice could still be heard above the hacking and groaning crowd, and he sounded delirious, full of insecurity and rage and confusion. One moment he was pleading for everyone to just calm down, and the next he was screaming at a small trickle of people hurrying from the pavilion.

Ed headed that way. He was surprised to see Margaret O'Brien out in front, guiding several adults and quite a few children away from the pavilion.

"Where are we going?" she asked.

"Head to the RVs. Where's Robin?"

"Back there," Margaret said, and pointed toward the pavilion. "Help her, Ed."

But he was already running as she said it.

* * *

He saw Robin herding her kids away from the pavilion, struggling with a few who were trying to break loose and run back to be with their parents.

One of the guards stepped out of the gas cloud behind her, hacking and coughing, ropes of snot hanging from his nose and mouth, a pistol held limply in his hands. His body was shaking, and there was an enormous open bite mark on his wrist. When he saw Robin, he fell on her. She screamed and tried to break free, but the guard held her with the last of his strength.

With his elbow, Ed hit the nerve bundle at the base of the man's neck, dropping him to his knees. He stared up at Ed and his eyes were rimmed with red, unfocused, turning the milky pale of the infected. His face was shiny with sweat and a chemical film. He tried to moan, but only managed a gargling sound. Ed kicked him in the chest and laid him out on his back, where he began to convulse.

Then Ed reached down and picked up the man's pistol, a 9mm Beretta, nice gun. U.S. Air Force written down the side. It was an officer's gun.

"Are you okay?" he said to Robin.

She nodded. Ed glanced over at the pavilion. The gas cloud was so thick now all he could see was the peaked top of the metal roof, and the gas was spreading, seeping down the hill toward them.

A moment later, Jeff Stavers emerged from the fog, holding his shirt over his face. He had a rifle on one shoulder and a struggling child on the other.

"Help him, Ed."

"I will. Go."

The kids were running across the playground in front of her. A few had made it to the large earth dome that marked the beginning of the fields, and they had crested the top. They were almost there.

Robin caught up with the stragglers and helped them along.

A little girl of two, maybe three was standing near the top of the hill, looking back toward the pavilion. She was crying for her mother and refused to go any farther. Before Robin could reach her, two other little girls stopped near her and started crying for their parents, too. Robin knelt beside them, begging them to move. One of the little girls slapped Robin's hand away from her shoulder and tried to run back to the pavilion. Robin managed to grab the girl, but she couldn't stop all three, and they ran around her.

They didn't make it far, though. Sandra Tellez scooped them up, both girls fighting and kicking and screaming, and she carried them back to the top of the hill.

"Come on," she said to Robin. "They've got the RVs ready to go."

Robin picked up the third struggling little girl, and they ran the rest of the way to the waiting RVs. Ben Richardson met them outside the closest RV and helped them get the children on board.

She heard a shot and saw Jeff leveling a rifle at a group of zombies who had followed them down from the pavilion. He was blocking a child with his body. He fired twice more before he ran out of ammunition.

There were still three more zombies in front of him.

"Jeff!" Robin yelled. "Come on!"

He turned and saw her waving at him.

"Come on," she said.

He picked up the child and ran for the RVs. She took the child from him and helped her up onto the RV.

"Where's Ed?" she asked.

"I don't know. He went back for some of the others."

She turned toward the pavilion and saw the gas cloud rising higher into the air. It had engulfed most of the center of the village and was starting to make its way around the slight rise of the hill at the edge of the road, long, narrow fingers poking through the gaps between the buildings and inching downhill.

"We don't have much time," Richardson said above them. "That cloud's going to be on us in another minute or two."

"We have to wait for him," Robin said. "We have to."

"I don't know if we—"

Richardson cut himself off abruptly. Robin watched his eyes go wide, his attention focused on something over her shoulder.

She turned.

Jasper was limping toward them up the snow-covered main road. Even from a distance of some thirty feet, Robin could tell the man's eyes were bright red. He was coughing. A runner of blood oozed down the corner of his mouth from his left nostril. His square face was shining like it had been sprayed with wax. And though he was limping, he was fueled by a rage so monomaniacal and intense that he still managed to outdistance Michael Barnes, who was coming up behind him.

"Give me back my children," Jasper shouted at them. "They are not yours. They are not yours to take. They are mine. Mine! You hear me? Give them to me now!"

Spit flew from his lips. He looked thoroughly deranged. He reached down and picked up a long piece of rebar that was leaning against the front of a nearby pickup and swung it wildly in their direction.

"Give me back my children. Give them to me, you little bitch."

"No," she murmured.

"Give them to me now!"

He was closing on them, barely ten feet away. Robin put up her hands to block the blow she knew was coming and a whimper passed her lips.

But the blow never came. She'd closed her eyes without realizing it. When she opened them, Ed Moore was standing between her and Jasper.

"Get everybody on board," Ed said to Richardson. "Get the RVs rolling."

"You," Jasper hissed. "You did this to us. You betrayed us."

Ed had a pistol in his hands. He had it centered on Jasper's chest, but Jasper wasn't looking at it. His eyes were drilling into Ed Moore's, every ounce of him consumed with rage.

Jasper drew the piece of rebar back to strike, and Ed shot him. One round, square in the chest.

Jasper sucked in a surprised breath, looked down at the hole in his body, and collapsed without a word. A second later, Barnes was at his side, his fingers groping for a pulse on the dead man's neck.

He closed Jasper's eyes, then looked up at Ed Moore.

"Stay there, Barnes." Barnes rose to his feet. "Don't move."

If Barnes understood him, he made no sign of it. He stared past the gun to Ed, his face inscrutable.

"You guys get moving," Ed said to Jeff and Robin, who were still watching from the doorway. "Hurry."

They climbed into the RV and Robin turned and looked back at Ed. He still had his gun trained on Michael Barnes.

"You guys go," Ed said. "I'll cover you."

She was about to motion to Richardson to drive away when Barnes suddenly reached under his shirt, drew his pistol, and fired at Ed. Barnes was amazingly fast, and the shot was ringing in her ears before her mind had a chance to process what had just happened.

But either the shot had gone wide or Ed was faster, for he'd hit the ground and rolled toward the vehicles to his right. Robin watched Barnes sprint forward, turn, and level his gun at the spot where Ed had slipped between a pair of trucks, but he didn't fire.

Ed wasn't there.

Barnes moved so fast.

Ed saw him ducking his shoulder to reach under his shirt, saw the flash of metal as the gun came out, saw the explosion as it went off, and the whole thing happened so fast he couldn't make himself react in time.

He felt the punch in his side even as he jumped to his right, hit the ground, and rolled between a pair of pickups. Moving quickly, he rolled under one of the pickups and out the other side. He had just enough time to see a small trail of blood behind him, and in that moment he knew he'd been hit. Ed looked down and saw blood seeping between his fingers, running down his hip inside his jeans. The wound was bleeding badly, but it wasn't especially deep. He could see that. Still, Barnes had drawn first blood.

Another shot rang out ahead of him and slammed into the windshield beside him. Exploded bits of glass dusted his cheek, making him cry out.

He immediately fell to the ground.

There were no more shots, and Ed pushed himself up onto his hands and knees and crawled around the back of the truck and came to a rest with his back against the truck's wheel. Glancing under the vehicle, he got a glimpse of Barnes running toward his hiding spot.

Ed was breathing hard. He knew he had to regain the offensive if he was going to have any chance at all of survival, but his aged body was screaming at him in pain. Everything hurt. Not just the wound in his side but his knees and his shoulders and his back, too. Even his heart was pounding like an engine that had been pushed too hard.

"Gotta do it," he said, and popped up behind the truck's tailgate right as Barnes rounded the corner. Ed fired, hitting Barnes in the shoulder and spinning him around in the air even as he was slammed to the ground.

He fired twice more, but Barnes was already on his feet and scrambling back around the corner of the truck, the shots slamming uselessly into the ground, kicking up snow and black mud.

Ed ran after him. He didn't want to let Barnes create distance on him. Younger, faster, and probably a better shot, too, Barnes would be able to use that distance to plant a bullet right in his forehead.

Plus Barnes was hit worse than he was.

He could use that.

Barnes turned around when he heard Ed running up behind him, but he was shot in the right shoulder, making that arm useless, and he had to cross over his body with his left hand in order to sight the gun on Ed.

Ed used the extra second to close the distance between them and tackle Barnes, knocking him backward over the hood of a truck and onto the snow-covered ground.

Barnes rolled away from him and got to his feet almost instantly. Ed took a moment longer. He managed to climb to his feet right as Barnes charged him and caught Ed under the jaw with a ferocious upper cut that turned everything in his world purple.

He fell back against the pickup.

Barnes charged him again, jabbing him twice in the mouth with his left, then stepping back and swinging his left again, this time catching Ed in the cheek. Ed fell back against the truck, stunned, his legs going weak beneath him. He'd never been hit so hard in his life.

Barnes swung another left at Ed's face, but this time Ed saw it coming. He slid down the front of the truck and came up just outside Barnes's wounded right shoulder. He snaked a finger into the wound and dug in.

Screaming in rage and pain, Barnes staggered backward.

Ed attacked. Leading with his right, he jabbed once at Barnes's throat, catching him on the windpipe before pulling back and then wading in with another punch to the solar plexus.

Barnes doubled over, the air leaving his chest in hacking rush.

Ed closed the distance between them again, this time meaning to slam the door shut on Barnes with a flurry of rights to the younger man's face. He swung, but Barnes came up under the blow and faded back as he sent a left across Ed's jaw.

Ed fell backward onto his butt. Dazed, he looked up at Barnes. He rolled over onto his elbow, but Barnes was on him so quickly he seemed like a blur. His fist crashed into Ed's chin with a crack that echoed across the unnaturally windless prairie.

Ed was flat on his back now, floating just above unconsciousness. Dimly, he watched Barnes walk casually down the slope that led to the west entrance. He reached down and picked up the pistol Ed had knocked from his hand earlier.

"You fight good, old man," he said. He rubbed his jaw. From the way Barnes winced, Ed could tell he'd done some damage. "Wonder what would have happened if we'd met when you were thirty."

"Fuck you," Ed said. The words sounded muddled coming from his busted lips.

Barnes raised the pistol at Ed and a shot rang out.

Ed flinched, and realized a moment later that he hadn't been hit.

In front of him, Barnes slumped to the ground, a spreading blossom of blood oozing from a hole in his neck.

Ed looked up and saw Billy Kline standing there, breathing hard, but smiling.

"You okay?" Billy asked.

Ed groaned. "You're kidding, right?"

Billy put a hand under Ed's arm and eased him up to his feet.

"So, was that an example of old age and guile triumphing over youth and raw talent? Cause if so, I gotta tell you, the lesson was a little murky."

Ed smiled. "You got a smart mouth on you, son. Just get me out of here."

"You got it, old man."

Billy led Ed onto the lead RV and put him down on the couch.

"Oh, Jesus," Sandra said. "Ed. Oh, my God."

She touched his battered face, but he pushed her hand away.

He looked up at Billy. "Get us out of here," he said. "Get us onto the road. Just drive."

"Right," said Billy.

Billy ran forward and climbed into the driver's seat. He'd never driven anything like this before, but everything looked familiar enough. Richardson had already gotten the engine running, and they were sitting on half a tank.

So far so good.

He looked to his left, making eye contact with the drivers of the other two RVs. Both drivers waved back.

"Hold on," he said over his shoulder.

He put the RV in gear and eased into the gas. He could feel the heavy vehicle sliding on the ice, but they were moving.

Richardson appeared at his side.

"You got more infected coming through the gate."

"I see 'em," Billy said. He checked his rearview mirror and saw that the other two RVs were falling in line behind him.

"Hang on," he said to Richardson, and he dipped into the throttle.

The big RV lurched forward, fishtailing a little on the ice and snow. Ahead of them was a knot of the infected. Billy braced for the impact and drove headlong through the crowd, bodies bouncing off the front bumper with dull-sounding thuds.

A moment later, they were through the crowds and through the gate and heading out of the Grasslands. The world was an endless white desert stretching out before them, the sky a dark gray mass of storm clouds stretching the length of the horizon.

"They all make it through?" Richardson asked.

Billy checked the rearview mirror. "Yeah," he said. "Yeah, we're all clear."

Less than ten minutes later, Richardson was pointing at a dark line of vehicles on the road ahead of them.

"I see it," Billy said. "Who do you suppose that is?"

The vehicles were moving slowly, deliberately. There were bodies on the road ahead of them, and as Billy slowed, they could see gunshot wounds.

"Whoa, Billy," said Richardson. "Stop!"

Billy hit the brakes and the big vehicle slid to a stop.

From behind them, Ed said, "What's going on? Why'd you stop?"

Richardson pointed out the window. "You see that?"

"Yeah," said Billy.

White shapes were sliding down the snowbanks along the side of the roads. Soldiers, black rifles in their hands standing out against the snow and their white snowsuits.

“What’s going on?” Ed said again.

Billy looked back over his shoulder. Ed was trying to stand; Sandra was trying to hold him down.

“The cavalry,” Billy said. “Day late and a dollar short, but looks like we’re saved.”

Beside him, Richardson laughed.

Epilogue

Nate Royal hurt everywhere. His first attempts to move, to roll over, went unheeded by his muscles. Every inch of his clothes, even his hands and his eyelids, were encrusted with ice.

At last, he managed to roll over onto his back. The room around him was entombed with ice.

His breath steamed in front of his face. He felt like some little bastard was going to town on the inside of his head with a sledgehammer. Every muscle was stiff, every joint frozen. His eyes burned. His chest felt like it was getting squeezed and it hurt to breathe. He couldn't feel his hands. He couldn't even curl his fingers into a fist.

Groaning, he rolled over onto his side and sat up. He recalled the beating he'd taken at the hands of Michael Barnes. They had forced him to tell about the cure and then gotten mad. They'd asked him about the cure, but they hadn't pushed the issue. He was glad for that. Lying was one thing, but lying while taking another of those beatings was another. He'd been lucky they stopped when they did.

The flash drive was still there. He could feel it.

He fumbled with his pants until he finally got them down around his thighs. Everything hurt, his gut especially, and taking down his pants felt like he was getting murdered all over again.

Wincing, he put fingers into his ass and pulled out a Ziploc baggie.

A low groan escaped his lips.

He opened the bag and took out the flash drive and dropped the lanyard over his neck.

Only then did he rise to his feet and walk outside.

There were bodies everywhere. One man was on his back, a hand raised skyward like he was trying to take something from a shelf. Icicles hung from his fingers. Dimly, Nate remembered the sounds of the fighting from the night before.

"Couldn't kill me," he said, and laughed. He was a cockroach, life's little symbol of endurance in the face of a dispassionate universe. The thought filled him with a mad sort of glee, and he laughed until the cold air caught in his lungs and made him cough.

He looked around.

He was standing in the field near one of the bigger buildings, looking toward the pavilion. There were hundreds of bodies over there, all of them encrusted with ice. It was too enormous to take in, all that death.

Nate wandered closer to the pavilion. He had to step over arms and legs bent and frozen at irregular angles. Here and there, he saw bodies on their backs, mucus frozen in tiny icicles from the corners of their open eyes and their nostrils. He saw men and women holding hands, their palms fused together by the cold. He saw young women clutching babies to their chests, and all that senseless wasting of life made him want to vomit. It was dreadful.

"Fucking maniacs," he muttered.

He turned away from the bodies and scanned his surroundings. The Grasslands compound was hugely vast and bleak. The sky was a deep, stormy gray. The wind blew snow, gritty as sand, across the fields to the north, where a single coyote loped across a barren plain. The fence was lost in fog, but he figured that the gate had been left open. There was no other way for a coyote to get in.

He wondered which way to go. Kellogg's words echoed in his mind. It didn't matter if he wanted this responsibility or not. You either chose to live, or chose to die. It was a yes-or-no question, no middle ground. Choosing to live was an acknowledgment that life has some sort of meaning. Whatever that meaning was, for him at least, was tied to the cure Kellogg had stored on the flash drive around his neck. For the time being, that was reason enough to go on living. He would bring this back to the world. What they did with it was their problem.

So he turned once again and found the rising sun. *That way is east*, he thought. *As good as any*.

And, shivering against the cold, the ice crunching beneath his boots, he made his silent, solitary way into daylight.